DEATH AND THRAXAS

MARTIN SCOTT

DEATH AND THRAXAS

This is a work of fiction. All the characters and events portrayed in this book are fictional, and any resemblance to real people or incidents is purely coincidental.

Thraxas at the Races copyright © 1999 by Martin Scott; *Thraxas and the Elvish Isles* copyright © 2000. Published by permission of Little, Brown U.K.

A Baen Book

Baen Publishing Enterprises
P.O. Box 1403
Riverdale, NY 10471
www.baen.com

ISBN: 0-7434-8850-4

Cover art by Tom Kidd

First U.S. printing, September 2004

Distributed by Simon & Schuster
1230 Avenue of the Americas
New York, NY 10020

Production by Windhaven Press, Auburn, NH
Typeset by Bell Road Press, Sherwood, OR
Printed in the United States of America

BUSINESS AS USUAL, DURING ALTERCATIONS

"So, what are you going to do when they take your license away?" Makri asks.

"I don't know," I say. "What are you going to do when you fail at the College?"

"I don't know."

A light tap comes on the outside door. In walks the dark-clad figure of Hanama. I fumble desperately for my sword. Hanama is number three in the Assassins Guild. The last time I saw her, she tossed a dart into the Chief Abbot of a temple of warrior monks, sending him off to paradise rather more quickly than he had anticipated.

"Relax, Investigator," she says, in her soft voice. "Had I been here on business, I would not have knocked."

I glare at her, sword now firmly in hand. "Then what do you want?"

"I've come to visit Makri."

Hanama looks at Makri. Makri looks puzzled but gets to her feet and they go off to Makri's room. Strange. I've never know Assassins to do much in the way of socializing.

The door crashes open. I whirl to face this new intruder. It's Sarija, wife of my former client, the late Senator Mursius. She trips and falls. She's wet through. Her face is drawn, with a yellowish hue. And she reeks of the narcotic dwa, easily discernible even among the multitudinous unpleasant odors from the street outside.

"I'm hiring you to find out who killed my husband," she says, then passes out in my arms. I dump her on the couch. I walk over to the door, close it, mutter my locking spell, then barricade it with a chair.

I notice there's an envelope pushed under the door. When did that arrive? I tear it open and read the message: *You'll be dead before the end of the rainy season*, it says.

"I will be if things go on like this," I mutter, and throw it in the bin.

BAEN BOOKS by MARTIN SCOTT:

Thraxas

Contents

THRAXAS
AT THE
RACES

Chapter One

I step out of the law courts. It's still raining. A huge clap of thunder explodes in the sky. I growl with annoyance.

"Terrific. The judge just fined me everything I have left, it's the rainy season and now the storms have started."

The sky is turning very ugly. My face is much the same. I can't remember being in a worse mood. Ex-Deputy Consul Rittius certainly managed to put one over on me this time. If I ever meet him in a dark alley I'll skewer him with a rusty dagger. It won't even have to be dark. Any alley will do.

"You still have some money left," says Makri.

"I lost a little at the out-of-town chariot races."

"A little? How much?"

I shake my head, which Makri correctly interprets to mean everything I had. Lightning splits the sky. Rain starts pelting down harder than ever. A small, mean-faced figure emerges from the law courts, the white of his official toga showing under his fur-lined cloak. It's Senator Rittius, formerly Deputy Consul of Turai, and still head of Palace Security. He's flanked by eight Guards. I consider running him through anyway, but hold myself back.

He sticks his thin face close to mine. "You were lucky, Thraxas," he says, with loathing in his voice. "The judge was far too lenient. If I had my way you'd be rowing a slave galley by now."

"Really? If you bother me any more, ratface, you'll be handing in your toga way ahead of schedule."

"Don't threaten me, fat man," hisses Rittius. "Or I'll have you back in court so fast it'll make you dizzy. I'm still head of Palace Security. You take one step outside the law and I'll be down on you like a bad spell. Your life in Turai is finished. I advise you to leave while you still can."

I stare at Rittius with hatred. I did him a very bad turn a while back. In the course of an investigation last summer I seriously dented his political ambitions and caused him to lose the election for Deputy Consul. I still feel good about it.

"Stay out my way," I tell him. "Your Guard won't stop me gutting you if I get a notion to."

My hand strays towards the sword at my hip. Rittius flinches, very slightly. He knows I could do it. He recovers himself quickly, and sneers at me.

"I think you'll find you've got far too much on your plate to go around inflicting violence on your betters," he says.

Rittius departs. His Guards march after him through the rain in good order.

"You certainly know how to make influential friends," says Makri. She offers to buy me a beer and we hurry through the ever increasing downpour to the tavern at the edge of the law courts where the accused steady their nerves before their ordeal and the barristers spend their fees afterwards.

"How long did you say this rain lasted?" asks Makri, who's only recently arrived in Turai, and has not yet become used to our seasons.

"A month. And it'll get worse now the storms have arrived. Last year Gurd had to shore up the walls of the Avenging Axe with sandbags."

Makri and I live at the Avenging Axe, a tavern in Twelve Seas. It's not much of a place to live, but nowhere is in Twelve Seas, the rough area by the docks. It's the sort of place you end up if your life isn't going too well. Like for instance if you're a highly paid Senior Investigator working at the Imperial Palace who is booted out of his job for alleged drunkenness, insubordination and whatever else it was I was accused of.

Rittius was my boss back then. He hated me then and since I put one over on him last summer it's become even worse. I helped clear a Royal Princess's name as well as the son of Rittius's opponent of serious charges. Rittius promptly lost the election. I knew he'd be out to get me but I never thought he'd stoop so low as to use his position at the Palace to drag me through the courts accused of assaulting an officer of the law.

"What the hell was I supposed to do?" I complain as I sink my flagon of ale and hold it out for a refill. "I needed that landus in a hurry. I could hardly stand around asking politely, could I? So I hauled the guy out and roughed him up a bit. I wasn't to know he was a Praetor's Assistant on a secret mission for the King. He wasn't even wearing an official toga."

I'm seething with the injustice of it all.

"I thought I'd get through the Hot Rainy Season without having to work. I hate investigating in the rain. Now I'm broke I'll have to."

Gurd, the ageing Barbarian who owns the Avenging Axe, is an old fighting companion. We were soldiers and mercenaries together. He tolerates a fair amount by having a Private Investigator like myself as a tenant. Only last month the place was practically wrecked when the Brotherhood, the local criminal gang, slugged it out with two bands of warrior monks in the downstairs bar. Gurd figures the least I can do is pay the rent on time. Which, until my unwise speculations on the recent out-of-town chariot races, I fully intended to do.

"Do you ever win at the races?"

"Of course, I win plenty."

Makri scoffs. She claims she could find more winners at the chariot races than me by simply throwing a dart at the form sheet. I remind her that she's an ignorant Barbarian with Orc blood in her veins who's so unused to civilisation she still finds it awkward to use cutlery.

"Stick to what you're good at, Makri."

"Like what?"

"Like killing people. You're good at that."

Makri accepts the compliment. It's true enough. Since Makri escaped from the Orcs' gladiator slave pits last year and headed on over to civilisation, she's proved herself pretty much invincible with a sword in her hand. This has been of great benefit to me on several occasions when my investigations have gotten nasty. They often do. During the attack of the warrior monks Makri demonstrated her skills in such a savage and devastating manner that Captain Rallee was left shaking his head in amazement, and Captain Rallee has seen a lot of fighting in his time.

"But superior fighting skills count for nothing at the race track. The problem was that the out-of-town meeting was fixed. You can't trust the resident Sorcerers at these small events. Not like here in the city. With Melus the Fair as Stadium Sorcerer you know everything is above board. She's practically the only honest person in Turai. She ensures that magic is never used at the Stadium Superbius. But that small meeting was a joke. I swear the chariot that won the last race wouldn't have made it out of the stable without a spell to show the horses which way to go. I should have known better than to gamble on it. There again, I wasn't expecting Rittius to drag me into court the following week."

"Could have been worse," says Makri, paying for my third beer. "You might be rowing a trireme by now. Rittius really hates you. How badly did you behave at his wedding anyway?"

"Pretty badly," I admit. "But if he wanted the guests to remain in order he shouldn't have provided so much free wine. That's strong stuff they ship up from the Elvish Islands. And his bride should have been better covered up. That dress was hardly modest."

I stare gloomily at the bar. Since the unfortunate incident at the wedding, the last few years have been pretty rough. Now I'll have to find a case and investigate it. Damn it. I really hate working in the rainy season.

Outside rain pours down and thunder rumbles overhead. I notice a Sorcerer walking towards us, easily identifiable by his rainbow cloak. He's a large man with a weighty-looking staff in his hand. He stops in front of me and pulls back his hood revealing a pair of steely eyes and a square jaw line. My heart sinks. It's Glixius Dragon Killer. I thought he'd left town.

"I'm going to kill you, Thraxas," he says, in his deep voice.

"What, right now? Or some other time when you've got nothing better to do?"

Glixius fixes me with his steely gaze for a second or two, then turns and marches off without another word.

Makri is shielding her eyes with her hand as if trying to pick out something on the horizon.

"What are you doing?"

"Seeing where the next deadly enemy is coming from."

"Very funny. Rittius and now Glixius. Some day."

Glixius Dragon Killer is a powerful Sorcerer associated with the Society of Friends, Turai's second major criminal organisation. Funnily enough, I did him a very bad turn this summer as well. It was a big summer for doing bad turns to powerful people. I foiled his plot to steal Red Elvish Cloth. I punched him in the face too, as I recall, though he was all out of magic at the time.

There isn't a landus to be found anywhere so we trudge home through the rain. I'm gloomier than ever. What a day. The state fines me all my money and two deadly enemies threaten me.

"It wouldn't be so bad if I ever made any profit out of this investigating business."

"You do," points out Makri. "But you spend most of it on beer and gamble the rest away."

Makri is a very hard worker. She works shifts as a barmaid at the Avenging Axe to pay for her classes at the Guild College. She's not above occasionally pointing out to me the error of my ways. Not that Makri doesn't have her share of faults. I strongly suspect that she's been experimenting with dwa, the powerful drug that has half the city in its grip, though she always denies it.

"Give me a turn with the magic dry cloak," she says.

"No chance," I reply. "I need it more than you. If I'm about to get attacked by Palace Security and a deadly Sorcerer, I need to be comfortable."

I wrap myself tighter in the magic dry cloak. Makri makes a face. It's odd. In her short life she's fought and defeated practically every kind of beast and warrior known and she will charge an impossible force of enemies without the slightest qualm, but she really detests getting wet.

"Damn this rain. At least it was dry in the gladiator slave pits," she grumbles. "I hate this Hot Rainy Season. How can it be hot as Orcish hell and wet as a Mermaid's blanket at the same time?"

She pulls her thin cloak over her vast mane of hair. If she's trying to make me feel guilty she's wasting her time. I didn't spend all that time studying sorcery to learn how to make a magic dry cloak just to hand it over to the first person that asks.

"Where are we going?" asks Makri, as I take a diversion down a series of twisting alleyways.

"I'm calling in at Honest Mox's."

"Honest Mox the bookie? But the Stadium Superbius is shut in the rainy season."

"There's a race meeting in Juval. It's dry there at this time of year."

Juval is a small nation, another member of the League of City-States to which Turai belongs. It's a couple of hundred miles southeast of Turai. Makri wonders how I can bet on chariot races so far away. I explain to her that the bookmakers here band together to pay a Sorcerer to transmit messages to another Sorcerer at the race track in Juval. He sends up the runners and the prices and afterwards transmits the results. It's not an uncommon practice among gamblers in Turai to bet on these races. Makri is impressed, though somewhat surprised to find Sorcerers engaged in such practices.

"I thought they all concerned themselves with higher callings."

"Well, mainly young Apprentices take the work. The Sorcerers Guild doesn't really approve but, hey, it's good practice for sending messages, which is handy in wartime."

"Haven't you lost enough recently?"

"That's why I have to win it back. I have an emergency supply for just this situation."

Mox the bookmaker is, as ever, pleased to see me. He's chalked the runners in the next race in Juval up on a board. I study the form.

"How do you know the Sorcerers transmit everything honestly?" asks Makri.

I admit that this can be a worry. Race Sorcerers have been known to be dishonest, but it's a risk I'm prepared to take. I've never had any trouble with the meeting in Juval. It's a small track, usually with only four chariots in each race. I can't see anything beating the favourite, a fine chariot from Samsarina called Glorious Warrior. It's only even money so I place twenty gurans on it.

"You're wasting your money," sniffs Makri.

"Oh, yes? You won't say that when I pick up my twenty gurans winnings tomorrow."

Chapter Two

— ❦ —

We trudge on down Moon and Stars Boulevard till we reach Twelve Seas. Around the law courts the rain was bouncing off the statues of past kings and heroes of Turai, running down the marble pavements into the well-maintained gutters. In the smarter parts of Turai public utilities such as drainage are a marvel of engineering. Not so in Twelve Seas. Here the downpour turns the dirt streets to mud. After ten days of rain the place looks pretty bad. Another twenty to go. Twelve Seas is hell in the Hot Rainy Season.

"My shift starts in two minutes and I'm wet as a Mermaid's blanket," complains Makri, and hurries off to change.

I climb the outside stairs leading directly from Quintessence Street into my office above the tavern. There's a sign outside my door: *Finest Sorcerous Investigator in the City of Turai*. The rain is starting to peel off the paint where it flaked in the burning summer sun.

11

Sorcerous Investigator. Big joke. I studied as an Apprentice but that was a long time ago. Now my powers are of the lowest grade, mere tricks compared with the skills of Turai's great Wizards.

I should do something about that sign. It looks cheap. I'm probably the cheapest Sorcerous Investigator in the whole of Turai but there's no need to brag about it. I'm forty-three, overweight, without ambition, prone to prolonged bouts of drinking and I take on the sort of case the Civil Guards won't help with for the sort of client that can't afford one of the high-class Investigators uptown. I charge ten gurans a day plus expenses which is never going to make me rich.

Things were looking up. This summer I solved a couple of important cases, earned myself a fair bit of reward money, improved my reputation in certain important circles. With a bit of luck I might have made it out of Twelve Seas back into proper society again. Now that I've been dragged through the courts on a charge of assaulting an official of the King, I'm back at square one. No money, and no reputation.

The atmosphere is cloying. The Hot Rainy Season is unbearable. It's like a steam bath out there. If it wasn't for my magic dry cloak I don't think I could cope. As my magic is so poor nowadays, I can generally only carry one or two spells around at a time. Usually I take a sleep spell, which is highly effective in rendering opponents unconscious, and maybe something like a loud explosion to cause a diversion. The days when I could work invisibility and levitation are long gone. Right now my entire sorcerous ability is concentrated on keeping dry. If I happen to meet five or six opponents at once I'll just have to rely on my sword.

My office is a mess. I kick some junk under the table, grab a beer from the supply in the sink and drop down on the couch muttering a few oaths about the unfairness of life. I fought for this damned city in the last Orc Wars. Helped throw back the savage horde that threatened to overwhelm us from the east. Not to mention the sterling service I gave the city in the war before that, with Nioj, when our enemies from the north swept through the mountain passes and damn near threw us all into the sea. And is anyone grateful? No chance. To hell with them all.

There's a knock on the outside door.

"To hell with you all," I shout.

The knock comes again. I'm in no mood for company. I shout out another curse, finish my beer and prepare to toss the bottle at the doorframe. The door opens and in walks Senator Mursius, one of Turai's greatest war heroes and my old commander from the Army. He's tall, erect, silver-haired and extremely vigorous-looking for a man of fifty. Pretty angry-looking as well.

"What is the meaning of this?" he demands in a voice that takes me straight back to the parade ground. "I am not accustomed to former soldiers treating me with disrespect."

I scramble to my feet. Senator Mursius was the last person I expected to walk into my office. Great heroes of Turai tend not to visit. It must be fifteen years since we last spoke, probably around the time when the platoon commanded by Mursius was holding out at a breach in our walls made by the besieging Orc Army, and I was one of the unfortunate soldiers forming a human shield to keep them at bay. I've seen him since of course, in one of the galleries reserved for Senators at the theatre or the Stadium Superbius, but I doubt if he ever noticed me.

Now he's noticed, he's not looking too impressed.

"You always were a disgusting apology for a soldier," he barks. "I see that time hasn't improved you."

Mursius is still a big man and he wears his white senatorial toga with a majestic air. I'm only in my underwear, which probably isn't helping things. I struggle back into my tunic and clear some junk from a chair.

"Won't you sit down, Senator Mursius?"

"You've put on a lot of weight," he says, eyeing my girth with the sort of disapproving gaze he used to reserve for ill-attired recruits. "And you've come down in the world."

He knows all about my fall from grace. He's not unsympathetic. As a soldier he has little time for Palace politics.

"A vipers' nest, the Palace. You should never have taken a job there in the first place. Why did you do it?"

"The pay was good."

"Look where it got you."

He looks around my shabby room. "Did Rittius clean you out in court?"

I nod.

"Rittius is a snake. Never did a day's fighting in his life. That's the sort of person who's running Turai these days. I take it you are looking for work?"

I nod again.

"I need the services of an Investigator. Nothing too complicated, or so I believe. I'd normally have hired a man closer to home, but I thought you might be in need of employment."

I ask him why exactly he thought that and he replies that he keeps an eye on most of the men who fought under him.

"You weren't too bad that day at the walls, Thraxas. I'd be sorry to see you starve. Though I see that would take a while. I hear you have a reputation as a good Investigator. When you can stay sober. How often can you stay sober?"

"Practically all the time if the case really calls for it."

A knock comes on the inner door that leads downstairs into the tavern. It opens before I get the chance to answer it. Makri has little concept of personal privacy. You have to make allowances for her. She grew up in a slave pit, after all.

For the first time Mursius shows some surprise. Makri can be a surprising sight if you're not prepared for it. Though only slightly taller than your average Turanian woman, she carries herself erect like a warrior, lithe and strong like a fierce chagra cat from the Simnian jungle. She has large dark eyes, almost black, a huge mane of dark hair and strikingly attractive features, but what usually impresses anyone visiting the Avenging Axe for the first time is Makri's shape. Makri has plenty of shape—and her shape is difficult to miss given the tiny chainmail bikini she wears while working as a barmaid. The purpose of this of course is to earn tips from the dockers, sailors and mercenaries who make up most of Gurd's clientele.

The next thing people generally notice about Makri is the reddish, slightly dark hue of her skin. Makri is one quarter Orc, and that means trouble. She's quarter Elf as well, which is fine in Turai, where everyone likes Elves, but the Orc blood leads to all sorts of difficulties. Everyone in Turai hates the Orcs. Though we are technically at peace with them now and have even signed a treaty and swapped Ambassadors, you don't need too long a memory to recall the days when they were besieging the city.

All of which means that Makri's Orc blood is bad news in Turai. The drinkers in the tavern are fairly used to it but Makri still wouldn't be allowed into a high-class tavern uptown, or various official buildings. She is often insulted in the street. I'd worry about her more if it wasn't for the fact that she's probably the most lethal fighter in Turai, if not the entire west. I've spent most of my life fighting, and I can't recall ever meeting anyone more deadly with a sword, an axe, or anything that comes to hand.

Senator Mursius stares at her in surprise. There is an awkward silence.

"I've got pointed ears as well," says Makri, which is true, though they're usually hidden beneath her huge mass of hair.

"Excuse me," says the Senator apologetically. He glances at the sword at her hip. "An Orc blade?"

Makri nods. "I brought it with me."

Mursius looks at it with interest. As a professional soldier he always was interested in weaponry.

"Fine work," he says with approval. "The Orcs are excellent armourers, whatever people say. Quite as good as the best Human smiths. You say you brought it with you?"

"From the Orc gladiator pits. I used to fight there. Before I killed the Orc Lord who owned me, slaughtered his entourage, escaped down a sheer cliff face and took a job as a barmaid instead."

"Interesting. Your attire seems hardly suitable for fighting, however."

"You're right," agrees Makri. "Only a fool would go fighting in a bikini. But it gets me tips. When I'm on duty I hide the sword behind the bar." She departs downstairs.

"A very interesting woman," says Mursius. "Half Orc?"

"A quarter. Quarter Elf as well. And half Human, though that doesn't make her act like one."

The Senator studies me with interest. He's wondering if he wants to hire an Investigator who's having a relationship with a quarter Orc. He needn't worry. I'm not having a relationship with Makri, or anyone else for that matter. Haven't had one for a long time. I went off women when my wife left me for a young Sorcerer's Apprentice some years ago. I took to drink instead. Actually I had taken to drink some time before she left, but afterwards I had much more time for it.

"So, how can I help you?"

The Senator tells me that he has suffered from a theft at his country house further down the coast, near to Ferai. Like any wealthy citizen, the Senator keeps a house in town and another in the country for retiring to when the weather gets too intense.

"My losses are not great. There wasn't much money at the villa, but various works of art have gone missing and I'd like them recovered. In particular I'd like you to find a painting which I hold very dear."

Remembering Mursius in his younger days, storming the Orc lines with a bloody sword in his hand, I never figured him as an art lover. You can never tell with these aristocrats, though. Men of Mursius's generation went naturally into war and fought bravely, but they learned their share of social graces as well. There used to be a theory among the aristocratic class that it was important to enrich every aspect of one's personality. But Turai was different in those days. Since the gold mines in the north started producing wealth and the drug trade brought dwa in from the south, the city is both much richer and much more corrupt. Today's young aristocrats spend their time in debauchery and bribe their way out of military service.

"What have the Civil Guards done about it?"

"I have not informed them."

I raise one eyebrow. Calling in the Guards would be the normal thing to do, unless there was some delicate aspect Mursius would rather not reveal in public. I was half expecting something like this. People do tend to come to me only in desperate circumstances.

"I have not informed them," continues Mursius, "because I strongly suspect that my wife was behind the theft."

"Your wife?"

The Senator expresses some anxiety about the private nature of his disclosures. I reassure him of my discretion. I have plenty of faults but I never blab about a client, even if it gets me thrown in jail. Which it does, often enough.

Outside the rain beats against the shutters, drowning out the other noise from the street. That's the only good thing about the Hot Rainy Season. It keeps most of the squealing brats that infest the area indoors.

"We have been estranged for some time. We stay together because it suits us not to part. I'm sure you understand."

I do. For a city as immoral as Turai, where almost everyone can be bought, the public still places a surprisingly high value on the morality of our public figures. If a Senator finds himself involved in a messy divorce case it can do great damage to his career and completely end his chances of advancing up the ladder of Prefect, Praetor, Deputy Consul and Consul. They tend to keep their problems hushed up and well away from the scandal sheets. Their wives generally go along with it. It suits them better to remain married and keep their wealth and social standing rather than risk finding themselves out on the market again.

"So, why would she rob you?"

"My wife is often desperate for money."

"You don't give her an allowance?"

"Not for dwa, no."

Right. Not for dwa. That makes sense. Since the southern trade routes were opened up, this powerful narcotic has flooded into the city. The effect on the population has been dramatic. Beggars, sailors, youthful apprentices, whores, itinerants, rich young things: all manner of people once content to alleviate their sufferings with ale and occasional doses of the much milder drug thazis now spend their days lost in the powerful dreams of dwa. Unfortunately dwa is both expensive and addictive. Once you take your dose you're as happy as an Elf in a tree, but when you come down you feel bad. Regular users who spend part of their lives lost in its pleasant grip are obliged to spend the other part raising money for more.

Since dwa swept Turai, crime has accelerated out of control. In many parts of Turai it's not safe to walk the streets at night for fear of violent robbery. The city is rotting. The poor are despairing and the rich are decadent. One day King Lamachus of Nioj will come down from the north and sweep us away.

"Is she a serious addict?"

"Very serious. She's tried to stop but—"

He holds his hands out in a hopeless gesture.

"For the past six months she's been down at the villa. It was her idea. Said it would help her to get straight. From what the servants tell me, it hasn't worked out. I've tried doctors, Sorcerers, herbalists, everything. Nothing does any good. She always comes back to dwa. Eventually I tried cutting off her money, just sending down a servant with supplies."

"As a result of which your wife sold some of the family treasures to feed her habit?"

"So it would seem."

I lean back in my chair and take a thazis stick from my drawer. I offer one to the Senator, but he declines. It's still technically illegal but since the arrival of dwa swept the city no one much cares about that. I light it up and inhale the smoke.

"What exactly do you want me to do?"

"Find my belongings. Particularly the painting. Without involving the Guard or the scandal sheets."

The Senator tells me in a frank, man-to-man sort of way that he's being pressed by the Traditionals to stand for the post of Prefect next year. He's fifty years old so it's about time for his political career to get started. As a war hero and a popular man with both the mob and the King, he's almost certain to get elected. Unless, of course, his name is blackened by scandal. The Populares, the powerful opposition party led by Senator Lodius, never hesitate to use any available dirt against their opponents.

I mull it over. It means travelling out of the city in the rain, which is a fairly unpleasant prospect with the country turning into swampland, but apart from that it sounds straightforward enough. No powerful criminal gangs involved. No mad Sorcerers out to get me. Just find out what she did with the goods and get them back. I can do that. I need the money. I take the case.

The Senator fills me in on the rest of the details and rises from his chair. He pauses at the door and glances round the room. "I hear you lost a great deal of money at the out-of-town chariot meeting."

I frown. I knew the Senator would have checked me out but a man never likes his gambling losses being made too public.

"I'll give you a good tip for the Turas Memorial Race."

I lean forward, suddenly eager.

"I'm entering a chariot in the Turas Memorial," says the Senator. "It's called Storm the Citadel. Back it. It's going to win."

I sit back, disappointed. I'm not too keen on this tip.

"Your chariot is going to win the Turas Memorial Race? Excuse me, Senator, you've had some good horse teams in the past, but there's an Elvish entrant in the Turas this year. Everyone knows Moonlit River is going to win. You can't even get a bet down on it any more."

The Senator treads softly back to my desk. "Storm the Citadel will win," he says, quite emphatically. "If you want to make up your losses, back it with everything you have."

With that he departs. I pick up a guran from the retainer he left me and head downstairs to the bar where I buy a flagon of Gurd's finest ale and muse about Senators' wives and the powerful addictive qualities of dwa. I tried it when I was younger, but it didn't do much for me. I guess I'm just not that sort of character. I finish my beer quickly, drink down another, and take a third flagon back up to my office.

There's a message on my desk. Odd. I break the seal and open it. It reads: *Thraxas, your death is near.*

I stare at it. I'm used to death threats but that doesn't mean I enjoy them. I check the outside door. It's locked. I'm sure no one came up the connecting stairs while I was at the bar. I put the letter under my nose, sensing around for any signs of sorcery. Is there a faint trace? Possibly.

My hand goes automatically to the spell protection charm at my throat. It's new. I hope it works.

I'm wary as I travel out to Mox's, but when I find that my chariot won and I pick up my twenty gurans winnings, I forget about the death threat. Afterwards I gloat to Makri.

"Yes, a man may have a few losses every now and then, but class will tell in the end. When it comes to picking winners I'm number one chariot around here. And I've a hot tip for tomorrow. You ought to join in and win a little money, Makri. Easier than working as a waitress."

Chapter Three

"What do you think of Storm the Citadel's chances in the Turas Memorial Race?" I ask Gurd as he hands me another beer. His biceps bulge as he passes it over the bar. His long hair is almost completely grey now but he's still as strong as a team of oxen.

"No chance," he says. "The Elves don't send a chariot all the way up from the Southern Islands unless they know it'll win."

I nod. That's what everyone in Turai thinks. Senator Mursius has produced some fine chariots in his time, but he's never going to beat the Elves.

Everyone is looking forward to the chariot races in the dry week after the rains stop, when the Turas Festival is held. Turas was the legendary founder of Turai, building a city after defeating several savage tribes and performing various heroic acts. It's always a good time for Turai. It cheers up the citizens before the onset of the bitter winter. This year the festivities will take on a larger scale than usual because they come at the time of the Triple-Moon conjunction festival, which only happens every fifteen years or so.

I'll be betting at the meeting, naturally, but I hadn't planned putting anything on the last and most prestigious event, the Turas Memorial Race. Not with the Elves entering Moonlit River. It's practically a shoo-in. The chariot belongs to Lisith-ar-Moh, a great Elvish Lord and a particular friend of Turai. Fifteen years ago Lisith-ar-Moh led a regiment of Elvish warriors through the Orc lines to the relief of Turai, arriving just as the Orcs breached our walls and various desperate Turanian soldiers, including myself, were trying to hold them back. He saved the city that day and we have never forgotten it. He's visited several times since, as guest of honour to our King, and it's because of his ties with the city that he's entered a chariot in the Turas Memorial Race.

Everyone is pleased about that. We all like Elves here. The only thing wrong is that the Elvish chariot has more or less finished the Turas Memorial as a serious competition. We don't breed horses up here the way the Elves do in the Southern Islands.

And yet . . . like any gambler I'm always interested when someone gives me a tip. I stood beside Senator Mursius when the east wall of the city was breached and watched him fight hand to hand with the savage Orcish force swarming over the debris and into the city. If Mursius hadn't been there to lead us we'd never have held out till the Elves arrived.

"He's not the sort of man to place his faith in a no-hoper," I point out to Gurd, who was there that day as well.

"True. But chariot-owners always think they're going to win," replies Gurd. "You've lost plenty at the races already. No point throwing more away."

Gurd and I reminisce about the war. We've done

that often recently. The imminent arrival of Lord Lisith
has certainly stirred up the memories. Orcs, dragons,
walls tumbling to the ground under sorcerous attack,
buildings on fire, the desperate battle, the sound of
trumpets and the sudden unexpected arrival of the
Elves. Even when they arrived it was no easy matter
to defeat the Orcs. The fight continued all day and all
night and all of the next day as well. It was quite an
experience. So I figure Gurd and I are fully justified
in bragging about our part in it, no matter what anyone might say when we wheel out our war stories for
another airing.

Gurd is right about the race of course. And
yet . . . Mursius is sharp as an Elf's ear when it comes
to chariot racing. He's had a lot of success. I can feel
myself being tempted. I banish it from my mind and
get back to the task in hand, namely recovering Senator Mursius's lost works of art. Gurd has a couple of
good horses out the back and I ask the stable lad to
saddle one of them up for me while Tanrose, the
tavern cook and object of Gurd's Barbarian affections,
fills me a basket of provisions for the journey. I tie
back my long hair and tuck it inside my tunic, then
wrap myself in my cloak.

Just as I'm leaving Makri enters the tavern.

"I'm wet as a Mermaid's blanket," she states. "What
a stupid climate this city has. If it isn't too hot, it's too
wet. Now it's both."

I have to agree. The weather in Turai is often unpleasant. We have four months of blazing sun, one month of
hot rain, about one month of a fairly temperate autumn,
then four months of extreme, biting cold. After that
there's another rainy season, cold this time, lasting a
month, before the month-long spring, which is pleasant.

"Which makes only two reasonable months a year,"
growls Makri.

"At least it's regular."

"Why the hell did anyone ever build a city here?"

"Good harbour. And we're on the main trade routes."

Makri curses in archaic Elvish. She's been learning the Royal Elvish language at her Guild classes and wants to practise.

"Not that the Elves ever curse the rain, or so I'm told," continues Makri. Apparently they all sit around in their trees thinking it's yet another fine part of nature. Stupid Elves."

Makri was already fluent in Common Elvish when she arrived in Turai. Presumably that was from her Elvish grandparent, but who that was I've never asked, and Makri has never exactly explained. Nor has she talked about her Orcish grandparent. I wouldn't dare ask. Anyway, both my Elvish and Orcish have improved a lot since she's been around.

I ask her what she was doing wandering around in the rain. She tells me she was looking for plants.

"What for?"

"Natural history class at the Guild College. The Professor wants us all to study some interesting local plants."

"That might be difficult in Twelve Seas. There aren't any."

"I know. I went to look in that small park behind Saint Rominius's Lane. Unfortunately the park's disappeared. Someone built a block of tenements right over it."

King Reeth-Akan lays down strict regulations concerning the number of parks for his subjects. Even the poorest of areas should have open spaces for the citizenry to take their exercise and forget their cares for a while. Unfortunately the Prefects who control planning in each district are very amenable to looking the other way if bribed by property developers. It's reached the stage now where there's hardly an open space left in Twelve Seas. The last Prefect, Tholius, was as corrupt as they come. He was recently forced to flee the city after being caught out trying to divert some of the King's gold into his own coffers. Obviously Drinius, his replacement, hasn't wasted any time in lining his own pockets. You can tell a man of aristocratic birth because his name ends in "ius." But you could work it out anyway by his amazing willingness to take money for favours. "Easy as bribing a Senator," as they say. Not like the solid working-class citizens, who tend to have "ox" or "ax" in their names. Like Thraxas, for instance. They're as honest as they come.

"I'm just heading off into the country," I tell Makri. "Come along and study the plant life."

Makri considers it. She has got the rest of the day free and she thinks she could use some exercise.

"Okay, I'll come along if I can share the magic dry cloak," she says, cunningly. "I need some interesting kind of plant. If I fail on this assignment Professor Toarius will be down on me like a bad spell."

Makri scowls. From her frequent complaints I know that Professor Toarius is high on the long list of people associated with the Guild College who think it would be a far better place if it didn't include Makri. It was him who forbade her to attend classes in her chainmail bikini because of the disturbance she was creating. Even the man's tunic she put over it didn't satisfy him.

"He said it showed too much of my thighs. Is that taboo in Turai?"

"No. Just distracting for young men trying to study philosophy."

As a result of which she now has to wrap herself up in a voluminous cloak before going to college, even when the sun is beating down and it's hot as Orcish hell, which it was all summer.

"Professor Toarius is as cold as an Orc's heart," grumbles Makri, and goes upstairs to get her axe.

Makri sticks at it though. She works hard, at the tavern and at the Guild College for the Education of the Sons of the Lower Classes. It's her ambition to go to the Imperial University. This, as I have frequently pointed out, is impossible. The University doesn't accept female students, especially ones with Orc blood in their veins. The Imperial University is such an exclusive institution, catering only for the offspring of aristocrats, that even our richest merchants have trouble getting their children in. It is a symbol of the complete control exercised by the ruling elite, which makes it even more impossible for Makri ever to attend. She refuses to be put off. "The Guild College didn't take female students either before I insisted," she points out. You have to admire her persistence.

She arrives back with her axe, two swords, a knife in her boot and a bag of throwing stars, an Assassins Guild weapon she's been experimenting with recently.

"Makri, you're only looking for a few plants. What the hell are you expecting to meet out there?"

"You never know. Any time I'm helping you on a case it always turns out worse than we expect. I still haven't forgotten the time we went looking for that missing dog and ended up fighting pirates. And look what happened the last time you made me go out without my axe. I ended up with a crossbow bolt in the chest and nearly died."

"And we'd have missed you terribly. Let's go."

"I found this envelope addressed to you on the stairs."

I rip it open.

You'll never make it past the Hot Rainy Season, says the message.

"Another death threat?"

I nod. I should have killed Glixius Dragon Killer when I had the chance.

Outside it's still hot. The rain has intensified and my old cloak keeps me dry for about thirty seconds. Meanwhile Makri is comfortably wrapped up in the magic dry cloak.

"The rain doesn't seem so bad when you get used to it," she says. "Where are we going?"

"Ferias. An exclusive little resort further down the coast."

"Then why aren't we heading for the west gate?"

"I'm calling in at Mox's. I have a hot tip."

Makri nods. She might not approve of betting but she was impressed when she saw me come home with a twenty-guran profit.

Mox's small, dingy premises is full of punters in the damp and grubby tunics and cloaks worn by the common Turanian masses. Most of the lower classes, including myself, wear grey. A few of the more adventurous youngsters might burst into colour occasionally but exotic clothes are beyond the budget of most people. Only the upper classes wear white.

A messenger arrives every now and then with the latest news from the Sorcerer at the track, hundreds of miles away in Juval. I'm here to bet on the first race tomorrow, just in case I don't make it back to the city tonight. Though I'm careful not to reveal anything I'm practically beside myself with glee. I've been looking forward to this race for a long time. It's my insurance policy.

The odds on the four chariots in the race are even money, six to four, six to one and eight to one. As a serious gambler I am not a man to throw away his cash on outsiders but I happen to know that Troll Mangler at six to one has a particularly good chance in this race. I whisper in Makri's ear.

"I know the owner, I was drinking with him just before he went south. He's been keeping this chariot in reserve, well out of sight. He told me he's never trained a better team of horses. That's why he's gone down to Juval, where he isn't known. He's going to make a bundle at six to one, and so am I."

Mox is slightly surprised when I confidently place forty gurans on Troll Mangler. Outside I do a little jig in the rain.

"Two hundred and forty gurans to Thraxas, thank you very much."

"What if it loses?" says Makri as she swings herself on to her horse.

"No chance. Trust me. I know what I'm doing."

The thunderstorm has passed but there will be plenty more of them in the month to come. It's a two-hour ride down the coast to Ferias. By the time we reach the city walls my good humour at placing the bet has disappeared and I'm starting to regret taking this case. When we're halfway there I seriously consider turning back.

"This is grim," I splutter. "I'm about as miserable as a Niojan whore. I haven't been this wet since Gurd and I swam underneath an enemy raft in the war against the Niojans and attacked them by surprise. And I was a lot younger then."

We stop for something to eat, sheltering under a tree. Makri looks around for some interesting plant life.

"I have to turn up with something really special. All I can see here is grass and bushes."

"They'll probably have some unusual plants in the grounds at Mursius's villa. Steal one of them."

We ride on.

"What are you meant to do when you get there? Isn't his wife going to find it rather offensive if you just march in and demand to know what she did with the loot?"

I look at Makri with interest. When she arrived in Turai I don't think she understood the concept of being offensive. The classes must be civilising her.

"Maybe. But Mursius doesn't care. Their relationship has passed the point of being polite. He just wants his paintings back."

The rain lashes down. I swear a few curses at Rittius. If he hadn't dragged me through the courts I wouldn't have to be doing this. Thank God he's not Deputy Consul any more. That post is now occupied by Cicerius, who belongs to the Traditionals, the party that supports the King. They'd been losing ground to the opposition Populares but Cicerius's victory stemmed the tide. I had a hand in the victory. Thanks to some smart work on my part Cicerius avoided losing his reputation. Not that I particularly support the Traditionals. The Populares have some things in their favour. The common people could do with a little more of the city's wealth. Unfortunately the Populares are led by Senator Lodius, as nakedly ambitious a tyrant as ever put on a toga.

"How come Cicerius didn't use his influence to protect you in court?" asks Makri. "After all, he's Deputy Consul now, and he owes you a favour."

That's a very sore point. First thing I did when the trouble arose was visit Cicerius but he would have to be the one man in Turai who is both absolutely incorruptible and a sworn upholder of the law. He expressed sympathy for my plight, but refused to use his influence to get the charges thrown out. Because, as he pointed out in his beautifully modulated orator's voice, I was actually guilty. I had dragged the King's representative from his landus and bludgeoned him to the ground. The fact that I needed the vehicle urgently was not, in Cicerius's considered legal opinion, a valid defence for roughing up a fellow citizen.

"Trust you to gain influence with the one official too honest to bend the rules in your favour."

We're now approaching the loose collection of large country dwellings that make up Ferias. Progress is slow. The ground is churned up and muddy and several streams have swollen, so it's difficult to get across. It's a long time since I've been here. When I was Senior Investigator at the Palace I visited regularly as the guest of various Senators, Praetors and wealthy Sorcerers. Now I'm about as welcome as an Orc at an Elvish wedding.

It's now well into the afternoon. My mood gets worse. The rain comes down in huge drops. After two hours it feels like rocks pounding on my head. I tell Makri it's my turn for the cloak and we swap over.

"If you were any good as a Sorcerer you could make two of them."

"If I was any good as a Sorcerer I wouldn't be here. I'd be safe in a big villa in Thamlin casting horoscopes for Princesses and courtiers and generally having an easy time of it. I should have studied more when I was an Apprentice."

We mount a small hill and there in the distance is Mursius's villa. Suddenly my horse whinnies and rears up. I struggle to regain control but the wet reins fly from my hands and I plunge to the ground. I struggle to my feet, sliding in the mud and cursing freely at the ignorant beast. Without warning three large Orcs with swords step out from behind the nearest tree.

Chapter Four

This doesn't make sense. You don't find Orcs in the Human Lands. Especially not in the excessively wealthy settlement of Ferias.

Orcs are larger than Humans, and generally a little stronger. I never met one that wasn't fierce, though as I've only met them on the battlefield, I suppose some might not be. Maybe the Orc poets all stay at home. I doubt it. Most Humans regard them as dumb animals but I haven't found that to be true. Their Ambassadors, for instance, have often proved to be shrewd negotiators, and Bhergaz the Fierce, the Great Orc leader of fifteen years ago who united all the Orcish nations and led them into the west, was a brilliant general. Only through a combination of luck, sorcery and desperation were the combined forces of Elves and Humans able to defeat him.

Makri hates them more fiercely than anyone. Despite this she refuses to acknowledge that Human civilisation is more advanced. She claims that contrary to what is believed in the west, Orcs do have music, literature and even a theatre of sorts, with extended performances of various religious rituals. If this is true, it's completely unknown to us, apart from the savage martial tunes they play when advancing into battle and the weird, shrieking pipe music they play from the backs of their dragons. Orcs can breed and control dragons, Humans can't. They're dark-skinned and wear their hair long, a style favoured by only the lower classes in Turai, and they dress in shaggy, tasselled black clothes. They're fond of silver jewellery. They make good weapons. They hate all Humans. And they can fight. So can I, which is fortunate as I'm not carrying any spells. I whip out my sword and my dagger and sink into my fighting stance.

The three Orcs are in the garb of young warriors, with black helmets and tunics and weapons at their hips. But they haven't attacked us yet. Strange. Orcs and Humans are implacable enemies. We waste no time when we meet. We just kill each other. I wonder if it might be worth asking them what they're doing here.

I don't get the chance. Makri's hatred of Orcs doesn't allow for conversation. With a decisive movement she rides one of them down and leaps off her horse to confront the others. Her axe and her sword are in her hands as she hits the ground and the first Orc's head flies from his shoulders before he has time to move. The second tries to draw his sword but Makri guts him and he slumps dead to the ground. I'm not the sort of man to let my companion fight on her own but I don't have the chance to join in. As the third Orc climbs to his feet Makri whips out a throwing star from her bag and tosses it with deadly accuracy right into his throat.

It's all over in seconds. Three dead Orcs lie sprawled at our feet. Seven years in the Orc gladiator pits, five of them as Supreme Champion, make a woman hard to beat.

Makri stalks around suspiciously, peering through the rain and sniffing the air for other Orcs.

There don't seem to be any more. There shouldn't have been any here in the first place. The Orcish nations are far away to the east. They don't wander around at will in the Human Lands. Any movement by a force of Orcs across the Wastelands that separate us would be detected by Human Sorcerers who scan continuously for just this sort of thing.

I wonder what they were doing here. There was something odd about their behaviour. We mount up and hurry on. A long white wall surrounds Mursius's villa. A heavy iron gate guards the front, behind which sits a bored-looking member of the Securitus Guild. I tell him my name and he nods as if expecting me. He opens the gate, and we ride in. When I tell him about the Orcs he looks at me with utter disbelief. I assure him it's true.

"Three warrior Orcs. Just up the hill. We dispatched them. You'd better have the local militia scour the area in case there's more."

Realising that I'm serious, he hurries away to raise the alarm while Makri and myself head towards the house. The villa's extensive gardens are partially submerged after the weeks of rain. Two servants take our mounts off to the stables.

The experience with the Orcs hasn't put me off my mission. I have a living to earn. My instructions from Mursius are to talk to his wife and find out what she did with the works of art she sold. He didn't require me to be subtle about it, and I'm not planning to be. Just a few quick questions, find out where the loot is, then recover it.

My plan for a few quick questions goes wrong right

away when a well-spoken young woman informs me
that Sarija, Mursius's wife, can't see anybody just now.

I wave this away.

"Mursius sent me."

"I know," she replies. "But you can't see her."

"Why not?"

"She's unconscious from dwa."

I stare at the young woman in surprise. One might
have expected something more subtle.

She shrugs. "It's the truth. I'm only paid to look after
her, not tell lies."

I get the strong impression that she's had more than
enough of taking care of Sarija.

"If you want to wait she'll probably recover in a few
hours. You can dry yourself in the guest rooms. I'll have
a servant bring you some refreshment."

The young woman's name is Carilis. She is pretty,
in a bland sort of way. She speaks with the cultured
voice of Turai's elite and is rather expensively dressed
in one of these long white gowns they charge a fortune for in the market. She was obviously disconcerted
by Makri's appearance. I wonder why she's playing
nursemaid to a Senator's wife.

Shortly afterwards I'm drying myself in front of a
fire as Makri roots around in the extensive window
boxes decorating the large bay window. There's a tray
of food in front of us and a flagon of wine on the table.
We wait for a while, which is okay with me. I charge
by the hour and if a few of these hours involve sitting around eating and drinking I'm not going to complain. I've just begun to feel comfortable when the door
opens and a woman walks in. She is as white as a ghost
and just about as healthy-looking.

"I'm Sarija," she says. "And it's time for you to get
the hell out of my house."

She picks up the flagon of wine. For a second I

think she's about to throw it at me—Senators' wives
are notoriously bad-tempered—but instead she puts it
to her lips and pours a healthy slug down her throat.
She coughs violently, throws up on a very expensive-
looking rug then keels over unconscious.

We stare at her body, prostrate on the floor in a pool
of wine, vomit and broken glass.

"I'll never really fit in with polite society," says
Makri.

I shake my head. "Senators' wives. They get worse
every year."

I think about helping her up but I'm not really in
the mood. I stride out into the corridor and holler for
someone to come and help. Round the corner marches
an Army Captain with eight armed men at his back.
That's more help than I was really expecting. They're
accompanied by the gatekeeper.

"He's the one."

The Captain wears a red tunic covered by a silver
breastplate. He's extremely wet and doesn't look
friendly.

"What's the idea of sending me on a fool's errand
looking for Orcs?" he demands.

I explain to him that it was not a fool's errand. The
Orcs were there and Makri killed them.

"Makri?"

I lead him into the room. When confronted by a
Senator's wife lying stretched out on the floor and a
young woman in a chainmail bikini with an axe slung
over her shoulder, the Captain becomes even more
agitated.

"What the hell is going on here?" he demands.

"Just looking," says Makri, and shifts around rather
furtively.

"Don't worry," I tell her. "They haven't come about
the plants."

The Captain strides over to Sarija. I'm thinking that we might have some awkward explaining to do but fortunately at that moment Carilis appears. The Captain seems to know her and makes no comment as she attends to the Senator's wife. He turns back to me.

"Well?"

"We're down here on business at the request of Senator Mursius. And we met some Orcs. Didn't you find the bodies?"

He didn't. Nor did he find any trace of a fight. Not even a footprint.

"The rain must have washed it all away."

"Very convenient. And would the rain also wash their aura away?"

"No, it wouldn't."

"Well, we went there with a Sorcerer. A very important local man. He wasn't at all pleased to have the Army dragging him outdoors on a day like this. He was just settling down with a glass of wine and a new book of spells. But we told him it was important. A sudden appearance of Orcs." The Captain fixes me with a grim stare. "The Sorcerer couldn't find any sign of them. Not the slightest trace of an Orc's aura. So what have you got to say about that?"

"Maybe he's out of practice . . ."

"Out of practice?" roars the Captain. "I'm talking about Kemlath Orc Slayer! Back in the war he detected enough Orcs to fill the Stadium Superbius."

"Really? Kemlath Orc Slayer? I'd no idea he lived down this way."

"Well, he does. And he's not at all pleased at being hauled out of his villa on a wild Orc chase. Thanks to you the country's in an uproar and I've spent the afternoon up to my knees in mud instead of sitting warm and dry in the barracks."

He goes on for some time, much of it in language

he really should not be using in front of a young female servant of good birth. I'm pretty sure he's about to turn us over to the local Civil Guards just to teach us a lesson but eventually he seems to run out of steam and simply tells us to leave and never come back.

"If we see you round this way again, you'll be sorry."

"What about our investigation?" protests Makri.

The Captain turns to his Sergeant. "This is what it's like in Turai these days. Degenerate. They have Orcs dressed in bikinis working as Investigators."

For a moment I think Makri's about to explode. I quickly pick up the magic dry cloak and toss it at her.

"Fine, Captain. Sorry to bother you. We'll be on our way . . ."

I drag Makri out of the room and outside as quick as I can.

"If you attack eight soldiers it'll only lead to more trouble."

We find our horses and start back to Turai. The rain is pouring down in torrents. Makri is in such a bad mood about the Captain calling her an Orc that I let her keep the magic dry cloak. Meanwhile I am as wet as a Mermaid's blanket. What a waste of time. As we pass the spot where the Orcs confronted us I halt and sniff the air, trying to pick up any trace of their aura. I certainly have enough of my old sorcerous skill left to detect the aura of Orcs for some time after they've departed.

"Nothing," I grunt. "It's gone. Someone has magically cleaned it away."

A huge flash of lightning rips the sky apart. Another storm. It's a two-hour ride home. A long journey in the pouring rain and all I get for my troubles is a Senator's wife throwing up over me.

"Hello, Thraxas!"

I recognise that voice. A Sorcerer, resplendent in

the most luxurious rainbow cloak I've ever seen, steps out from his shelter underneath a tree.

"Never did learn to control the weather!" he booms, in a loud, hearty voice I haven't heard for fifteen years.

"Kemlath!"

"Any good with weather spells?" he asks.

"I'm no good at any spells," I admit. "I never took up my studies after the war."

I introduce Makri. Kemlath, being a powerful Sorcerer, will of course immediately realise that she is one quarter Orc but for once it makes no difference. He's a large, hearty man with a great black beard and mounds of gold and silver jewellery. He's obviously done well for himself since we last met.

"Kemlath and I fought beside each other in the Orc Wars," I explain to Makri, who's puzzled at the appearance of this large, colourful stranger. He earned the name of Orc Slayer from the fine military power of his spells. He sent many an Orc to an early grave and brought the Orcish war dragons crashing down from the sky. Afterwards he was held high in the city's esteem and became an important man in the Sorcerers Guild. He was a brave man too. He didn't just hide behind his sorcery. When his magic ran out, as every Sorcerer's did eventually during the relentless assault, he picked up a sword and stood with us in the last desperate defence.

"What brings you here?"

I tell him I'm doing a little work for Senator Mursius.

"I didn't know you'd moved down to Ferias."

"Yes. It suits me well here, on the coast. The weather's milder—apart from this damned rain—and I've built a villa. I grew fed up with the city some years ago. It's not the place it used to be."

I agree with him there.

"What's this about Orcs?" he asks me.

I tell him the story.

He nods. "Well, Thraxas, if it was anybody but an old fighting companion I'd say they were lying, or hallucinating, but I know you too well for that. If you say there were Orcs here, that's good enough for me. But I can find no trace of them. And tracking Orcs is a speciality of mine. I'd swear I could tell if an Orc had been here, no matter how much another Sorcerer might have cleaned the area."

The rain beats down. Kemlath invites us back to his villa. We refuse, albeit reluctantly, as we both have to get back to Turai. He promises to look into the matter more fully, and report to me if he comes up with anything.

"Now you know where I am. Be sure to visit!" he says in parting.

"Not a bad guy for a Sorcerer," says Makri, as we ride off.

"One of the best," I agree. "I always liked him. When the weather clears up I'll take him up on his invitation. As King's Sorcerer in Ferias he is bound to be rich. Did you see the amount of gold and silver he was wearing?"

It's deep into the night when we arrive back at the city. Our horses are exhausted from plodding through mud. It's past the time when the gates are normally shut but I know the gatekeeper and he lets us in.

"Working late, Thraxas?" he calls down from his vantage point.

"Sure am."

"Going well?"

"Better than rowing a slave galley."

Makri, as ever, is impressed at my wide range of acquaintances. Most people south of the river know Thraxas.

It's forbidden to ride in the city at night, but it's so wet and we are so miserable that we risk it. I can't see many Civil Guard patrols out doing their duty on a night like this, with the thunder still rolling overhead and the rain coming down in sheets.

In the Avenging Axe late-night drinking is well under way, fuelled by some raucous singing to the accompaniment of Palax and Kaby, two street musicians who live in a horse-drawn caravan out the back. They spend their days busking and their nights playing and drinking in the tavern. Gurd gives them free drinks for entertaining the customers, which makes me feel somewhat jealous as I grab a beer and he chalks it up on my slate. If I don't make some progress on the Mursius case I'm going to have difficulty paying my bill at the end of the month.

Makri takes a beer and joins me at a table.

"What a waste of time that was."

She nods in agreement. "Although I did pick up these," she says, drawing out some small plants from her bag. They have tiny blue flowers, quite unlike anything I've ever seen before.

"Unusual, I think. I took them from the window box while the soldiers were berating you."

"Well done. I hope it keeps the Professor happy."

We wonder what the Orcs were doing in Ferias. Makri asks me if I'm going to report it to the authorities. I shake my head. The city isn't under attack, so I presume it was some private business being carried out by one of the rich citizens of Ferias. Something to do with dwa, probably. A lot of it comes in from the east. I can't see why anyone would want to make life difficult for themselves by involving Orcs, but who knows what goes on behind closed doors in a place like that?

I grab another beer and a few pastries Tanrose has

left over from dinner. Palax and Kaby take a break from playing music and join me at my table. They share some of their thazis with me; they always manage to have the best thazis in town. I start to mellow out. Today was a waste of time but at least I'm sitting comfortably with a few beers and some happy drinkers. Usually, when I'm on a case, things get much worse than this.

Makri has changed into her man's tunic. Some sailors shout across, asking where her bikini is. Makri shouts back that she's not working tonight. They look disappointed. She notices that I'm cheerful, despite the arduous day we've had. I tell her I'm always happy when I'm about to win two hundred and forty gurans. She's still sceptical.

"You might lose. It wasn't even the favourite."

"Troll Mangler is not going to lose. I keep telling you, I know the owner. It's by far the best chariot in that race. It was only six to one because they hadn't heard of it down in Juval. It's the surest thing I've backed in years. If you had any sense you'd go out early tomorrow and back it yourself."

Makri doesn't seem to approve. That's the trouble with people who are always working. It annoys them when you pick up a little spare money without making an effort.

Chapter Five

Next day I sleep late and don't wake until I'm disturbed by noises in my office. I only have two rooms, one for sleeping and the other for working. It's small but it ought to be private. I rise quietly and creep to the connecting door, sword in hand. There's someone in there all right. I burst through, ready to confront intruders.

It's Makri. She appears to be searching under the couch.

"What the hell are you doing under my couch?" I demand, not particularly pleased to have been woken up after last night's drinking session.

Makri leaps to her feet, a furious expression on her face.

"You idiot," she yells, and then carries on with some harsh abuse. I'm not fully awake and I find this hard to take in.

"What have I done?"

"I lost my money because of you."

"What money?"

"The money I was collecting for the Association of Gentlewomen!"

Makri insults me some more. I can't understand what she's talking about till I hear the words Troll Mangler mixed in with her tirade.

"Troll Mangler? Are you talking about the race in Juval?"

"Of course I'm talking about the race. You said Troll Mangler couldn't lose! You and your stupid tips!"

"Didn't it win?"

"No it didn't," cries Makri. "A wheel fell off at the first corner! And I went out this morning and put all my money on it!"

This is a staggering piece of news. I sink on to the couch, a broken man. "Are you sure?"

Makri's sure. She's been down at Mox's watching the gamblers who bet on the favourite pick up their winnings, and she's not very pleased about it. I'm stunned by these terrible tidings and struggle to defend myself against Makri's accusations.

"I didn't force you to bet your money on it, did I? This is bad enough for me, without you making it worse. Troll Mangler beaten! I can't believe it. I was depending on that chariot. There's been some dirty sorcery afoot in Juval."

"The only thing that's afoot is your inability to pick a winner! I never should've listened to you. Now what am I going to do? I'm broke and I need fifty gurans—today!"

Makri's behaviour starts to make sense. I have a fifty-guran piece hidden under my couch. It's my emergency reserve and is meant to be a secret.

"Is that what you were doing under my couch?" I demand.

"Yes."

"You thought you'd just take it while I was sleeping?"

"Yes."

"Why?"

"Because it was your fault I lost my money and I need it in a hurry. I promised it to the A.G. today."

This is such an outrageous statement that I am left practically gasping for breath.

"You promised it to the A.G.? The Association of Gentlewomen? You promised that bunch of harridans fifty gurans of my money?"

"No," replies Makri. "Any fifty gurans would do. But I need it today. And they're not a bunch of harridans. You don't mind me borrowing it, do you? You know I'm good for it. It's the least you can do in the circumstances."

"That fifty gurans is my emergency reserve," I roar, dragging Makri away from the couch. "You go anywhere near it and I'll run you through like a dog. You already owe me the forty gurans I lent you to pay for last term's exam fees."

Makri is now madder than a mad dragon. So am I.

"How dare you rob my office! You think I want to donate the last of my money to that lunatic women's organisation? Are you insane?"

"I only wanted to borrow it," protests Makri, wiping some dust off her knees.

"Why do you need fifty gurans for the A.G. anyway?"

"It's the money I collected for them. I spent two months raising that cash. You know how hard it is in Twelve Seas. Everyone's poor and the men won't give anything anyway. I had to move heaven, earth and the three moons to raise even that. I've had easier times fighting dragons."

"Don't tell me about fighting dragons," I retort. "I was fighting dragons before you were born."

I seem to be straying from the point here. I get back to berating the Association of Gentlewomen, which, while not illegal, is not exactly well thought of by a large part of the city, namely the male part.

The King doesn't like it, the True Church fulminates against it from the pulpit and the Senate has condemned it as seditious. It was established to raise the status of women in the city. After a slow start it has gathered an increasing amount of support from the most unlikely quarters. Membership is not made public, but I happen to know that Princess Du-Akai is a supporter, as are various powerful female Sorcerers.

The Sorcerers Guild admits women. Most other guilds do not, which is something the Association intends to put right. Or put wrong, depending on your point of view. The Association has official recognition and admittance into the Revered Federation of Guilds as its first objective, but that's an expensive business, with fees and bribes needed all along the line. Fifty thousand was the figure Makri mentioned, I believe.

"So, can I borrow it?"

"Of course you can't borrow it. If you promised that money to the A.G. you shouldn't have gambled it away. It's unethical."

"Don't lecture me on ethics, you fraud!" roars Makri.

I start to laugh. I can't help it.

"So. You lost your money on a chariot. Very amusing. Miss Austerity herself gambled it away. The Queen of Sensible Behaviour blows her cash at the races."

Makri doesn't take this too well. "It was your fault, you Orc lover! I'd never have backed that chariot if you hadn't said it was a sure thing."

Makri is livid at me for giving her a bad tip, but she's even angrier at herself for losing the money. She's had to work hard to get the respect of the local business-women who support the A.G. and this isn't going to help.

"I've got to take it Minarixa the baker by noon! You have to help!"

I wave this away. "I'll forgive you for trying to burgle my offices. I'll put it down to the rashness of youth. But let this be a valuable lesson to you. Never blow the last of your money at the races."

Makri stares at me. I stare back at her.

"I really worked hard collecting that money. And I came and supported you in court. I'll pay you back."

I shake my head.

"Come on, Thraxas. It's not like you to be as mean as a Pontifex when it comes to money."

"I need that fifty gurans," I tell her

"What for?"

"To win back my money at Mox's. Now depart. I need to be alone with the bad news about Troll Mangler."

There's a knock at my outside door. Makri departs, looking dispirited. I shake my head. Give my last fifty gurans to the Association of Gentlewomen indeed. Big joke.

The knock sounds again, angry and urgent. My door is generally sealed with a locking spell. This is a common minor spell that I can use at will without having to learn it afresh every time, like one of the major spells, but it can be employed by anyone with the slightest knowledge of the mystical arts. While it's reasonably effective against petty theft, it wouldn't keep out someone who was seriously determined. A few months ago Hanama the Assassin came here uninvited and it didn't keep her out for more than a second. I mutter the appropriate incantation, and the door springs open.

It turns out to be Carilis, the not very friendly employee whom we met yesterday in Ferias, looking after Sarija. She has mud all over her fancy black boots and water drips from her elegant blue cloak.

She strides in and looks around with disapproval. "What a mess."

"If I knew you were coming I'd have had it cleaned."

"How can you live in such squalor? It's disgusting."

I glare at her. I'm starting to feel some disgust myself.

"Did you just come here to lecture me about the state of my office?"

"Doesn't everyone?"

"Some people are too polite. The rest are in too much trouble to care."

"Well, I find it very offputting. You should do something about it."

"I will. I'll throw you out on your ear if you don't get down to business. What do you want?"

She stares at me like I'm something that just crawled out from under a rock, but swallows the rest of her criticism and gets down to business.

"Mursius's belongings."

"What about them?"

"He's hired you to find them?"

"Maybe."

She leans over the desk and drops a scrap of paper in front of me.

"You'll find them there if you hurry," she says. She rises swiftly and departs without a backward glance.

I look at the paper. It has an address written on it. One of the old warehouses next to the docks.

I find my magic dry cloak. This case might be even easier than I thought.

The rain has halted and a hot breeze blows in from the sea, raising steam from the streets. The stals, the small black birds that infest the city, risk a few chir-rups and venture from their perches high up on the tenement roofs. In the Hot Rainy Season they usually hang around looking miserable like everyone else.

When I'm halfway down Quintessence Street I realise I haven't had any breakfast. I'm hungry. It strikes me that it will soon be time for prayers. I hurry through the mud, keen to get indoors before Sabam, the call for morning prayers which rings out through the city as regularly as clockwork every morning. It's a legal obligation for all citizens to kneel and pray, no matter where they are. Anyone found not complying is charged with impiety, and there's no way round it. Naturally, most citizens take care to be in some suit-able place, but if you happen to be in the street at the time, then you have to pray there. Three times a day. It gets me down. It could be worse. Up in Nioj, where things are much more strict, they have six prayer calls a day. Last time I was there on a case my knees ached for a month.

I make it to the harbour and head for the ware-house. Unfortunately, before I reach it, the call rings out from the tower of the nearest church and I am obliged to kneel and pray. I'm seething with frustra-tion. This sort of thing makes it hard to be an Inves-tigator. If anything is going on in that warehouse, the culprit will have plenty of time to cover it up before I arrive.

All around the dock workers are kneeling down so I can't risk ignoring the call. I'd be reported for sure and hauled in front of the special clerical court for impious behaviour. Bishop Gzekius, head of the True Church locally, would relish the chance to send me away for a long trip on a prison galley. He hasn't forgiven me for putting a stop to some nefarious operations he was engaged in earlier this year.

As I'm kneeling, the rain starts again. I pull my cloak tighter around me and wonder how anyone is meant to pray in such circumstances. Finally prayers are over. I hurry towards the warehouse and step inside. The interior is set up with pens and feeding troughs for receiving livestock but the warehouse is empty. I follow my instincts and mount the metal staircase to where the manager's office should be. I find the office, but there's no sign of any manager. No sign of anyone at all.

The door is locked. I bark out the common opening spell and it springs open. I walk in. It's dark apart from a narrow shaft of light coming through the shutters. I wrench them open. Light floods in, and I look around me. The room is full of artwork. Nine or ten sculptures, a few paintings and what looks like a very fine old antique chest inlaid with gold and ivory. I nod. I can't help feeling some satisfaction. When it comes to investigating I'm number one chariot for sure. Hire Thraxas to find your missing works of art, and what happens? He finds your missing works of art the very next day.

It looks like quality goods. There's a small statue of an Elf Maiden which might even be by Xixias, the famed Turanian sculptor who lived in the last century and whose work is now highly prized. I glance at the paintings. High quality again. One catches my eye immediately. It's the painting Mursius was most keen to get back. It depicts a group of young men, one of whom is Mursius. He's in the uniform of a Captain and he's standing with a group of other soldiers, all in dress uniform with swords at their hips and long spears over their shoulders. The inscription on the bottom reads: *Officers of the King's Fourth Regiment after the successful defence of Turai against the Orc Invaders.*

I was there as well, doing my share of defending. No one painted me afterwards.

If I'd prepared for this eventuality I might have been able to load some carrying spell into my mind enabling me to take this lot home with me. But I didn't. Which means I need some form of transport, and quick. I hurry out of the warehouse and look around. The dockers are unloading crates of what looks like Elvish wine from a small vessel tied up in the dock. I approach the foreman, a man I know slightly from drinking in the Avenging Axe. I ask him if I can hire his wagon.

He shakes his head. I take out ten gurans. He shakes his head again. I take out another ten. He tells his men it's time to take a break.

"Have it back in half an hour," he says, and pockets his twenty gurans. That's quite a sum for hiring a wagon, but I'm sure Senator Mursius won't mind the expense. As I'm leading the horse-drawn vehicle back towards the warehouse I suddenly sense something unusual. Nothing I can name, just unusual. I halt, trying to identify it. Sorcery? I can't tell, it's too faint for my senses. A clap of thunder overhead breaks my concentration but the feeling returns as soon as I re-enter the warehouse and it quickly gets stronger. Everything looks the same but I know that something has happened. This place reeks of sorcery. I draw my sword and tread softly up the stairs.

I pause outside the office door. My senses are going crazy. I take a deep breath and kick the door with all my might then charge in with my sword raised. There's no one inside. The room is empty. And when I say empty I mean empty. Of the sculptures and paintings, there is no sign. Damn.

I swear out loud. In the few minutes I've been outside I've been outsmarted by a Sorcerer. I vent my frustration by kicking a cupboard door. It swings open slowly, propelled by some weight behind it. I watch with horror as a body slumps forward to lie sprawled at my feet. It's Senator Mursius. Blood seeps out of a wound in his back. He's dead.

I stand there staring stupidly at the corpse, trying to work out what's happened. Suddenly heavy boots sound from outside, thundering up the stairs. There's no time to flee and nowhere to hide. A platoon of Civil Guards bursts into the office. As soon as they see me standing beside the body they surround me, swords drawn. Their Captain bends down and examines the body.

"It's Senator Mursius!" he exclaims.

I'm arrested on the spot. Within a minute I'm in the back of a covered Guard wagon on my way to the main Twelve Seas Civil Guard station.

"You're in serious trouble," mutters one of the Guards.

Senator Mursius was a hero of Turai. It doesn't take a genius to work out that I am the number one suspect for murdering him. I am in trouble. Lightning flashes overhead as I'm led out of the wagon and into a cell.

I was right. My cases usually do turn bad. This one just went very bad indeed.

Chapter Six

At the Guard station they fling me into an underground cell which is as hot as Orcish hell and stinks like a sewer. The Guards all know me but there's no one likely to do me any favours apart from young Guardsman Jevox, and he's nowhere to be seen. Civil Guards don't like Investigators. In particular, they don't like me. The Guards are under the control of the Prefects in their area. The last Prefect of Twelve Seas, Galwinius, was a man of such corruption that they should have given me a medal for my part in running him out of town, but the Guards don't appreciate a Private Investigator cutting off their supply of bribes. I haven't met Galwinius's replacement Drinius yet, but I doubt he's any better.

A Sergeant questions me for a while. I tell him I had nothing to do with the murder and I'll give him the full story when my lawyer arrives. He tells me that that will probably be a long time.

"Why did you kill the Senator?" he demands.

I shake my head wearily. If he didn't believe my denial the first ten times, I doubt I'm going to convince him now, so I clam up and wait for someone else to arrive. Everyone in a Guard cell is entitled to a Public Defender, but that doesn't mean you'll actually get one. They don't go out of their way to respect your civil liberties in Twelve Seas. I should have my own lawyer on a retainer, but I can't afford it.

It seems obvious that Carilis has set me up for the murder, but I have no idea why. The door opens and in walks Prefect Drinius, his toga edged in yellow to denote his rank. He's a tall, lean man with aquiline features and close-cropped hair, still dark. He can't be much more than a couple of years older than me. I've an idea he fought in the war, which says something for his character. Many city officials managed to avoid it. He has the well-modulated voice of the aristocrat who learned rhetoric at school.

"Did you kill Senator Mursius?"

"No."

"Explain to me what you were doing there."

I repeat my request for a lawyer. It's never a good idea to give statements to the Guard without one present. And I'd as soon not have to blacken Mursius's reputation by spilling the truth about his wife. Even though Mursius is dead I still feel some obligation to protect my client's good name.

Drinius informs me that I'll get a lawyer when he's ready to provide me with one. "I am aware of your reputation, Thraxas. You take pleasure in interfering in the business of the Civil Guards. I do not intend to let you meddle now that I am in command."

"You ought to be grateful. There wouldn't have been a vacancy if I hadn't exposed Galwinius's corruption."

Drinius almost smiles. "Perhaps. I understand the Consul himself was pleased. But as you are no doubt aware, it did not increase your popularity among the Civil Guards."

"I've never been really popular with the Guards. I try and try but they still don't like me."

Drinius motions for his scribe to come to his side.

"Put it on record that the prisoner refused to make a statement."

The scribe puts it on record. Drinius dismisses him and the Sergeant.

"Thraxas, I am not the sort of man to leap to conclusions. You may have a good explanation for what you were doing in that warehouse, but as things stand just now, it looks bad for you. You were found next to Mursius's body. He had been dead for a very short while. The Guard Sorcerer who checked the office found no trace that anyone else had been there. No one at all. Just you and Mursius. Well?"

"Well, he's wrong."

"I doubt it. Furthermore, our Sorcerer reports that no sorcery was used in the area."

This surprises me. I wasn't expecting the Prefect to try and trick me with such an obvious untruth. The room reeked of sorcery, which would have lingered for a long time after I'd left. Drinius sees my surprise.

"Are you claiming that sorcery had been used? If so, you're lying. No sorcery was found. Our Sorcerer is quite certain on that point. Which just leaves you and Senator Mursius. And he's dead. Is there anything you'd like to say?"

"Yes. How about some food? I haven't eaten today."

Drinius shrugs, and departs.

A Guard locks the cell and insults me through the barred slot in the door. "Things were good when Galwinius was Prefect. Then you stuck your nose in. Now we're going to hang you."

I don't know what to make of Drinius. I'd assumed

he was your standard corrupt Prefect but in reality he
doesn't seem so unreasonable. But why bother lying
that no sorcery had been used in the warehouse? That
wouldn't stand up at the trial. A Guard Sorcerer
wouldn't perjure himself about something like that.
Even weeks after the event a really good Sorcerer
working for my defence could prove that magic had
been used at the scene. The Guard Sorcerer would look
foolish in court and the Sorcerers Guild would be down
on him like a bad spell for abusing his skills. Odd.

The door opens. Breakfast arrives. Bread, cheese and
water. All fresh. Perhaps Drinius isn't so bad. Prefect
Galwinius would have let me starve.

I wonder who did kill the Senator. Strictly speaking I shouldn't have to worry about it. I only work when
I'm paid. The Senator hired me to recover his works
of art. I recovered them. Then they went missing again.
But now he's dead there's no one to pay me to find
them again, which kind of ends my involvement. Unless
they do accuse me of the murder, and I end up having to clear my name. I sigh. If that happens, I'll end
up investigating with no one to pay me. Private Investigator. What a life.

The door opens. Young Guardsman Jevox appears.
I helped him in the past, and he owes me a few
favours.

"Thraxas," he says urgently. "You're in serious
trouble."

"So they keep telling me."

"I can't stay here. But I've sent a message to the
Avenging Axe."

He disappears. The day gets hotter and I feel more
and more in need of a beer. Sabap, the call for afternoon prayers, rings through the city. I kneel and pray.
No sense in giving them something else to get me on.
Shortly afterwards the door opens.

"Someone to see you."

Makri walks in. The door closes behind her.

"In the cells again, Thraxas? They ought to put your name on the door."

"Very funny. How did you get in here?"

"I said I was your wife. And they believed me, which doesn't say much for your reputation. Or mine, come to that."

"Well, thanks for coming. I need you to—"

Makri interrupts me. "Let me guess. The case you were working on has now gone drastically wrong. You have annoyed the hell out of the local Prefect and to make matters worse you are now a prime suspect for murder. You need a lawyer, but they won't bring you a Public Defender so you want me to get you one. Correct?"

"In every detail."

"Funny how it always happens that way," says Makri, grinning.

Gurd and Tanrose tell me that Makri has a very attractive smile. I don't really see it myself.

"So, have you seen Gosax?"

Makri sneers.

"Gosax? That cheap crook? He's about as much use as a eunuch in a brothel."

"Maybe, but he's the only lawyer I can afford."

Makri looks serious.

"I saw Kerk."

Kerk is a dwa addict and dealer who, on occasion, passes me information he picks up on his travels.

"He says this time you're really in trouble."

"So everybody tells me. Why does Kerk say that?"

"Because Senator Mursius is a hero of Turai and the Guards really think you killed him. You've been thrown in jail on trumped-up stuff in the past, Thraxas, but this time they think it's for real. Did you kill him?"

"Of course not! Why would I?"

Makri shrugs. "Who knows? Maybe someone paid you. After the Troll Mangler debacle you need a stake for the big race meeting."

"Makri, I liked it better when you'd just arrived in the city and hadn't learned how to make smart comments all the time. I've no idea who killed Mursius but when I was there the place stank of sorcery and now the Guards tell me that their own Sorcerer couldn't detect any traces of magic at all. Which means either they're lying spectacularly, or I'm involved with someone with great sorcerous power. Enough to completely clean up all traces of his actions, which isn't easy."

Makri's hand keeps straying to her hip. She had to check in her sword at the desk and she doesn't feel comfortable without it.

"You should get a good lawyer," she says.

"Makri, is there something behind this?"

"Of course not. I'm just concerned for your welfare. I'll get you a good lawyer. By the way, could you lend me some money?"

Makri has not yet developed the art of subtlety.

"Haven't you already removed it from my room?"

"No," says Makri. "I was going to, but then I realised Samanatius wouldn't approve."

Samanatius is a philosopher who sometimes teaches at the Guild College. He's quite famous. He teaches for free, and gives every appearance of being genuine, unlike some of the charlatans we get round here. Makri likes him. He makes me feel uncomfortable.

"I told Minarixa I'd lent out the money I collected to a woman in distress and I'd have it back in a few days. I promised her sixty gurans."

"I thought you owed them fifty."

"Minarixa seemed so disappointed I pretended I'd collected an extra ten."

Makri pulls a sheet of paper from her tunic. It's a form sheet from Mox's.

"So lend me thirty," she says. "And this time pick something good."

"I only have twenty," I confess.

"What about your emergency reserve?"

"I'm talking about my emergency reserve." Sensing that Makri is on the point of lecturing me about drinking my money away, I explain to her about the hefty bribe I had to pay out down at the docks. "To make things worse, my boots fell apart in the rain. You know how much it costs to get a new pair of boots? Anyway, I can only lend you ten. And I'm not forgetting the forty you already owe me."

Makri nods. She runs her fingers through her wet, tousled hair.

"Do you know any good lawyers?"

"None that will do me any favours," I admit.

"How about Cicerius?"

"He's the Deputy Consul."

"But isn't he a lawyer as well? I'm sure I read some courtroom speeches he made in my law class."

I explain that while Cicerius is a fine lawyer, he isn't the sort of man you can drag down to Twelve Seas to get you out of the slammer.

"He only works on cases of national importance."

"Well, I'll see what I can do," she says.

I study the form sheet for the day's races at Juval. The best bet I can see is Orc Crusher, a good chariot who's won for me in the past. Unfortunately he's a strong favourite and the odds are five to four on. When I explain to Makri that this means if she bets five gurans she'll win only four she's a little disappointed. I tell her there's nothing else really worth gambling on, particularly as we're not in a position to take chances.

"I hope you're right about this one, Thraxas. I'll bet my ten gurans. If I win eight it'll be a start."

I tell her to put the same bet on for me. Makri bangs on the door, summoning the Guard. He lets her out.

"So what's it like being married to a half Orc?" he asks me when she's gone.

"She's only a quarter," I reply.

"I reckon you'd be better off being hanged," he says, and slams the door.

I wait in the cell for hours. No one comes to see me. I feel so starved of company I'd be glad if they interrogated me again, but all that happens is a stony-faced guard brings me more bread, cheese and water. Maybe they're trying to bore me into a confession.

Finally Drinius returns. There's a strange, troubled expression on his aristocratic face. He gazes at me for a few seconds before speaking.

"Your lawyer is here."

"Good."

"I was unaware that you were represented by Deputy Consul Cicerius."

So was I. I can't believe that Makri has managed to bring him here. No wonder Drinius looks troubled. If you're starting out on your political career in Turai you don't want to be caught maltreating a prisoner by the Deputy Consul. Cicerius has little in the way of human warmth, but he's a stickler for the law.

The Prefect departs and Cicerius enters, wearing the green-edged toga that denotes his rank. I notice his sandals are quite dry despite the rain outside. Of course an important man like Cicerius would be ferried here in a wagon and escorted to the door by a servant with a parasol. They might even have laid out a special carpet to protect him from the mud.

"I understand you need a lawyer," he says, some-what dryly.

Deputy Consul Cicerius is by far the best orator in the city and has won numerous sensational cases for the defence in the law courts. He's not a crowd-pleaser but he is respected by all for his irreproachable honesty. Although he is a bastion of the Traditional Party and a strong supporter of the Royal Family, he has not hesitated to defend opponents of the King in court if they happen to be innocent. But while everyone trusts Cicerius, he is not exactly well liked. His character is too austere, and he exudes too little warmth to be genuinely loved by the masses. And he is not well born enough to be totally accepted by the aristocracy. He's aware of his brilliance, and his vanity shows. He's a self-made man, respected by all. I wonder if it bothers him that no one much likes him. Possibly.

I thank him for coming, telling him I'm glad I was able to help such an esteemed character as himself with his recent difficulties. He informs me sharply that he did not come out of any sense of obligation.

"You were adequately paid for your services. You should not expect any favours from me, Thraxas. If you do, you will be disappointed."

I'm disappointed already.

"Then why are you here?"

He tells me he is repaying Makri for a service. I blink. Service from Makri?

"My official wagon became trapped in the mud as we progressed along Royal Way. Some hooligans from the Populares seized the occasion to toss mud and rocks at me. I was in a most uncomfortable position. Your friend Makri fortunately appeared on the scene. She dealt with my tormentors in a most convincing manner."

This sort of political violence is common in Turai. When it comes round to election times it's swords instead of rocks.

"As a result of which I agreed to her request to help you. In truth, I was not unhappy to do so, because you have featured in my thoughts recently. I believe you may be able to be of service to me. However, that can wait. Firstly, I must get you released from this cell. Tell me the circumstances surrounding your arrest."

I tell him the full story, omitting nothing.

"In that case they have nothing to hold you on. The case against you is entirely circumstantial. I will arrange your release immediately."

He leaves the cell. He arranges my release immediately. I am instructed to stay in the city. We leave the Guard station.

"Thank you, Cicerius. What now?"

"Now we have an appointment with Makri at the Avenging Axe. Come."

He leads me to his official wagon, which takes us slowly through the sodden streets of Twelve Seas.

"She is an interesting woman," says the Deputy Consul, suddenly.

"Who?"

"Makri. Is that her only name?"

"As far as I know."

"I had planned to introduce a bill banishing all people with Orc blood from the city. They only cause trouble and are rarely loyal citizens. But I may delay it for a while."

Somehow this doesn't surprise me. Makri has this odd attribute of making herself popular with the most unlikely people. I used to put it down merely to the sight of her bursting out of her chainmail bikini, but it seems to go further than that. Cicerius has no known track record of being impressed by any young woman's shape, but already he seems to have taken to her.

We pull up at the Avenging Axe. Vendors still grimly try to sell their cheap wares and the prostitutes still ply their trade with any soul brave enough to face the weather. The beggars, having nowhere else to go, still sit in useless misery in the mud, homeless, hopeless, deformed, a sight to raise pity in anyone's breast, anyone apart from the entire population of Twelve Seas, who see it every day.

To my annoyance Kerk chooses this moment to waylay me. Kerk deals dwa but he uses far too much of his own product. He's around thirty, gaunt, with large eyes, possibly displaying a faint trace of Elvish blood, no doubt the result of some distant union of an Elvish visitor and a Twelve Seas whore. Even Elves have to enjoy themselves sometime, I suppose, when they're not sitting in trees singing about stars and rainbows.

Cicerius looks on with disapproval as the bedraggled Kerk plants himself in front of me. I tell him I can't talk now but if he comes across any of Mursius's missing works of art I'll be interested to hear about it. I give him a small coin, which he glances at with disgust before tramping off through the mud and rain.

Makri is waiting for us inside. She looks pleased with herself.

"Thanks for the lawyer. Did you put on the bet?"

She nods. I make a fast trip to the bar. Deputy Consul or not, I haven't eaten properly all day. Bread and cheese are nowhere near enough to satisfy the healthy appetite of a man my size. And I haven't had a beer for more hours than I care to think about. I order a fair selection from Tanrose's dinner menu and a "Happy Guildsman" jumbo-sized tankard of ale, and then proceed to get them inside me as quickly as I can.

Cicerius is more accustomed to the Senate and the law courts than Twelve Seas and is uncomfortable in the public bar. Everyone is staring at him, wondering what an important man like him is doing here. He insists that we retreat to my office immediately. I nod, but stop off on the way for another "Happy Guildsman." You can't expect me to function properly if you starve me of beer. It just can't be done.

Chapter Seven

Cicerius's crisp white toga stands out like a beacon in the shabby surroundings of my office.

"To business," he declares. "I need the services of a man who has experience of the seamier side of this city, someone who also has a knowledge of chariot racing and all its mechanisms. You qualify for that, I believe."

"Absolutely."

"Since our recent encounter, Thraxas, I have looked into your career. I find that though you were a notably bad student as a Sorcerer, and have rarely held down a regular job, you did serve well in the Army. Senator Mursius himself spoke highly of your fighting qualities.

"It is unfortunate," he continues, fixing me with the sort of stare that can terrify an opponent in court, "that you could not apply yourself properly in the rest of your life. Your time as Senior Investigator at the Palace was continually marred by periods of drunkenness and insubordination, of which I myself have seen evidence. And where has such behaviour got you?" He gestures round at the squalor of my office. "Do you not even have a servant to clean for you?"

I can't afford a servant, but I'm not going to admit that to Cicerius. I remain silent.

"Well, it is your affair. If you choose to squander your talents instead of using them for the good of our nation, no one can prevent you. But I think that you might be of use to me, and I wish to hire you."

He addresses Makri. "I believe that you may also be of service. I understand that you speak fluent Orcish, both Common Orcish and the pidgin Orcish spoken in the Wastelands?"

Makri nods. Her eyes narrow at the mention of Orcs.

The Deputy Consul turns back to me. "You are aware of the Turas Memorial Race, and the entry of a chariot by the Elf Lord Lisith-ar-Moh, who has always been a great friend of Turai?"

"Certainly. I'm looking forward to it. The whole town is."

"It may surprise you to know that Lord Rezaz Caseg also wishes to enter a chariot in the race."

I frown. "Lord Rezaz Caseg? I've never heard of him."

"You may know him better as Rezaz the Butcher."

I explode in astonishment. Beer flies everywhere. "Rezaz the Butcher? That Lord Rezaz? But he's an *Orc*, for God's sake! The last time he was in the area he damn near wiped us off the map. What do you mean, he wants to enter a chariot?"

It's one of the most outrageous things I've ever heard. An Orc entering a chariot in the Turas Memorial? And not just any Orc—Rezaz the Butcher! One of the fiercest, most bloodthirsty warlords ever to lay waste to a human settlement. And also, unfortunately for us, one of the cleverest generals ever to destroy a Human army. He was by far the best commander in the Army of King Bhergaz the Fierce, who united all the Orcish lands and led them against us. I pound my fist on the table.

"You don't have to say any more, Deputy Consul. Just tell me what I have to do and I'll do it. I'll prevent that Orc from ever reaching the city. You can depend on me!"

Cicerius looks at me with that steely gaze again. "That is not what I require you to do. I do not wish you to prevent him reaching the city. Rather I am hiring you to look after the Orcs while they are here. There may be attempts to sabotage their chariot. I need someone to protect against that and see that they are given a fair deal."

It's not often that I'm speechless. But at Cicerius's words I'm struck dumb. I can't even move my lips. I stand there, staring, wondering which one of us has gone mad. Makri fares no better. She's actually drawn a sword and is looking round her suspiciously as if an Orc might enter right now.

"I see you are surprised," says Cicerius, breaking the silence.

I'm feeling weak. I fumble for the remains of my beer and try to formulate a reply. Meanwhile I'm straining my mental powers for any sign of sorcery, in case this isn't actually Cicerius but some magical impostor sent to torment me. Finally I utter a few words.

"You can't be serious. Rezaz the Butcher can't really be entering a chariot in the Turas Memorial race. And if he is, you can't expect me to play nursemaid to an Orc! Especially not that Orc. He was leading the assault when the wall caved in. I was there. I lost almost everyone I knew to the Butcher's soldiers."

"Times change," replies the Deputy Consul.

"I know. But not that much. Okay, we're at peace just now, but for how long? The Orcish Ambassadors never appear in public for fear of causing a riot. And this Orc Lord wants to walk right into the Stadium Superbius and enter a chariot? Why? And what does the King think about it?"

"The King is strongly in favour of the idea. You see, Thraxas, the politics of running a city involves us in many strange alliances. It so happens that at this moment it is vital to the interests of Turai that we maintain good relations with Lord Rezaz Caseg. Are you aware that exploration and prospecting of the various minerals in the furthest northeast of our territory has advanced to such an extent that we are about to open several new copper mines?"

"No."

"Prospecting has been continuing for some years, and is now about to pay dividends. You will appreciate the importance of this to the state. Small as we are in size, we depend on our wealth for our security. You are of course aware that there have for some years been border disputes with Nioj?"

Nioj, our northern neighbour, is always finding some reason to start a border dispute. We already have gold mines along the boundaries of our two nations and they would love to get their hands on them. In fact, right before the last Orc War Nioj invaded Turai. Only the arrival of the Orcs brought that war to an end as we Humans were obliged to forget our differences and unite to face the common enemy.

"Well, once more, the territory is disputed. Although the deposits of copper are clearly on land that belongs historically to Turai, Nioj has been making inroads and may even be about to claim it as hers."

Cicerius pulls a map from his toga and spreads it

on the desk. He points to the mountainous area where the northeastern part of our territory meets the far larger state of Nioj.

"The next territory along is Carsan, populated mainly by nomadic tribes with little state authority. Carsan is in fact under the strong influence of its eastern neighbour Soraz, which sits firmly in the Wastelands between us and the Orcs. And its effective ruler is Lord Rezaz Caseg. To make things as simple as possible, we need support from Carsan to keep hold of the copper mines. And we can't get support from Carsan unless Soraz allows it."

"So we have to be nice to Lord Rezaz Caseg?"

I look at the map. Soraz looks a long way away.

"Do we really need support from them? What about the League of City-States?" About a hundred years ago all the small states in the region banded together to protect ourselves from large predatory countries like Nioj.

"We can no longer count on much support from that direction."

I knew that before I asked. The League has been crumbling for a decade, pulled to pieces by the selfishness of its members, including Turai.

"Now do you understand why we wish to accommodate the Orc Lord?"

"Just about. But I don't like it."

"Your likes are of no concern to the King or the Consul."

"So I understand. But what's this got to do with chariot racing anyway?"

"Lord Rezaz Caseg is a keen racer, apparently. Furthermore, he has let us know, through diplomatic channels, that he has not forgotten the Elf Lord Lisith-ar-Moh. They fought hand to hand underneath the walls of Turai, but were separated by the press of

bodies before a fatal blow could be struck. He tells us
that while he respects Lord Lisith-ar-Moh as a soldier
he would be pleased to match him in the Stadium.

"The King believes that Rezaz may have other
motives. He is under some pressure at home in Soraz
from his rival, Prince Kalazar, who is supported by
Makeza the Thunderer, a very powerful Orcish Sorcerer. Together they have had some success in gaining support. We believe that Lord Rezaz may be
seeking to increase his prestige by defeating the Elvish
chariot. Furthermore, with a powerful rival like Prince
Kalazar waiting in the wings, he can't allow any insta-
bility in the region. If this understanding ensures peace,
everyone will benefit."

I don't believe that we'll ever get any benefit from
co-operating with Orcs but Cicerius isn't interested in
my opinion.

"The arrival of an Orcish chariot and racing crew
will cause some concern in the city," continues Cicerius.
"It is possible that there may be objections."

"Objections? There'll be a riot."

"Let the government deal with riots. You protect
against sabotage. If anything goes wrong, you may have
the chance to use your investigative powers to put it
right. The King is depending on you."

Cicerius turns to Makri. "You will appreciate why I
also need your help. Very few people in Turai have your
grasp of the Orcish language. That, allied with your
fighting skills, makes you an ideal person to assist
Thraxas in this potentially difficult endeavour."

Makri has been standing there all this time speechless. She now raises her sword slightly—a terrible
breach of etiquette in the presence of the Deputy
Consul—and then spits on my floor.

"I'd kill you, the King and all his children before I
protected an Orc."

Well, you can't make it clearer than that.

Cicerius looks puzzled.

"You are particularly averse to Orcs?"

"I am," explodes Makri. "I was born in an Orcish slave pit. I lived as a slave till I killed my own Orc Lord and most of his household a year ago. And if you take on the job, Thraxas, I'm leaving."

"I'm not taking it," I say, quite emphatically. "Already people talk about bad luck falling on Turai because we have Orcish Ambassadors here. If more of them appear then every time something goes wrong—from a cup getting broken to a child dying—it will be blamed on them. Senator Lodius's Populares won't have to encourage the population to riot. They'll be out doing it for themselves in no time. Anyone trying to protect the Orcs would soon find their life wasn't worth living. He'd be the most hated man in the city. Protect an Orc? Not me."

Cicerius leans towards me. "Yes, Thraxas, you will. The alternative is losing your Investigator's licence."

"That's not fair!"

"Not fair? I doubt the King would worry himself overmuch about some slight injustice if his wishes were ignored. I myself would not countenance a breach of the law, but consider. You have recently been convicted in court of assaulting an officer of the King. You are at present on bail, suspected of murdering Senator Mursius. It would be entirely right and proper to remove your licence. However, I will stretch a point, provided you do as I request. And you will be well paid."

"Doesn't it worry you that Orcs are sneaking, treacherous, murderous animals who'd like nothing more than to wipe us off the face of the earth?" I fume.

"Not at this moment," replies the Deputy Consul. "We need that copper."

I ask him when the Orcs are arriving.

"The chariot is coming in by ship in a week or so. Lord Rezaz is already in the city. So is his charioteer. We brought them in discreetly a few days ago. Do not mention this to anyone."

I won't. The thought that Rezaz the Butcher is actually in Turai at this moment makes me tremble with rage.

Cicerius turns to Makri.

"How is Professor Toarius?"

"What?" says Makri, surprised.

"Your Professor at the Guild College. I understand he dislikes you."

"How do you know that?"

"He told me when he was my guest for dinner last week."

Makri shifts uncomfortably, not liking the way this conversation is going.

"He does not approve of women attending the College and would rather you were not there. He can fail you at any time, and fully intends to do so."

"But I'm a good student!"

"I don't doubt it. Unfortunately the Professor's word will be final. After all, his academic status far outshines that of anyone else at the Guild College. He is seconded there from the Imperial University as a favour to the lower orders by the Consul. If he refuses to pass you then you will not proceed to the next year. If that happens you will never gain the qualifications you require for the University."

Makri takes a stride back towards Cicerius. She tells him straight out that she doesn't like being blackmailed into doing anything. Cicerius gives the slightest of shrugs, implying that it doesn't matter to him if she likes it or not.

"Are you saying you'll get me into the University if I help?"

"No. The Imperial University does not accept women. Nor anyone with Orcish blood. That is more than I can promise. But I will persuade Professor Toarius to pass you at College, providing your work is acceptable. I understand from other sources that it is indeed of good quality."

Cicerius stands up to leave. "Of course, when the time comes, I might be persuaded to use some influence in the matter of the Imperial University. I may well be Consul by then, and I am a very good friend of the Professor in charge of admissions. Who knows how he might react if the Consul were to promise additional funds. Farewell. In the next few days I shall send my assistant with details of what I require from you."

He leaves the room.

Makri yells in anger and tosses her sword, blade first, into my couch.

"I refuse to protect an Orc!" she shouts.

"And so do I," I agree.

We light up some thazis to calm us down. I scrabble under the desk for my store of klee, the locally distilled spirit. There are times when beer won't do. The klee burns my throat as it goes down. Makri makes a face, and holds out her glass for more. We sit in silence, letting the day's events sink in. The rain beats on the door and windows. The light fades into evening gloom. After a while Makri breaks the silence.

"So, what are you going to do when they take your licence away?"

"I don't know. What are you going to do when you fail at the College?"

"I don't know."

We sit in silence a while longer, and smoke some more thazis.

"It's not fair," says Makri eventually. "I don't want to protect an Orc."

"Me neither," I sigh. "But it looks like we're stuck with it. Maybe we won't have to do anything. If nothing goes wrong for the Orcs, Cicerius won't need our services."

"How likely is that?"

"Not likely," I admit. "As soon as the chariot arrives the city will be in uproar. The Butcher will be hacked to pieces and we'll get the job of sorting it out."

Neither of us wants to be involved, but Cicerius has left us no choice.

I pour us some more klee. Makri shudders as she drinks it.

"Why do you buy this firewater?"

"Top-quality klee. It's good for you. You know, I learned long ago to expect strange things to happen. But I never thought I'd end up playing nursemaid to an Orc Lord at the Turas Memorial. I'm tired. I'd better get some sleep before anything else weird happens."

A light tap comes on the outside door. It opens. In walks the delicate, dark-clad figure of Hanama. I fumble desperately for my sword. Hanama is number three in the Assassins Guild. The last time I saw her she tossed a dart into the Chief Abbot of a temple of warrior monks, sending him off to paradise rather more quickly than he had anticipated. I make ready to defend myself.

"Relax, Investigator," she says, in her soft voice. "Had I been here on business, I would not have knocked."

I glare at her, sword now firmly in hand. "Then what do you want?"

"I've come to visit Makri."

"Just a social call?"

"That is correct."

Hanama looks at Makri. Makri looks puzzled but gets to her feet and they go off to Makri's room.

Strange. I've never known Assassins to do much in the way of socialising.

The door crashes open in the most violent manner. I whirl to face this new intruder. It's Sarija, wife of the late Senator Mursius. She trips and falls. She's wet through. Her face is drawn, with a yellowish hue. And she reeks of dwa, easily discernible even among the multitudinous unpleasant odours that waft in from the street outside.

"I'm hiring you to find out who killed my husband," she says, then passes out in my arms. I dump her on the couch. I walk over to the door, close it, mutter my locking spell, then barricade it with a chair.

"I don't care who it is," I grunt. "No one else is getting in here tonight."

I notice there's an envelope pushed under the door. When did that arrive? I tear it open and read the message.

You'll be dead before the end of the rainy season, says the message.

"I will be if things go on like this," I mutter, and throw it in the bin.

Chapter Eight

———◆———

The Deputy Consul is blackmailing me into protecting a hated Orcish enemy. A murderous Assassin has just called in to visit Makri. The dwa-addicted wife of Senator Mursius has collapsed in my office after asking me to find out who killed her husband, although I am in fact the main suspect. And now there's another death threat. I hurry downstairs for a beer.

The bar is crowded with thirsty dockers relaxing after their day's work. I squeeze past some mercenaries singing a raucous drinking song and work my way to the bar.

Gurd and I have known each other a long time. As soon as he sees me he can tell I'm troubled.

"You're looking as miserable as a Niojan whore. Guards still after you for Senator Mursius?"

"Much worse," I reply, and lean over to whisper in his ear. His eyes widen when I tell him about Cicerius and he lets out a Barbarian oath.

"You better get ready to move to another city. Are there any where you aren't wanted by the law?"

"A couple. Nowhere good though. That Deputy Consul is as cold as an Orc's heart. How dare he blackmail me like this?"

Tanrose is stirring a cauldron of soup. I ask her if she can come upstairs and take a look at Sarija. As well as being an excellent cook, Tanrose is handy with a herbal potion and is competent at dealing with life's little injuries. Since dwa swept the city, she's become competent at dealing with overdoses as well.

We meet Makri and Hanama in the corridor. Hanama is so small, pale and generally childlike it's hard to reconcile her appearance with her reputation. But all the stories are true. People still talk in whispers of the small, anonymous figure who eluded one hundred Simnian soldiers and crawled along the rafters of our Consul's private banqueting hall to fire an arrow into the Simnian Ambassador's heart at the exact moment he undid his impenetrable magic cloak to scratch himself. The Ambassador had plenty of protection with him. I was still at Palace Security at the time and I'd have sworn he couldn't be touched. A great many questions were asked, particularly by the Simnians, but no one was ever tried for the murder. The King swore to the Simnians that he'd track down the killer, but as his own agents had discreetly hired Hanama to do the job, the investigation didn't get very far.

Hanama is distressingly good at killing people. I don't like her at all. I don't like the Assassins, period. Coldblooded killers, dealing death for money. I've suspected for a while that Makri might be rather closer to the Assassin than she admits and the social call seems to bear it out. It's probably something to do with the Association of Gentlewomen, which I believe Hanama secretly supports. That's Assassins for you, very unpredictable. You can't read their emotions or motives. They're trained not to show them.

Makri bids farewell to Hanama and follows me back into my office where Tanrose turns Sarija on her side to prevent her from choking on her own vomit. I frown. I don't mind too much whether she chokes or not, but I'd rather she didn't do it in my office. It's untidy enough.

My last client, a rich woman by the name of Soolanis, was a hopeless drunk. Now I have a Senator's wife who's a dwa addict. What's the matter with these aristocratic women? They all have nice villas up in Thamlin and plenty of money to spread around. You'd think that would be enough.

Tanrose thinks she'll be fine in the morning, so I dump a blanket on her and leave her on the couch. And then I bid Makri and Tanrose good night, walk into my bedroom, lock the door, put a spell on it, and go to sleep. I've had more than enough for one day. Unfortunately I sleep badly. I'm troubled by dreams of huge Orcish armies rumbling over the Wastelands led by Rezaz the Butcher, on their way to sack Turai.

I wake up sweating, feeling the heat of the city burning around me. I can still hear the screams of my comrades-in-arms as they fell beneath the blades and sorcerous attacks of the Orcs. I was a regular soldier at the time. Gurd was there beside me; he'd joined up as a mercenary. We stood alongside Mursius and a very few others, grimly holding out, seconds from death. A ragged collection of survivors from the regiments had been posted to defend the east wall before it was torn down by the catapults and dragon fire of the invaders. Kemlath Orc Slayer was with us too, I remember. Though young, he'd already gained a great reputation for the military power of his sorcery, and he'd scattered and broken many an Orc battalion with his magic. But by then his sorcery was all used up and he stood alongside us with only a sword for his protection. He was brave, and a good fighter for a Sorcerer.

I remember Captain Rallee, a private like myself in those days, his long golden hair tied back in a braid, picking up a rock to throw as a final act of defiance after his spear was broken and his sword was shattered in the last assault. As the Orcs prepared to overwhelm us, suddenly there was the sound of Elvish trumpets, cutting through the terrible din of battle. Having given up even hoping for it, we were saved by the arrival of Lord Lisith-ar-Moh and the combined Elvish forces from the Southern Islands who'd slipped through the Orc naval blockade in the night and landed just outside the walls of the city.

When the Elves fell upon the rear of the Orc Army it broke and fled. The Elves hunted a great many of them down. Most of us defenders were too badly wounded or too fatigued to join in the chase. All I remember is rescuing a case of klee from a burning tavern and getting so drunk I had to be held upright by Gurd when the Consul came round to congratulate us on our sterling efforts.

Now Rezaz the Butcher and Lisith-ar-Moh are going to race their chariots against each other. Strange times.

I can't get back to sleep. Who killed Mursius? And why? Because of the stolen artwork? They hardly seem sufficient reason. What was he doing in the warehouse anyway? I suppose it's possible he'd somehow tracked down the items himself and had been killed by the thief to prevent him being identified, but I'm not convinced. And what happened to the works of art after that? I know they were removed from the warehouse by sorcery, but it doesn't make sense. Any Sorcerer powerful enough to do that shouldn't need to go around stealing a few statues and paintings. He'd have his own collection.

There aren't that many rogue Sorcerers around, which is fortunate. The Sorcerers Guild regulates its members pretty carefully. There's always Glixius Dragon Killer, I suppose. He seems to operate outside the law when it suits him, although so far he has never been convicted of any crime. I strongly suspect that the death threats are coming from him. It's just the sort of petty malice he'd enjoy. They might be some sort of diversion to distract me from his nefarious schemes. He's wasting his time. I don't have any ideas what his nefarious schemes might be.

I can hear the rain beating down outside. In another couple of days the streets will start to resemble canals and no wheeled vehicle will be able to travel. I get up, light my lantern and go next door. Sarija is still sleeping on the couch. A masked man with a sword is standing over her, about to cut her throat. I wasn't expecting that.

I fling my lamp in his direction. He raises his arm to ward it off and it smashes on the floor. Now there's no light in the room, and I'm facing an armed opponent. Before my eyes have time to adjust I hear him leap at me so I jump sideways, crash into something and fall heavily to the floor.

I'm on my feet in an instant and as my eyes adjust to the gloom I see my assailant trying to outflank me. I let him think I haven't seen him. He thrusts at me with his blade, but I'm ready for it and slide out of the way. I grab his wrist and he grunts in surprise. I drag him towards me.

"You're better than you look, fat man," he snarls, kicking out at my shin. It hurts but I don't let go till I've pulled him right up to me, then I butt him in the face. He yells in pain as his nose caves in. I like that.

He swings his sword wildly, but he's lost concentration. I stay calm and wait my chance. He makes another rash lunge towards me. I leap nimbly over the still comatose figure of Sarija and he stumbles into her body. I grab a dagger from my desk and fling it at him. It sinks into his chest, and he slumps dead to the floor.

I stare at the body. He wasn't much of a fighter. He should have known better than to attack me. I've had a great deal of experience.

Makri bounds naked into the room with a sword in her hand, alerted by the noise.

"Who is it?"

"I don't know."

I light a lamp so we can see better. I still don't know. Just some anonymous-looking thug I've never seen before.

"What happened?"

"I found him about to kill Sarija."

Sarija has not woken up. Powerful stuff, dwa. Maybe it would make me sleep better.

I haul the body out of my room and carry it along the street, where I dump it in an alley. I don't want to report this to the Civil Guards because it'll only give them an excuse to make my life even more difficult. The rain immediately washes out all trace of my footprints, not that the Guards will spend a lot of time looking for clues anyway. If you're found dead in an alley in Twelve Seas it tends to be regarded as the natural order of things. When I return Makri has put a tunic on.

"Couldn't you have done that before you came in the first time?"

"What for?"

"Just one of these civilisation things. Round here young women don't rush naked into men's rooms."

"You wouldn't be saying that if there had been four of them and you needed me to help."

"I suppose not. Don't you wear anything when you sleep?"

"No. Do you?"

"Of course. Sleeping naked is only for Barbarians. Like eating with your fingers."

"What if you're in bed with someone?"

"You still use cutlery."

Makri says that now she's up she'll use the few hours before dawn to study some philosophy. She attended a public lecture in the forum by Samanatius and she's been puzzling about eternal forms ever since.

"Do you think it's true that somewhere in the universe there is one great, perfect axe of which my own axe is just a pale reflection?"

"No."

"Samanatius says it's true. And he's the wisest man in the west."

"Says who?"

"Everyone."

I start on a joke but bite it back. Makri is keen on her philosophy and can get upset if I mock. As she rushed into my room to save me I figure I might as well be polite for a while. She asks me if I'm going to take on the case for Sarija. I tell her I will, if Sarija ever wakes up.

"I need the money. Anyway, I want to know who killed Senator Mursius. He was my commander. I owe him. What did Hanama want?"

"Some advice on gambling."

"Gambling? Hanama? What for?"

"It's private," replies Makri.

"Why would she ask you about gambling?"

"Why not? After all, I'm a woman who just won eight gurans on Orc Crusher."

The chariot came in an easy winner, winning eight gurans each for Makri and myself.

"So now I have eighteen gurans," says Makri. "What's the next bet?"

I see that Makri is not going to tell me any more about Hanama the Assassin, so I let it pass for now. Makri takes tomorrow's form sheet from my desk and spreads it out.

"You're keen on the chariots, all of a sudden."

"I've no choice. If I don't come up with sixty gurans pretty soon I'll be in disgrace with the Association of Gentlewomen. It's all your fault really."

I promise to study the form for the next races.

Sarija wakes with the dawn. For a woman rich enough to buy the finest food, cosmetics and hair-dressing skills that Turai has to offer, she's looking pretty rough. I try and get a little breakfast inside her but she has no appetite and barely manages a mouthful of bread. I eat heartily and ask her for some details of the case.

"I'll find the killer. I have to. I'm the main suspect."

Sarija asks me if I did kill him. I assure her I didn't. She seems to believe me.

"Who do you suspect?"

I admit I have no real suspect. Apart from Sarija, possibly.

"Why me?"

"You can't have been getting on too well together. He won't give you money in case you spend it on dwa. In return you sell off a few works of art and he hires an Investigator to get them back. It doesn't add up to a very harmonious household."

She admits that what I say is true but points out that she had no reason to kill Mursius.

Not strictly true, I reason. If Mursius wasn't around to interfere, all the family money would revert to the control of Sarija, giving her unlimited access to dwa. Dwa has already proved an ample motive for murder many times in Turai. I ask her where she was when Mursius got killed.

"In Ferias. The servants can testify to that."

"Servants can generally testify to anything. Did anyone else see you, anyone not connected with the household?"

She shakes her head. It doesn't seem to have occurred to her that she might well be a suspect. "Surely any Sorcerer could clear me?"

"Maybe. A powerful Sorcerer like Old Hasius the Brilliant at the Abode of Justice can sometimes look back in time and see what happened. But it's a hard thing to do. Depends on the moons being correctly aligned at both the time of the crime and the time of the enquiry. More often than not it's not reliable. That's why we still have people like me to investigate things. Do you know why Carilis came to see me yesterday?"

At the mention of Carilis, Sarija makes a face. "I've no idea."

"You didn't like Carilis?"

"She was sent by my husband to make sure I didn't get any dwa. Of course I didn't like her. And I think she had an idea in her head of replacing me."

"Replacing you? As Mursius's wife?"

Sarija nods. "That's why I was still able to buy dwa. Carilis was meant to be preventing it, but she'd always turn a blind eye, hoping I'd die from an overdose so that she could move in. She figured it was time she married into some wealth. She comes from a good family, but her father lost all his money in some land scandal. They were cousins of Mursius. He took her in."

I see. I wondered why an obviously aristocratic young woman like Carilis was working as a nursemaid.

"Have you ever considered giving up dwa?"

"Every day. It's not so easy."

I talk to her a while more. Now her mind is clearer she's not nearly so unpleasant. In fact, I end up rather liking her, particularly when she tells me about the trouble she had with Mursius's relatives after they married. Sarija comes from a decidedly lower class than the Senator and they didn't like that at all.

"My mother was a dancer from Simnia. I kept up the tradition. I used to work at the Mermaid. It was a rough place in those days."

"It still is. Roughest place in Twelve Seas. I can see why Mursius's relatives didn't like you. How did you meet?"

"During the Orc Wars. You know how class divisions relaxed for a while when the Orcs were at the gate. Mursius used to come into the tavern with some of his men when they were off duty. We fell in love. After the war was over he came back to Twelve Seas, whisked me off in his carriage and married me. I wasn't expecting it. It was good for a while . . ." She spreads her hands. "But his family never accepted me."

I sympathise. I suffered much the same sort of thing with my wife's relatives. You can usually tell the birth of a Turanian from their name. High-class women's names generally end in "is," like Carilis. No one would mistake Sarija for an aristocrat, even if she acted like one.

"Do you have any beer?"

I give her a bottle.

She drinks it with some relish. "You know the upper classes only drink wine? I haven't had a beer in years."

I don't tell her about the man I found trying to cut her throat. Maybe he was just a burglar with a mean streak. I doubt it.

She drinks her beer quickly and asks for another. I'm starting to like her. Any friend of beer is a friend of mine. I hope she didn't kill Mursius. We talk about him a while more. Suddenly she starts to cry. Not hysterical, just a slow, sad kind of weeping.

I hate it when my clients cry, particularly the women. I never know what to do. I try patting her hand. It doesn't help much.

"I'll find the killer," I tell her.

She seems a little comforted, but it doesn't stop her from crying.

An official messenger arrives from the Senate. I rip open the scroll and eye it warily.

Come immediately to the Stadium Superbius, it reads. It's signed by Cicerius. I suspect it's bad news, but really I'm pleased at an excuse to run away from Sarija's tears.

Chapter Nine

The Stadium Superbius is situated outside the east gate of the city walls. It's huge, the largest arena in any of the League of City-States. The chariot-racing track is the longest you'll find in this part of the world. Samsarina's is longer of course, but Samsarina is way out west of here, and far bigger than Turai.

I travel through the pleasure gardens to the east gate. Usually I'm excited by the journey but as the pleasure gardens are half underwater they're a sorry sight and I'm apprehensive as to why Cicerius has summoned me. I guess I'm about to meet an Orc. Furthermore I currently as wet as a Mermaid's blanket, because I've left the Avenging Axe without my magic dry cloak. Instead I've used my sorcerous capacity to load the sleep spell into my mind. No matter if Lord Rezaz is here at the invitation of the King. I'm not meeting Orcs without some means of protecting myself.

Prince Frisen-Akan owns a villa right next to the

Stadium and it is here that Lord Rezaz is staying. His presence in the city is not yet publicly known. A Guard takes me to Cicerius.

"We have a problem," says the Deputy Consul.

"Already?"

"I am afraid so. Come with me."

He leads me through the villa. It's as splendid as you might expect but I'm in no mood for appreciating fine furnishings. Before I've prepared myself properly Cicerius has led me into a large reception room. There, standing in front of the window, is the Orc I last saw at the foot of the crumbling city walls fifteen years ago.

"Lord Rezaz Caseg," says Cicerius, and introduces me.

Lord Rezaz is large, even for an Orc, and looks much the same as I remember him, slightly more gnarled, though it's hard to tell. Orcs tend to be gnarled anyway. Despite his rank he wears the standard black tunic of an Orcish warrior. Over it he has a sumptuous dark red cloak and he carries a golden mace. With him are two other Orcs, both rather small for the race. Each has dark shaggy hair, as is normal, and one wears the black garb of a warrior. He looks mean. The other is unarmed and turns out to be Rezaz's charioteer.

I am extremely uncomfortable. I'm in a room with three Orcs and only Cicerius for Human support. Cicerius was never much of a fighter, even in his youth. I can't shake the feeling that, diplomatic mission or not, these Orcs are going to attack me. I prepare the sleep spell.

"I remember you," says Lord Rezaz, startling me.

"You remember me?"

"From the walls. You fought that day. I saw you. You were thinner then."

I'm even more startled, and a little annoyed. The

last thing I was expecting was for Rezaz the Butcher to comment on my weight.

"I am pleased that the man assigned to aid us is a warrior," says the Orc Lord.

Cicerius looks satisfied that I've got off to a good start. A servant brings us wine. Before coming I had determined to decline all such hospitality. I will not share drinks with an Orc, I told Gurd. "To hell with it," I think, and take the wine. No point making life difficult for myself.

"Would someone like to tell me what the problem is?"

"Sabotage," says the Deputy Consul.

"Already? But the chariot isn't here yet."

"My charioteer's prayer mat has been stolen," says Lord Rezaz. "And without it he cannot ride."

I stare at them, uncomprehending. "His prayer mat?"

"It is necessary for an Orcish charioteer to place his prayer mat under his feet before competing. Without it he cannot race. Last night someone stole my charioteer's."

"Can't you give him another one?"

Apparently not. It seems that an Orc gets his own prayer mat from a priest when he comes of age and losing it is a serious matter. A replacement can only be obtained from an Orcish temple and the nearest Orcish temple is some weeks' ride away. As I know nothing about Orcish religion this is all news to me. I wasn't even sure if they prayed.

I turn to Cicerius. "Isn't this place guarded?"

"Heavily. But the theft still happened."

"We foresaw that there may be some difficulties during our stay," says Lord Rezaz. "But we did not foresee that the moment we arrived in Turai, under the protection of the King, our religion would be insulted and our persons robbed."

Cicerius is troubled. He can see the copper mines

disappearing from under his nose, and with them his favour with the King.

I ask the Deputy Consul if a Sorcerer is working on the case. He looks uncomfortable and confesses that he's worried about asking for sorcerous help. He's concerned that any Sorcerer asked to find an Orc's prayer mat might tell him to go to hell. The True Church in Turai is permanently suspicious of sorcery and consequently the Sorcerers Guild is always wary of any action that might be seen as impious. He says he'll try and arrange some sorcerous help, but meantime I better start looking.

"Who knew that Lord Rezaz was in Turai?"

"The King and his family. The Consul and myself. That's all, apart from the battalion that brought him in. And they're the most loyal troops the King has."

Few people are so loyal in Turai that they can't be bought, though I don't say this out loud, not wanting to run us down in front of an Orc. I turn to Rezaz.

"Okay, better fill me in on the details."

He looks blank.

"It's what Investigators do. Take details. Don't you have Investigators in your country?"

"No," replies the Orc Lord. "There is nothing to investigate. In my country, no one would be unwise enough to steal my charioteer's prayer mat."

I take some details. I take some more wine. It's a fine vintage. Being in a room with three Orcs doesn't seem to spoil it at all. Then I take my leave. As he escorts me to the door, Cicerius lectures me about the importance of this matter. I get the impression Cicerius is never happier than when lecturing me about the importance of something.

Back in Twelve Seas Kerk is waiting at my door, looking like a man who needs dwa. Even the rain cannot entirely wash its smell from his clothes.

He's brought me a small bronze cup that's just turned up at the premises of one of Twelve Seas' numerous dispensaries of stolen goods. He thinks it might be from Mursius's collection. In truth, Kerk has no idea where it comes from and has simply brought me the first vaguely suitable thing he found in order to raise a little money. For all he knows the cup could have been made yesterday.

I let him know I'm not impressed, but pay him a small amount for his trouble. Later I permit myself a satisfied smile. I remember this cup. It was in the warehouse along with the paintings and sculptures.

"Made in distant Samsarina in the last century, if I'm not mistaken," I tell Makri. "It was Mursius's all right. I seem to remember he once bounced it off my head after I fell asleep on duty."

"Right, Thraxas, you know I'm always interested in your war stories. Have you studied the form yet?"

"Makri, you've made a very quick transition from stern moralist to demon of the race track. Give me a chance."

"No time," says Makri. "I have to hand over that sixty gurans soon. The women are starting to talk."

I take out the latest form sheet from Mox. It's damp, like everything else in the city now. It costs me and Makri more to take these form sheets away. Paper isn't cheap in Turai. Like *The Renowned and Truthful Chronicle,* it's written out by a scribe and copies are then produced by a Sorcerer, or in Mox's case, a Sorcerer's Apprentice, complete with misspellings.

"Let's see. I don't like anything in the first race. Or the second. Maybe the third . . . Sword of Vengeance, six to four. That's a good chariot."

"What about Castle of Doom?" says Makri suspiciously. Castle of Doom is the even-money favourite and Makri is now dubious of anything that seems risky.

I shake my head. One of its horses injured a leg last season and I'm not convinced it has fully recovered.

"Sword of Vengeance ran two good seconds last year and they've been out training in the west. I reckon it'll win."

"Well, I hope so," grumbles Makri. "My life was stressful enough already before you started me worrying about chariot racing."

She hands me her eighteen gurans. "Are you sure that Stadium Sorcerer in Juval is honest?" she demands.

"I think so. More honest than Astrath Triple Moon was anyway. Incidentally I went up to see Lord Rezaz Caseg today."

Makri reels in surprise. "What?"

"Up at the Stadium. He's staying at the Prince's racing villa."

Makri starts preparing for her inevitable bad mood about Orcs. I brush this aside and tell her about the day's events.

"Good," she says. "Maybe they'll go home."

"Afraid not. They're staying. And I'm helping find the prayer mat. Bit of a weird crime. Not what I was expecting."

Makri tells me that it was a very smart crime. "What better way would there be to make sure the Orcs don't enter the race? If someone sabotages the chariot after it arrives, it could always be fixed. I presume the King will place the services of Turai's wagonsmiths at the disposal of Rezaz. Even the horses would be difficult to harm because Cicerius said they're bringing a spare team. But the prayer mat is a clever target. No Orcish charioteer will ride without his mat. If he dies in the race he wouldn't get to heaven. And there's no chance of getting another one to Turai in time, not in this weather. Didn't you know about Orcish charioteers and their prayer mats?"

"No. And neither did anybody else in Turai, apart from whoever stole it. Why didn't you mention it earlier?"

Makri looks annoyed. "No one asked me. I don't go around giving out lectures about Orcs. It's not my fault if you're all completely ignorant about their culture."

"Well, it's fortunate you know so much, Makri, because you're helping me find it. Don't start protesting, you know you have to. If the Orcish chariot doesn't run then Rezaz withdraws his protection from the copper mines. Cicerius will be down on us like a bad spell. I'll lose my licence and you'll fail college. First thing I have to know is who in the city wants the Orcs not to run."

"Wouldn't that be everyone?"

"Yes. That makes things difficult. But there must be someone with a stronger reason than most. And who would have enough knowledge to pull this off? There can't be many people who know enough about Orcish culture to realise that taking the prayer mat would have such an effect."

Makri stops being angry and gets depressed. All this involvement with Orcs is really upsetting her. She doesn't like to think about her time as a gladiator slave. "It's okay when I can just kill them. But I can't stand this collaboration."

I sympathise. I'm not enjoying it either. And there's still the matter of Mursius's murder to be cleared up. More tramping round in the torrential rain asking questions of people who don't want to answer them. Not for the first time, I curse Rittius for plunging me into poverty and making me work.

I'll take the bronze cup up to Astrath Triple Moon. He's a good Sorcerer and may be able to learn something from it. Before I can do that Captain Rallee appears. He's the officer in charge of the small Civil

Guard station next to the docks. The Captain and I go back a long way. We were in the same unit in the Army and fought against the Niojans and then the Orcs. Most times we meet now I annoy the hell out of him. He thinks that when I'm investigating criminal activities I should go running to the Guard every time I find out something. I rarely do.

Incidentally, our careers both took a sharp downward turn around the same time. When I was sacked from the job as a Senior Investigator at the Palace the Captain was moved out of his comfy job at the Abode of Justice due to some political manoeuvring by Rittius, who was then still Deputy Consul. The Captain ended up pounding the beat and he doesn't like it at all. The small station next to the harbour is not the most comfortable place for a man to spend his time, and certainly not a suitable reward for a man who fought bravely for his city. But in the corrupt city that Turai has now become, advancement comes to those with good connections, not to those who have served her well. This, plus the fact that Turai is currently struggling under a dwa-fuelled crime wave, puts the Captain in a more or less permanent bad mood.

I'm generally pleased enough to see my old fighting companion though a visit from him usually means trouble.

"You're in trouble," says Captain Rallee.

"Trouble is my middle name," I reply.

It doesn't raise a smile. "The name Lisox mean anything to you?"

I shake my head.

"Small-time thug. We just found him dead in an alley, not far from here. He had a knife wound in his chest. Thrown, not stabbed, according to my medical expert. Not many men can throw a knife that accurately, Thraxas. Specialised art." He eyes me.

"Lots of men learn how to do it in the Army," I point out.

"Not many as well as you."

"I expect it was the Brotherhood. They have a lock on crime in the area. You know how they hate any independent men trying to muscle in."

"You care to hand over your knife for sorcerous examination?"

"I would. But I haven't seen my knife for some time. I lost it on a case and never got round to replacing it."

"Then perhaps we better just get a Guard Sorcerer down from the Abode of Justice and have him check the aura on the body. See if it has any connection with your office, perhaps."

"Come on, Captain. The Abode of Justice isn't going to send down a high-class Sorcerer just to check on some vagabond found dead in Twelve Seas."

"Probably not," agrees Captain Rallee, realistically. "So why don't you just tell me what it was about?"

I remain silent.

"What's the idea of reporting Orcs in Ferias?" he demands, taking me by surprise.

"I met some. You don't expect me to ignore them, do you?"

"Well, no one else met them. I hear that Kemlath Orc Slayer himself was down there. If he says there were no Orcs around it means there were no Orcs around."

The Captain looks thoughtful. I know he's reliving memories similar to mine, of when we knew the young Kemlath and how he fought at the walls.

"Except, Captain, you know I wouldn't make up a story like that. I don't know why Kemlath couldn't find any trace. Someone must have cleaned up the area with sorcery. It was good seeing old Kemlath again. You remember that day when he brought down a war dragon and Gurd was furious because it crushed his tent?"

"Never mind the war stories. What were you doing out in Ferias?"

"Working for Senator Mursius. Not that Ferias falls within your jurisdiction."

"The Senator was murdered at the docks. That does. Prefect Drinius thinks you killed him."

"Well what do Prefects know about anything?"

"Drinius is much smarter than Galwinius was. How come you suddenly have the Deputy Consul on your side?"

"Cicerius is always willing to come to the assistance of an honest citizen."

"So why's he helping you then?"

I decline to answer. I offer the Captain a beer but he doesn't accept it.

He's around the same age as me but much better preserved; tall, strong, broad-shouldered. His hair hangs down his back in a long pony tail. So does mine, but mine is brown, fast going grey, and the Captain's is still golden. A ladies' man, or used to be before he grew too tired of trying to keep the lid on the spiralling crime wave to do anything except work and sleep.

"Last time the Guards met Lisox he was working for Glixius Dragon Killer. Remember him? So maybe you're running into trouble, Thraxas. Now, do you want to tell me about it?"

"There's nothing to tell."

"Then if Glixius starts getting on your tail don't come running to us for help. And if I find you stepping out of line on this one I'll be down on you like a bad spell. I've enough problems without you adding to my grief."

He slings his heavy rainproof cape over his shoulders.

"I hate the Hot Rainy Season. It's pouring down out there and I'm still sweating like a pig. If I have to wade through Quintessence Street to visit you again I'm not going to be pleased.'

Weather shouldn't be like this. Thirteenth day of the Hot Rainy Season. Seventeen more to go. Makri was right. It was a dumb place to build a city.

I ponder his news. Glixius Dragon Killer. He's a powerful Sorcerer. Not up to the standards of the greats, but a lot more powerful than me. It seems likely he's behind the death threats. And now one of his thugs is creeping into my rooms, disturbing the occupants. Glixius is a known criminal associate of the Society of Friends. He's never been convicted of anything. Too smart, too many connections. I eat some breakfast, and wonder what it's all about.

I've had a few strange experiences recently. There were the Orcs in Ferias. Then Carilis leads me to the warehouse and Mursius turns up dead. I found the lost works of art and straight away they went missing again. Surely sorcery must have been involved there, though the Guard found no trace of it. And now I'm getting death threats. I finger my spell protection necklace. It's made from Red Elvish Cloth, which forms a barrier against magic. I have a strong feeling that Glixius Dragon Killer is behind this. If he is, I'm going to nail him.

I wonder what Hanama wants with Makri. No time to think about that, not with this business of the prayer mat. Where do I start on that one? Practically the whole city would be willing to sabotage the Orcs. But no one was meant to know they were here yet. Finding out who had advance information seems like the thing to do.

I try the kuriya pool, without success. Kuriya, a dark liquid from the furthest west, is a mysterious substance in which a skilled practitioner can sometimes see events that happened in the past. It's fabulously expensive and I thought long and hard before replenishing my supply recently. It turns out to be a waste anyway, because I draw a complete blank. Maybe there's nothing to see, or maybe with so much going on I just can't work myself into the required trance. Whatever the reason, when I sit down, concentrate the best I can and stare into a saucer full of the liquid, all I see is a saucer full of liquid.

You can't use the same kuriya twice. I pour it out and curse the expense. I ditch the sleep spell from my mind, use my sorcerous capacity to renew my magic dry cloak, and hit the streets.

The rain pours down. First thing I want to do is locate Carilis and find out how she knew Mursius's goods were at the warehouse. After that I'll pay a visit to Astrath Triple Moon and show him the bronze cup.

A young lad at the next corner is selling *The Renowned and Truthful Chronicle of All the World's Events*. As ever, it is written hastily by a scribe and then turned into thousands of copies by their Sorcerer. It purports to cover all important events in the city but in reality it concentrates mainly on scandalous matters, detailed accounts of clandestine meetings between Senators' sons and notorious actresses and such like. I notice that the vendor is looking as happy as an Elf in a tree as he sets out his papers in his stall.

He tilts back his head and lets out a cry. "Orcs coming to Turai! Orcish chariot due to race in the Turas Memorial!"

Rarely can a newsboy's cry have had such a dramatic effect. Even when the *Chronicle* mistakenly announced that Prince Frisen-Akan was dead from a dwa overdose I didn't see people running through the rain to get their hands on a copy. No wonder the vendor is happy.

When word starts to spread that Rezaz the Butcher is really entering an Orcish chariot in the race there's immediate uproar. Ignoring the rain, people pour out of their homes and workplaces to vent their anger. Soon an angry mob is gathering and voices are raised in furious protest. Among the crowd are the usual collection of troublemakers and criminals but alongside them are many honest citizens, outraged by the shocking news. With the single exception of the Ambassadors secreted away in the grounds of the Imperial Palace, no Orc has ever entered Turai.

"Death to the Orcs!"

"Kill them!"

"No Orcs in Turai!"

"The city will be cursed!"

The most obvious representative of the King in Twelve Seas is Prefect Drinius. His house is close to the Civil Guard station down Tranquillity Lane and people start marching in that direction. I presume this news has leaked out without the knowledge of the authorities because the Guards seem unprepared for trouble and are slow to react.

The poor of Turai are not averse to rioting but it's not easy to get one going in the downpour. When the Civil Guards finally realise the extent of the problem and start flooding into the area at least there are no burning buildings to hinder them.

I'm as interested in a good riot as the next man but I probably should get on with my investigation. If the Guards seal off the area I'll be stuck in Twelve Seas, and I have to make my way to the rich part of town if I want to find Carilis. I start muscling my way through the crowd. My weight gives me a decided advantage and I barge through the mob. I'm used to this sort of thing. Only this summer there was a massive citywide riot after Horm the Dead, a particularly malignant Half-Orc

Sorcerer, unleashed his Eight-Mile Terror Spell on the city. Even now the damage has not been fully repaired. The workmen will be back at their tasks after the rain stops.

What troubles me is the thought that if the Consul's plans to allow an Orc chariot to race in Turai have leaked out already, then my part in the affair might become public knowledge sooner than expected. It's going to make looking for this prayer mat much harder. I'd better ask Astrath Triple Moon if he can help me with a decent spell for protecting the Avenging Axe from being burned to the ground by an angry mob.

Bricks start to fly. The crowd is turning nastier and the noise of their anger is loud enough to wake Old King Kiben. Finally I make it through Quintessence Street and turn right up Moon and Stars Boulevard. This takes me into Pashish, which, though poor, is generally a quieter part of town. But even here angry crowds are on the streets and squadrons of Civil Guards are out with their shields, spears extending from the front of their ranks to keep back the mob. Kalius the Consul is the subject of vociferous criticism for allowing such a thing to happen. Some voices even berate the King which makes me wonder about the wisdom of this whole policy. I suppose he needs the copper, but this can only bring more support to the Populares, who want to get rid of the monarchy. I find myself next to Derlex, the young Pontifex in charge of the local church. He's not rioting, being a Pontifex, but he's certainly outraged by the news.

"A shameful thing!" he thunders.

"Absolutely." I agree. "Orcs in the city—disgraceful. I imagine the True Church will not be pleased?"

"Of course not! We will drive them out."

"And yet," I add, "who knows? Might they pray to the same God as us?"

The Pontifex gasps with horror at this terrible blasphemy. He screams at me that Orcs don't pray to any God that he knows of.

I apologise for my stupidity. The Pontifex moves away. Now there's a man who obviously knows nothing about Orc prayer mats.

I struggle on. When I reach the business and market districts the violence fades away, but even here the atmosphere is tense and angry. The news has spread all over the city and the rich merchants don't like it any better than the poor workers. Everyone hates Orcs here.

The heat that has been building up over the past few days now erupts into an enormous thunderstorm. The sky explodes in flash after flash of lightning and the thunder booms over the city. The rain comes down in such sheets that it's impossible to see where I'm going and I'm driven into a doorway for shelter.

I find myself next to a well-dressed man, a lawyer from the cut of his cloak and tunic.

"We're cursed," he says, shaking his head, as the storm rages above us. "You can't invite Orcs into the city and expect nothing bad to happen."

"Perhaps the King has good reasons for it?" I venture.

The lawyer looks at me furiously. "Orc lover," he spits, and strides out into the rain, preferring the torrential downpour to the company of a man who doesn't mind a few Orcs coming for a visit.

I stare out gloomily at the rain. I can see these next few weeks are going to be tough.

Chapter Ten

Carilis is back at Mursius's villa up in Thamlin, close to the Palace. I used to live around here. My old house is occupied by a Palace Sorcerer now. He's a dwa addict, but he keeps it quiet. He makes a healthy living from drawing up horoscopes for ambitious courtiers. Many of Turai's Sorcerers are independently wealthy. Those that have to work earn their money from generally useless tasks, pandering to the rich. Comparatively few do any good for the city, other than Old Hasius the Brilliant, chief Investigating Sorcerer at the Abode of Justice, or Melus the Fair, resident Sorcerer at the Stadium Superbius.

The servants show me in. Carilis laughs when she sees me.

"What's funny?"

"You. You're so fat and your feet are wet."

"Maybe you can help me with some things I don't already know."

"Like what?"

No servant has come to offer me wine, or even take my cloak. I dump it on a chair. It's still dry. Good spell.

"Like who killed Mursius?"

"I understand you're a prime suspect."

"Only in the eyes of the law. So who really did it?"

Carilis doesn't know and she says she's too upset to talk about it. Whether that's because she's lost her lover or her meal ticket, I can't tell.

"How did you know Mursius's artwork was at the warehouse?"

She won't say.

"Were you having an affair with Senator Mursius?" I demand, just to shake her up a bit.

"No," she replies, and doesn't look shaken.

"Sarija thinks you were."

"What would that dwa-riddled fool know about anything?"

"That's no way to talk about your employer."

"Sarija didn't employ me. Mursius did. And I didn't enjoy having to look after his wife."

I bet she didn't. No young aristocratic woman would enjoy being reduced to the role of servant. That's a terrible loss of status, and status is very important to these people.

"If you want to find out who killed Mursius you'd be better off coming clean. The Guards won't find out anything."

"I somehow can't imagine that you will either, fat man."

For an elegant young lady she has very bad manners. I tell her I'm suspicious she set me up for the murder. This infuriates her.

"Are you saying I was involved? I was trying to help Mursius. If you'd done your job he'd still be alive."

She turns on her heel and walks out of the room. The interview is over. On the way out I pick up a peach

from a bowl of fruit and cram it in my mouth. No
sense in letting the visit be a complete waste of time.
I haven't learned much apart from the fact that Carilis
is still living at Mursius's house, though with her
employer dead, it surely won't be long before Sarija
slings her out.

The thunderstorm has abated, but the rain hasn't
let up. Here in Thamlin the effect isn't so bad. Most
of the water flows off the tiled roads and pavements
into the sewers. The houses round here won't be
collapsing when the ground gives way beneath them,
as happens every year in Twelve Seas.

My cloak is still dry but my shoes are wet through.
I start to wince as the incessant rain pounds into my
face. The cloying heat sends torrents of sweat running
down my back. A wagon rumbles up, its wheels making a dull noise on the tiled road. Prefect Drinius
emerges, followed by three Civil Guards.

"You're under arrest," he says.

"Fine," I reply. "I was getting tired of the rain
anyway. What's the charge?"

"Murder. We found the knife that killed Senator
Mursius. And guess whose aura is all over the handle?"

"Archbishop Xerius's?"

"Wrong. It's yours."

The Guards throw me in the back of the carriage.

"Watch him closely. If he tries uttering a spell use
your swords."

Little do they know I'm using my entire magical
capacity to keep dry. The Guards keep a careful eye
on me as we ride west through Thamlin. The ground
rises slowly, sloping up through the wooded area that
leads to the Palace. The Abode of Justice, headquarters of the Civil Guards, is located just outside the
Palace grounds.

I can make no sense of this development, so I don't

try to. I'm an important man in the city, at least for a few weeks. The Deputy Consul needs me to look after the Orcs. He'll get me off from whatever phoney charge Drinius and Rittius have cooked up this time.

The Abode of Justice is a large building, fairly splendid I suppose, though you can't see it in this rain. I used to know everyone here when I was Senior Investigator at the Palace, although Palace Security and the Civil Guards are rivals, and generally fail to co-operate on anything. It takes us a few minutes to enter. The Sorcerer who checks us in takes an age to utter the spells to open the doors and close them behind us. With the unrest in the city, they've stepped up security.

I often get thrown in the cells but twice in two days is excessive. I'll never get anything done at this rate. Damn that Rittius, he's really out to get me. It strikes me how much I want a beer, and how long it will be before I can get one. Once they put you in a cell, they never hurry to question you, the theory being that if they give you some time to worry about things you'll be easier to break. Sound theory for most people, maybe, but I've been in far too many cells to let it bother me. And I get a good break because there's someone in my cell already who turns out to be a big racing fan. When he informs me that Sword of Vengeance cruised home an easy winner I'm so pleased I almost forget I'm incarcerated. I matched Makri's eighteen-guran bet at six to four which means we both won twenty-seven gurans. Makri is edging closer to the sixty she needs. Another couple of wins and she'll be off my back. What's more, I'll have a reasonable stake for the Turas Memorial.

I'm soon deep in conversation about the upcoming race meeting with my cellmate, Drasius. He's a banker by trade, who's been having a little difficulty persuading his customers that his accounts are entirely honest. He's just heard the news of the Orcish chariot coming to town and he's of the opinion that it might give the Elves a good run for their money.

For the first time it strikes me that there is actually an interesting sporting contest coming up. I've been so appalled at my unwilling role in it that I haven't considered this before. Moonlit River will certainly be a superb four-horse chariot. Lord Lisith-ar-Moh wouldn't send it up from the Southern Islands if it wasn't. I've seen many Elvish chariots and I've rarely seen one that couldn't cruise past anything we Humans had to offer. It's said that the Elvish horsemen can talk to the horses, which gives them an advantage. There again, what about the Orcish team? I hadn't given them any chance, but Drasius the banker points out that Lord Rezaz Caseg wouldn't send his chariot if it didn't have a chance of winning.

"Why would he? The Orc wants revenge on the Elf Lord. He wouldn't enter something that was guaranteed to lose. I figure it's worth making a sizeable investment with the bookmakers on the Orcs."

I can see why Drasius might be in trouble with his customers at the bank. But what he says makes sense. So far the only reaction I've encountered to the affair has been the outright hostility to Orcs shown by the rioting citizens. I'm a little surprised to find someone who's more interested in the sporting aspect. It starts to make me feel interested too. Okay, the Orcs are hated enemies and the only good Orc is a dead Orc, but from another point of view, a chariot race is a chariot race and I love chariot races more than a Senator loves a bribe.

"They'll be giving good odds on the Orcs," adds Drasius. "Even if the bookies rate it, it's not going to get many backers in Turai. The Elves will be strong favourites. The bookies might even push the price out on the Orcs to attract a little money."

This is true. The Orcs are going to be unpopular, so their price is bound to be high. Bookmakers set their odds partly by the chance they give the chariot of winning, but the amount of support for a chariot comes into it as well. A popular charioteer can attract a load of bets, even if he's not actually riding the best chariot, and when this happens the bookies have to cut the odds just in case he happens to win. Conversely, a good chariot with a chance of winning but which no one wanted to bet on would stay at higher odds. That's an unlikely occurrence normally—why would a chariot with a chance of winning not be popular? But the Orcs might be a special case. Even if their chariot could win, I can't see it being heavily backed by Orc-hating Turanians. There might be an opportunity here. To put it bluntly, it might be a good idea to bet on the Orcs. I hate Orcs as much as anybody else, but one has to be realistic about these things. It certainly offers me an incentive to find their prayer mat.

"I expect Senator Mursius's chariot will have some support for sentimental reasons but only a fool would back it against the Elves," says Drasius

I didn't realise that Mursius's chariot was still in the race.

"Didn't you hear? His wife's taken over the stable."

That's interesting. You have to admire Sarija for this. Mursius's chariot is by far the best in Turai. The public would be disappointed not to see it run.

"At least the race will be fair now," says Drasius.

"How do you mean?"

"I heard a rumour that the Society of Friends was planning some sort of betting coup but I doubt they'll try it now with the Orcish chariot coming. Too much attention."

"I don't see how they could've planned anything anyway," I object.

Betting coups, horse doping and various other examples of nefarious behaviour designed to cheat honest punters like myself are not unknown in the out-of-town meetings, but you can't do that sort of thing at the Stadium Superbius. It's too carefully regulated. Melus the Fair, bless her name, is Stadium Sorcerer and she makes sure everything is above board. Powerful, clever and incorruptible, Melus is the only person in the whole city apart from Cicerius that everyone trusts. Since she took over the job from Astrath Triple Moon, there hasn't been a breath of scandal at the Stadium.

Drasius agrees.

"It's certainly been better. I lost a bundle while that crook Astrath was meant to be keeping things in order. Damn him."

Astrath Triple Moon was accused of letting sorcerous involvement in the races go unreported after he was heavily bribed to do so. I helped with his defence. I didn't exactly prove him innocent—it would have been difficult as he was guilty as hell—but I muddied the evidence enough for him to be able to resign without prosecution. I was as outraged as the next man at the idea of cheating at the Stadium, but Astrath was a friend. And he paid me a bundle. I don't mention any of this to Drasius.

"All the races have been fair since Melus took over. But that's what I heard anyway, the Society was planning something."

The Society of Friends control the north of the city. It's not impossible they'd make some attempt at cheating, though I really can't see how they could pull the wool over the eyes of Melus the Fair.

When a guard comes along and takes Drasius away, I'm sorry to see him go.

"Delighted to share a cell with you," I tell him. "Remember my name. If you need any help, just call on me."

Not long afterwards I'm taken to see Praetor Samilius. For a small state Turai has far too much officialdom. We're ruled by the King but beneath him are a whole host of elected officials, all of them jostling for power. Next in line to the King is the Consul, followed by the Deputy Consul, and then there are the four Praetors, one of whom, Praetor Samilius, is head of the Civil Guard and based at the Abode of Justice. Then you've got the ten Prefects, and a whole Senate to advise them all, and various powerful pressure groups like the Honourable Association of Merchants and the Revered Federation of Guilds and the True Church, not to mention the Army, the Civil Guard and Palace Security.

It didn't used to be like this. Fifty years ago there was the King, a few officials and a whole host of loyal citizens ready to fight for Turai. We were poor, but strong. Now we're rich and weak. It's only a matter of time before Nioj wipes us off the face of the earth.

Praetor Samilius isn't too corrupt by our standards, but he's a harsh man with little feeling of sympathy towards the struggling masses. He is a renowned snob. Like many of our upper classes, he has adopted some rather decadent foreign manners, though he did fight in the war, so he's not soft, despite the vastness of his belly and the rolls of fat around his neck.

"Don't you people in Twelve Seas ever get your hair cut?" he says by way of an opening insult.

"We're wearing it long this season."

The Praetor's hair is short, grey, and beautifully conditioned. His nails are perfectly manicured, and he smells of perfume. He looks at me with distaste.

"We really should have them washed before we bring them into this office," he says to his secretary.

He takes a sheet of paper from his desk and tosses it down in front of me.

"What's that?"

"Your confession. Sign it."

This gives me my first good laugh of the day.

"What am I meant to confess to?"

The Praetor's eyes narrow. "You know."

I remain silent. Samilius adjusts his bulk in his chair. He takes a bite from a peach and drops the rest in a wastebasket.

"Thraxas, I can't be bothered getting tough with you. There's no point. Your aura was on the knife that killed Senator Mursius."

"Says who?"

"Old Hasius the Brilliant."

I'm shaken by this, though I don't let it show. Old Hasius the Brilliant, chief Investigating Sorcerer of the Civil Guard, never makes mistakes and is almost impossible to fool. What's worse, he's honest. I remain silent.

"Nothing to say? Not going to ask for a lawyer? Maybe you expect the Deputy Consul to come to your aid?" He chuckles. "He's not going to get involved. Very bad for his reputation. You're on your way to the gallows. Even Cicerius and his famous oratory couldn't help you in court. Not for this. Not when you were found at the scene and Hasius places your aura on the knife. Why don't you make our lives simple and sign the confession?"

I remain silent.

"Very well," says the Praetor.

He makes a big show of signing some official documents, then informs me that I am being arraigned for the murder of Senator Mursius. I will be held in custody until I appear in court, where the charges will be laid against me. The Guards lead me back to my cell. I'm not feeling too happy with the way things are going. I was depending on Cicerius to get me out of this, but Samilius is right. No matter how much the Deputy Consul wants my help he's not going to come to my rescue if it's certain I killed Mursius. It would be too damaging politically.

I can't understand it. Hasius says my aura was on the knife. How can that be? A really good Sorcerer can fake an aura, just about, but it's difficult, and it would be almost impossible to fool Hasius. He might be a hundred years old, but he's still sharp as an Elf's ear on such matters. If someone stole a knife from me and used it on Mursius my aura would be on it, but so would theirs. Hasius only found my aura. It's looking worse with each passing second. A jury will convict me on this evidence. If I was in the jury, I'd convict me.

The call for prayers rings out through the Abode of Justice. I get down on my knees and pray. It seems like the smart thing to do. As I finish the door opens.

"Deputy Consul Cicerius and Government Sorcerer Kemlath Orc Slayer to visit Thraxas," barks the Guard, who sticks his chest out as he stands to attention.

I leap to my feet. "Kemlath! Am I pleased to see you. And you, Deputy Consul."

Cicerius looks at me very severely. "Are you incapable of staying out of prison for more than one day? I would not be here had I not been persuaded to come by Kemlath. How strong is the evidence against you?"

"Strong," I admit. "I was there when Mursius was killed and now Old Hasius the Brilliant says my aura was on the murder weapon."

"And what do you have to say in your defence?"

"I didn't do it."

"Is that all?"

"What else can I say?"

"That depends on how keen you are to avoid the gallows. This is most inconvenient, Thraxas. I need you to find that prayer mat."

"And there's nothing I'm looking forward to doing more. But what can I do if Rittius and his gang are out to get me?"

"Are you saying Rittius has manufactured the evidence?"

"Someone has."

"I'm sure of it," agrees Kemlath Orc Slayer. "That's why I persuaded Cicerius to come. An old soldier like Thraxas wouldn't murder his ex-commander. Who knows what may have happened to the evidence?"

Cicerius is looking very dubious. As Deputy Consul he really can't be seen to be continually pulling strings to release a man from prison if that man then turns out to have murdered a Turanian war hero. It would be political suicide. On the other hand, he's relying on me to find the Orc charioteer's prayer mat.

"In view of Kemlath Orc Slayer's opinion that the evidence against you may have been manufactured, I am willing to once more use my influence on your behalf. I shall instruct Praetor Samilius to release you."

I thank him profusely. He waves it away. "Just try and stay out of trouble this time."

He turns to Kemlath. "Kindly report your findings to me as soon as possible. It is vital that you come up with something quickly. With the evidence being so strong, I will be unable to keep Thraxas out of prison for long."

Chapter Eleven

Praetor Samilius is about as angry as a Troll with a toothache.

"If you try to flee the city I'll have you hacked down at the gates."

Murder trials are traditionally not held during either of the rainy seasons, nor during festivals. But as soon as the rain dries up, and the Turas and Triple-Moon Conjunction festivals are over, I'm due back in court.

"Cicerius won't protect you forever."

"Samilius," I reply, with dignity, "I don't need Cicerius to protect me from you. As a Praetor you are about as much use as a eunuch in a brothel, besides which you are dumb as an Orc. Feel free to contact me any time. Now good day."

Kemlath meets me outside the Abode of Justice. He's hugging his cloak round him and notices that I'm not getting wet.

"Using one of your spells to keep dry?"

"I'm using my only spell to keep dry."

"Your only spell? Aren't you carrying a few others to help with your business? A couple of fighting spells and maybe something for reading hidden documents?"

I admit that I can't really carry around more than one or two these days. "It's taking all my powers just to keep dry. I don't let on how little magic I can use. How do you think my aura got on the knife?"

Kemlath isn't sure. He's well aware that Old Hasius the Brilliant is not easy to fool. "But there are ways. I'll apply myself and see what I can come up with. Meanwhile, you'd better tell me everything. It might give me some clues as to who is attacking you."

I'm grateful to Kemlath. We did fight together, but that was a long time ago and he doesn't owe me anything.

There are always plenty of landuses for hire in Thamlin, unlike Twelve Seas. The drivers aren't so keen to take you down there either.

"The nearest bar," I instruct the driver. "And then the Royal Library."

Kemlath is surprised. "Are you planning on some reading?"

"No, talking."

The driver pulls up at an elegant hostelry at the edge of the sloping woodlands between the Palace grounds and Thamlin. The clientele here—senior Palace servants and officials, one or two Senators and their secretaries, even a Sorcerer or two—sit sipping wine in private alcoves. I march in, grab a waitress and instruct her to bring me their largest flagon of ale and to keep them coming till I tell her to stop.

"And food," I add.

I used to come here to eat when I worked at the Palace. They had a good chef in those days, I hope he's still in the kitchen.

The waitress hands me a menu.

"Bring me everything. And extra bread."

"One way of faking an aura—" begins Kemlath.

I wave him quiet. "Too hungry. Wait."

I down my tankard in one, start on the second and signal to the bartender to bring me another. The first courses start to arrive, bread and some fancy fish entrees. I can't scoop up enough food using the small spoon provided, so I shovel it in with my fingers and the aid of the bread.

"More beer," I tell the waitress before she leaves. "Quickly. And bring the next courses."

She smiles. No doubt the staff appreciate a man with a healthy appetite. Inside the hostelry it is cool and pleasant. I haven't been this comfortable for weeks. The waitress wheels up a cart carrying six main courses and a hefty selection of side dishes. She looks at me enquiringly.

"Just leave the cart," I tell her. "And bring me another beer. Have you any bigger flagons?"

Kemlath looks on in some surprise as I demolish the contents of the food cart. He's sipping a glass of wine and picking at a small plate of roast fowl.

"I have to be careful with my stomach," he says, apologetically.

That's sorcery. It can't guarantee a healthy appetite and a good digestion.

"Can I bring you anything else?" says the waitress. I tell her to bring another wagonload of main courses.

"But pile it up higher. And one of each dessert. And more bread. Did you bring me beer? Better bring another."

I undo my belt and my sword clatters to the floor. I let it lie there and carry on eating. Some time later I'm feeling Human again.

"More beer," I tell the waitress.

I notice the kitchen boy is peering out from the kitchen with awe on his face.

"Must be a while since they had a good eater in here," I mutter to Kemlath, and get down to the wide range of desserts.

Later, when I'm imbibing another beer and finishing off a few scraps, the chef appears at our table.

"Thraxas!" he says, throwing his hands in the air with pleasure. "I should have known it was you! We miss you!"

Outside the landus driver is wet as a Mermaid's blanket and looks as miserable as a Niojan whore. Landus drivers are notoriously bad-tempered.

"The Library," I instruct.

"I've never seen such an appetite," says Kemlath Orc Slayer admiringly, as we drive off.

"I need a lot of fuel. I've serious investigating to do. And the way I keep getting thrown in prison these days I never know when my next meal might be."

I take a drink from the flagon of ale I brought out with me. I'll have to finish it before we enter the Royal Library. I know from experience that the curators are touchy about anyone getting too close to their books and manuscripts while carrying a flagon of ale.

"Who are you meeting?" asks Kemlath as the vast marble building comes into view.

"Makri."

"The woman who killed the Orcs? Can she read?"

"She certainly can. And don't let her hear you doubting it. Makri's a budding intellectual and she's very touchy with men who give her a hard time about it. Apart from me, but then I taught her the skills needed to survive in the city."

"Why do you want to see her now?"

"Because she's smart. I want to tell her what's been happening and see if she has any ideas. Also I have some good news for her."

This is Makri's regular study time. Not surprisingly, the Library staff were taken aback when a young woman with Orc blood started to appear asking for manuscripts about philosophy and rhetoric, but as the Library extends membership to all people attending the Guild College they were obliged to let her in. Now they're used to her, the staff are pleased to see her, rather like the chef being pleased to see me: they like anyone who appreciates what they do.

I leave Kemlath in the landus after arranging to meet him in an hour at the Avenging Axe. The Royal Library is vast, with two huge wings and a massive central dome housing one of the finest collections of works in the west.

"Please leave your wet cloak in the cloakroom," says the doorkeeper.

"Completely dry," I say, pointing.

He looks impressed. Everything else in the city is soaking wet but I'm walking round dry and cosy. What a superb spell.

I head for the extensive philosophy section, housed in another smaller dome at the back. All around are thousands of books and manuscripts. Small busts of kings, saints and heroes are set into alcoves in the walls and the ceiling is painted with a magnificent fresco of Saint Quatinius banishing the Orcs, painted by the great Usax, the finest ever Turanian artist, who lived around a hundred years ago. That's certainly a lot of culture for one building. Makri likes it. I had never been to the place before Makri arrived in the city.

That was one reason she chose Turai. Plenty of culture. And she heard there was a lot of fighting as well. She was right on both counts, but she says she wasn't expecting us to be so degenerate. There again, she wasn't expecting to be able to earn money from her shape. She never even knew she had an impressive figure when she was a gladiator. Orcs don't find Human women attractive, so no one ever mentioned it.

I find her engrossed in some old scroll. She looks at me suspiciously.

"Have you got beer hidden somewhere?"

"Of course not."

"You had last time. The librarian was upset."

"Well, I haven't this time."

"It's not very considerate, you know, Thraxas. I need to come here to study. It's been awkward for me, as you well know. The last thing I need is for you to arrive drunk and spilling beer all over the manuscripts."

"For God's sake, Makri, I've just got out of prison. I'm on a murder charge. Will you pick some other time to lecture me about my drinking? I've got good news for you."

A librarian in a toga strides forwards and tells me to be quiet and stop disturbing the other readers. Makri gives me a foul look then stands up and motions for me to accompany her to another small room where we can talk.

"What good news?"

"Sword of Vengeance won."

Makri lets out a cry of pleasure and practically dances round the table. I'm feeling smug.

"You see? Didn't I tell you I could pick winners? Easy as bribing a Senator for a man of my talents. Okay, I may have the odd bad day, but when you want some expert help with chariot racing, Thraxas is the man to come to."

Makri tots up her winnings in her head.

"Twenty-seven gurans. And I have eighteen already except I owe you ten—that means I now have thirty-five. Is the race meeting in Juval still on?"

"Another couple of days. If you can call in at Mox's for a form sheet I'll study it tonight."

"The form sheet always gets wet when I walk back

from Mox's," says Makri cunningly. "Lend me the magic dry cloak."

I hand it over with a sigh. "Great spell," says Makri, wrapping it around her comfortably. "What's happening with the murder case?"

Makri listens while I recount the latest developments. "I still don't know anything about Lisox, that guy trying to kill Sarija. Captain Rallee says he used to work for Glixius Dragon Killer. Remember him?"

"Sure. He must be behind it all," she says. "He doesn't like you, and he's a Sorcerer."

"Maybe. He's a powerful fighter, but I'm not sure his sorcery is good enough to fool Hasius the Brilliant about the murder weapon. But he could have improved. He's certainly my number one suspect."

"Are you really in trouble?" asks Makri.

"I am. It's fairly normal for the Guards to suspect me of every crime they can't find a better suspect for, but someone is really fitting me up for this one. Even Cicerius has his doubts. If I don't crack the case soon I'm in serious trouble. I can't work out if it's all connected to the murder, or if it's more of Rittius's campaign to get me."

Makri wonders if I have any good leads. I admit I have not. I made no progress with Carilis. I think the next step is to speak to Mursius's wife Sarija.

"I expect she'll be full of dwa again. It gets me down trying to get any sense out of dwa addicts."

"Maybe she won't use so much dwa now she's taken responsibility for entering Mursius's chariot in the Turas Memorial."

I'm surprised to hear Makri say this. "How did you know about that?"

"It's all over town. The students at the college are talking about nothing else. Everyone is wondering about the race with the Elves and the Orcs. Has Sarija's chariot got any chance?"

"None at all. You weren't thinking of betting on it, were you?"

"Maybe."

"Bet on the Elf. Unless the Orcish chariot turns out to be better than we expect. That's if the Orcish chariot runs. I haven't made any progress with the prayer mat yet. I'm hoping Cicerius can persuade some Sorcerer to find it. What are Orcs like with racing chariots, anyway? They seemed pretty handy in the war."

"They're good," says Makri. "Some of them are good with horses too. I wouldn't be surprised if Rezaz the Butcher is bringing something hot to Turai."

I notice that despite her hatred of all things Orcish even Makri is getting caught up in the excitement of the race. Before I depart I ask her if she has any suggestions for finding the prayer mat. She hasn't.

I call in on my friend Astrath Triple Moon but it's another fruitless meeting. He can't tell me anything about the bronze cup Kerk brought me.

"It's been cleaned."

Every single thing I need to know about these days has been sorcerously tampered with. Damned Sorcerers.

I ask Astrath if he can look back in time and pick up something about the three Orcs I encountered in Ferias, but he draws a blank on that too.

"Whoever cleaned the area is too powerful for me, Thraxas," he says, looking gloomy because he's stuck in the city in the rain along with the rest of us, and doesn't have a nice villa in Thamlin to shelter in like the other Sorcerers.

"How much would Turai's Sorcerers know about Orcs? Specifically their religion?"

"Do Orcs have a religion?" asks Astrath.

"They might have. You know, temples and bishops and things like that. And prayer mats."

Astrath chuckles. "I doubt it. They're too savage to spend any time praying."

So it seems that even Sorcerers are ignorant of Orcish prayers. Someone in this city must be aware. Someone knew enough to remove the prayer mat.

Back in Twelve Seas the mood is still ugly. The Civil Guards have pacified the area, but you can feel the sullen resentment everywhere. The drinkers in the Avenging Axe mutter complaints against the King and the Consul for allowing it.

"I didn't risk my life against the Orcs just so they could run chariots at the Turas Memorial," growls old Parax the shoemaker. His cronies nod in angry agreement.

I don't remember Parax risking his life at the time— I seem to recall he spent the war hiding in his mother's attic—but he catches the mood of the moment in the Avenging Axe. Gurd is bewildered. As a Barbarian he never had much grasp of grand strategy and stolidly subscribes to the idea of killing all Orcs on sight.

"Maybe we're just luring Rezaz here so we can ambush him," he says hopefully.

Makri squeezes her body into her bikini but the gloom that pervades the place is bad for tips. Drinker after drinker arrives in the tavern, curses the rain, curses the Orcs and sits brooding over a flagon of ale. Even when she adopts emergency tactics of removing a couple of links from the garment, making it so small she might as well be wandering around naked, it doesn't bring much of a result.

"These copper mines might be good for the King's treasury, but it's ruining my income," she complains, slamming a few beers down at a table full of dockers who barely glance at her before getting back to muttering to each other.

A few people ask me about my hunt for Mursius's killer. They know the Guards suspect me but, at least in the Avenging Axe, no one takes me for a murderer. I tell everybody I'm making good progress.

"Mursius knew how to treat Orcs," says Parax. "Fling them off the battlements, that's what you do with Orcs." He leaps to his feet, banging his fist on the table. "I'd kill any man who helped an Orc!" he roars.

"We're going to be popular when news leaks out," whispers Makri as she passes.

Kemlath arrives. His sumptuous rainbow cloak creates a minor sensation in the Avenging Axe. We don't get many high-class Sorcerers down this way. With his large frame, his jovial laugh and his collection of gold necklaces, Kemlath is hard to ignore. The jewellery alone would attract plenty of attention as no one would normally be foolish enough to walk through Twelve Seas wearing such valuable items. Kemlath is safe of course. No one is going to try and rob a Sorcerer. Not even a dwa addict would be confused enough to do that. Sorcerers Guild rules allow them to respond to personal attacks with as much force as necessary, and an angry Sorcerer might well decide it's necessary to fry you to a crisp.

He's come to get a full description of recent events and see what he can find out by sorcerous means.

"Good tavern," he says, as I lead him upstairs. "Can you smell burning?"

I can. There's smoke in the upstairs corridor, coming from beneath my office door. I rush in and my desk is on fire. My desk?

I run to the bucket under the sink to get water. The bucket's empty. I haven't been bringing up water for bathing these last few days. No real need, with all the rain.

"It's all right," calls Kemlath before he utters some

word of power. The fire immediately dies away. Yet again I regret not studying more when I was an Apprentice. I open the outside door and the smoke clears slowly out of my room, mingling with the steam rising from the streets outside as the sun beats down during a break in the rain.

A message is scorched on the surface in spidery, blackened letters.

Do not attempt to find the works of art, it says.

I stare at the warning. Bit of an odd message.

"It isn't easy to send a burning message like that," muses Kemlath Orc Slayer. "He must be a powerful Sorcerer. Or she."

"Well, he or she is going to get a nasty shock when I catch up with them," I growl. "No one burns my desk and gets away with it. Do not attempt to find the works of art, indeed. I'll find them and ram them down his throat."

Kemlath looks around, seeing if he can pick up any trace of where the attack came from. Could it be Glixius Dragon Killer? If so, he's much more skilled than he used to be. Makri said she saw him in the Royal Library last week. Perhaps he's been studying.

The smoke clears. I drink some klee and note with dissatisfaction that it's my last bottle. I now have very little money left, and every time I turn around I'm being warned, attacked, arrested and generally harassed half to death. I'm making little progress in any direction and Sarija has been sending me messages asking what I'm doing about finding Mursius's murderer. I send back a message saying I'm doing everything I can. In which case, I suppose, I'd better do something.

Chapter Twelve

Unfortunately during the week that follows I achieve very little. The rain pours down, the streets turn into rivers of mud, and I run into dead end after dead end. It's been raining for twenty-two days and I'm no nearer to finding either Mursius's killer or the Orcish prayer mat. Cicerius keeps demanding to know when I'm going to come up with something, and I'm fast running out of excuses.

I've asked representatives from every conceivable group of people in Turai what they know about Orcish religion, and the sum total is nothing at all. The Honourable Association of Merchants, the Sorcerers, the Guard, the Brotherhood, the Transport Guild, the True Church, the Goldsmiths, and plenty more besides. As far as I can see no one in Turai knows enough about Orcs to even guess they have a religion, let alone deliberately set out to steal their prayer mat. I'm starting to wonder if the whole thing is a coincidence. Maybe someone took the mat to keep their feet dry.

Furthermore these questions are very bad for my reputation, with the city being so touchy about Orcs just now.

I wouldn't be floundering around in quite such a hopeless manner if Cicerius could tell me anything useful, but he can't. No one who shouldn't have been there was seen near the Prince's villa. And when Old Hasius the Brilliant gets round to checking the scene, he can't find anything.

"How is it that Sorcerers can never find anything?" I complain loudly to Makri. "The damned city is top heavy with Sorcerers yet every time there's a crime and I could use a little help there's nothing they can do. Either the moons are in the wrong conjunction or the whole area's been mysteriously cleaned up. What's the point of having so many Sorcerers if all they can do is make up horoscopes for handmaidens? It's not like that when I get accused of something, of course. No chance. Then it's, 'We found Thraxas's aura on the knife so let's throw him in the slammer.' I tell you, Makri, they're useless. Damned Sorcerers. I hate them."

"What about Kemlath?"

I admit I don't hate Kemlath. At least he's trying to be helpful. He keeps hanging round anyway, though I think there might be more to it than helping me.

"I think he's taken a shine to Sarija," I say.

"Sarija? Wouldn't he regard her as beneath him? And kindly don't turn that into one of your crude jokes."

"Who knows? Sorcerers aren't quite as hidebound about that sort of thing as other aristocrats. And Kemlath comes from the far west originally, same as Astrath. He's certainly been spending a lot of time with her. Says he's helping her to kick dwa."

Makri agrees that this does seem to be working. "But that might be because you got her addicted to beer instead."

"Well it's far healthier. Build her up. She'll need her energy if she's still planning to enter Storm the Citadel in the Turas Memorial."

I stare glumly out of the window. Magic dry cloak or not, I can hardly bear going out in the rain again. Yesterday the aqueduct that runs down to Twelve Seas collapsed with the weight of water. Workers sent by the local branch of the Revered Federation of Guilds are now struggling to repair it. The guilds are blaming Prefect Drinius for the lack of maintenance. The Prefect is accusing the guilds of inflating their workmen's fees. Strikes and litigation are threatened on all sides. It's standard Hot Rainy Season stuff, and adds to the general gloom.

Kerk's seller of stolen goods claims to know nothing of the bronze cup. He has no more of the works of art and won't even admit that the cup came from his shop. His business is under the protection of the Brotherhood so there's little I can do to threaten him. I ask Kerk to notify me if anything else comes on to the market.

Neither Astrath or Kemlath could learn anything from the cup, and I'm no further on with the murder of Mursius. Even though Sarija is my client I haven't neglected to have her checked out, or Carilis. Nothing useful turns up. Close questioning of servants, relatives, local shopkeepers and various others fails to reveal if Carilis was having an affair with Senator Mursius. Some think she might have been. Others don't. No one knows for sure. And even if she was, so what? There's nothing particularly unusual in a Senator having an affair with another woman. If that woman is young, attractive and engaged in looking after the dwa-ridden shell of Mursius's wife, it seems quite probable, but no reason for a man to get murdered. Even if his wife Sarija was the jealous type, I doubt she could have stayed on her feet long enough to do it.

Carilis has gone to ground and refuses to speak to me. She won't tell me how she knew where the goods were. I think she's scared.

I've no idea why Mursius was in the warehouse in the first place. No one reports any strange behaviour on his part and his personal attendant claims not to know what he did that day.

"The Senator gave me the day off," he tells me. Very convenient for him, if not for me.

Guardsman Jevox tells me that the Civil Guard still thinks I'm the culprit. Even so, it's carrying on with its investigations under pressure from Rittius and Samilius, trying to dig up more evidence to nail me. They haven't turned up anything new. This gives *The Renowned Chronicle* something to whine about, though it spends most of its time complaining about the imminent arrival of the Orcish chariot. The city is still simmering. The True Church is particularly upset and its Pontifexes thunder against the notion from their pulpits. Even Archbishop Xerius, a strong supporter of the King, lets it be known in private that he's not happy.

I do turn up one interesting fact. Drasius the banker wasn't the only one to hear the rumour about the Society of Friends planning a major betting coup on the Turas Memorial. The story has certainly passed around town among the betting fraternity. This doesn't prove anything—such rumours are common enough among Turai's perpetually paranoid gamblers—but it's interesting if only because Glixius Dragon Killer is a known associate of the Society. A man of his sorcerous power might be expected to be in on the plot. I've received two more sorcerous warnings, presumably from Glixius, so I'm interested in anything he does right now.

I wonder about the Turas Memorial. Even though Senator Mursius knew the Elves were entering, he advised me to back Storm the Citadel with everything I had. Why was he so confident? Could he possibly have been involved in the plot somehow? Might the Society of Friends have been planning to help Storm the Citadel win? I doubt it but I can't absolutely dismiss it. Nor can I dismiss the other possibility, that Mursius just stumbled into the picture somehow and was murdered by the Society to keep him quiet. Nothing really points that way, however.

I sit downstairs with a flagon of ale in front of me. Makri brings me another as she finishes her shift. She notices that my face fails to light up as the beer arrives.

"No progress?"

"Nothing."

"Can I borrow the magic dry cloak for College tonight?"

"Okay."

"Really?"

"I've no use for it. I've investigated everything and found nothing. I'm just going to sit here drinking till Praetor Samilius comes and arrests me for the murder."

"When will that be?"

"Probably right before Glixius kills me with a spell."

"Come on, Thraxas," says Makri. "There's no point sitting round being as miserable as a Niojan whore about everything."

"Fine," I say. "You have cheered me immensely. I am now as happy as a drunken mercenary."

"Don't get angry with me," says Makri.

Makri is easily annoyed these days. The constant downpour, the strain of her studies and the amount of shifts she has to work are getting to her. And she still hasn't collected the sixty gurans she promised Minarixa. The race meeting in Juval ended without us finding another chariot worth backing. Makri asked Gurd for a loan, but Gurd's trade has been poor and he's also had the expense of fixing the roof, which sprang several leaks in one of last week's storms. So he claims, anyway, though I suspect that Gurd may just be unwilling to lend out any money for the purposes of helping the Association of Gentlewomen. In the northern Barbarian lands where Gurd comes from, women have a lower social status than horses, and he finds it difficult to adapt to our more civilised ways.

Makri's only hope of raising the sixty in time is at another race meet even further south in Simnia. She's frustrated with the delay. In truth sixty gurans isn't going to get the Association of Gentlewomen very far. They've run into problems with their attempt to have themselves recognised by the Revered Federation Council. They need money to pay a bribe to the Praetor in charge of Guild Affairs and they need it quickly else the whole process will be delayed for a year. The local group has been going round Twelve Seas with collection boxes and getting precious little reward for their troubles. Maybe the rich women up in Thamlin are doing better. Lisutaris, Mistress of the Sky, is a member, I believe. She's a very powerful Sorcerer.

"Get Lisutaris to magic you some money," I suggest to Makri.

"Could she do that?" asks Makri, eagerly.

"Of course not," I reply, having a good laugh at Makri's naivete.

Makri storms off annoyed. I never like to let a day pass without upsetting someone, as my ex-wife used to say. I gather up another beer and slump back in my chair.

Parax the shoemaker stumbles through the door.

"Goddamn it, I'm wet," he says. "It's the Orcs."

Parax is a fool. It's day twenty-two of the Hot Rainy Season. He knows as well as everyone else that there's another eight days to go, Orcs or no Orcs. Gurd points this out to him.

"Well, it's heavier than usual," counters Parax, continuing to insist that we're cursed. I wonder what he'd say if he knew that Rezaz the Butcher was here already.

I study the form for the chariots in the upcoming meeting in Simnia. Far south of Turai, it's hot there. Too hot, really, but at least they don't have a Hot Rainy Season. I wish I was there just now, far away from this damp, stinking, corrupt and crime-ridden city.

I turn the sheet of paper listing the chariots over to study the other side. Except on the other side there don't seem to be any chariots. Just a message printed in red ink: *Take care, Thraxas, you have little time left.*

I slam it down in a fury. This has gone too far. Now I can't even read the racing form without a sorcerous warning appearing and messing it up.

Kemlath Orc Slayer arrives later in the day and I show him the message.

"Can't you pick up anything from it?"

So far Kemlath has been unable to say for sure where any of the sorcerous warnings have come from. He stares hard at the document for a long time.

"I think he's getting careless," says Kemlath, eventually. "I wouldn't stake my reputation on it in a court of law, but I think this message has faint traces of Glixius Dragon Killer on it."

I pound the table. "So! It is Glixius! He's trying to scare me off the investigation."

Kemlath, as ever, is wearing plenty of jewellery: gold chains, silver bracelets, and a distinctive antique ring on his finger with a fabulous blue stone in it. He buys

me a beer and asks how the case is going. I tell him
I've made little progress.

"I can't seem to get a handle on it somehow. But
I'm still hopeful more of Mursius's art will turn up.
If the cup did, there's no reason why a few more pieces
shouldn't find their way on to the market. Once they
do, it might give me an opening."

"Do you think the same person that stole the works
of art murdered Mursius?"

"Probably. Either that or they know who did."

"You think it's Glixius?"

I nod. "He's never been convicted of anything.
Thinks he's safe with his sorcery and his aristocratic
connections. Well, he's wrong. If he killed Mursius, I'm
going to nail him."

"You were always a dogged soldier," says Kemlath,
which I take as a compliment, along with another
beer.

Three days later, I'm beginning to wonder if Parax
might have been right about us being cursed. The rain
is heavier than anyone can ever remember. Usually
there are periods where it stops, the sun shines and
the city gets a chance to breathe. This year the downpour is relentless. Life in Twelve Seas becomes unbearable. Quintessence Street is a sea of mud and some
of the small streets running off it are completely
impassable. A few cheap tenements have crumbled to
the ground, their foundations undermined. Everywhere
you look someone is desperately trying to shore up a
building, repair a roof or bail themselves out of trouble.
Trade in the city slows to a crawl and the anger about
the Orcs lies over Turai in a simmering cloud.

All the while the heat produces thunderstorms so
terrifying that our more nervous citizens start looking
up old prophesies, wondering if the end of the world
might be nigh. Makri shakes her sword angrily at the

sky while practising her fighting skills in the back yard in defiance of the elements.

I receive another warning. This time it's magically etched into my own flagon, which I take as a very personal attack. I'm late with the rent but for once Gurd understands that there's nothing much I can do about it. I'm not the only one finding it hard to earn a living these days. Street vendors, messengers, whores, wagon drivers—all give up the struggle with the elements and huddle indoors, waiting for it to pass.

"I've tramped over half this city looking for that damned prayer mat," I tell Makri. "It's one of the most frustrating cases I've ever come across."

"What about Mursius's murder?"

"That's one of the most frustrating cases I've ever come across as well. Do you know—"

"Yes, fine," interrupts Makri. "So, who are we betting on in the first race at Simnia?"

"Thank you for your support. Okay, the first race in Simnia. I reckon the second favourite in the first race is a reasonable bet."

"Only a reasonable bet? I'm running out of excuses for Minarixa. Everyone was looking at me at last night's meeting. Do you think they know I gambled the money away?"

"I doubt it. Who would suspect you, an escaped slave gladiator with Orcish blood in her veins, of acting with anything except impeccable honesty?"

We leave for Mox's.

"You might lend me the magic dry cloak."

"No. It's mine. Who is it has to say a spell over it every day?"

I have my own reasons for needing a win at the races. I'm running severely short of money and soon won't have enough for my daily supply of beer.

"I can't function without beer."

"Aren't you the person who always ridicules these dwa addicts for wasting their lives on a stupid drug?"

"That's not the same thing at all," I inform my smart young companion. "Beer is a normal healthy part of any man's diet, particularly a vigorous man like myself. It's part of our culture and heritage. Dwa is for degenerates. Let's go."

We walk out into the swamp that used to be Quintessence Street. A gale is blowing the storm in from the sea. The rain lashes into my face and the lightning splits the sky above. I grit my teeth and struggle on. Mox's is close to the harbour, right next to Prisox's pawn shop, another establishment with which I am very familiar. Despite the adverse weather, it will be business as usual there. Prisox always has a healthy supply of sad customers trying to raise a little cash for life's necessities.

Makri, after her initial inclination to splash out on wild bets on chariots with long odds, has settled into a careful strategy and is content to go along with my suggestion of a modest gamble on Bear Baiter. She bets fifteen of her thirty-five gurans. As Bear Baiter is quoted at evens, she stands to win fifteen gurans, which will bring her close to her target. I bet a similar amount.

As we leave we run into a throng of people. The crowd seems quite cheerful, or as cheerful as it's possible to be when lightning is searing the rooftops and wind and rain are pinning you to the walls.

"What's happening?" I yell to the nearest passer-by.

"Elves are coming in," he roars back, above the din.

Of course. The Elvish chariot is due to land at the docks today. Everyone is heading for the harbour. I can't miss this. Like any true gambler I want to see the Elvish chariot and horses in order to form some opinions of their chances in the race. And it's not just gambling that brings people here. Everyone likes Elves and Lord Lisith-ar-Moh is still a hero in Turai.

At the harbour crowds of people are straining their eyes for the first sight of the Elvish ship, and a podium has been set up for welcoming speeches. No one seems worried that the Elves might not arrive on schedule. They're renowned for their sailing skills, and have probably used sorcery to calm the waters on the way. Sure enough, a cry goes up that there's a sail on the horizon. A pleasant ripple of anticipation runs through the crowd. Everyone forgets their rain-soaked misery as the green sails gradually grow in size as the Elvish ship approaches the harbour.

Cheers go up as the Elves take down the sails and manoeuvre into the harbour. A bigger cheer goes up when Lord Lisith-ar-Moh himself is spotted on deck. He has a silver band around his brow, and his green cloak flaps in the wind. Around him are various attendants, all tall and fair. As the ship draws into the pier Elvish sailors wave to the crowd.

Elves are always tall, fair and golden-eyed. They generally wear green. Their ears are slightly pointed at the top. It's never difficult to recognise an Elf. It cheers me to see them. It cheers me further to think that if the Orcish chariot is given any chance by the bookmakers, the odds on the Elves might just stretch out far enough to be worth a bet.

Consul Kalius, Turai's most important official, is here to welcome the Elves on behalf of the King. He's standing on a podium with an attendant holding an umbrella over his head, but with the storm still raging he cuts his speech short, simply welcoming the Elves to the city, thanking them for their help in the past, wishing them good luck in the race, then departing with Lord Lisith in a convoy of official carriages. The crowd applaud, and crane their necks to see the chariot being unloaded. The horses snort apprehensively as they are lowered in harnesses from the ship to the pier, but their Elvish grooms call to them, calming them down, before leading them off to the shelter of a nearby warehouse. I note with interest that this is the same warehouse in which Senator Mursius was murdered.

Do the Elves who have just arrived know they're going to be up against an Orc? I wonder. I follow as young Elves wheel their chariot into the warehouse. They're lithe and strong and show no ill effects from their long voyage through rough seas from the Southern Islands to Turai.

Makri has remained silent throughout all this activity. When it comes to Elves she has mixed emotions. She's always attracted to Elves, partly because she is quarter Elf herself and partly because she thinks that the men in Turai are such scum. On the other hand, Elves annoy the hell out of her because they always react badly to her quarter-Orc blood.

The chariot is loaded safely into the warehouse. I'm right up at the doors, peering in past the attendants. I slip past an Elf distracted by the sight of Makri and poke my head in the door. I can't believe it's a coincidence that the Elf chariot is being stored in the same place that Mursius was murdered.

Civil Guards are in attendance to keep order and to prevent anyone from touching the chariot. One of them spots me, and calls to me to get out.

"What do you think you're doing?"

"Nothing," I grunt, though this is not quite true. In reality I'm staring at the wall of the warehouse where I've just noticed, scratched in tiny letters close to the floor, a pair of clasped hands, very crudely drawn. Just a piece of graffiti, a common enough sight in the city.

But not that particular sign, I muse, as the Guards

eject me and the rest of the overly curious crowd. Two clasped hands is the sign of the Society of Friends, who don't hang around in Twelve Seas, which is controlled by the Brotherhood, their deadly enemies. Any known Society man wandering around in Twelve Seas would soon end up dead. But who else other than a Society of Friends man would make such a mark? With the Brotherhood being so powerful in the south of the city, it's not the sort of thing that even a bored youth would do. Scrawling Society of Friends graffiti is liable to earn you a good beating, or worse.

Outside Makri is talking to a young Elf in Elvish. The heavy rain has flattened her hair so her pointed ears show through. The Elf looks intrigued but troubled. Soon an Elf commander calls to him and he hurries away.

I tell Makri about the Society of Friends graffiti. Has the Society been in the warehouse in which Mursius was murdered? The same place in which the Elvish horses and chariot are now being stored prior to removal to the stables at the Stadium?

"Are you coming home, or do you want to hang around waiting for more Elves to appear?"

"Stupid Elves," says Makri, walking rapidly away. The crowd make optimistic noises about the Orc curse being lifted now that Lord Lisith has arrived. I catch up with Makri. She's in a bad mood after meeting the Elves. Poor Makri. They're never going to welcome her like a long-lost sister.

At the end of Quintessence Street I sense magic close by and spin around in case I'm under attack. Right behind me a tall man in a grey cloak is approaching through the rain. His face looks down towards the ground but I recognise him anyway. It's Glixius Dragon Killer. I grab him as he passes, which is rash, given Glixius's power, but I'm still annoyed at the damage to my own personal tankard. He looks up in surprise.

"Leave your rainbow cloak at home, did you?"

"Thraxas! How dare you lay a hand on me. Do you wish to be blasted into the next world?"

"How dare you send me sorcerous warnings!" I counter. "That tankard was very dear to me. And I don't appreciate you writing all over my racing form either."

"Have you gone insane?" roars the Sorcerer. "I have no time for your petty stupidities. Be gone!"

He raises his arm to cast some spell at me. I brace myself, hoping that my spell protection charm is in good working order. I don't get to find out because before Glixius can utter a word Makri slugs him on the back of his head with the pommel of her sword. He slumps unconscious to the ground.

"Nice work, Makri."

"I needed that," she says, and looks a little more cheerful. We leave Glixius lying in the mud.

"That'll teach him to meddle with me."

At the Avenging Axe four Civil Guards and a Praetor's assistant are waiting for me. The official hands me a paper and informs me I'm due in court the day after the Triple-Moon Conjunction festival ends.

"Care to buy me a beer to celebrate?" I ask the Praetor's assistant.

He doesn't care. They depart.

"Have they charged you with the murder?" enquires Makri.

"Not exactly. Cicerius managed to have that delayed. I have to go before the examining magistrate, who looks at the evidence."

"What happens then?"

"Then he charges me with murder."

Later in the day I receive the news that Bear Baiter romped home a clear winner, which gives me enough money for a few beers and Makri another fifteen gurans to add to her total. She now has fifty and needs only ten more.

"Stop sitting around drinking beer," says Makri, interrupting my late-night relaxation. "Start studying the form sheet."

I sigh. Life was easier when Makri disapproved of gambling. Cicerius's Aedile, or Assistant, arrives on horseback looking for news. The Deputy Consul is extremely agitated at my lack of progress in locating the prayer mat. Lord Rezaz Caseg is increasingly unhappy at his charioteer's loss and may quit the city any day. I tell the Aedile I'm doing everything I can. I have a beer in one hand and the racing sheet in the other which might give him the wrong impression. He doesn't look too impressed when he rides away.

Chapter Thirteen

I make no progress in the next few days. I'm sitting gloomily at my desk, beer in hand, when I hear voices in the corridor outside. Makri's voice and another one, softer. I creep over and place my ear to the door. The other voice belongs to Hanama. Another social call from the Assassin?

"I won fifteen gurans on Bear Baiter," Makri is telling her. "Evens favourite at Simnia. He won by three lengths after a slow start. But Bear Baiter always starts slowly. I wasn't worried."

"I didn't know you were so informed about betting," says Hanama, sounding impressed.

"I picked it up here and there," replies Makri. "If you come to the Turas Memorial I'll show you how it's done."

I wrench open the door. "Will you stop discussing gambling with Assassins outside my room? I'm trying to work in here."

"So, what's eating you?" asks Makri.

"Her," I retort, indicating Hanama. "You might be buddies, but she still gives me the creeps. Since when have Assassins placed bets? Shouldn't you be out murdering people?"

Hanama eyes me calmly and retreats down the corridor without comment, followed by Makri. Damned Assassins. How come she's so friendly with Makri recently?

"And it was me that picked Bear Baiter," I yell after them.

I get out the magic dry cloak. It's time to visit the Brotherhood. They are very powerful in Turai. They started off as a bunch of small-time crooks operating round the harbour about two hundred years ago. Now they're one of the most powerful groups in the whole city-state. Since dwa started flooding into the city, bringing with it vast profits and a whole new class of people dependent on crime, their influence has grown alarmingly. They're behind most criminal activity in the south of the city, but they also have their fingers in various legitimate businesses. Many of our banking houses, for instance, are now suspected of using dwa money to fund their enterprises, and when a Senator makes a speech in favour of some particular venture you can never be sure if he isn't being heavily influenced by the vast wealth and influence of the Brotherhood.

While I am too small-time to really irritate the Brotherhood, I couldn't claim that they like me. Casax, their boss in Twelve Seas, was particularly displeased with me when I prevented him from making off with the King's gold which had originally been stolen by Galwinius, our ex-Prefect. He warned me then to stay well out of his way. So some might say it is unwise of me to walk into the Mermaid, Twelve Seas' most dangerous tavern and local Brotherhood headquarters, and demand to see him.

Several thugs confer with each other then send a message upstairs. Karlox, a huge bruiser whom I have had several run-ins with in the past, appears at the top and motions me up. He shows me into the large room at the back, where Casax is sitting at a table. I greet him politely and take a seat without waiting to be asked.

He stares at me silently for a few minutes. The table is huge, beautifully carved. On the walls around us are valuable tapestries showing scenes from Turai's legendary past. Casax is not especially ostentatious as gang chiefs go but he needs to remind visitors of his power.

"Didn't I tell you to stay well out of my way, Investigator?" he says eventually.

"Probably," I reply. "But most people say that to me, one time or another."

"So what do you want?"

"A chat about the Society of Friends."

This gets his attention. The Society operate way out of my territory. I have no contacts there and no real means of gaining information about them, so I'm hoping that I might learn something from the Brotherhood. Even though they don't like me, they like the Society a lot less.

"Well?" says Casax.

I can feel Karlox's eyes boring into the back of my neck. Last time we met I was on a horse and I rode him down. He'd like to repay the compliment.

"I think they've been working down at the docks. I wondered if you might know anything about it."

"Since when have the Brotherhood discussed their affairs with cheap Investigators?"

"I'm not asking you to discuss your affairs. I'm talking about the Society of Friends. I take it you don't know anything about the warehouse where Mursius was killed?"

I tell him about my suspicions that the Society have

been at work in the warehouse. Casax asks if I have any evidence apart from the graffiti.

"No. But it all fits, more or less. You've heard the rumours that the Society are planning some sort of betting coup. Senator Mursius was entering his chariot in the Turas Memorial. His stolen artworks ended up at that warehouse. And then he ended up there too, dead. And now it turns out to be the same warehouse where the Elvish chariot is stored when it's brought off the ship. I don't know what that all means, but it seems like too much of a coincidence to me."

Casax ponders my words. Like all Brotherhood chiefs he's capable of brutality, but he's not dumb. If the Society has been operating secretly in his territory he wants to know all about it.

"So, what do you want from me, Investigator?"

"Information. In exchange for what I've told you. Anything you know or find out about the warehouse. And I'll tell you anything else I learn about the Society working in Twelve Seas."

Casax remains silent for a time. The only sound is the rain beating down outside. Finally he nods. "Okay." He looks at me intently. "I hear you've not been doing too well at the races."

Casax wants me to be impressed that he knows my business. I shrug, and don't look impressed.

"You're not going to be a popular man in this city," he continues. "No one's going to like the man who's looking after the Orcs."

This is a blow. I curse silently. I suppose it was bound to leak out eventually. I can't entirely hide my discomfiture. Casax smiles; at least, the tiny twitching of his lips is probably meant to be a smile. Karlox shows me out.

"I'll kill you one day, fat man," he says as a parting shot.

I don't bother replying. I receive too many death threats to be always coming up with smart answers.

The rain is heavier than ever. It's almost the end of the Hot Rainy Season. The water in Quintessence Street is deep enough to drown dogs and small children. There are far too many dogs and small children around here anyway. It takes me a long time to walk back to the Avenging Axe. Sweat pours down inside my cloak. The Hot Rainy Season. I hate it. I thank God that this is the last day. Tomorrow, according to Turai's regular calendar, the rain will dry up and we'll have a month or so of pleasant autumn weather before winter arrives.

The prospect of the rain ending has restored some cheer to the inhabitants of Turai, but it's overshadowed by the knowledge that this is also the day that the Orcish chariot is due to arrive. As the land route from the east is impassable at this time of year they'll be coming by sea like the Elves, though without the welcoming reception party. Twelve Seas is crawling with Civil Guards, posted to keep order. Even though this is the King's idea he's not going to risk lowering himself in public opinion by officially greeting the Orcs, and even Consul Kalius seems to be distancing himself. The only officials there to greet them will be Cicerius and Melus the Fair, Stadium Sorcerer.

I practically bump into Captain Rallee at the foot of my stairs. "Don't expect the Guards to protect you over this one," he says.

"I take it you've heard the news."

"I have. Never thought I'd see the day when you'd be guarding Orcs, Thraxas."

"Me neither."

"Why are you doing it?"

I explain to the Captain upstairs in my office. He understands how I've been forced into it, but he doesn't think that your average Turanian will have much sympathy. "The way the scandal sheets will report it you'll have volunteered for the job."

The Captain crosses over to the window and stares out at the rain. "Last day, thank God," he mutters. I ask him if he'll be putting in an appearance at the Avenging Axe tonight. There's always a prolonged celebration on the night of the last day of the Hot Rainy Season and the Captain's not averse to a spot of celebrating himself. He shakes his head.

"I'm on duty. They've cancelled all leave. The city's restless. The rain's been keeping the lid on, but no one's happy about the Orcs coming. I don't like the way things are shaping up, Thraxas. Too many strange things are happening. You know it's rumoured the Society of Friends are planning some sort of betting coup?"

"Yeah, I heard."

"You know I even heard a whisper that the Assassins are placing bets? It's like some sort of fever's gripped the city since it was learned the Elves and the Orcs are coming."

The Captain tosses down the rest of his klee, fastens his cloak and departs abruptly. Melus the Fair is going to have to be in good form to keep things legal. Talking of Melus the Fair, she's due back in town today. She's been away out west on a goodwill mission to study sorcery in Samsarina. She's due to welcome the Orcish chariot into town.

There's a knock at the door. I answer it with a sword in my hand, ready for anything. It turns out to be a bedraggled messenger who hands over a scroll then departs. I unroll it and read it:

Found more artwork, it says. Kerk's signature is at the bottom. Good. At last something is going well.

Makri arrives. "Are we going to Mox's?"

"Sure you don't want to go with your Assassin friend?" I say.

Makri doesn't rise to the bait. We sneak down Quintessence Street, which isn't too difficult as the torrential downpour cuts visibility almost to zero. We're sneaking because Minarixa the baker is annoyed at Makri for failing to come up with the sixty gurans as promised.

"I've really offended the Association of Gentlewomen. It's hell. Last night Chulani the carpet-weaver said very pointedly that she was surprised to hear that certain members had been gambling with the Association's money and was Minarixa planning to do anything about running these members out of Turai."

"She might not have been referring to you," I point out. "Half the city is gripped by gambling fever just now. You're probably not the only member of the A.G. who's diverted funds to the bookies."

"I'm sure someone's been spreading rumours."

"Well don't look at me. The only contact I have with the Association of Gentlewomen is my daily order for two large meat pies and three loaves of bread at Minarixa's bakery. Face it, Makri, you haven't been that discreet. Anyone could have seen you hanging round Honest Mox's."

Makri screws up her face in near anguish. "How did I ever get into this?" she demands, staring accusingly at me.

We're on our way to place a bet before joining in the welcoming committee for the Orcish chariot. Makri's fifty gurans have shrunk to thirty, the result of a very poor performance by the favourite in the last race in Simnia. Makri spent most of the evening cursing all horses, chariots and race meetings and demanded to know if the Sorcerer at Simnia is honest.

"If I find he's been taking bribes I'll ride down to

Simnia myself and gut him like a pig," she raged. More or less standard behaviour for any gambler in Turai. It gets into the blood somehow. The streets are thick with Civil Guards and the Palace has sent down wagonloads of troops to back them up in case serious trouble erupts.

I sense a certain coldness in the air as Makri and I enter Mox's. News of my cursed mission must be spreading.

"Just can't keep away from Orcs," whispers someone.

"He's brought one with him," whispers someone else.

Makri's eyes widen and her hand flashes to her sword as she prepares to wreak mayhem for being called an Orc, but she remembers what she's doing here and checks herself. She needs to win another thirty gurans urgently and she's not going to be able to do that if she destroys Mox's shop and everyone in it. She's tense enough already at the bet she's putting on. Victory or Death is even money but is only joint favourite and I'm not at all certain about its chances. Makri, however, has no choice. She's run out of time and must now place her whole remaining thirty gurans on the chariot and hope it comes in a winner.

"Shame you haven't found the prayer mat, Thraxas. I'd have given it a try."

We wait at the queue. The man in front of me, a large, ugly individual I've never seen before, suddenly turns to me and snarls "Orc lover" right in my face.

Like Makri, I hold myself back. I don't want to get into a fight, not before I've placed a bet.

"Merely helping the King out," I answer pleasantly. It doesn't placate him. I draw myself up and try to look like a Sorcerer who might just blast everyone to hell if they're not careful. This sometimes works, as most people in Twelve Seas don't realise how insignificant my powers really are. Many hostile eyes follow me as I advance up the queue. At the counter Mox is sullen. Despite the fact that I've been one of his finest customers for years he refuses to greet me, and takes my bet in silence.

Outside the shop I hurry away, with Makri at my heels.

"This is bad. Damn that Cicerius."

Makri is bristling about her treatment. She says that if her chariot doesn't win she's going to go back and kill everyone in Mox's for daring to call her an Orc.

"What if it wins?"

"I'll let some of them live."

I figure I might as well take a look at the Orcish chariot that's causing me so much grief. The rain beats down and another storm rolls in off the sea. By the time we reach the harbour the sky is black and the crowd is wailing that we're cursed.

"God will destroy us for welcoming them into the city," yells a young Pontifex, who urges the crowd to repent while they still have the chance.

Visibility is so poor that the Orcish ship is not seen until its monstrous black sails suddenly loom out of the darkness right at the mouth of the harbour. The mob yells in fury and the Civil Guards and soldiers struggle to keep order. Thunder roars in one long continuous explosion and the rain batters down like hailstones from hell. As the ship draws slowly alongside the pier Lord Rezaz Caseg and his attendants suddenly appear to welcome their fellow Orcs. His black cloak billows in the wind. His features are hidden by a black and gold helmet. The crowd explodes with rage and the soldiers beat them back with staffs.

Suddenly, at the podium set up for the welcoming committee, green and blue shafts of light cut through the air. The shafts grow in intensity before bursting into star shapes which float over the heads of the crowd. They hang in the rain-darkened atmosphere before changing again into huge yellow flowers which slowly drift off towards the clouds. The crowd stop rioting, their attention drawn by the fine pyrotechnic display.

Melus the Fair steps forward on to the podium, her staff in her hand. I have my own illuminated staff with me, hanging from my belt. It's pretty feeble compared with Melus's. The crowd applauds. Melus the Fair is a popular favourite. As she raises her hands, the crowd becomes almost peaceful and the Orcs begin to disembark without trouble.

"Nice trick," I mutter to Makri. "Lets hope she's in as good form at the Turas Memorial."

We all watch as Lord Rezaz removes his helmet and marches forward, flanked by eight warrior Orcs, to meet Melus. Cicerius has now appeared at her side and he holds his hand up, palm outwards, in formal greeting. I notice that Melus has put a magic dry spell on her cloak, which is the smart thing to do, but poor old Cicerius is getting very wet indeed. His toga clings to his bony frame.

The crowd watch, partly in anger and partly in fascination. Many of our younger citizens have never even seen an Orc before. The Orc Lord marches with more dignity than I would have credited, and greets his compatriots and Melus. Speeches are extremely brief. Everyone knows this is not an occasion to spend too much time over.

Lord Rezaz mutters an order that is transmitted from his attendants to the crew of the ship. A huge covered crate is lowered from the ship to the pier. The Orc chariot. Attendants are strapping the Orc steeds into the harnesses they use at the docks for unloading livestock.

To the disappointment of the crowd, the chariot is drawn into the warehouse without being uncovered. Now that the Orcs are here, and trouble has been kept at bay, not a few of the onlookers are keen for a sight of the chariot, if only to help them judge which way to bet. The horses look impressive enough—large and jet black, with fiery eyes and long manes, groomed to perfection.

"They're here," says a voice in my ear.

It's Kemlath. This must be very strange for him. One of Turai's most notable killers of Orcs, and he's forced to watch them arriving in the city as guests of the King.

Melus, Cicerius and the Orcs quickly depart in a string of carriages. The soldiers advance to clear away the crowds. We make our way back to the Avenging Axe via Honest Mox's.

As soon as I step inside I know we've lost our bets. I can always tell. I glance at the board on which Mox has just chalked up the result, fresh up from the Sorcerer in Simnia. Victory or Death lost by a short head.

Makri's head droops. We make to leave.

"Been seeing your Orcish friends up at the harbour?" sneers a large docker with arms like tree trunks and fists to match. Makri spins on her heel so fast it's hard to catch exactly what she does but at the end of it her elbow is sunk about eight inches into the docker's stomach. His mouth opens. No sound comes out and he collapses to the floor. Makri walks out slowly and with dignity. I hurry after her. Kemlath is impressed.

"Fine technique," he says, but Makri is in too bad a mood to acknowledge the compliment. Instead she curses the rain.

"It'll be sunny tomorrow," I say.

"But I still won't have any money," says Makri. "I can't believe I went through all that and I'm back where I started. These chariot races are fixed."

A woman with a basket appears through the gloom and Makri hurls herself down an alleyway out of sight.

"Member of the A.G.?" I enquire, after she's gone.

"Coxi the fishwife. Very militant."

We make our way home through the impossible mud. I offer Makri my magic dry cloak but she says she's so wet already it doesn't matter.

Chapter Fourteen

Two messages are waiting for me at the Avenging Axe. One of them, etched in magical letters of fire on my front door, says: *Beware, your death approaches.* Now I'll have to get the door repainted. At least the rain put the fire out.

The other one is from Cicerius. In it he informs me that Lord Rezaz is again threatening to leave the city if he doesn't get his charioteer's prayer mat back quickly. Now his chariot is here he wants to practise.

I curse. This is the last night of the Hot Rainy Season. Everyone celebrates. Can't they leave a man in peace for one day? How am I meant to find their damned prayer mat? If it's so important to these Orcs, why did they lose it in the first place? Cicerius tells me that it'll be another couple of weeks until the moons are in the correct alignment for Old Hasius to check back in time. That's no use to anyone.

I'm uptown, wondering what to do next. I have a couple of beers in a small tavern frequented by the

young apprentices from the local silversmith. Inspiration
fails to strike. I decide to visit Makri in the Library.
Maybe she'll have some good ideas. I find her sitting
with a bundle of old scrolls, but she is too disconsolate about losing her money to have any good ideas.

"Last day of the rain. Major celebration tonight."

"I don't feel like celebrating," replies Makri.

"Neither do I."

A bearded scholar at the next table looks at us
pointedly and we lower our voices. I glance at the scroll
in front of Makri. It's entitled *Comparative Religion*
and is some deathly dull treatise on the subtle differences between religious practices in Turai and its
neighbours. We pray three times a day in Turai. In Nioj
it's six. In Mattesh it's four. Fascinating stuff.

A germ of an idea appears. I lean forward to whisper
to Makri. "Would this library have anything about Orc
religion?"

Makri doesn't know. "If anything has ever been
written about it, it'll be here. Why?"

"Sudden Investigator's intuition," I tell her.

There's a very large and comprehensive catalogue,
which Makri, with her superior knowledge, starts checking. After a fair amount of shuttling back and forth
between various volumes, she finally locates a relevant
entry.

"There is a scroll about Orcish religion. Just one.
Written in the last century by some scholar I've never
heard of."

Makri leads me to the centre of the library where
the librarians sit behind a large counter decorated with
paintings of the saints, most of whom seem to be
reading manuscripts. She approaches a young man and
asks him for the scroll. He blushes, then goes off to
find it.

"He has a crush on me," whispers Makri.

He's gone a long time. When he finally returns he's carrying a small scroll, the entire sum of knowledge in Turai about Orcish religion. I take it to a table and start to unroll it. The scroll is dusty with age, but I notice that some of the dust has recently been shifted.

"Here. Chapter Three. Prayer mats."

It's a very full description of the role of prayer mats in the Orcish Lands. I read it through.

"*The importance extends to the class of charioteers, who will not ride their chariot unless standing firmly on their mat. Failure to do so would mean they risked being sent to the place of damnation should they die in an accident whilst riding.* Well, how about that?"

I ask Makri to enquire of the young librarian if anyone has borrowed this scroll recently. I see him blushing, and then sorting through some records. Makri comes back to the table.

"Pontifex Derlex," she says. "He borrowed it last week. As far as the librarian can tell, he's the first person to look at it in fifty years."

I rise to my feet. "A sudden breakthrough."

"Looks like it," agrees Makri. "What made you think of it?"

"Intuition. Some days it's sharp as an Elf's ear. Let's go."

Makri leaves the library with me. She can't concentrate on her studies because of her worries about the money.

"Forget about the money. Cicerius will pay me a bundle when I take the prayer mat back. I'll give you your share."

We find a landus to take us down to Twelve Seas. I ask Makri why she was discussing gambling with Hanama, but her reply is noncommittal and I don't pursue it. I'm elated at finally making some progress. Pontifex Derlex. The man who claimed that the Orcs didn't even have a religion. And here he is, reading all about it. Then removing the prayer mat no doubt. It makes sense. The True Church was always a strong candidate for sabotaging the Orcs, and the Pontifex is an ambitious young man. If Bishop Gzekius was casting around for volunteers he'd be first in line.

Derlex lives in a small house in the grounds of the church in Saint Volinius's Street. We march right up and knock on the door. The door swings open. I draw my sword and we advance cautiously. I note that the house is poorly furnished, in contrast to the splendid mansion inhabited by Bishop Gzekius. No lamps are lit in the evening gloom so I take out my illuminated staff and speak the command to give us more light.

A groan comes from somewhere along the corridor. As we arrive in the main room Derlex is struggling to rise from the floor. There's a large candlestick beside him and it looks like he's been clubbed to the ground. I feel his pulse and check his wound.

"You'll live."

Derlex groans again and struggles to focus his eyes.

"Was this connected with a certain Orcish prayer mat?" I demand.

His hand reaches out to the chair behind him. There's nothing on it. "It's gone," he says, and slumps back to the floor.

"Who told you to steal it?" I ask, but Derlex isn't talking any more. He slips back into unconsciousness. I have a quick look round, but don't find anything.

"Too late," I mutter to Makri. At least we're on the trail."

I send a message to the Bishop informing him that his Pontifex might not be able to take services for a day or two. Then I send another message to Cicerius giving him a full description of events. At least he'll know I'm busy.

"Who do you think took it?" enquires Makri.

"No idea. I'll think about it tomorrow. Right now it's time for food, beer and some celebration."

After that smart piece of investigating, I figure I'm fully entitled to some relaxation. I head back to the Avenging Axe for a bite to eat, an early beer, and then a nap to prepare me for the full rigours of the night.

By the time midnight rolls around on the last day of the Hot Rainy Season, celebrations are in full swing all over the city, nowhere more so than in the Avenging Axe. Nowhere more so than at my table, actually. Palax and Kaby are perched on the bar playing a flute and a mandolin. They're looking as weird as ever. No one else in Turai has pierced eyebrows and they actually dye their hair bright colours, something I didn't even know was possible till they arrived. Gave me quite a shock when I first saw them. They're leading the revellers in raucous renditions of popular favourites while Gurd, Makri, Tanrose and another couple of bar staff hired specially for the occasion fill flagon after flagon of ale.

The bar is full of singing mercenaries, dancing dockers, drunken fish vendors and smiling labourers. Everyone, including me, forgets their troubles for the night. Outside the rain is still pounding down, but tomorrow the clouds will roll away, the sun will shine and preparations for the Turas and Triple-Moon Conjunction festivals will get under way. I forget all about Mursius, Orcs, prayer mats, death threats and crime in general and concentrate on getting as many giant "Happy Guildsmen" tankards of ale down my throat as is humanly possible.

Kemlath is sitting by my side and he's about as happy as a drunken mercenary. "I haven't had such a good time since the celebrations after the war," he tells me. "I'd forgotten what a good night in a tavern was like."

A young prostitute sits down on his lap and admires his rainbow cloak and his fine jewellery, Kemlath takes off a bracelet and gives it to her. He's a generous man, the big Sorcerer, and he buys drinks all round, which makes him popular. The only person who doesn't seem to be smiling is Makri. She doesn't have any money and Minarixa the baker is sitting right at the bar, which is embarrassing for her.

"What's the matter with your friend?" asks Kemlath.

I explain to him that Makri has made somewhat of a blunder in gambling away the money she'd collected for the Association of Gentlewomen. Kemlath roars with laughter.

"The Association of Gentlewomen," he thunders. "A bunch of harridans. A plague on them!" He laughs some more, and catches Makri as she sways past with a tray of beers on her arm. She frowns.

"Don't frown," cries Kemlath. He taps his illuminated staff on the floor, causing a rainbow to magically appear in the room. Everyone cheers, but Makri remains unmoved. Kemlath reaches into some corner of his voluminous robe and pulls out a fat purse.

"How much do you owe them?"

"Sixty gurans."

"A woman like you shouldn't owe sixty gurans," cries Kemlath. He says that he hasn't seen such an impressive demonstration of unarmed combat as Makri showed at Mox's shop this evening since he himself knocked three Orcs off the city walls after his spells had run out. Without hesitation the Sorcerer counts out twelve five-guran pieces and hands them to Makri. Makri is too wise to question such a gift. She grabs them, stuffs them in her purse, wriggles her way through the crowd to deliver her tray of beer, then beats a path to Minarixa and her friends at the bar. Through the haze of thazis smoke I see her handing over the money. From Minarixa's reaction and Makri's smile, it seems to do the trick. Makri is back in the good books of the A.G.

She struggles her way back to us.

"Thanks," she says to Kemlath. "I'll pay you back."

"Don't worry about it," says the Sorcerer.

A flicker of suspicion crosses Makri's face as she wonders exactly what Kemlath might expect in return for his sixty gurans, but he doesn't seem to want anything. He's just carried away by the good time he's having in the Avenging Axe. It can hit you like that, sometimes, when you're only used to the refined and rather dull pleasures of the upper classes.

So now Makri is happy too. In the heat of the tavern, sweat pours down her near-naked figure. Makri has discovered that glistening skin seems to be good for tips and reckons she might as well use it to her advantage. The purse that hangs on a long string round her neck is bulging.

"I was going to give you a hard time for that chariot losing," she tells me. "I won't now. But you're still a lousy gambler."

"Nonsense. Didn't I pick you plenty of winners? No one can do it all the time. Just wait till the Turas Memorial. I'm going to leave that race meeting a wealthy man. The Stadium Superbius has never seen anything like the damage I'm going to inflict on the bookmakers."

Makri grins. "Won't you be too busy looking after the Orcs?"

"Don't remind me. They won't even be racing if I don't find that prayer mat. But now I've made a start I expect I'll track it down soon enough. You know me, dogged."

Gurd takes a break to join Kemlath and me, and we start swapping war stories. The arrival of Lord

Rezaz has stirred a lot of memories and we reminisce about this and that till Gurd is called away to change a barrel of beer in the cellar.

A woman falls on top of me. It's Sarija. Her cloak is wet and mud-splattered and she's full of dwa.

"I thought you'd be having a good time in Twelve Seas," she says, and falls off my lap and on to the floor. Kemlath helps her into a seat.

"Where does a woman get a beer around here?" she demands, banging on the table till Makri arrives.

"Wish I had your figure," says Sarija. "But bring me a beer anyway."

Another wet hand paws at my shoulder. It's Kerk, who's just arrived looking very poorly indeed. He doesn't waste any time but thrusts a small bust of an Elf into my hand.

"From Mursius's collection," he yells, above the din. "Found it at Axa's." Axa is another purveyor of stolen goods who operates around the harbour.

He holds out his hand for payment. His face carries the haunted look that descends on a man when he needs dwa more than anyone has ever needed anything in the world before. It takes me a few seconds to register. I nod dumbly, and fish in my purse for some gurans, and probably end up paying him too much. He departs without a word. I give the bust a quick glance then stuff it in my bag.

"More evidence?" says Kemlath. "Do you want me to study it?"

"Tomorrow," I reply. "It can wait."

Kemlath expresses some surprise at my casual manner. I spread my hands.

"It's okay. You see, Kemlath, criminals in this city aren't really that smart. They always leave some trail behind them. People think I must be doing something pretty dammed clever to keep catching them. That's why I keep up the pretence of Sorcerous Investigator when really I can hardly do any sorcery. Good for the reputation. I like people to think I'm moving heaven, earth and the three moons to put these crooks behind bars. In reality I just plod along the trail till I catch up with them."

"What if you run up against someone really smart?"

"Hasn't happened yet. More beer?"

The revelry continues all through the night. Kemlath shows me a good trick for conjuring rainbows out of my illuminated staff. I send rainbows all over the tavern, up people's legs and into their drinks, which keeps me entertained. It's years since anyone taught me any new magic. Sarija drinks herself unconscious and falls asleep on Kemlath's lap. I smoke so much thazis I can barely join in with the soldiers' drinking songs initiated by Gurd.

"You're a fine man," I tell Kemlath, putting my arm round his shoulder. "One of the best. These other Sorcerers are all stuck-up snobs. I hate them. But you, you're a soldier. I always did like you."

Makri is happy. She's back in favour with the A.G. and she's making loads of tips. She swings lithely through the crowd, dealing out beers to customers and slaps to anyone whose hands show signs of straying as she passes, though in quite a friendly way for Makri. No bones are broken. When she takes another break she joins us for a while and gets into conversation with Kemlath, who seems quite taken with her. As the big Sorcerer is definitely a more cultured man than your average Twelve Seas drinker, Makri finds him interesting. She tells him about her current projects at the Guild College and mentions the plants she brought back from Ferias for her natural history class.

"Strange things," she says. "Even my tutor isn't sure what they are."

Something nags at me. I try and ignore it. I don't want things to nag at me when I'm having a good time. I drink another beer. No good, it's still nagging. Why did Mursius have rare unknown plants in his window boxes? No reason, probably. I drink another beer. Again it's no good. It won't go away. Sometimes I hate these Investigator's intuitions. Won't leave a man alone to enjoy himself. I drag myself out of my chair and upstairs, along to Makri's room. This is furnished with extreme simplicity, as Makri has very few possessions. Nothing but a cloak, some books and a lot of weapons. In contrast to me, Makri is very tidy and her few belongings are neatly positioned around the room.

She's rooted the plants in little pots of earth beside the window. I grab one of them and take it downstairs, fighting my way through the throng to where Chiaraxi the healer and Cospali the herbalist are sitting at a table in the corner. Both women are unusual in that they run shops in Twelve Seas, a rare activity for a woman. Both are, incidentally, supporters of the Association of Gentlewomen, probably because they are not allowed to join the trade Guilds, which is bad for their business.

"Either of you ever see this plant before?"

They study it. Chiaraxi shakes her head but Cospali thinks it might be a variety of the coix plant, which they use in the far west for treating delirium.

"What would its effect be if used on a horse?"

"A sedative, maybe, if it's the same sort of plant."

I work my way back to Makri and Kemlath. I clap Makri a little too enthusiastically on the shoulder.

"What you trying to do, break my arm?"

"Sorry."

I brandish the plant. "You know what this is for?"

"No."

"Doping horses, that's what it's for. That's why Mursius was so optimistic about his chances in the race. He was planning to dope the other horses."

Sarija, Mursius's wife, is slumped beside us. I ask her about the plants, but she's too drunk to make any sort of sensible reply. I shake her shoulder. Suddenly Kemlath grabs my arm.

"Don't do that," he says.

They've been drinking together. Obviously the Sorcerer's manners are better than mine.

He apologises to me for speaking sharply, but points out that Sarija has been having a hard time and is entitled to some stress-free relaxation. I'm sure he's developed a passion for her.

I trust my intuition. Senator Mursius, war hero of Turai, was about to engage in some very dubious business at the races. I wonder if Sarija knew about it. She's planning to enter Mursius's chariot in the race. Is she still planning to cheat? Right now she is incapable of administering sweets to a child, let alone carrying out a large-scale doping operation, but who knows, the Senator might have engaged others to do the work for him. He might have been working with the Society of Friends, for instance.

I'm too full of beer to think it through. Tomorrow I'll come up with something.

Palax and Kaby work up a furious rhythm loud enough to wake Old King Kiben and the place starts swaying as the drinkers bang their tankards on the tables. I join in heartily and stamp my staff on the floor in time to the music, sending rainbows out in all directions. Tomorrow the rain will end. Everyone is happy.

The last thing I remember is berating the Sorcerers Guild for being too snobbish to let an honest workman like myself be a member, and then criticising the

King, the Consul and the Deputy Consul for being too useless to run the city properly. After that it's all a bit of a blur and I fall asleep in my chair with a flagon of ale in one hand and a thazis stick in the other.

Chapter Fifteen

I wake up in the chair. My back hurts and my neck is stiff. I'm too old to be falling asleep in chairs. Sarija is sleeping on the floor. She's wrapped up in Kemlath's rainbow cloak and the Sorcerer slumbers alongside, his arm draped protectively over her. Various other people are slumped all around. Gurd is usually careful to clear the Avenging Axe at night, but as he himself is unconscious at the bar I guess he didn't have the energy.

I check my bag for the small statue Kerk brought me last night. It's gone.

Dim light filters through the windows. I can hear the rain battering down outside. That's strange. The Hot Rainy Season ended last night.

I struggle to the door. Sure enough, the rain is still pouring down out of a grey sky. In all my years in Turai I can't ever remember this happening before. The seasons might be grim, but they're regular. The effort of moving has made my head hurt. I'm feeling rough. What I need is a lesada leaf. I trudge upstairs to find one.

Makri is creeping along the upstairs landing looking one step ahead of death. She groans as I appear.

"I should never have come to this city. You're all
decadent. My head hurts. Got any leaves left?"

I nod. She follows me into my room and I remove
a small pouch from my desk. Inside are my twenty or
so remaining lesada leaves. I took them from a dead
Elf a few months ago. He was killed after trying to
cross Hanama. Before making the mistake of thinking
he could outwit the Assassins he had been a healer and
used the lesada leaves for treating all sorts of mala-
dies. I've found them highly effective against hangovers.
Best thing I ever got from an Elf in fact.

Makri struggles to swallow her leaf then sits silently
beside me while we wait for them to take effect.

"Have you noticed there's a threat painted on your
wall?" she says, after a while.

I hadn't.

Stay away from the Mursius investigation, it says.
The message is written in blood. Or a magical imita-
tion of it. I hope it washes off.

Underneath is a letter G. Glixius Dragon Killer, presumably. I wonder why he doesn't just attack, instead
of leaving these stupid messages. I tell Makri that the
bust of the Elf has disappeared during the night.

"It's my own fault. Never fall asleep from too much
beer when you're carrying vital evidence. First thing
I learned as an Investigator."

"You think Glixius sneaked in during the night and
stole it?"

"Maybe. He's just the sort of evil character who
wouldn't be celebrating like everyone else."

We lapse back into silence. "Thank God for these
leaves," says Makri some time later, as the colour
returns to her face. "But you ought to go easy. They're
running out."

"I know. I'll have to mount an expedition to the Southern Islands to get some more."

The fabulous Southern Islands, home to the Elves, are far, far away, and difficult to reach. You need a well-equipped ship to cross the ocean and the Elves are extremely wary of who they let visit. I went there a long time ago, but very few others in Turai have. The idea of actually going back there just to pick up a hangover cure makes us smile.

"Did you notice it's still raining?"

"Oh no!" wails Makri and hurries to the door. She stares in fury at the rain and starts complaining as if it's my fault.

"You promised it would stop. I can't stand any more rain. What's wrong with this place?"

I'm stuck for an answer. It's never happened before.

The celebratory joy evaporates immediately and the entire city plunges back into depression and anxiety. The continuing rainfall is regarded as the gravest of omens. No one has to look far for the cause.

"It's the Orcs!" thunders Bishop Gzekius.

Bishop Gzekius is standing in for his subordinate, Derlex, who'll be absent from the pulpit for a while.

"The rains shall wash us away!"

It's a powerful sermon from the Bishop, much more passionate than you'd normally hear in Saint Volinius's Church, I imagine, though I'm not really one to judge. I never attend church and have only come today to ask Bishop Gzekius what exactly he thinks he's doing, organising the theft of the Orcish charioteer's prayer mat.

It's an unsatisfactory interview. The Bishop refuses to acknowledge any part in the theft of the prayer mat.

"It is ridiculous to think that Pontifex Derlex could have spirited away the prayer mat from a villa which was heavily guarded."

"You have influence all over the city, Bishop. Enough to make a few Guards turn a blind eye if necessary."

Gzekius denies it. He claims to have no knowledge of Orcish religion and when I tell him that Pontifex Derlex has been reading up on it in the Imperial Library he says it is none of his business what his young Pontifexes get up to in their spare time.

I ask Gzekius who slugged Derlex and made off with the mat, but again the Bishop is saying nothing. I can't tell if he organised the sabotage of the Orcs as part of some wider politicking or simply for reasons of faith. Sometimes members of the True Church have surprised me by acting from the sincerity of their beliefs. Not often though.

Either way, the Bishop doesn't know where the prayer mat is now. He says that if I pursue the matter he will see that charges are brought against me for burgling Derlex's house. I tell him that if he wants to start threatening me he'll have to wait his place in the queue.

"You do seem to be in considerable trouble these days," agrees the Bishop, maliciously. He hands me a copy of *The Renowned and Truthful Chronicle of All the World's Events*. It devotes one full side of its single sheet to the shocking continuation of the rain, joining in with the general cry that the arrival of Lord Rezaz and his cursed chariot is to blame. *Only the True Church speaks up for the people*, it says, and compliments the staunchness of our local Bishop. Nice publicity for Gzekius. I flip it over. The other side is devoted entirely to me, unfortunately.

How can it happen, thunders the *Chronicle*, *that the number one suspect for the murder of the Turanian hero, Senator Mursius, has been employed by the government to protect an official Orcish chariot? Is there no end to the corruption in this city? Surely in any honest*

civilisation Investigator Thraxas would at this moment
be climbing the steps to the gallows to receive due pay-
ment for his crimes, rather than receiving payment from
the King for protecting these foul enemies of humanity.
It is bad enough that the Civil Guard, with all the
resources of the state behind it, has not yet secured a
conviction. Surely it is intolerable in a civilised society
that the chief suspect, Thraxas, a man, it must be said,
with the most dubious of characters . . .

And so it goes on. It's a thorough piece. Even I had
forgotten about the time I was hauled up in court for
stealing a loaf of bread while everyone was engaged
in morning prayers. I was very young when it happened
and got off with a warning.

"I'd say you were in enough trouble without bothering a Bishop of the True Church," says Gzekius,
summoning a servant to show me out.

Everywhere I go I meet with sullen anger. Even
Minarixa seems annoyed when I call in for some provisions, though it could just be the result of the effects
of last night's revels. Guardsman Jevox is surprised to
see me.

"I was wondering why they let you out of jail. You've
been working for Cicerius."

"That's right. Did you find out anything about the
warehouse?"

Jevox hasn't. If he does he'll send me a message.

"You have any idea who broke in to the Pontifex's
house last night?"

No crime was reported at the Pontifex's. I suppose
that was to be expected. It's baffling though. It was
hard enough finding one person who'd know enough
to steal that prayer mat. How come someone else
suddenly knows enough to steal it from Derlex? The
entire city can't have been studying Orcish religion. The
library only has one scroll.

I walk down to the Mermaid and there Casax the Boss is almost pleased to see me.

"You were right, Investigator. The Society of Friends had infiltrated Twelve Seas. Four of their men were in that warehouse for a week, posing as common labourers."

Casax isn't sure what they were doing there, though he presumes it was connected with the arrival of the Elvish and Orcish chariots, both of which were stabled temporarily in that very warehouse.

"I figured that myself. And I think I know what they were planning. A doping operation."

Casax looks sceptical. "Doping? For the Turas Memorial? No chance, Investigator. The King's Master of Horse inspects every entrant and Melus the Fair checks for doping as well as sorcery. You couldn't get a doped horse past them."

"Usually you couldn't. But I think the Society came up with something special this time. Namely the coix plant."

I take out a small fragment of the plant that Makri brought back from Mursius's villa and hand it to him.

"Comes from the far west. Doesn't look anything special, I know. But I've a strong hunch it'll act as a powerful sedative on horses, and it's completely unknown here in Turai. I reckon there's every chance that if the Society managed to feed the correct dose of this to the Orcish and Elvish teams they'd both crawl round the track on the day and neither Melus the Fair nor the Master of Horse would be able to detect a thing."

Casax stares at the green leaf. "I'll have it checked out," he says.

The Brotherhood prefer muscle to magic but they have Sorcerers on call if they need them.

"So, who was behind it?"

I admit I'm not certain but I imagine it must have been Senator Mursius. After all, the plant came from his house.

"And it makes sense. If the Society were planning something like this, who better to work it for them than the man who was entering the strongest Human chariot team? Mursius was very confident about his chances, far too confident for a man who's up against an Elf. I know that Glixius Dragon Killer is involved. He might be the murderer. Maybe they argued over the cut. People like that always do."

Casax shakes his head sadly. Not even a gangster likes to see a Turanian war hero exposed as a cheat at the races.

"Perhaps he wasn't thinking straight," I say. "He had problems with his wife."

"I hear his wife is entering the chariot anyway. I also hear she likes to soak up dwa. You think she's carrying on the doping operation?"

"I don't know. I doubt it. Anyway, I'll pass some of the leaf on to Melus the Fair. Once she's studied it, it won't get past her."

Casax smiles. I don't think I've ever seen him do that before. "Congratulations, Investigator. You seem to have thwarted a Society operation. I like that. I'll tell my men to keep a lookout for Glixius. We'll make sure he doesn't venture down this way again."

When I leave the Mermaid I reflect that I've never had such a productive meeting with the Brotherhood. Casax might even feel he owes me a favour.

I head off up to the Palace to find Cicerius. The streets down here are impassable for wheeled vehicles and I have to walk a long way up Moon and Stars Boulevard till I find a landus to take me to the Palace. It still looks splendid, despite the deluge, but even here the gardeners are losing the battle with the volume of rain and huge swaths of land lie under water. The numerous officials scurrying around these parts do so with their cloaks pulled tightly round them and their faces downcast, looking no happier than the denizens of Twelve Seas. Cicerius greets me briskly. The Deputy Consul may be the only person in the entire city unaffected by the weather. He gets down to business right away.

"I'm due in the law courts in an hour. I'm defending a Senator on a corruption charge, so I can't spare you much time I'm afraid. Have you found the prayer mat?"

"Almost."

"Almost is not good enough."

I relate the full story of Derlex and Gzekius.

Cicerius nods.

"The True Church will have to learn not to meddle in state affairs. Who do you think took the mat from Derlex?"

"I don't have any suspects. It's very strange, Deputy Consul. Not that people are trying to sabotage the Orcs, we were expecting that. But who else could possibly know of the importance of that mat?"

Cicerius and the Consul are coming under increasing pressure from the King. Cicerius is fair-minded enough to realise that I've been doing my best, but he needs more than that.

"You have to find the mat by tomorrow. If you don't, we lose the copper mines."

Before I go I tell him a few details of the Mursius case. He takes the news about the Senator and the doping attempt calmly.

"Once I would have been shocked. Not any longer. Nothing surprises me in Turai any more."

Last summer I helped Cicerius when his son had been supplying dwa to Prince Frisen-Akan, the heir to our throne. Cicerius can have no illusions about the state of our nation. Rotten, in a word.

At my request the Deputy Consul asked a clerk to examine the state of Mursius's finances. He was in grave financial trouble. He'd lost a great deal of money speculating and he was hit badly when several ships to which he had joined with others to offer insurance sank last year in a storm. Much of his land was mortgaged and he had more debts than he could hope to meet.

Poor Senator Mursius. The man fights off the Orcs from our city and becomes a hero. Fifteen years on and he's broke and his wife's addicted to dwa. No wonder he tried to cheat at the races.

Cicerius summons his official carriage and we ride down to Truth is Beauty Lane, where the Sorcerers live. Melus has a large villa here, luxurious enough though not too ostentatious.

Melus is a powerful Sorcerer from a long line of Sorcerers. She came to public prominence when she was appointed to the job at the Stadium, since when she's become a national favourite. Everyone trusts Melus. She's around the same age as me and fought in the last war. All our Sorcerers did, and their Apprentices. She stood beside her father as he was killed by dragon flame, so I don't imagine she's too happy about having to help the Orc Lord either. I tell Melus the Fair about Senator Mursius's plans for cheating in the races and hand her a leaf from the coix plant. She's grateful though she doesn't admit that it would have fooled her.

"I'd have picked up that something was wrong. Easy as bribing a Senator."

Sorcerers always have a very high opinion of their own sorcery.

"Who do you fancy for the big race?" I ask her. She laughs. "I'm not allowed to speculate."

I inform her of developments, and admit that I don't know where to look next for the prayer mat.

"I take it Rezaz the Butcher isn't pleased?" I say.

"No he is not," says Lord Rezaz Caseg, stepping into the room.

I look at Melus reproachfully. She might have told me there was an Orc Lord next door. If I'd known he could hear me I'd have used his proper title.

"So, Investigator, you have failed to locate my charioteer's prayer mat?"

"That's right."

"Then we shall leave the city tomorrow."

"There is no need to leave," says Cicerius, calmly. "You may have complete confidence in Thraxas. He will locate the missing item."

Cicerius proclaims this with complete conviction, though I know he doesn't believe it. Lord Rezaz looks thoughtful. With everyone on their best behaviour you might think this was a gathering of old friends. Deputy Consul Cicerius, Melus the Fair and Lord Rezaz Caseg, in white toga, rainbow cloak and black cloak respectively, maintain a high level of dignity. It's left to me to spoil it all. I've been having a hard time keeping calm. I manage until Rezaz's attendant, a short, muscular Orc with a sword at each hip, makes a comment to his Lord in Common Orcish.

Very few people in Turai speak any Orcish. Since Makri arrived, mine has become quite fluent. The attendant's remark produces the slightest of smiles from the Lord Caseg. I turn to Cicerius, bristling with anger. "That's it, I'm leaving. I refuse to work for an Orc who says I'm too fat to find my own feet."

I let the attendant have a choice insult, also in Orcish, that I've heard Makri use on occasion.

"How dare you say that about my mother," he says, drawing his sword.

I draw mine. I've had enough of being polite to Orcs. I like this better.

"Please!" cries Cicerius as he tries to get between us. There's a commotion at the door and Lord Lisith-ar-Moh walks in with his Elvish attendants. He stares in surprise at the sight of myself and the Orc facing each other with swords in our hands.

"What is going on?" demands the Elf Lord.

"Have you met the man responsible for seeing that the Orcs are treated fairly?" says Melus.

Everyone looks at me. I still have my sword in my hand. I suddenly feel very conspicuous.

"Well, he started it," I say.

The Deputy Consul shoots me a glance that speaks volumes. I sheath my weapon. Cicerius explains to Lisith what has been happening.

The Lords exchange formal bows.

"An epic battle, that day at the walls," says Rezaz. "I regretted that my allies were foolish enough to allow your ships to land. Had I been overall Commander of our forces, I would not have permitted it."

The Elf Lord allows this to pass without comment. Both of them, each with great power, are too skilful and experienced to give anything away in terms of emotions. They hate each other, but they're not going to let it show, not here.

"I hear that your Orcish chariot is a fine vehicle," says Lisith politely.

"It is. My pride and joy, in these days when warriors must seek their diversions elsewhere. I was looking forward to the race."

They enter into a discussion, but I don't pay much attention. I'm still insulted at the Orc commenting on my weight. So it is that on this momentous occasion, the first in recorded history in which Orcs, Elves and Humans have a discussion without there being a war going on, I spend my time staring glumly out the window at the rain, drinking wine.

I'm interrupted by a loud cough from Cicerius.

"So, are you in agreement?" he says.

I look blank. "Sorry, I wasn't listening."

Cicerius restrains his ire. "It is suggested that Melus, Azgiz and Lothian will go with you immediately in an effort to find the prayer mat."

"Azgiz and Lothian? Who are they?"

A tall young Elf steps forward, bows, and introduces himself as Lothian.

"My personal swordsman," says Lord Lisith.

The Orc who insulted me also steps forward.

"Azgiz," he says. "Personal swordsman to Lord Rezaz Caseg."

I turn to Cicerius. "You want me to wander round the city with an Orc and an Elf in tow, looking for a prayer mat? Forget it."

"What choice do we have? I appreciate that you came close to locating it. As does Lord Rezaz. Had you not been so occupied with your wine you might have heard him compliment your powers of investigation. But time is running short. Both Melus and Lothian should be able to sense any Orcish item. And it seems reasonable that Azgiz should accompany you."

"Hasn't it struck you that we're not exactly going to be inconspicuous? Not much chance of going anywhere discreetly."

"Melus can discard her rainbow cloak. Azgiz and Lothian can cover themselves with hoods. No more objections. There isn't time. You must locate the prayer mat before tomorrow morning. Now go."

And thus it is that I find myself hunting through the city with the Stadium Sorcerer, an Orc and an Elf. Another momentous and historical occasion, I suppose.

Orcs and Elves have never cooperated before. Neither of them looks happy about it.

I tell them that we'll have to call in for Makri. I refuse to accompany these three on my own. God knows what might happen. Also, I want to see Makri's face when I turn up with an Orc in tow. If she kills him on the spot we can always flee the city. At least we'd get out of the rain.

"It's your fault," I say to the Orc, as we take our leave.

"What is my fault?"

"The rain. You've cursed the city."

"Orcs are not perturbed by rain."

"That's because they're stupid," I say.

It's not much of an insult. With a few beers inside me I'm sure I can come up with something better.

Chapter Sixteen

The rain continues. Some areas of Turai are now under three feet of water. Parts of Twelve Seas can only be reached by raft. Whole communities have to be evacuated to higher ground and across the city miserable groups of refugees are huddled in warehouses, sick, wet and hungry. The death toll from accidental drowning is the highest ever recorded and food is now unavailable in many districts.

Everyone is suffering. Even the sophisticated drainage engineered in Thamlin can no longer cope and the gardens of the rich have turned into swampland. Prayers are being said for an end to the deluge. Even I have added my voice to them. If this keeps up, the Turas Memorial Race will be cancelled. The races are due to begin in two days' time but the chariots can't run in this.

We form a strange company as we troop to my office. One large-sized Investigator and three mysterious hooded figures. Melus walks between Lothian and

Azgiz for fear that the natural antipathy between Orcs and Elves may make them forget our mission and start fighting. Lothian has already intimated that he finds it difficult to walk down the same street as an Orc, and Azgiz has let it be known that personally he'd rather descend to the fiery pits of Orcish hell than cooperate with an Elf. I am now obliged to be on my best behaviour because Melus promised that if I started any trouble she'd ban me from the Stadium Superbius. As we enter my office, Makri is scrabbling under the couch.

"I was just looking for—" she begins.

"Forget it. You're needed."

"What for?"

"We're looking for the prayer mat. You already know Melus the Fair, I believe. Allow me to introduce Lothian the Elf and Azgiz the Orc. Don't make a fuss, there isn't time."

Makri is horrified as the Orc and the Elf draw back their hoods.

"You can't be serious," she says.

To make matters worse, Azgiz greets her in a friendly manner while Lothian the Elf regards her with suspicion.

"I saw you fight in the arena," says the Orc swordsman.

He addresses me. "She was undefeated. She was regarded as one of the finest gladiators in history." He bows to her.

Makri doesn't know how to react to this so she falls back on what she knows and hurries to her room to find a few weapons.

Lothian's Elvish senses detect Makri's background. He looks displeased. "Orc and Elf and Human?" he says. "That is meant to be impossible."

"Yeah, she's a marvel."

Makri reappears with a fierce scowl, a sword at each hip, an axe at her belt and knives stuck into her waistband and boots. Round her neck she carries a bag of throwing stars.

"What were you doing under my couch?" I enquire as we make our way through the muddy street.

"Needed money."

"Don't you learn any morals at these ethics classes?"

"Never mind that. What's the idea of bringing Orcs to the Avenging Axe?"

I fill her in on the details.

"It's outrageous. Cicerius better get me into the University," says Makri. "Did you see the way that stupid Elf ignored me?"

I nod. "At least the Orc was polite. He said you were number one gladiator."

Makri makes a face. She's none too pleased to encounter anyone who saw her fight in the arena. Too much of a reminder of her days as a slave.

We arrive at Saint Volinius's Church.

"I tracked the prayer mat to the Pontifex's house."

"What now?" asks Melus the Fair.

I admit I've no idea.

"Then why did you bring us here?"

"Where else would I bring you? I never claimed to know where the mat is now. It was you and Cicerius who demanded we all troop off and look for it. This is its last known resting place. Now it's up to you."

Melus turns enquiringly to Lothian.

"I seem to have misunderstood the role of an Investigator," says the Elf, dryly. He starts to sniff the air, trying to detect any sign of Orcish artefacts. "It's no use," he says, shaking his head. "I can't sense anything. Too much Orcish smell around here already." He looks pointedly at Azgiz.

"The stench of Elves fills my nostrils," retorts the Orc.

"Quiet," demands Melus the Fair. She concentrates for a long time. The distant sound of thunder reaches our ears. Another storm heading in. "This way," she says finally. She sets off towards the harbour.

I trudge along behind with Makri at my side.

"This is the worst thing you've ever got me into, Thraxas."

I offer my flask of klee. Only Makri accepts. Melus strides through the mud and the rain with the Orc and the Elf on either side, while we tag along behind. I warn Makri that she'd better not lose control and attack Azgiz.

"Melus has threatened to ban me from the Stadium if I step out of line. I'm worried she might mean it. How's a man supposed to concentrate on his betting with all this going on?" I drink some more klee. "Not that I can concentrate anyway," I continue, warming to the subject. "Not with half the people in the city trying to fix the races. It's scandalous. Some things in life should be sacred, beyond interference, and the Turas Memorial is one of them. When I was young no one would've dreamed of tampering with it. I tell you, Makri, things are getting out of hand. If I suspect any cheating I'm going straight to the Consul to tell him what's what. I will demand he calls a special meeting of the Senate."

Makri is looking at me with something approaching awe. "I've never heard you get so worked up before."

"Well, there's some things in life a man has to care about."

"Beer and chariot racing?"

"That's right. Beer and chariot racing made me what I am today. And I'm proud of it!"

Melus has led us right down to the waterfront, to some warehouses just west of the harbour. She asks

Lothian if he can sense anything, but he shakes his head. Melus looks around doubtfully.

"I thought I could sense something Orcish. But it was so faint . . . I've lost it."

The door of the warehouse opens and four large Orc warriors march out.

"How faint did you say the traces were?"

More Orcs start pouring out waving scimitars and axes.

"Good," says Makri, who couldn't take much more sneaking about in this company. I grope for my sleep spell and realise that I'm not carrying it. I'm still using all my magic to keep my cloak dry. This is a tactical error. A dry corpse is not such a great thing to be. I have to discard my cloak anyway to free my arms for fighting.

Melus the Fair reacts quickly, raising her hand and blasting the Orcs with a spell. The front row falls down but there's a tangible jolt as the spell runs against something and dissipates into the air. The warehouse door opens again and an Orc in a plain black cloak steps out. Around his head is a small black band holding a black jewel in place on his forehead. I haven't seen that for fifteen years. The black band is the mark of an Orcish Sorcerer, and the black jewel denotes mastery of his art. This Orc can bring down city walls. My spell protection charm is about to be severely tested.

The Orcish Sorcerer barks out a spell. The air turns red and I'm thrown backwards, but my protection charm holds. Melus has placed a barrier between us and the Orcish Sorcerer, preventing his magic from harming our party. It doesn't hold back the Orcish warriors though. They charge through the crackling, red-tinged air, and Makri, Lothian and myself find ourselves in the middle of a desperate battle for survival.

I'm surprised to see Azgiz at our side. Something wrong there, surely. He should be fighting with the Orcs. I'm glad he's not, though the odds are bad enough as it is. He has a sword in each hand, a manner of fighting rare in the west. Makri is a master of this style, though on this occasion she is using a sword and an axe, to deadly effect. Both Lothian and myself use a sword and a knife. I'd be better off with a shield but it's not the sort of thing you carry around the city. We're hard pressed. We have our backs to the warehouse wall but although we repel the first assailants we're soon in trouble as the Orcs swarm round our flanks.

I parry a sword thrust from an Orc then stick my knife in him. As I do so he lands a painful cut on my shoulder and I'm only saved from going under by Lothian who brings his sword down on the Orc's arm then kicks him out of the way.

Suddenly there's a flash of light. Melus has used a spell to give us an escape route. Part of the wall caves in behind us, and we flee back into the warehouse. Melus is unable to bring her full power into play because she's already occupied with keeping the Orcish Sorcerer at bay, but she manages to place a stream of fire behind us, giving us enough time to make it to the door at the far side. It opens. More Orcs pour in.

"Isn't this meant to be a Human city?" I snarl.

"The wagons," yells Lothian.

In one corner of the warehouse are four or five empty carriages, waiting to be loaded. We charge over and drag one of them out.

"Look," cries Azgiz. "The prayer mat."

The prayer mat indeed. We've found it, but it doesn't seem likely we're ever going to return it.

With our backs to the corner and the wagon in front of us we at least have some sort of cover against the superior numbers. I ask Melus to send for assistance and she gasps that she has already sorcerously contacted her Apprentice, telling her to bring help. Twenty or so Orcs remain. As they advance Melus releases a powerful attack and an explosion sends five Orcs hurtling into the air. Unfortunately this gives their Sorcerer an opening. Without warning, the wagon we're using as a barricade bursts into flames.

Makri screams an utterly savage war cry and charges out to make her death stand. The flames are licking round us, and there's no choice but to follow her. I see her whirling into the fray, hacking down Orcs left and right, and I plunge after her. Azgiz is at my side and between us we deal with a couple of them, but there are far too many. Azgiz goes down and I find myself desperately trying to protect him. I see Lothian sliding his sword elegantly into a huge Orcish warrior, but then he too falls under a blow from an axe. Makri leaps to his side and wards off his attackers but then she is surrounded. We're still on our feet, but we're seconds from death. I take a blow from a mace and sink to my knees.

At that moment whistles sound and a squadron of the King's soldiers flood into the warehouse followed by Civil Guards. Melus's message to her Apprentice reached its destination. I struggle to my feet.

"Thraxas, are you all right?"

It's Makri, cut and bruised, but still in one piece. I nod. I notice I smell strongly of klee. "They broke my flask."

Both Lothian and Azgiz are lying on the ground. Melus is kneeling over the Orc, protecting him from the soldiers and Civil Guards who are mopping up. I suddenly feel faint from the blow I received, and sit down heavily next to a wagon. There's something uncomfortable underneath me. I drag it out. It's a small silver statue of a Mermaid, a strange thing to find in a deserted warehouse.

Down on all fours I crawl under the wagon.

"Look, Makri," I say, emerging with another small statue and a painting. "I just found the rest of Mursius's stolen artwork."

"You just can't stop investigating, can you?"

"I know. I amaze myself sometimes."

"Careful," says Makri. "You're bleeding over them."

She's right. We both are. I shout to Melus. "How about a little medical attention round here?"

There is a great deal of confusion as the Guards send out patrols in pursuit of the Orcs who escaped, and messages are sent to dignitaries all over the city. Some time later I find myself comfortably seated in a large reception room in Prefect Drinius's official residence in Twelve Seas, drinking wine. I am here as his guest, which makes a change. After our desperate battle we are all heroes. Makri and I are in fairly good shape, having been attended to by both Melus the Fair and Chiaraxi the healer. Lothian and Azgiz were more seriously wounded and will take a few days to recover fully.

"My superior street-fighting skills," I tell Captain Rallee, by way of explanation. "The Elf is not a bad fighter. No doubt in a forest he'd be hard to beat. But when it comes to slugging it out in the slums, I'm number one chariot. Incidentally, what were all the Orcs doing there?"

The Captain doesn't know. "You're a busy man these days. If you keep up the hero act they might let you off with murdering Senator Mursius."

"Very funny. I didn't kill him."

"Then who did?"

"Glixius Dragon Killer."

"Have you got any evidence?"

I shake my head. "But I'll find it. He's not getting away from me this time."

Drinius's residence is full of senior Guard Captains, Army officers, Sorcerers from the Palace and various other important city officials. The mysterious appearance of so many Orcs in the city has stirred the government into action. As I'm talking to Captain Rallee, the Consul and the Deputy Consul arrive. Cicerius acknowledges me but immediately goes into conference with Melus the Fair and Old Hasius the Brilliant.

The Captain doesn't know what the Orcs were doing there. I guess I'll find out soon enough. I summon a servant and ask him for some beer. He tells me there is none and offers me some wine.

"I need beer. Send out for some. Remember, I just saved you from a load of Orcs."

Lord Lisith-ar-Moh walks majestically into the room, flanked by his tall Elvish attendants. He walks right past the Consul and comes over to Makri and me.

"Lothian has told me of the battle," he says to us. "I understand that you stood over him when he fell. He would certainly have been killed had it not been for you. He has asked me to thank you, which I now do. And you have my personal thanks as well."

He bows lightly to me, and then, with the sort of courteous gesture you find among important Elves, he takes Makri's hand and kisses it. She gapes at him in surprise and stammers out a thank you. Lisith walks off to confer with Kalius and Cicerius, leaving me and Makri with our social status greatly improved. Not everyone in this city gets personally thanked by an Elf Lord. Everyone looks impressed.

A young Elf, who may be the one that stared in surprise at Makri when the ship was being unloaded, also walks over to thank us. His salutation to me is brief and formal. I suspect the real reason is that he has suddenly had a desire to kiss Makri's hand as well, which he does, though formal Elvish etiquette doesn't absolutely demand it. Makri blushes. I've never see her do that before. The Elf hopes he'll see her at the Turas Memorial, then departs after his Lord.

Makri is left confused, unused to having her hand kissed by Elves.

"You're blushing."

"What?"

"Blushing."

Makri claims not to know what the word means. I explain it. "That's the most stupid thing I've ever heard," she says. "I don't believe it happens."

A tall figure swathed in a black cloak arrives in the now crowded reception room. Even among the city's important figures few have been introduced to Lord Rezaz Caseg and there is a frisson of shock as he draws back his hood. Many of these government officials, Army commanders and Sorcerers were young soldiers themselves the last time Rezaz the Butcher was here and they're reliving similar memories to the ones which have flooded my own mind recently. Consul Kalius prepares to greet him but the Orc walks right over to me.

"Azgiz wishes me to thank you for saving his life," says the Orc Lord.

"Think nothing of it," I reply.

He turns to Makri and thanks her. I dig down into my bag and bring out the prayer mat.

"Tell your charioteer I was as careful with it as I could be."

Lord Rezaz's eyes light up. He takes the prayer mat with every sign of pleasure, and then holds out his hands in a gesture that encompasses both myself and Makri.

"This is excellent! Now the race can go ahead. I am

indebted to you both. I proclaim you friends of the Orcish nation of Soraz!"

He walks off with the mat in his hands, talking animatedly with his attendants. I notice that everyone seems to be looking at me. I'm not sure if my social status just went up or down. A friend of the Orc nations is not necessarily such a good thing to be.

"I can't take much more of this," says Makri. "Did that servant bring you any beer? Pass it over." She downs a large gulp from my goblet. "What were the Orcs doing there anyway?"

No one has provided an official explanation as yet, but I'm fairly sure I know.

"I think they were agents of Prince Kalazar, Rezaz's rival for the throne of Soraz. They were here to kill Lord Rezaz. We just helped save the life of an Orcish monarch. You ought to be proud, Makri. I know I am."

"Is that a joke?"

"Yes."

We depart. It's still raining.

"Will the races go ahead now?" asks Makri.

"Not if this doesn't stop."

Makri is perturbed. "Stupid place to build a city," she says, not for the first time.

Chapter Seventeen

I wake up early. It's the day of the Turas Memorial Race. The rain is still beating down. For the first time ever, the race looks like it might be cancelled.

A faint tap comes at my door. It's Casax, with a huge cape protecting him from the elements. It's unusual for the Brotherhood Boss to go anywhere without a few strong-arm men to protect him. Normally such a visit would be cause for concern but right now we seem to be cooperating.

"I thought I'd fill you in on a few details, Investigator. This is private. As far as anyone else is concerned, you heard nothing from me."

I nod.

"I found out some more from Axilan, this guy we picked up last night, who was trying to sell us some information. You were right about the warehouse. The Society of Friends was using it. They had men hiding there, waiting to drug the Elvish horses with that coix plant from the far west. But it seems they were taken by surprise when they were offered some works of art for sale."

"You mean Mursius's art?"

"That's right." Casax glances at the pile of artefacts in the corner. "I see you've recovered the junk."

"Some of it's quite valuable."

"I never was an art lover. According to Axilan they were hiding out when suddenly this Sorcerer appeared."

"What Sorcerer? Glixius?"

"That's right. And he tells them to use their contacts to sell the goods. They were surprised, but they knew Glixius was well connected to the Society of Friends and was part of the doping operation. So they dumped the stuff upstairs, planning to remove it when it was all over. They couldn't work out why Glixius didn't dispose of the goods in the north of the city, where he had plenty of contacts, but he was too scary to argue with. Anyway, it was valuable stuff and they stood to make a good profit.

"So Axilan carries on waiting for the Elves to arrive when one day he hears a terrible argument upstairs, which surprises him as he didn't know there was anyone up there. He goes upstairs afterwards and finds Senator Mursius dead. I figure the story is true so far, because he says he saw you come into the warehouse, which you did around that time."

"What happened next?"

"The Society men panicked. They didn't want to be found in the warehouse with Mursius dead upstairs, so they grabbed a few valuables and ran. They sold them as soon as they could to raise a stake to get out of the city. They didn't want to go back north after bungling the operation. That's why you found a few pieces in the local shops."

I tell Casax that the goods they left behind were

later removed by sorcery. "I found them in another warehouse close by."

"I heard," says Casax. "When you were being a hero, fighting Orcs. Were they in on the theft?"

"No. Just a coincidence that the rest of the art ended up there. It was the nearest empty warehouse."

I ask if I can speak to Axilan. Casax shakes his head. "He doesn't seem to be around any more."

"You mean he's floating in the harbour?"

"No idea. But he did say he wanted to leave the city quickly."

I thank Casax for the information.

"No racing in this rain. Must be bad for your business."

Casax shrugs. "If people aren't gambling at the Stadium they'll be drinking in our taverns or visiting our whores."

He departs. I light another thazis stick, and think about Glixius. How did he get hold of Mursius's belongings? I wonder if Sarija sold them directly to him. She used to be a dancer at the Mermaid. Who knows what contacts she might still have in the city. But why did Glixius take them to the warehouse in Twelve Seas? There must have been plenty of other places where he could have disposed of them. It doesn't make much sense. But it does more or less confirm that he killed Mursius.

Glixius Dragon Killer. He's been sending me death threats, interfering with the races, stealing valuables, and murdering a Turanian hero. And putting my aura on the knife that did it, if I'm not mistaken. The man is a plague. I resolve that he is not going to get away with it. I'll see Glixius in court if it's the last thing I do.

The prospect of no race meeting robs me of my appetite for breakfast. I drag out a bottle of beer and drink it while staring gloomily out at the rain. Makri arrives in my room.

"How's life?" she asks.

"Better than rowing a slave galley. No, I take that back. It isn't."

"Can't the chariots run in the rain?"

"Not if the track's waterlogged."

Makri scowls. She was looking forward to the races, even if she has no money to gamble with. I told her to keep a little back from the money she promised the A.G. but she wouldn't.

"I can't do that. It's stealing."

"What about burrowing under my couch looking for my emergency reserve?"

"That's different."

A carriage pulls up outside and the Deputy Consul alights to wade through the mud. He walks in with his toga still gleaming white, if somewhat damp.

"Important news," he says.

"The races are on?"

Cicerius shakes his head. "No. It is unfortunate. It does rather negate the effort we put in to ensuring that the Orcish chariot could compete. Lord Rezaz has no complaint against us however, and the agreement will be honoured. The King is very pleased, Thraxas, and the government fully appreciates the part you played in the recovery of the prayer mat."

He turns to Makri and thanks her as well. He seems surprised that neither of us leaps around with glee. He notices the collection of fine art I now have dumped in a corner.

"Belonging to the late Senator Mursius? Have you found the killer yet?"

"I'm close. Though I guess I'm still the Guard's main suspect."

"The Guard doesn't really suspect you, Thraxas," says Cicerius.

"They give a good impression of it. Or was that just

to put pressure on me so I'd agree to protect the Orcs?"

"I wouldn't say that," replies Cicerius. "After all, there is evidence against you. Your aura really was on the knife, and that circumstance has still to be explained. But I doubt if charges would have been brought."

He takes out a purse and hands it to me. Reward for services to the city.

"Enough for a few good bets," I say. "If there was anything to bet on. Was I right about the Orcs being in the pay of Prince Kalazar?"

"You were. They were transported here by his chief Sorcerer, Makeza the Thunderer, for the purpose of assassinating Lord Rezaz. It was a clever plot. Lord Rezaz's security in his homeland was too thorough to allow his assassination, but there seemed every likelihood that it could be achieved in Turai where he would have only a few attendants with him. Furthermore, while our own Sorcerers would normally detect the arrival of any Orcs in the west, Makeza the Thunderer was able to disguise the presence of Kalazar's Orcs by mixing their aura with that of Rezaz and his attendants. Makeza is a dangerous opponent."

"Did the Guards pick him up at the warehouse?"

"No, he was long gone by then. Back to the safety of the Wastelands, I imagine."

"Why did the Orcs steal the prayer mat from Pontifex Derlex?" enquires Makri.

The Deputy Consul smiles. "To return it, strangely enough. Their assassination was planned for the Stadium Superbius. It was vital for them that Lord Rezaz did not leave the city before it occurred. Makeza the Thunderer learned of its theft through his sorcerous probing, then located it and sent his Orcs to recover it. Pontifex Derlex can count himself extremely fortunate to be alive. The Orcs planned to return it anonymously. Then they would mingle with Rezaz's entourage and murder him on the way to the Stadium."

"Is there no chance of the race meeting going ahead?" I ask.

Cicerius looks irritated. "I am told that it cannot go ahead in these conditions. But surely that is of only marginal importance. I never cared much for chariot racing myself," he says.

"You should take it up," I tell him. "Give your image a boost in time for the next election."

Cicerius is not the sort of man to give his image a boost in this manner. He relies on honesty and integrity. He'll never make Consul. Outside his driver is having problems. The carriage is stuck in the mud. Thus it is that I find myself out in the rain trying to pull Cicerius's official carriage free while the local street vendors look on with amusement. The combined force of two horses, two attendants, two Guards, Makri and myself fails to budge it.

"Can't we just leave him?" says Makri.

"Not if you want Professor Toarius to pass your work at college."

It's useless. The carriage won't move. Cicerius himself gets out and lends a hand, making a fairly amusing sight in his white toga. Its green edges are soon coated in filth. While we're pushing, the call for morning prayers, Sabam, sounds around the city. I'm appalled. How could I be so careless? Makri lets out a despairing groan.

"I'm already as wet as a Mermaid's blanket. You expect me to kneel down in this?"

With Guards, attendants and the Deputy Consul right beside us, there is no escaping it. Even the Deputy Consul, a pious man, does not look particularly pleased to kneel down in the mud and the rain to pray. I whisper to Makri to stop grumbling.

"Pray for the rain to stop and we might get to the races."

I send up a devoted prayer while sinking into the swamp. By the time the call for the end of prayers sounds I'm embedded about a foot deep and have some difficulty extracting myself. I'm covered in mud. With the mess, the rain, and the prospect of a cancelled race meeting, I am about as miserable as a Niojan whore and see no possibility of things improving.

"The rain's stopped," says one of Cicerius's attendants.

We all look up. It's true. The rain has stopped. Furthermore, blue sky is visible on the horizon.

"The rain has stopped!"

I practically dance for joy as the sun begins to shine. Word spreads and happy people start to appear on the streets.

Kemlath Orc Slayer appears from the tavern.

"Having some trouble?" he says, seeing Cicerius's plight. He makes a motion with his hand and a little jolt runs through the carriage. The horses whinny and suddenly it's free.

"Nice spell, Kemlath. Pity you didn't get here earlier."

I accost the Deputy Consul before he drives off. "How's the drainage system at the Stadium? Well maintained?"

"Certainly," he replies. "I allocated the budget myself. And I'll send over extra men to clear up."

"You think the race meeting will start on time?"

"It will," says Cicerius, whose political reputation might now take a knock if it doesn't.

We tell Gurd and Tanrose the good news.

"I said a prayer and the rain stopped," says Makri. There's bustle and excitement as everyone prepares to travel up to the Stadium Superbius. Gurd will shut the tavern for the day and come along with Tanrose. Palax and Kaby are planning to busk to the crowds, and maybe place a few bets if they earn enough. Myself and Makri are in reasonable shape after the reward money from Cicerius. He gave me sixty gurans. I extract ten to repair the damage to my rooms inflicted by various sorcerous warning messages and such like, and split the rest with Makri, which gives her twenty-five gurans. I have fifty, which puzzles Makri.

"Where did you get the extra twenty-five?" she asks suspiciously.

"I pawned my illuminated staff. Still not much of a stake, but I'll soon build it up. Follow me, and you won't go wrong. I'm going to make these bookmakers wish they'd joined the Army."

Makri wonders if anyone will try to sabotage the Orcish chariot again.

"I doubt it. It's too late. The Consul has Guards everywhere and Old Hasius the Brilliant is watching out in case the Thunderer shows his face again."

For the first time in a month I don't bother putting the dry spell on my cloak. Instead I use my magical capacity to load up with the sleep spell. I'm not expecting any more trouble but it's best to be prepared. I'm in a notably good mood.

"It's amazing how the prospect of gambling cheers you up, Thraxas. Only yesterday you were complaining that everything was a disaster. You said your reputation was in shreds because everyone was calling you an Orc friend and what's more you hadn't found Mursius's killer."

I wave this away. "Minor problems, Makri. I found the artwork, didn't I? I'll track down the killer soon enough. If some high-class Sorcerer at the Abode of Justice can find a link between the stolen goods and Glixius it'll be enough to take him to court. If not, I'll

just have to do a little more leg work. Either way, I'll
sort it out after the races."

Kemlath Orc Slayer compliments me on my perse-
verance. "You're right, Thraxas, you are a hard man to
shake off. Glixius should have known better than to
tangle with you."

Kemlath is travelling with us up to the Stadium,
where he's planning to meet Sarija and lend her support for the chariot she's entering in the big race.

Mursius's stuff is still in my room: fancy cups, statues, and the painting of him as a young man after the
Orc wars.

"How come you weren't in the painting?" asks Makri.

"I was a common soldier. They only painted the
officers and Sorcerers."

"It's a lousy painting," says Makri, who, along with
everything else, is now an art critic. I wouldn't know.
At least you can recognise the people in it. I always
think a painting can't be that bad if you can recognise
the people. It was this item which Mursius particularly
wanted to recover. I stare at it. Mursius, Kemlath, a
few other officers I recall. I have memories of the war
again, but banish them, and we continue with the
business of the day. Tanrose is bustling about merrily,
packing food for the trip.

"I really thought the race would be cancelled."

"I just said a prayer and the rain stopped," says
Makri. I have a bag of thazis sticks, a few beers and
fifty gurans. It's time to go racing.

Chapter Eighteen

The Stadium Superbius is an enormous stone amphi-theatre built by King Varquius a hundred years ago. It's the setting for circuses, theatrical performances, religious ceremonies, gladiatorial shows and, best of all, the chariot races. During the racing season the amphi-theatre is packed full of racegoers from every stratum of Turanian society. Praetors, Prefects, Senators, priests, society ladies, Sorcerers and high-ranking Guild offi-cials all mingle with the huge mass of proletarian Turanians out to enjoy themselves for the day, and maybe pick up a little money on the side. Today, for the Turas Memorial Race, the place will be bursting at the seams.

The gloom that has recently enveloped the city disappears with the rain. Being able to walk around without getting wet is enough to make most people cheerful and the prospect of the race definitely tak-ing place brings a smile to the faces of even those who only yesterday were confidently predicting that we were all cursed by the gods. The relief is so great that anger about the Orcs is largely replaced with anticipation to see the race between them and the Elves. The Elf is a strong favourite. Few Turanians will bet money on the Orcs, even if some do suspect that they might have a chance of victory. Sarija has entered Storm the Citadel, and although I personally think it has no chance of winning it's the best of the Human entrants and will also gather a large amount of popular support.

Entering the Stadium is tough. I have to use my weight to force my way through, with Makri bringing up the rear.

"I admit your bulk does have some advantages," she says, as I forcefully negotiate a path for us through a large group of schoolchildren who are far too tardy in finding their seats. We settle down in a good position near to the track, with easy access to both the bookmakers and a beer tent. All Turai is here. Tumblers and jugglers cavort before the crowds. The great mass of the people sits in the huge banks of terraces that run round the banks of the Stadium, and the Senators and other important people are up in the reserved galleries. I catch sight of a few green Elvish hoods up there and possibly a black Orcish one well back from public view.

Right at the front of this gallery, very visible to the public, is Melus the Fair in her rainbow cloak. The sight gives everyone confidence. Melus the Fair, bless her name, will protect us gamblers from unwanted outside interference.

I have fifty gurans. Makri has twenty-five. I'm surprised that the normally cautious Makri has brought all her money with her. I would've expected her to put some aside for necessities.

"I'm feeling confident," she says. "I think I have the hang of this now."

Makri is happy. Here in the Stadium everyone is too busy with the racing to bother about minor distractions such as a young woman with one-quarter Orc blood wearing a man's tunic and carrying two swords. At times like this such things fade into insignificance. The whole place is still damp and steam rises in the mid-day heat, but the track is in reasonable condition. It is wide enough to allow eight chariots to run at once, which makes for an exciting spectacle. We settle down with some beers.

"I'm feeling sharp as an Elf's ear today," I say, and get down to studying the form sheet.

The favourite is Glorious North Wind at six to five on.

"Glorious North Wind for the first race. Certain winner."

"I don't fancy it," replies Makri, surprising me. "I like the look of Eastern Beauty."

Eastern Beauty is the close second favourite in the race, quoted at evens by the bookmakers. It's not a bad bet, actually, though I prefer the favourite. When I ask Makri why she prefers Eastern Beauty she says she likes the name.

"You can't just bet on a chariot because you like the name."

Makri won't be swayed. Obviously she wishes to demonstrate that she can make up her own mind and, as I say, Eastern Beauty isn't such a bad prospect. There's nothing else in the race worth backing. None of the other chariots are fancied any better than sixteen to one and I'm in no mood for incautious speculation. Honest Mox has set up a stall in the stadium, manned by his son, and we make our way over to place our bets. I bet five of my fifty and Makri bets four of her twenty-five, then we settle down in the sunshine to watch.

After a fanfare of trumpets and a speech from the Consul the chariots make their way out from the stables. It's one of my favourite sights. Eight chariots, eight riders, thirty-two horses, poised to do four laps of the track. Terrific.

The starter drops a flag, the chariots set off, and the crowd erupts with a mighty roar. Glorious North Wind takes an early lead and by the end of the first lap is in a commanding position. The charioteers flog the beasts mercilessly as they thunder around the track. There's an early collision as three chariots get tangled up in each other's wheels and crash out of the race. A team of amphitheatre officials rushes on to clear the wreckage before the others come round again.

At the end of the third lap Glorious North Wind has a substantial lead with the other four disputing second place. Eastern Beauty, Makri's choice, is not making much of a showing. I'm on my feet along with everyone else, screaming encouragement at the favourite.

I have often thought that the gods are displeased with me. Perhaps it's the way I keep missing prayers. With half a lap to go and a clear run to the finish, Glorious North Wind loses a wheel and skids to a messy halt in the centre of the track. Three of the pursuing chariots crash into the wreckage, spilling their unfortunate charioteers heavily on to the ground. Eastern Beauty, currently in last place, swerves to avoid the pile-up and trots home an easy winner. There's a great groan from the crowd. Makri is still on her feet, however, shouting and yelling, and she practically tramples her neighbours to death in her eagerness to collect her winnings. She arrives back brandishing a fist full of coins.

"I won four gurans!"

I manage a grin. I'm not very pleased but I can't

begrudge my companion a bit of good fortune, so long as it doesn't happen too often.

"What're you betting on next, Thraxas?"

I study the sheet. "Dragon's Breath," I announce finally.

Makri makes a face. "Don't like the sound of that. I'm going for Lilac Paradise."

"Lilac Paradise? What sort of a name is that for a chariot?"

"I like it," insists Makri.

"It's got no form whatsoever."

I stare suspiciously at my companion. This seems like a very rash bet by Makri's standards. Lilac Paradise is a rank outsider at twenty to one. It's one of the chariots owned by Magadis, a very rich aristocratic widow. She's a racing enthusiast and has been training chariots for years, but she's not one of our more successful racers. Lilac Paradise is a poor chariot, even by her standards.

"I still like it," says Makri.

"Five gurans on Lilac Paradise," says Makri, handing over her money to Mox's son

Dragon's Breath is second favourite at three to one. I place a modest three gurans on it, which is just as well because on the first corner the chariot is involved in an ugly collision and crashes out of the race. Several more collisions follow and to the amazement of the crowd Lilac Paradise wins by half a lap.

There is a great deal of grumbling in the crowd, much of it from me.

"How is a man meant to make a bet when the wheels fall off his chariot at the first corner?" I complain, and stand up to hurl abuse at the charioteer as he is carried off on a stretcher.

"Orc lover!" I yell. "Who told you you could ride a chariot?"

My fifty gurans has now shrunk to forty-two. Makri, having picked up an astonishing hundred gurans on Lilac Paradise, now has one hundred and twenty-nine. Rarely have I seen a bookmaker so unwilling to hand over one hundred gurans.

The owner of Dragon's Breath appears on the track, supervising the removal of his mangled chariot.

"Come over here and I'll mangle you as well!" I scream at him.

"Cheating dog!" roars a woman behind me, brandishing a tankard. She has to be restrained by her companions from invading the arena and assaulting the owner.

"The population of Turai doesn't like losing," observes Makri.

"Damn right we don't," I grunt.

I'm in no mood for Makri's philosophical observations. I muscle my way to the beer stall and buy a drink. I don't get one for Makri. She's just won a hundred gurans. She can buy her own.

"I like it here," says Makri, as I return. "Who do you fancy in the next race?"

The sun beats down. The Stadium is now as hot as Orcish hell and the crowd is restive. What we need here is a popular favourite romping home an easy winner, not a load of outsiders carrying off the prizes. The woman behind me is particularly virulent. I nod in agreement as she roundly lambasts the chariot owners for carving it all up among themselves, cheating the honest punters out of their hard-earned money. I think I recognise her from Twelve Seas and I chat with her about the iniquities of chariot owners while we wait for the next race to get under way.

I note with relief that Warrior Chief, one of the finest chariots in Turai, is due to run. Okay, he's odds-on favourite and I'm not going to win much, but it'll

get me back on course. Warrior Chief is an absolute
certainty. I back him with twenty gurans at two to
one on.

Makri plumps for Serenity of Love, a useless wreck
of a chariot pulled by four crippled old horses and
ridden by a man who last won a race some time during
the Orc Wars. It's another of Magadis's chariots and
is something of a joke. The bookies are offering sixteen to one and there are few takers even at that price,
apart from Makri. She says she likes the name, and
backs it to the tune of thirty gurans.

"You're throwing your money away. Serenity of Love
wouldn't win a chariot race if all the other chariots were
eaten by a dragon."

When Warrior Chief fails to complete the race and
Serenity of Love strolls in an easy winner I'm not the
only one up on my feet baying my disapproval.

"Cheats! Fix!" cries the crowd, along with other
things much ruder. Fists are waved angrily and cush-
ions and ripped-up form sheets cascade on to the
track. The Civil Guards on duty stand up and face
the crowd, nervous about the possibility of a riot.
There is massive discontent. The stadium is packed
full of punters all seeing their hard-earned cash going
down the drain as one unlikely chariot after another
comes home a winner. I've rarely seen a race crowd
look so ugly. It's fortunate that Melus the Fair has
such an impregnable reputation for incorruptibility,
else there would be great suspicion that magic was
involved. Even so, mistrustful glances are cast in her
direction and some slanderous accusations are mut-
tered by the more degenerate members of the lower
classes, like myself, for instance.

"Damn that Melus, someone's been bribing her."

"Nonsense," replies Makri, cheerfully. "You said
yourself she got the job because of her honesty."

"Well, you can't tell me that wheel fell off by accident. Even the Sorcerers up in the royal box looked surprised."

"You're a poor loser, Thraxas."

"You're damn right I am."

Makri is now rolling in money, having picked up an astounding four hundred and eighty gurans on Serenity of Love.

"I have six hundred and nine gurans," she says.

"I don't remember asking you for an exact count."

I'm now down to twenty-two and facing the prospect of having nothing left for the final race. I remember that Makri owes me fifty—forty for her exam fees and ten that I lent her for betting.

"Hand it over," I demand.

Makri repays me the fifty gurans with a bright smile, which puts me in a even worse mood. There are a couple of races to go before the big Turas Memorial and the trumpets sound for a break in the proceedings. Makri asks if I want to go with her to find something to eat, but I am in too bad a mood to accompany her.

"I prefer to take luncheon on my own," I say.

I'm furious about the day's events. There's something strange going on here and I'm going to move heaven, earth and the three moons to get to the bottom of it. Leaving Makri to gloat over her winnings, I depart in the direction of the nearest food vendor.

I'm musing over a large meat pie—one of the Superbius Specials—when I run into the woman from the seat behind me.

"I haven't seen such injustice since they cancelled the races during the Orc Wars," she says.

I recognise her now. She was the landlady at the Mermaid tavern back in those days. She served me many a drink when I was a thirsty young soldier. She tells me that she married a man with a good position in the Barrel-Makers Guild and moved up to Pashish.

"How's the barrel-making business?"

"Good. It'll have to be, after the amount I've dropped here today."

I wander away, going nowhere in particular. With the money that Makri repaid me I still have seventy-two gurans, but my confidence has been badly shaken. Near the Senators' boxes I meet Kemlath Orc Slayer. He's on his way down to the owners' enclosure to wish good luck to Sarija, whose chariot will be competing soon.

"I don't suppose she has much chance against the Orcs and Elves," he says, truthfully. "But you have to admire her for making the effort. She's a fine woman, Sarija."

"I noticed you were getting to like her."

I complain to Kemlath about my bad luck so far.

"You haven't noticed any sorcery being used I don't suppose?"

"Sorcery?" says Kemlath. "Certainly not. You know Melus wouldn't allow it."

"I suppose not."

"Incidentally," says Kemlath. "I noticed Glixius Dragon Killer back there."

He waves his hand, indicating a throng of people. His large ring glints in the sunlight.

"Glixius Dragon Killer. Really?"

I'm reminded of the longstanding rumours about the Society of Friends and their purported betting coup at the races. Could these strange events be the result of that? Have the Society somehow been manipulating things in their favour? I decide to nose around.

Kemlath warns me to be careful, reminding me of Glixius Dragon Killer's sorcerous power.

"To hell with his sorcerous power. I'll make him wish he took up basket-weaving instead."

I spot quite a few Sorcerers in their rainbow cloaks around the stadium but Glixius's size makes him easily visible. I wade through the crowd towards him. When I reach him he has his back to me and is talking to a Senator.

"I can't understand it," he's saying. "Warrior Chief should have won. It was obviously the best chariot in the race. I'm down two hundred gurans today."

The Senator nods in sympathy; obviously he's suffered heavy losses himself.

"Don't give me that," I snarl, grabbing Glixius's shoulder. "You and your Society friends are behind all this."

He whirls round, a look of contempt and fury on his face. "Must you harass me everywhere I go?" demands the Sorcerer. "Were we not in the stadium where sorcery is forbidden I would tear your heart from your chest and jump on it."

I repeat my accusation. The Senator looks interested. Glixius notices this and he becomes defensive.

"You accuse me of fixing the races? Me? How dare you. I personally have suffered grievous losses."

"So? You could pretend to do that to throw suspicion off yourself."

Even as I'm saying this, I'm not entirely convinced. I have long, long experience of gamblers and their reactions to adversity. I hate to admit it, but Glixius Dragon Killer sounds more like a man genuinely aggrieved at his bad luck than a man who's behind it all.

"Do you have any evidence for these accusations?" demands the Senator.

Do I? Not really. Glixius and the Society of Friends were certainly planning some doping, but I can't prove it. I don't even know if the operation carried on after they were interrupted by Mursius getting killed, or if it was cancelled. When it comes right down to it, I have no firm evidence against Glixius, and I don't want to show my hand to him before I do. If I'm going to prove he killed Mursius I shouldn't be giving him advance warning of what I already know. It was rash of me to approach him. My emotions got the better of me.

"Anyone making such accusations without good grounds faces severe penalties in the courts," says the Senator.

I turn on my heel and march away, annoyed with myself. So far today, nothing is going very well.

I find myself next to the Senators' enclosure, which is protected by a low wall. Inside, Melus the Fair is in conversation with Cicerius. I walk up and demand admittance. The Deputy Consul nods to the attendant to let me in.

I march up to the pair of them. Cicerius looks glad to see me.

"I'm pleased you're taking your work seriously," he says.

"What work?"

"Looking out for sabotage of the Orcish chariot, of course."

"Sabotage of the Orcish chariot? Sabotage of me, more like." I turn to Melus the Fair. "What is going on here? Are you trying to tell me that Serenity of Love won that last race without magical help?"

As I say this, various Senators and Praetors nod their heads in sympathy. It's not only the poor who are suffering in the great gambling disaster that's unfolding here.

Melus smiles. "It has been a string of unexpected results, I grant you, Thraxas. But I have been monitoring everything very carefully. I can assure you that no sorcery has been used in the stadium. Nor has there been any attempt at doping."

The Senators all around sigh. It looks like we're all just stuck with our losses.

I'm flummoxed. If Melus says it, then it's true. Besides, there are plenty of other Sorcerers here as spectators. They all specialise in different types of sorcery but surely one of them would notice if anything odd had been happening. I decide to go down to the chariot pen underground and see if I can find out anything there. Maybe someone has been sawing through a few axles.

Cicerius draws me aside as I make to leave. "You are still in the employ of the city," he hisses severely. "Rather than wasting time gambling, I expect you to keep a vigilant lookout for the welfare of the Orcs."

"To hell with the Orcs," I hiss back. "I've more important things on my mind right now."

I storm off, having again caused my status to plummet in government circles. To hell with them all. I grab a beer and start shoving my way through the crowd again. It's too hot. I wish I hadn't broken my flask of klee. A blind beggar gets in my way. I push him to one side and he falls to the ground, protesting angrily. I ignore him. He was probably putting it on anyway. These beggars, you can never trust them.

At the foot of the terraces there's another row of bookmakers' stalls. People stand in line waiting to place bets and there, of all people, is Hanama the Assassin. I'm astonished. I didn't really believe she was actually going to be here gambling but there she is. She's wearing a cheap blue robe, the sort of thing worn by your average not-so-well-off Turanian woman on a day out, and she is completely indistinguishable from the rest of the crowd. In fact, with her thin, pale body she looks rather like a schoolgirl who's bunked off for the day to place a bet.

I can't understand it. It's completely unheard of. Assassins dedicate their lives to not having fun. I wonder if she might be here in disguise to assassinate someone. The chariot owners with any luck. I'd be happy to see the owner of Warrior Chief carried out of the Stadium with a knife in his back.

Chapter Nineteen

"Find out anything?" asks Makri as I return to my seat.

I've never seen her so cheerful. It's really irritating.

"No, I didn't."

"I expect there's nothing to find out," says Makri. "It's just one of those days when the favourites don't come in. Didn't you tell me that happens sometimes? Statistically it's bound to."

I have twenty gurans on Demon Killer. Makri has thirty on Joyous Sunrise. Joyous Sunrise wins by a length and a half and Makri collects another sixty gurans. Next race I back Venomous Death Adder, the favourite. Makri backs Fairy Rainbow, a rank outsider at twenty-five to one. Fairy Rainbow records its first ever win. Even the charioteer looks surprised. The crowd rises to its feet to protest. The Guards are again obliged to fan out to keep them from invading the track. Bottles and broken chairs rain down on them. I've lost another twenty gurans.

Makri picks up five hundred gurans for her twenty-guran stake and now has the incredible total of one thousand, one hundred and nineteen gurans.

"Easy as bribing a Senator," she says.

I can't understand it. I've never known anyone be so successful at the race track simply by backing every chariot with a nice-sounding name.

Honest Mox's son looks glum as he hands over her winnings, though in truth he's doing well. The way the favourites keep losing means he's raking in the public's money. The public is not amused. Only the appearance of the Orcish and Elvish chariots keeps the crowd from staging an uprising. The race officials wisely usher the alien chariots out early knowing that the interest in them will quieten the crowd. It works. As Lord Lisith's chariot appears there is great cheering but when the Orcish chariot rolls out after it there is a tremendous wave of booing and jeering. Frustrations are put to one side as the major race of the day approaches. The Orcish charioteer has long black hair, plaited and tied in a black ribbon. Despite the hostility around him he rides with an air of assurance. I expect he's feeling confident now he has his prayer mat back.

Storm the Citadel comes out next, with Sarija and Kemlath walking behind it. The crowd cheer again. Popular support has brought the odds on Storm the Citadel down to two to one, the same price as the Elvish Moonlit River. The Orcish chariot, Destroyer, is quoted at four to one. Certain astute punters have been backing it, feeling that a sensible bet is more important than patriotism. Nothing else figures much, the five other chariots in the race being quoted at prices between sixteen to one and eighty to one.

I'm still undecided how to bet. I fancy the Elves to win but I'm not convinced the Orcs won't pull it off. I could do with a nice piece of four to one. I'm down to thirty-two gurans and facing ruin. I delay my bet. The Orcish chariot drifts out to five to one. I'm tempted. I get a strange feeling. It's similar to the one I had down at the warehouse when the Orcs appeared. Nothing strange about that. After all, there are Orcs here.

My senses are picking up something else. A man walks past, a very normal-looking man in a plain tunic and sandals. I notice a slight scar on his forehead. I've never seen him before. Without quite knowing why, I follow him.

He heads up through the terraces. He seems to be in a hurry and I have to use my weight again to keep up. He pays no attention to either the bookmakers or the punters. At the top of the terraces he turns left and makes his way towards the Senators' box. I'm close behind him, still with no idea of why my senses are detecting something unusual.

As he halts in front of the Senators' box I glance at his face. Am I imagining it, or is the scar on his forehead beginning to glow? Cicerius is standing near the front of the box. Right beside him is Lord Rezaz Caseg. I suddenly realise what's happening and make a dive for the stranger. I land on him with all my weight and as we go down a terrific bolt of energy flies straight up in the air. Next second I find myself grappling hand to hand with Makeza the Thunderer. This Orcish Sorcerer is way out of my league in every way, apart from girth. I've prevented the assassination of Rezaz the Butcher, but I might not live to tell the tale.

I have my hands around his neck and I am desperately trying to keep out of the way of the jewel on his forehead. He manages to turn his head enough to send a piercing bolt into my shoulder and I cry out in pain. My spell protection charm has kept me alive, but it's not strong enough to resist a close-range blast of Orcish sorcery.

I yell for help, but the Guards at the Senators' enclosure are slow to react. I remember that I'm carrying my sleep spell. I use it, charging it with as much power as I can. This spell can knock a company of men unconscious, but it has little effect on the powerful Orcish Sorcerer, other than to make him loosen his grip a fraction. I break free, kick him in the ribs, then hurdle the wall into the Senators' enclosure.

"You expect me to do everything?" I gasp, and get myself behind Melus the Fair. Let someone with a bit of power take over.

Makeza the Thunderer, now back in his true form as an Orc Sorcerer, springs to his feet. His eyes are smouldering with fury as he advances. Three Civil Guards leap at him but he brushes them away with a word and they fly through the air. When he comes to the low wall, Makeza doesn't bother to climb. He barks at it and it crumbles before him. Melus the Fair steps in front of him and I'm relieved to notice several other Turanian Sorcerers hurrying to the scene. Makeza isn't going to be easy to beat.

Meanwhile Rezaz the Butcher has drawn his sword in readiness, and so have his attendants. This creates further confusion as the Senators find themselves standing among a group of armed Orcs and aren't quite sure what's going on. The Civil Guards present don't seem to know who they're meant to be protecting. Rezaz steps forward to confront Makeza and the Thunderer immediately releases a powerful blasting spell. The Orc Lord is thrown backwards and slumps to the ground.

Melus spreads her arms and directs all her power against Makeza. She is enveloped by a great burst of yellow light and struggles to free herself. She emerges unscathed and directs a counter-spell at the Thunderer. Again he seems unshaken, and continues to advance towards the prone figure of Rezaz. Two of the Butcher's guards fling themselves in front of the Sorcerer but they too are brushed aside like flies. Another powerful Turanian Sorcerer, Lisutaris, Mistress of the Sky, arrives, but Makeza the Thunderer keeps on coming.

I've seen these Orcish Sorcerers in action before. I know how powerful they can be. Even when Harmon Half-Elf rushes up (with several losing betting tickets sticking out of his pockets, incidentally) and adds his power to that of Melus and Lisutaris, the issue still seems to be in the balance. Fire crackles through the air and great bolts of lightning strike sparks from the metal railings.

My shoulder hurts. None of my chariots have won. I've lost a lot of gurans. I'm in a really bad mood. If Makeza the Thunderer succeeds in killing Lord Rezaz the Turas Memorial race will be cancelled and I'll never win my money back. I'm completely fed up with this continual disruption at the races. I grab a glass of klee from the hands of a Senator's wife, toss it back, then pick up a heavy chair and start circling around the back of the warring Sorcerers.

A huge maelstrom of fiery colour now envelops most of the Senators' enclosure. I step into the middle of it, offering up a prayer that my charm will protect me. Inside the maelstrom I can't breathe. I grit my teeth and struggle on. Space seems to be warped. I can see Makeza, but he's a long way away. As I struggle forward he takes on the aspect of a huge Orcish war dragon. The dragon turns his long neck towards me, baring its fangs. Through its nose it wears a great ring of power, with a dazzling blue jewel sending out poisonous rays. It reminds me of something, I don't know what. I crash the chair down with all my might on the dragon's head. It disappears with a deafening explosion, and I find myself back in the Senators' enclosure with a broken chair in my hands and an unconscious

Orcish Sorcerer at my feet. In front of me Melus the Fair, Lisutaris, Mistress of the Sky, and Harmon Half-Elf are standing in a line looking exhausted. Melus the Fair wipes sweat from her brow.

"It's a long time since I fought an Orc," she says, breathing heavily. "For a moment there I thought I was going to be handing in my toga. Nicely done, Thraxas. How did you know that would work?"

"A trick I remembered from the war. When an enemy Sorcerer is fully engaged in sorcerous combat he's often vulnerable to being beaten over the head with a heavy object. Incidentally, I thought that Old Hasius the Brilliant was supposed to be keeping an eye out for Makeza."

"He's at home with a cold—it's his age," explains Melus.

Lord Rezaz Caseg struggles to his feet. He thanks the Sorcerers, and me too. It is commonly admitted that it was smart work on my part to recognise Makeza the Thunderer as he walked through the crowd in Human guise.

The congratulations pass me by. I'm a little dazed. Not so much by the battle—the three Sorcerers bore the brunt of Makeza's attack—but by the sudden inspiration that hit me when I walked into the magical maelstrom. I've often found that close involvement with sorcery gets my intuition working. As soon as I saw the dragon with its ring of power I realised who killed Senator Mursius. Foolish of me not to have realised before.

The Senators and their wives troop back into the enclosure. Consul Kalius looks as if he might be about to shake my hand, but he thinks better of it and offers me a stiff thank you instead.

"Don't mention it. Do they sell beer in this enclosure?"

They don't. It's wine only for Senators.

Kalius takes control and issues orders for the races to resume as quickly as possible, so that the crowd does not become restive. Makeza the Thunderer is bound and taken off under heavy sorcerous guard.

I shake my head to clear it, then walk out of the enclosure, very thoughtful. I find a messenger and hand him over a small coin to take a note to Captain Rallee.

Chapter Twenty

"What happened up there?" asks Makri.

"Thraxas once more saves the day for Rezaz the Butcher. I may now be the greatest friend of the Orcs in the west."

The chariots are lining up behind the tape. I still haven't placed my bet. I can't make up my mind. I notice Hanama in the queue and sneak up behind her. As she reaches the front I strain to hear what she says. It's difficult to make out her soft voice above the noise of the crowd. I think I hear her say Peaceful Dreams of Heaven.

Peaceful Dreams of Heaven is the most useless chariot ever seen in Turai. It was brought in to make up the numbers after a late withdrawal. It was eighty to one at the start of the day and has come in to fifty to one, so a little money must have been placed on it. Not much though. Why would it? It doesn't have a chance.

Hanama disappears into the crowd, gliding easily

through the mass of bodies. The trumpets sound for the start of the race. I swallow hard. This goes against the grain.

"Eighteen gurans on Peaceful Dreams of Heaven."

I rush back to my seat.

"What did you back?" I ask Makri.

"Peaceful Dreams of Heaven,"

"I thought you might," I say. "It has a very nice name."

I glare hard at her. She glares right back at me. The race starts. As the long-awaited contest between the champion chariots of the Orcs and the Elves gets under way the Stadium Superbius explodes with excitement. By the time the chariots reach the first corner not a person is left in their seat. Everyone is up on their feet, screaming encouragement. Not only the ill-behaved masses are carried away. Up in the private enclosure the Senators, Sorcerers and city officials are caught up in the excitement. The Elvish supporters of Lord Lisith are up on their feet waving green banners and the Orcs are standing on their chairs shouting out encouragement in their jagged, guttural language.

For the first time Makri and I have backed the same chariot. Unfortunately it's the worst vehicle in the city. Round the first lap things don't look good. The Elvish Moonlit River has taken an early lead with Sarija's Storm the Citadel close behind. The Orcish Destroyer is going along easily in fourth place. Peaceful Dreams of Heaven is last. Things don't improve much in the second. I scream some abuse at the charioteer. Two chariots collide and another pulls up with a lamed leading horse, leaving Peaceful Dreams fifth out of five going into the third lap.

I can see the Elvish charioteer speaking to his horses, giving them encouragement. The Orcish rider uses his whip. Less kind, but effective, as he moves

easily up into third place to lie in wait just behind
Storm the Citadel.

The chariot behind the Orcish Destroyer tries to
overtake but gets the worst of it when the Orcish
charioteer lashes his whip into his opponent's face,
sending him crashing into the central barrier. You have
to hand it to the Orc, that's good technique. The crowd
erupts in a frenzy. As the last lap begins, Moonlit River,
Storm the Citadel and Destroyer are nose to tail and
going well. The only other remaining chariot, Peaceful Dreams of Heaven, is almost a whole lap behind.
I curse myself. I can't believe I put money on this
collection of rusted metal and broken-down nags.

"Please send a mighty collision," I say, raising my
eyes briefly to heaven.

Makri is gripped by the madness and seems close
to losing control. She's screaming encouragement to
Peaceful Dreams and waving her sword in the air,
which is illegal in the Stadium, even when your chariot
loses.

On the final straight Destroyer makes its move and
glides past Storm the Citadel like it was standing still.
It draws level with the Elf and they start jostling each
other as they come round the bend. The Orcish charioteer lashes his whip at the Elf, who starts lashing him
back. Sparks fly as their wheels grind together and the
horses hurtle onwards at speeds never before seen in
the Stadium. The volume is deafening. I've never seen
such madness in a race crowd. Young Sorcerers' Apprentices with whole months' wages staked on the Elf wave
their staffs in the air. I see Gurd up on his seat with
sweat pouring in torrents down his mighty neck, screaming encouragement.

In the final straight the Elf is ahead by a nose but
it seems to me that the Orc is finishing stronger.

"It's all over," I cry, and hang my head in despair.

Suddenly their wheels lock. There is a spectacular collision and both chariots leave the ground. They land in a terrible jumble of Orcs, Elves, wood, metal and horses. Storm the Citadel, racing into the final straight, has no chance. The charioteer tries to pull up but there is no time and he too is thrown into the air as his chariot hits the wreckage and slews across the track.

Peaceful Dreams of Heaven, a long way behind, has plenty of time to slow down and pick its way carefully past the carnage. It trots over the line, the only chariot to complete the race, and the winner. There's a huge collective groan of despair from the crowd. Not in our corner of the crowd, however. Makri goes berserk, and so do I. I practically dance my way down to Honest Mox's to pick up my winnings. I'm as happy as a drunken mercenary. In fact, I'm happier. Eighteen gurans at fifty to one. Nine hundred gurans.

Near Mox's stall an irate mercenary is bemoaning his fate. He's lost all his money and is complaining that the race was fixed.

"Nonsense," I tell him brusquely. "Just one of those things. Take it like a man."

There are some more complaints about the way things have gone but after the incredible excitement of the final race the crowd seems stunned. Most people sit quietly as the race attendants clear away the ruined chariots and give the charioteers some medical attention.

Makri's winnings are almost beyond belief. She has thousands of gurans and has to buy a new bag to carry them. She pulls the coins out in handfuls just to look at them.

I ask her if she'll put it in the track vault for a while. "What for?"

"I need your help before we go home."

Captain Rallee taps me on the shoulder. "Got your

message. What's happening?" The Captain has lost all his money and isn't very pleased. "I'm not convinced this was all fair and square," he says. "What do you want?"

"More Civil Guards and a couple of powerful Sorcerers."

We walk down to the race track. Standing there are Lord Lisith-ar-Moh and Lord Rezaz Caseg, examining the remains of their chariots and checking on the health of their riders and horses. While not exactly friendly, they appear to have reached a truce.

"A fine race."

"A fine race indeed."

Sarija is also there. The Elf Lord compliments her politely on the form showed by Storm the Citadel. She replies politely in return, both to Lisith and Rezaz. Melus the Fair appears, along with Kalius and Cicerius. Everyone is polite to everyone else. If the outcome of the race left much to be desired for your average Turanian gambler, in diplomatic terms it was just fine. No one is about to declare war on Turai.

It's a rare moment of peace between Orcs, Elves and Humans. I hate to be the one to spoil the mood but I don't like to drag it out. I walk up to Kemlath Orc Slayer.

"An exciting day, Kemlath. I notice you're wearing your favourite ring. The ring you stole from Senator Mursius when you killed him."

Captain Rallee looks at me sharply. So do the Consul and the Deputy Consul.

"I suppose it meant something to you, Kemlath, but it was careless of you to take it." I turn to the Captain. "That ring belonged to Senator Mursius. And I can prove it. You can see it clearly in the painting of him done after the Orc Wars. It was presented to him by the Consul for bravery."

Sarija shakes her head, protesting. "It's Kemlath's ring. The Consul presented them to all the officers."

I shake my head. "Afraid not. Kemlath told you that to keep you from suspecting. But I checked the records in the Library. That was the only ring presented by the Consul. Kemlath took it from Mursius because he was jealous of his war record and jealous of you. I've been looking at that painting for days, but it never struck me till now. You know, Kemlath, I wondered why you were paying such close attention to this case. I thought for a while it was just because of your interest in Sarija. But there was more to it than that. You removed the stolen art from the warehouse, but the Society of Friends got there first and took a few items. One of these items was the painting. And you knew you were in trouble if that turned up and someone put two and two together. Like I just did.

"And even if no one connected the ring, the rest of the stolen goods might still incriminate you, because you hadn't had time to clean them all properly. It was smart, sticking close to me. Every time a piece of evidence appeared, like the bronze cup, you sorcerously cleaned all traces of the crime from it. No wonder I drew a blank everywhere I looked."

Flocks of black stals flop around the track, picking up scraps from the crowd. I never liked these birds.

"The sorcerous messages were going a bit far though. Glixius sent the first and you followed on. You were probably just amusing yourself. Incidentally, you remember that time you told me you detected Glixius's aura on one of them? You never met Glixius. You just made that up. It's funny, really, the way I kept blaming everything on Glixius, when it was you all along."

Kemlath remains calm. He neither blusters nor protests.

"Why would I wish to kill my good friend Mursius?" he says.

"Because you were as jealous as hell of your good friend Mursius for stealing Sarija out from under your nose, that's why. I talked to the old landlady of the Mermaid. You both used to go there during the war when you were stationed on the walls at Twelve Seas. She remembers very well that you asked Sarija to marry you first, and she turned you down for Mursius. I think you've hated him ever since."

Unruffled, Kemlath continues to deny my accusations.

Captain Rallee is unsure of how to proceed. It's not as if I've produced a cast-iron case, and Kemlath is an important man, another war hero. He looks at Kalius for guidance. Kalius questions me.

"Is the ring all the evidence you have? It seems to me that the ring could have been transferred from Mursius to Kemlath at any time."

I turn to Sarija. "Well? Was it?"

She shakes her head. "Mursius was wearing it the day he disappeared."

Sarija is wide-eyed with horror. She believes me. There's a woman who'll be deep into her supply of dwa tonight, or maybe sooner. Kalius orders Kemlath's arrest, pending further investigations.

Afterwards Captain Rallee is still troubled. "Why did he wait twenty years to kill him?"

"I don't really know. Maybe he just brooded on it till it all became too much for him. It might never have happened if he hadn't found himself face to face with Mursius at the warehouse. That was unplanned. Mursius was part of the plot with the Society of Friends to dope the horses. I think Kemlath found out about it and decided to expose him. Unfortunately Sarija chose this time to sell a load of Mursius's art to Axilan, a minor Society of Friends figure, when he was up at the villa collecting the doping plants.

"Kemlath didn't like that. He didn't want anything at the warehouse that might lead to Sarija. If he exposed Mursius, he didn't want Sarija to be arrested as well. So he tried to remove the goods. Unfortunately his visit coincided with Mursius's. I figure Kemlath told Mursius he was going to inform the authorities about the doping and they got into a fight. Kemlath might not have meant to kill him, but that's what happened. It suited him fine anyway. Left him free to woo Sarija."

Captain Rallee is taking mental notes through all this. He has a powerful memory, the captain. I've never known him to forget anything.

"I think you're probably right, Thraxas. But I'm not at all sure we have enough evidence to make it stick in court. Why didn't you wait before denouncing him?"

"Because I was sick of it all, that's why. I've been arrested, made to look foolish and generally given a hard time by everyone. I'm fed up with Kemlath and fed up with the weather and I'm especially fed up with the way the races have gone. I've done my job, I found the killer. If you need more evidence, I'm sure the Guard can dig it up. And now I'm going home."

"One last thing, Thraxas—the Orcs you said you met down at Ferias, were they for real?"

"Of course! Do you think I'd make that up? They were part of Prince Kalazar's assassination force. Makeza the Thunderer was hiding them there until the race meeting. Probably picked Ferias because the weather was better."

I walk off. Makri follows me. As we pass Melus they studiously pretend not to know each other.

"Don't bother faking it," I mutter. "I know what was going on here today."

In the landus back to Twelve Seas, Makri plays with

her bags of money. I have nine hundred gurans of my own, but now the euphoria of winning has faded I'm in a very bad mood.

"A very fortunate day's gambling," I say.

"It sure was," she says, brightly.

"Odd that all those unfancied chariots came in. Very odd. I won nine hundred on the last race. I backed Peaceful Dreams of Heaven even though it was the worst chariot in the race. You want to know why? Because I noticed Hanama betting on it, that's why."

Makri looks uncomfortable.

"How much of it do you get to keep?" I ask.

"What do you mean?"

"Do you get to spend any of it? Or did you promise to pay it all over to the Association of Gentlewomen?"

"Stop talking rubbish, Thraxas."

"I'm not talking rubbish. If you're going to tell me that the number three in the Assassins Guild puts on a summer robe and goes to the chariot races for pleasure, I'm not going to believe it. The whole meeting was fixed, Makri, as you well know. And it was nothing to do with the Society of Friends or the Brotherhood. These favourites didn't all break their axles and rear up in fright for no reason. There was sorcery at work there."

"You can't work sorcery at the Stadium Superbius," says Makri stubbornly.

"You can if you've recruited the Stadium Sorcerer. You should mention to Melus the Fair that if she wants to pull that scam again she better be a bit more discreet. I know the A.G. needs money in a hurry, but Lilac Paradise a winner? And Peaceful Dreams of Heaven? I figure she picked up some new racing magic on her trip to Samsarina that no one here was familiar with, but if she keeps doing it there will be serious trouble.

If the male population of Turai ever finds out that our resident Stadium Sorcerer is casting spells to help win money for the Association of Gentlewomen, they'll tear you all to pieces. And I'll help them.

"I'm disgusted, Makri. I must have seen twenty A.G. supporters in the Stadium, all raking in the money. I wouldn't mind so much if you hadn't tried to throw me off the scent. All that standing around outside my room, talking about betting with Hanama in stage whispers. As if I would think she'd suddenly become interested in the sporting life. She'll end up with a dagger in her back if the Assassins Guild finds out she's spending time working for the Association of Gentlewomen."

"I guess she's responsible enough to work for who she likes."

"She's a disgusting killer. So that should suit you well enough. Who do you think you are, messing around with the races?"

"We need the money," protests Makri.

"So do all the poor wagon drivers, carpenters and sailors who thought that everything was honest. I tell you, Makri, I'm not pleased. The Stadium Sorcerer cheating the public. Melus the Fair, of all people! I only refrain from denouncing you all to *The Renowned and Truthful Chronicle* because you personally would be thrown off the city walls. The population's had enough of Orcs in the past month. They're not going to take kindly to another one cheating them."

Makri reacts furiously to this.

"Are you implying that I'm an Orc?"

"Well, you don't have Human values, that's for sure."

Makri sticks her head out of the landus, yells for the driver to stop, and then leaps out into the street.

"Never speak to me again, you obese drunkard!" she shouts.

"Cheating Orc!" I shout back. She storms off.

"And don't try robbing my room again, pointy ears!" I yell at her departing figure.

The sun is beating down. It's hot as Orcish hell. Even though I've won nine hundred gurans I'm as mad as a mad dragon. I can't stand it that the Association of Gentlewomen outsmarted everyone.

Chapter Twenty One

The city, overstimulated in the past month of discontent, starts to return to normal when the Turas and Triple-Moon Conjunction festivals get under way. The temperature starts to drop as autumn slides into winter.

There was great unhappiness after the race meeting, but surprisingly little suspicion. Everyone trusts Melus the Fair, bless her name. I understand that the Association of Gentlewomen have succeeded in moving their application for Guild status further up the ladder.

Cicerius is pleased with me. The race was run, the Elves still like us and Lord Rezaz will provide protection for the mining territory. If things keep on like this, I may get back to the Palace one day.

The Civil Guards dig more deeply into Kemlath's role in the death of Mursius and succeed in building a reasonable case against him. Even Captain Rallee admits that I was sharp as an Elf's ear on this one.

Kemlath doesn't come to trial however. Unless it's a case of high treason any citizen as important as Kemlath, especially one who was a hero in the war, is usually given the opportunity to flee the city before going to court. A member of the aristocracy is most unlikely to face the scaffold, or a long spell in the prison galleys. Instead they retire into exile, which Kemlath does.

Sarija remains in the city, spending her inheritance on dwa. Glixius Dragon Killer sends me a message. He likes me even less than before and will kill me at the first opportunity. Given the way I mistakenly harried him over the Mursius case, I can't exactly blame him.

At least I picked up nine hundred gurans at the races, and won't have to work for a while. That's the only bright spot on the horizon. With winter around the corner I'd like to spend a few months just sitting in the warmth of the Avenging Axe with my feet up, drinking beer. Unfortunately Makri makes it impossible for me to relax.

"I've never seen her this mad," says Tanrose.

Gurd nods his agreement.

"Yesterday she damned near demolished the wall out the back with her axe. Said she was practising fighting, but I noticed she'd chalked a picture of you on it, Thraxas. Why did you call her an Orc?"

"We were arguing."

As no one else in Turai seems to realise that the Association of Gentlewomen fixed the races I've decided that I'm not going to be the one to expose them. Partly I'm concerned for Makri's safety. Also there might be attempts to take back the nine hundred gurans I won. But I'm still as mad as hell at Makri. She can chop down as many pictures of me as she likes, I refuse to apologise. Cheating at the Turas Memorial is despicable behaviour.

Even Astrath Triple Moon confined his larceny to the minor meetings.

Makri appears from the street outside.

"Come for your evening shift?" says Gurd.

She shakes her head. "I'm leaving. I refuse to live in the same tavern as a fat useless drunk who called me an Orc." She storms upstairs.

"What are you looking at me for?" I demand. "How come I'm the one that always has to apologise around here? You heard what she called me."

"Come on, Thraxas. You know you should make up. You'd hate it if Makri really left. Who'll protect your back when you go up against these villains?"

"I managed to protect my own back just fine before she came along. Let her leave. She annoys the hell out of me anyway. If it's not that damned women's group then it's some stupidity she's picked up from Samanatius the Philosopher. Who ever heard of a Barbarian from the east going to the Guild College anyway? The whole thing is ridiculous."

Gurd and Tanrose continue to look at me accusingly. I start to feel persecuted.

"Well goddamn it, if it means that much to the pair of you, I'll say I'm sorry. Not that it'll do any good. Even Makri isn't naive enough to fall for a bunch of flowers three times in a row."

On two previous occasions when Makri was apparently irreconcilably annoyed at me I had given her a bunch of flowers, at the suggestion of Tanrose. It seemed like a lousy way of apologising to me but it had a spectacular effect on Makri. She burst into tears and ran out of the room in fact. Both times. Tanrose put it down to her growing up in a gladiator slave pit and never really getting any presents before.

Makri appears downstairs with a bag over her shoulder.

"And tell that corpulent slug if he buys me flowers I'll ram them down his throat," she says, storming out of the door.

"She's just saying that," says Tanrose. "I'm sure it would work again."

I stare at her in amazement. Tanrose seems to have an almost mystical belief in the power of a small bunch of flowers. It's ridiculous.

"Buy her a new axe," suggests Gurd. "I think she damaged her favourite one hacking down the wall."

Which is why I find myself tramping through Quintessence Street and up to the market on my way to the armourer's. The weather is pleasant, with the warm autumn air showing the first sign of cooling. Winter is not far away. Winter in Turai is hell. I'm really going to regret it if I can't spend it comfortably in front of a roaring fire at the Avenging Axe.

I reach the armourer. There's a sign on it saying: "Closed due to bereavement." I forgot that the armourer's third son was killed in a crossbow incident last week. The fourth son is due in court any day now.

It's too late to reach another armourer. It'll have to wait till tomorrow. I make my way back into Quintessence Street. I buy a pastry from the bakery. Minarixa is less friendly than usual. Probably Makri has been spreading bad stories about me.

I stop in the street to eat.

"Come for some flowers?" says Baxos the flower seller.

"Hey, Rox," he calls over to the fish vendor. "Thraxas is buying flowers again."

"Still got his lady friend, has he?" yells back Rox, loud enough for the entire street to hear.

"You treat her nicely, Thraxas!" screams Birix, one of Twelve Seas' busiest prostitutes.

I glare at Baxos and toss him a coin just to get away. I arrive back in the Avenging Axe holding a large bunch of flowers.

"I thought you were buying an axe?"

"The axe shop was shut."

It sounds a bit lame. I thrust the flowers into Makri's hand. My hand strays to my sword, just in case she gets violent.

Makri raises the flowers to dash them to the ground. Suddenly a tear trickles from her eye. She refrains from dashing them to the ground and instead rushes forward, embraces me then runs out of the room in tears. I'm unsure of what this means.

"Did it work again?"

"Of course," says Tanrose.

I can't understand it. Neither can Gurd.

"This is a woman who once fought a dragon. She killed a nine-foot Troll when she was thirteen."

Tanrose shrugs. "I imagine it was really grim growing up where she did. There's obviously a lot of mileage left in small presents where Makri is concerned."

Gurd snorts. "The women in my village were not like that. It took at least a new plough to impress them."

"That must be why you never married," says Tanrose. "You should have ignored the ploughs and tried flowers."

She looks rather pointedly at Gurd. He seems embarrassed. He's been attracted to Tanrose for a long time, but any mention of the subject makes him uneasy. These northern Barbarians. No romance. I leave them to it.

Upstairs I check on my supplies. I need plenty of klee and thazis to get me through the winter. And maybe some new blankets. I have nine hundred gurans. Enough for plenty of thick blankets. I might even buy one for Makri. She doesn't have much money and she handed over all her winnings to the A.G. Foolish behaviour, it seemed to me, but that's the problem with being idealistic. It makes you do foolish things. Personally, I'd have kept every guran.

THRAXAS
AND
THE ELVISH
ISLES

Chapter One

It's well past midnight and the air in the tavern is thick with thazis smoke. In front of me the table is groaning from the weight of money in the pot. Every week the Avenging Axe plays host to a game of rak, but there's rarely been this much money riding on a single hand. There are six of us left in and Captain Rallee is next to bet. He stares at his cards for a long time.

"I reckon Thraxas is bluffing," he says, and pushes forward his fifty gurans.

Next to him is Old Grax the wine merchant. Grax is a wily card player. He once won a thousand gurans off General Acarius, and General Acarius is universally acknowledged to be the finest gambler in the Turanian army. It's never easy to read Old Grax's intentions. From the confident way he slides his money into the centre of the table you might think he's got one hell of a hand. I'm not so sure. I'm guessing he hasn't.

Outside the streets are dark and silent. The front door of the Avenging Axe is locked. Light from the fire and the torches on the walls flickers over the faces of the dozen or so spectators. They nurse their drinks in silence, caught up in the tension as the game nears its climax.

"I'm out," says Ravenius, a young guy from uptown who joins us most weeks. He's a big loser on the night and looks disappointed, but he's the son of a wealthy Senator so he'll be back next week with another bag of money.

Gurd the landlord is still in the game, and next to bet. The heat from the fire brings sweat to his brow. He pushes back some strands of grey hair from his face and stares at his cards, which are dwarfed by his great hands. Gurd is a Barbarian from the north. In our younger days we fought all over the world together as mercenaries. We also played rak. Gurd's a shrewd gambler. He thinks he knows everything there is to know about my technique at the card table. He doesn't.

"I'm in," he grunts, pushing his money forward with his brawny arm.

Captain Rallee raises his flagon and sips his ale. Two of his men, Civil Guards still in uniform with their swords at their hips, sit close to him, their interest fixed on the game. Tanrose, the tavern's cook, has abandoned her position at the bar and edges closer to peer at the players.

Last person to bet is Casax, head of the local chapter of the Brotherhood, the powerful criminal gang that runs the southern half of the city of Turai. It's not often you'll see Captain Rallee at the same table as a Brotherhood boss. Unlike most of our city officials, the Captain is way too honest to socialise with figures from the underworld. But the Captain loves to gamble at rak so he makes an exception for our weekly meeting.

Nor would Casax normally be sitting down with me. Brotherhood bosses don't take kindly to Private

Investigators. More than once Casax has threatened to have me killed. Karlox, his oxlike henchman, who sits by his shoulder, would like nothing better than to gut me with his sword. He'll have to wait. There is never any violence at this table, which is why it attracts such diverse people as rich wine merchants and Senators' sons down to Twelve Seas, a rough part of town they'd normally work hard to avoid.

Casax glares round at us. He tugs at his earrings. Might be a sign of tension. Might not be. Casax is a very hard man to read. We wait for him to make his move. We wait a long time, in silence.

"I'll cover," he grunts, eventually. "And raise."

Casax reaches out a hand and Karlox drops a fat purse into his palm. Casax rips it open and counts rapidly.

"Your fifty gurans and another two hundred."

The onlookers whisper in excitement. Two hundred gurans. It takes an honest citizen a long time to earn that amount. It takes me a long time to earn it, and I'm not that honest.

Makri appears with a tray of drinks. Ravenius studies her with interest. She's worth studying if you're a young man with the energy for that sort of thing. Strong, beautiful, and possibly the only person in the West to have Orc, Elf and Human blood in her veins, Makri is quite a sight. She wears a tiny chainmail bikini at work for the sole purpose of earning tips and as Makri has the sort of figure men dream about when they're far from home, and maybe dream about even more when they're actually at home, she earns a lot of tips.

My five cards lie face down on the table in front of me. I don't bother looking at them again. I don't react to Casax's raise too slowly or too quickly. Two hundred gurans on a single hand might be getting out of my league in the normal course of things, but last month I walked out of the Turas Memorial Chariot Race with an extremely handsome profit, thanks to some very astute gambling on my part. I still have most of my winnings. I can cover Casax's bet. I take a beer from Makri's tray and edge my chair back an inch to give my belly a little more room. I take my purse from my lap and count out two hundred gurans and I push it into the centre of the table.

The tavern is completely silent apart from the spitting of the fire. Makri stares at me. She's one of my very few friends in the city. I can tell from her expression she thinks I'm a fool who's about to be parted from his money.

The betting has gone too far for Captain Rallee. That'll teach him to be honest. To compete at this level he ought to be taking a bribe every now and then. He hands in his cards with a look of disgust.

Old Grax is next. Despite the heat he's still wearing the dark green cloak with the fur collar that denotes his high ranking in the Honourable Association of Merchants. He's a wealthy man—he should be, with the amount of wine drunk in Turai—but he doesn't seem so keen on risking two hundred gurans on the card he holds.

I guessed right. He folds, his face betraying neither anger nor disappointment. He motions to Makri for some wine. I motion for another beer. I'm not the sort of man who needs to stay entirely sober at the card table. So I like to believe anyway.

Gurd sighs deeply. He's already a loser on the night and another two hundred gurans would make a substantial hole in his tavern's profits. Gurd had a lot of expense rebuilding after the city-wide riots last year and maybe this influences him. He hands in his cards, reluctantly. I notice Tanrose smiling. She doesn't like to see him lose. Tanrose is sweet on the old Barbarian. Also, he pays her wages.

Makri hands me my beer and stands next to me. Here in the Avenging Axe everyone is more or less used to her by now, but in much of the city her appearance still draws a lot of attention. It's not just her looks and figure. The reddish hue of her skin and her pointed ears reveal her Orc blood and anyone with Orc blood is regarded as cursed, a social outcast, and totally unwelcome in Turai. Everyone hates Orcs, even though we're at peace with them just now. Makri's only a quarter Orc, but that's more than enough to get you into trouble in many places.

Casax has a glass of water in front of him. No alcohol has passed his lips since he sat down at the table almost six hours ago. His eyes are deepest black and in the torchlight they shine with malevolent intelligence. He snaps his fingers. Karlox the enforcer digs deep into his robe, producing a larger bag of money.

"Count me out a thousand," says Casax, casually, as if betting a thousand gurans on a hand of cards is an everyday occurrence.

The spectators can't help showing surprise and there are excited whispers as they crane their necks to see the action.

Karlox counts. Casax looks me straight in the eye. I stare straight back at him and I don't allow the slightest flicker of expression to show on my face. I don't think the Brotherhood boss is bluffing. He has a good hand. That's fine with me. I have a good hand too. I have four black dragons. Four black dragons is practically unbeatable at rak. The only thing higher would be a full royal mansion, and if Casax turns up with a full royal mansion at the same time as I have four black dragons I'm liable to suspect that things have not been entirely above board, and to start asking a few questions with my sword.

I calmly sip some beer, and make ready to clean out the gangster. While my face is devoid of expression, inside I'm feeling pretty damn good. I've fought all over the world, I've seen Orcs, Elves and dragons, I've been employed at the Imperial Palace and I've been down and out in the gutters. I've talked, drunk and gambled with Kings, Princes, Sorcerers and beggars. And now I'm about to walk off with the largest pot of winnings ever seen in Twelve Seas. I've been waiting for this moment all my life.

"One thousand," mutters Karlox, and hands the money over to his boss. Casax gets ready to make his bet.

"You mind if I sit down on the edge of your chair?" says Makri to me, breaking the silence. "I'm feeling a bit weary. I've got a heavy blood flow this month."

I blink at her. "What?"

"My period. You know, it can make a woman tired."

For a split second a profound, awestricken hush descends in the room, followed immediately by the most God-awful racket as people rise from their chairs in a panic. To my certain knowledge no woman has ever said such words in public in Turai before. Menstruation is high up the list of taboo subjects in this city and in the assembled company of gamblers and drinkers the words fall like a fiery blast from a war dragon. Casax freezes. He might have once killed a lion with his bare hands but he's not up to this sort of thing. Beside him Gurd's face assumes a look of terror the like of which I've not seen since we were tramping through the Macian Hills and a large and venomous snake suddenly reared up and bit him on the leg.

Chairs crash as people start heading for the exits. Young Pontifex Derlex, the local Priest, shrieks as he runs out the tavern.

"I'll open the church for immediate purification," he yells over his shoulder, and bursts out through the door to safety.

"You filthy whore!" yells Karlox, helping his boss to

his feet. Casax is looking shaky and has to be led away. His other companions scoop up his money before they depart, taking not only his thousand but the other money he's already put into the pot.

"You can't do that!" I yell, rising to my feet and fumbling for my sword, but they've already got their blades out. From the way Captain Rallee is buttoning up his cloak I can tell he's not going to hang around to help me out. Gurd, my trusty companion in adversity, is disappearing into the back room muttering that if this sort of behaviour continues he's going to close the tavern and move back north.

About thirty seconds after Makri's grim utterance I'm staring at a scene of total desolation. Everyone has fled, either to the safety of their homes or straight to church for ritual purification. I stare at Makri. I try to shout at her but nothing comes out. I'm too shocked even to yell. Makri is looking puzzled.

"What just happened?" she asks.

My arms are shaking. It takes me a while to get my tankard up to my mouth. The ale revives me a little, enough to get some words out.

"You . . . you . . . you . . ."

"Come on, Thraxas. It's not like you to splutter. What's going on? Did I say something wrong?"

"*Something wrong!*" I bellow, my voice finally returning in fury. "Something wrong? "Can I sit down because I've got a heavy blood flow?" Are you completely insane? Have you no shame?"

"I don't see what all the fuss is about."

"It's completely taboo to mention . . . to mention . . ." Somehow I can't say the word.

"Menstruation?" says Makri, helpfully.

"Stop saying that!" I scream. "Look what you did! I was about to rake in a thousand gurans from Casax and you scared him away!"

I'm livid. Strange emotions well up inside me. I'm forty-three years old. As far as I can remember I haven't cried since I was eight, when my father caught me raiding his beer cellar and chased me round the city walls with a sword in his hand. But at the thought of Casax's thousand gurans, rightfully mine but now disappearing into the depths of Twelve Seas, I'm pretty close to tears. I consider attacking Makri. She might be a lethal swordswoman but I'm the best street fighter in town and I figure I could take her low down with a surprise kick.

"Don't try it," says Makri, taking a step backwards towards the bar, where she keeps her sword hidden during working hours.

I advance towards her. "I'll kill you, you pointy-eared freak!" I yell, and get ready to charge. Makri grabs for her sword and I draw mine swiftly from its scabbard.

Tanrose appears and plants herself between us. "Stop this at once!" she demands. "I'm surprised at you, Thraxas, drawing your sword against your friend Makri."

"That pointy-eared Orc freak is no friend of mine. She just cost me a thousand gurans."

"How dare you call me a pointy-eared Orc freak," screams Makri, and advances towards me, blade in hand.

"Desist!" yells Tanrose. "Thraxas, put that sword away or I promise I will never cook you a venison pie again. I mean it. And Makri, put your weapon down or I'll have Gurd get you to clean out the stables and sweep the yard. I'm surprised at you both."

I hesitate. It shames me to admit it, but I do more or less depend on Tanrose's venison pies. My life would be far poorer without them.

"It's not Makri's fault if she didn't know she shouldn't say that. After all, she grew up in an Orcish gladiator slave pit."

"Quite right," says Makri. "We couldn't mess around with social taboos. We were too busy fighting. Just get a towel in place and chop up the next enemy. When you've got four Trolls with clubs trying to knock your head off, no one worries about whether you're menstruating or not."

I can't take any more. I swear that when Makri says this Tanrose actually smiles. I begin to suspect that these women are conspiring against me. I am now madder than a mad dragon, and maybe a little more.

"Makri," I say with dignity. "For the first time in my life, I find myself in complete agreement with Karlox. You are a filthy whore and you have the manners of an Orcish dog. No, Orcish dogs have many social graces which you lack. I am now going upstairs to my room. Kindly never talk to me again. And in future please keep your disgusting revelations about your bodily functions to yourself. Here in the civilised world we prefer not to know what goes on between the legs of the Orcish half-breeds who sometimes see fit to infest our city."

Somewhere in the middle of this speech Makri explodes in fury and tries to rush forward and sink her sword in my guts, but fortunately Gurd has re-emerged from the back room and places his brawny arms around her shoulders to restrain her. As I mount the stairs, still with dignity, I hear her screaming that she looks forward to the day when her sword pierces my heart.

"If it can make it through all that blubber, that is," she adds, quite unnecessarily referring to my excess weight.

I place a locking spell on both my doors, grab a bottle of beer, drink it down, then slump on my couch. I hate this stinking city. Always have. Nothing goes right for a man in this place.

Chapter Two

———

Next morning I'm woken up by the shrill voice of a street vendor outside, eager to sell her wares in the last week of autumn before the evil winter takes hold of the city. It doesn't improve my mood.

Winter in Turai is grim: bitter cold, howling gales, freezing rain and enough snow to bury the homeless beggars that huddle miserably in the streets of Twelve Seas. Back in the days when I was a Senior Investigator at the Imperial Palace, winter didn't trouble me. I hardly even saw it, just remained within the comfortable confines of the Palace walls, where a combination of engineering skill and sorcery prevented the inhabitants from feeling any discomfort. If any investigating needed doing, I sent a subordinate. Since I was booted out by my boss, Rittius, my life has changed considerably for the worse. I'm a Private Investigator in a dangerous part of town where there is plenty of crime to be investigated but precious little money to pay me for the investigating. I'm reduced to living in two rooms above a tavern, eking out my existence by risking my life against the sort of violent criminals who'll happily gut a man for a few gurans or a small dose of dwa.

The sign outside my door says *Sorcerous Investigator* but that is somewhat misleading. A more accurate version would say *Investigator Who Once Did Study Sorcery But Now Has Only The Feeblest Of Magical Powers. And Works Cheap.*

I sigh. It's true that my winnings at the chariot races will enable me to make it through the winter in more comfort than I otherwise might have. But if I'd taken that huge pot at rak last night I'd have been a good way towards moving out of this dump. I've had my fill of the slums. I don't have the energy for it any more.

I need some beer for breakfast but that means going downstairs and facing Makri. She will be out for vengeance. The woman—I use the term loosely—has in the past refused to speak to me after far less wounding accusations. What she'll do after the things I said last night, God only knows. Attack me, probably. Let her. I'm feeling angry enough to attack her right back. I tuck my sword in its scabbard and am on the point of marching right downstairs to confront Makri with her many crimes when there's a knock on my outside door and a voice I recognise calls out my name.

I banish the minor locking spell from the door and haul it open.

"Vas-ar-Methet! What are you doing in the city? Come right in!"

Vas-ar-Methet walks in, dumps his green cloak on the floor, and embraces me warmly. I embrace him back, equally warmly. I haven't seen him in fifteen years but you don't forget an Elf who once saved your life during the last great Orc War.

I saved his life too. And we both saved Gurd. The .

last Orc War was grim. There were plenty of occasions when lives needed saving.

Like all Elves, Vas-ar-Methet is tall and fair, with golden eyes, but even among the upright Elvish Folk Vas-ar-Methet stands out as a distinguished figure. He's a healer, an Elf of great skill, and well respected among his folk.

"Would you like some klee?"

Klee is the local spirit, distilled in the hills. Elves in general are not given to strong drink, but I seem to remember that Vas, after the months we spent together fighting, was not averse to something to keep the circulation going.

"I see you haven't changed," he laughs.

Vas always laughed easily. He's rather more emotional than your average Elf. He's some years older than me but, as is the way with Elves, shows little sign of advancing age. If he's reached fifty, which he probably has, you'd be hard pushed to guess.

He brings out a small packet from within his green tunic. "I thought you might like these."

"Lesada leaves? Thank you. I just finished my last one!"

I'm grateful. Lesada leaves grow only on the Elvish Isles and they're hard to acquire in Turai. They're used as a cure for many things and have a great purifying effect on the body. I use them for hangovers, and can personally state that there is no finer remedy.

The memory of where I obtained my last supply of lesada leaves causes me to frown.

"Did you hear about the two Elves I encountered last year?" I ask.

Vas-ar-Methet nods. They'd arrived at my door claiming to be friends of his and hired me under false pretences to work for them. As it turned out, they were Elves of the criminal variety—rare, but not unheard of—who had been using me for their own ends. It got them killed in the end, though not by me, and I've worried slightly since then that they might really have been friends of Vas.

He reassures me. "No, not friends, nor relatives. We heard the full tale on the islands eventually. They used my name and the name of my Lord only to gain influence with you, Thraxas. It is I who should apologise to you."

We beam at each other. I clap him heartily on the back, break open the klee, and tell him to fill me in on the last fifteen years.

"How's life on the Elvish Isles? Still paradise on Earth?"

"Much the same as when you visited, Thraxas. Apart from . . ." He frowns and breaks off.

My Investigator's intuition lumbers into action. In the excitement of seeing old Vas again it had temporarily switched off, but now, looking at his troubled face, I can tell that something is wrong.

"Is this a professional visit, Vas? Do you need my help?"

"I am afraid so. And if you can forgive my rudeness, I must explain my business quickly, though I would far rather talk with you a while of old times. Is Gurd still alive?"

"Still alive? He certainly is. He owns this dump. I'm his tenant."

Vas guffaws at the thought of Gurd turning into a businessman. And when Vas-ar-Methet guffaws, he really lets it out. He's pretty unrestrained for an Elf. Not the sort to sit around in a tree all night, watching the stars. I always liked him.

"What's the rush?"

"I am here as part of the retinue of Lord Kalith-ar-Yil. We sailed in early this morning, earlier than

expected. Lord Kalith has been keen to complete the
voyage as he is anticipating bad weather on the return
journey."

I'd heard that Lord Kalith-ar-Yil was due in Turai.
He's the ruler of Avula, one of the Elvish Isles to the
south, and a friend and ally of our city. Some of our
Turanian officials are going down to visit as guests of
the Elves for the Avulan festival, which is held every
five years, I believe. The invitation was sent up by way
of Lord Lisith-ar-Moh, another Elvish ally, who visited
Turai recently. Lisith-ar-Moh is the ruler of Ven, an
island close to Avula.

"I heard you were of some service to Lord Lisith,"
says Vas.

"I was. I helped make sure the great chariot race
actually happened, though that involved helping the
Orcs' entrant as well, which I could have done without. A man doesn't want too much of a reputation as
an Orc helper. So you're here to pick up our Prince
and take him to the Avulan festival?"

"We are. And as we are earlier than expected, and
Lord Kalith wishes to sail tonight, I imagine there is
some amount of panic at the Imperial Palace. I myself
have much to do and can't spend long here."

"Well, tell me the trouble, Vas. We can reminisce
another time."

Elves can be a little wordy. I heard Lord Lisith when
he proffered the Avulans' invitation to their festival,
and to be honest it dragged a little. We all like Elves
in this city, and we're pleased they've invited our young
Prince to the island of Avula, but we don't necessarily want to hear endless speeches about it. Fortunately
Vas is more direct than an Elf Lord.

"Two months ago our Hesuni Tree was damaged by
fire."

My eyes widen in surprise. Every Elvish island is

inhabited by one clan of Elves and every clan has its Hesuni Tree. It's said to record the history of the clan. In some ways it's their soul. I've never heard of one catching fire.

"It never has happened before. And it was not completely burned, though it suffered considerable damage. The tree-tenders of our tribe have saved it, though it will be some time before it is strong again. This is not public knowledge. I know that Lord Kalith will have informed your Royal Family of the occurrence, but we would not wish for people to know the true state of affairs."

I light up a thazis stick. Vas frowns.

"These narcotic substances are bad for a man, Thraxas."

I shrug this off. Thazis is a very mild drug, calms the nerves, nothing more. Compared to the plague of dwa that has recently gripped the city, its effects are negligible. Since dwa started flooding in from the south, Turai has advanced several giant steps on its way to hell, damnation and destruction. Crime has mushroomed on all fronts, which is good for my business, I suppose.

"Tell me about the Tree."

"Someone attacked it with an axe, and then with fire. It took the greatest efforts of our tribe to save it."

He pauses to sip some klee.

"No Elvish tribe has ever suffered such an attack. The Hesuni Tree of the Uratha Clan was struck by lightning and killed three hundred years ago, and this calamity has ever since plagued the Uratha. That, however, was an act of God. It is without precedent for a Hesuni Tree to be attacked. You have been among the Elves, Thraxas; you may have some idea of what the Hesuni means to the clan."

I nod. I know enough to realise the seeming impossibility of any Elf harming it.

"Coming before our Festival it is particularly unfortunate. Many Elves from the neighbouring islands visit Avula and it has cast a shadow over the occasion."

"Who was responsible? Has Orcish sorcery extended its arm so far south?"

Vas's eyes mist over. "My daughter stands accused of the crime."

Unexpectedly, a tear rolls down the face of Vas-ar-Methet.

I see too much misery on the streets every day to be much affected by it, but I'm greatly touched by the sight of my old companion-in-arms reduced to tears.

He tells me that his daughter is currently under lock and key on the island, accused of the terrible and unprecedented crime.

"I swear she is innocent, Thraxas. My daughter is not capable of such a terrible act. I need someone to help her but there is no one on the islands who can do what you do. No one has any experience of investigating . . . we have no crime to investigate . . . till this . . ."

I finish off my klee and bang my fist on the table in a reassuring manner. "Don't worry, Vas. I'll sort it out. When do we sail?"

You can trust me in a crisis. Thraxas will always come to your aid. What's more, it will get me away from the terrible Turanian winter, which is all to the good.

"We sail with the evening tide. The winter storms will soon be here and we must be well clear of your coast before then."

The thought of winter storms makes me wonder if I might have leaped in too hastily here. I've sailed enough to take another long voyage in my stride, but even under the fine seamanship of Lord Kalith and his Elvish crew I don't relish the prospect of battling though the icy winter gales. Vas reassures me: Avula is one of the closest of the Elvish Isles, about three or four weeks' journey due south, and we should be able to pass through the most dangerous waters before they become too troubled.

"I appreciate this more than I can say, Thraxas. It is no light thing for a man to drop everything at a moment's notice to travel far, even in answer to a call from help from an old friend."

"Think nothing of it, Vas. I owe you. Anyway, who wants to sit through another Turanian winter? You ever been here in winter? It's hell. Last year I had to spend three weeks at the harbour sorting out some shipping fraud. I was colder than a frozen pixie and you couldn't move without tripping over some poor beggar's corpse. Anyway, I've a little personal trouble at the moment I wouldn't mind being far away from."

"Personal trouble? What sort of . . ."

An almighty crash comes at my inside door. It's still protected by my locking spell but this minor incantation isn't going to hold out for long against such a determined assault.

"An angry woman," I grunt. "If you can call her that."

I grab my sword and bark a few ancient words at the door, removing the spell. It bursts open and Makri practically flies into the room. She has an axe in one hand and is trying to fend off Gurd with the other. She makes good progress towards me before Gurd manages to get his arms round her and bring her to a grinding halt.

"Let go of me, damn you," yells Makri. "I don't care what you say, I'm going to kill him."

Gurd hangs on, using his extra body weight to his advantage. Makri struggles furiously. Normally in this sort of situation she would produce a dagger from somewhere around her body and stab whoever was unwise enough to be hanging on to her but she has the disadvantage of not actually wishing to kill Gurd, who is her employer and has always treated her rather kindly.

Vas has stood up in astonishment at the sight of Makri and Gurd struggling at the door. Like any Elf, he can sense Orc blood, and Elves hate Orcs even more than Humans do. But of course he can also sense Makri's Elf blood. Elves are always confused by Makri, while Makri herself finds relating to Elves troubling, so troubling that, at the sight of the dignified presence of the healer, she stops struggling and eyes him coldly.

"Who the hell are you?" she demands, in fluent Elvish.

"A friend of Thraxas," replies Vas.

"Well you better say your goodbyes," grunts Makri. "I'm about to send him to hell. No one calls me a pointy-eared Orc bitch and lives."

Vas walks up to her, bows politely, then looks her in the eye. "I have rarely heard our language spoken so gracefully by someone not born on the islands," he says. "You speak it quite beautifully."

Makri is not placated. She spits out an Orcish curse at him. I wince. I myself am fluent in the Common Elvish tongue and since Makri arrived my Orcish has greatly improved. I can't believe that she just said that to a well-bred Elf. I hope he didn't understand. It's about the rudest thing you can do to an Elf to speak Orcish in front of him.

Vas does the last thing I'm expecting, which is to put his head back and laugh heartily.

"You speak Orcish very well also. I picked up quite a lot during the war. Please tell me, young lady, who are you that you live here in a tavern in Twelve Seas and have such command of three languages?"

"Four," says Makri. "I've been learning the Royal Elvish language as well."

"Really? That is unheard of. You must be a person of unusual intelligence."

Makri has now stopped struggling. Having this cultured Elf compliment her on her high intelligence puts her in a quandary. Makri is not short of compliments on her looks, her figure, her spectacular hair. She hardly notices them any more, unless they are accompanied by a hefty tip. The main reason she stays around here is to attend the Guild College. Makri is a budding intellectual of a serious nature and an Elf complimenting her intelligence can't fail to have some effect.

"Well, I've been reading the scrolls at the library . . . you know . . ."

"Have you read the tale of Queen Leeuven?"

"Yes," replies Makri. "I loved it."

Vas is delighted. "Our finest epic. So fine that it has never been translated from the Royal language for fear of spoiling its beauty. You know it originated on Avula, my island? It is one of the glories of my tribe. I am indeed pleased to meet you."

He bows to her again. Makri bows back. Gurd lets her go. Makri frowns, realising that she can't really hit me with her axe. It would completely spoil the good impression she just made.

"Calmed down now?" says Gurd.

"No," grunts Makri. "But I'll save it for later."

Tanrose calls from downstairs, something about a man arriving with a load of fresh venison, and Gurd hurries off. Makri is about to turn and leave when Vas calls her back.

"I am pleased to have met you. I sail on tonight's tide and may not see you again. But the Elves of my island will be pleased to learn of the person in Turai who respects our tale of Queen Leeuven."

It's struck me before as peculiar the way Makri can make all sorts of people like her. Every time she comes across some well-bred or high-up member of society, the sort of person who would, not without reason, regard her as an ignorant Barbarian not worthy of notice, she always seems to end up creating a good impression. Cicerius, our Deputy Consul, was practically eating out of her hand the last time I worked for him. And now my friend Vas, an Elf of the highest repute, who quite possibly has never so much as spoken a word to any creature with a speck of Orc blood in them, is chatting away to her when really we should be discussing business. Any moment now they'll be reciting poetry together.

Just because Makri and Vas have hit it off in a big way doesn't mean I'm keen to spend time with the woman. I'm still mad as hell about the money she cost me.

"How long till we sail?" I say, muscling into the conversation.

"About eight hours."

"Where are you going?" asks Makri, immediately interested.

"To Avula," I reply. "Far away from you. Vas, I'll need to make preparations. I'm going out to buy a few things. There will be plenty of time to fill me in on the details while we're sailing."

"I want to come," says Makri.

I laugh. "No chance. As the well-known saying goes, you'd be as welcome as an Orc at an Elvish wedding."

"It's the Avulan festival, isn't it?" says Makri. "I've read about it. Three staged versions of the tale of Queen Leeuven and competitions in choral singing, dance and poetry. I want to come."

"Well you can't," I say. "The Avulan festival is not open to everyone. It's strictly an Elf-only affair, plus a few honoured guests. Like me, for instance. I'll see you on board, Vas. If you wish to stay here and discuss poetry with this barmaid, I must warn you that she is not fully trained in the ways of civilisation."

And with that I depart. As I head down the stairs I can feel the air getting colder. The voyage may well be chilly till we reach the warmer waters of the south. I'll need a warm, waterproof cloak for the journey and maybe a new pair of boots. And some beer. I'll get Gurd to load a barrel on to a wagon for me when I get back. The Elves have fine wine but it wouldn't surprise me if there was no beer at all on board their ship, and that's a chance I'm not prepared to take.

Chapter Three

———◆———

Around seven and a half hours later I'm ready to sail. I arrive at the harbour on a wagon and load my belongings on board. The Turanian soldiers on guard duty look at me suspiciously as I roll up with a small bag of provisions and a large barrel of beer, but as the Elves are expecting me they let me past. The Elvish crew assume that as I am a guest of Vas-ar-Methet I'm probably part of the official Turanian party heading south for the festival, and I don't bother to correct them.

This festival is held every five years and, as far as I know, is mainly attended by Elves from the three neighbouring islands of Avula, Ven and Corinthal. There are several distinct great tribal groupings of Elves on the Southern Islands, and all the Elves from these three islands, while forming separate nations, belong to the great Ossuni tribe. Whether Elves from further afield will be in attendance I'm not sure, but there will certainly be few Humans there. It is regarded as a great

256

honour in Turai that our representatives have been invited, a mark of the continuing friendship between our nations.

Turai needs this friendship. We have declined in importance in the last fifty years or so, mainly as a result of the internal strife within the League of City-States. It is now pretty much politically impotent. When the League was strong Turai could speak with a powerful voice. Now we're weak. Despite this we are still high among the nations who are regarded as friends of the Elves. They saved us during the last great Orc War and if the Orc nations ever unite again and start heading west over the Wastelands, which is more than likely, we'll be relying on the Elves again. Hence the importance of this invitation. Prince Dees-Akan won't just be attending a festival, he'll be cementing our diplomatic ties.

Turai is sending the young Prince, second in line to the throne, and Deputy Consul Cicerius, the city's second highest official, along with a few other minor dignitaries, a couple of Sorcerers and various royal bodyguards and attendants, a party of twenty or so, which is why the Elves sent up such a large ship. It's a bireme with twin banks of oars along each side, although it's unlikely that these will be much in use. Elves don't enjoy rowing any more than they have to and they'll be planning on running with the wind for most of the journey.

It's against the law for the city's highest official, the Consul, to leave the state during his term of office, which is why our government will be represented by his Deputy, Cicerius. I've worked for Cicerius on several occasions, and he's been satisfied with my achievements, but I couldn't claim to be friends. I know he has neither forgiven nor forgotten the time I was carried drunk into the Palace, singing songs. I'm not under any illusions that he'll be pleased to have me along.

I expect that the Elves have proffered other invitations to Humans. Turai was not the only city to fight alongside Lord Lisith-ar-Moh and Lord Kalith-ar-Yil. Important politicians from other sea-going nations will be gathered on Avula. Maybe I can pick up some business.

As I'm lugging my travelling bag up the gangplank I notice Lanius Suncatcher striding nimbly on board, followed by his apprentice struggling with the heavy baggage. Lanius is wrapped in his rainbow cloak, denoting him as a member of the Sorcerers Guild. I used to know him back in the days when I was a Senior Investigator at the Palace. A nice young guy, as I remember. He's been recently promoted to a senior spot in Palace Security because of several unfortunate deaths among our more experienced Sorcerers.

He greets me as I reach the deck. "Thraxas. Wasn't expecting to see you here. Are you back in favour with the Palace?"

"Afraid not. Still pounding the streets in a private capacity. I'm not part of the official party, just here as a guest of the Elves."

I congratulate the young Sorcerer on his promotion. "You've come a long way. Last time I saw you, you were still running errands for Old Hasius the Brilliant."

"The way our Sorcerers have been handing in their togas recently has been good for my career," he admits. "I'm Chief Sorcerer at Palace Security these days, promoted after Mirius Eagle Rider got himself killed. It would be just fine if it wasn't for Rittius."

He makes a face. So do I. Rittius, head of Palace Security, is not a popular man with his staff. He was the man responsible for my sacking and any time our paths cross there is trouble.

"He's not part of the delegation, is he?"

"Fortunately not. Cicerius refused to sanction his coming. You're not going to Avula to work, are you?" asks Lanius Suncatcher, suddenly suspicious.

"Work? Of course not. No call for an Investigator in those parts. Purely a social visit."

Lanius might be an old acquaintance, but I'm not in the habit of sharing my business secrets with Palace officials. I wonder how powerful his sorcery is these days. As often happens when I encounter a young Sorcerer on the way up, I grow suddenly depressed at the sad decline in my powers. I admit I was never the most powerful Sorcerer on the block, but I used to be able to perform a trick or two. These days I'm lucky if I can put an opponent to sleep, or temporarily blind him with flashing lights, and even these small spells wear me out. It's a long time since I've been able to carry around more than two spells in my head. A powerful Sorcerer can carry four or five.

I sigh. Too much drinking and high living. But I've had bad luck as well. I never did get the breaks I deserved. As a man who fought loyally for his city, I shouldn't be having to scratch a living in Twelve Seas, declining powers or not.

Harmon Half-Elf, another of our important Sorcerers, arrives on deck. He greets me with a nod before going off with Lanius Suncatcher, discussing the probability of their needing to calm the ocean on the way. The harbour at Twelve Seas is well protected and the ship is lying calmly on the water, but already the open seas are rough. It's not unusual for the winter storms to descend early, though on an Elvish ship, with extra Sorcerers in attendance, I figure I'm safe enough.

I hunt for Vas-ar-Methet, taking care not to run into any Turanian official who might not be delighted to find me aboard. Vas has reserved for me a tiny cabin where I dump my stuff, haul my boots off, drink some beer and wait for us to sail. Vas arrives and I tell him that an unexpected voyage to the Elvish Isles is just what a man needs after his idiot companion has cost him a thousand gurans at cards.

Vas still seems impressed by my idiot companion. "After you departed she told me of her studies at the Guild College. I just cannot believe that any woman with Orc blood should be so civilised and intelligent."

"What do you mean, civilised? The first time you saw her she was trying to plant an axe in my head."

"Well, Thraxas, you had grossly insulted her. She also told me about the card game."

"Oh yes? Did she tell you about the outrage she caused by wilfully offending public decency?"

Vas laughs. "She did. And I can understand why it caused such a disturbance. The subject is calanith among Elves also."

"Calanith" roughly translates as "taboo." The Ossuni Elves have a lot of them.

"Often during my healing it has caused awkwardness. But the young woman was surely unaware of the offence it would cause. I feel you must make allowances for her. Had you not abused her so virulently at the time, she would quite probably have apologised for the loss she caused you."

I snort in derision. Makri would probably leap from the highest part of the city walls rather than apologise. Stubborn, that's what she is. It's a very bad trait and one she would do well to overcome. But Elves are always keen to see the positive side.

"Try living in a tavern with her. Then you'd see how likely she is to apologise. And anyway, what good is an apology to a man who's just been cheated out of a thousand gurans? I tell you, Vas, I'm desperate to get out of Twelve Seas. If I don't raise enough money soon for a villa in Thamlin, you're going to find me swimming south looking for a permanent residence in your tree. Any chance of a game of rak down on your island?"

This makes Vas smile, troubled though he is. He shakes his head. "Elves are not fond of cards as a rule. We play niarit though. I remember you used to be keen on that."

"Still am," I inform him. "Local champion in fact. I'm hell at the niarit board."

Niarit is a complicated board game involving two armies of Hoplites, Trolls and Cavalry along with assorted other pieces—Harpers, Sorcerers, Plague Carriers and such like. The aim is to defeat your opponent's army and storm his castle. I brought my board with me, thinking that it might while away a few idle hours on the long voyage. When it comes to niarit I'm sharp as an Elf's ear and undefeated champion of Twelve Seas. Since I taught Makri how to play she's never come close to beating me, for all her much vaunted intellect. Drives her crazy. Whether or not I find a game of rak or niarit anywhere along the way, at least Makri will not be along to ruin it, and that's a bonus.

"Well, if you find yourself on the wrong side of Lord Kalith," says Vas-ar-Methet, "try challenging him to a game of niarit. He's the finest player on Avula, and can't resist a game."

"That's good to know. I could do with a little practice."

I break open another beer. I've brought as many bottles as I could carry and a barrel for when they run out. I'm still sketchy on the details of the case I'm being asked to investigate. All I really know is that Vas's daughter Elith is currently imprisoned on a charge of attempting to kill the Hesuni Tree. I'm about to ask Vas-ar-Methet to fill me in, but before I can he is called away. Vas is not only Lord Kalith's chief healer, he is close enough to him to be his trusted adviser as well, and this makes him a busy man. Well, there will be plenty of opportunity to learn the full facts of the case before I arrive on Avula. And once I'm in command of the facts, I'm confident I'll be able to sort it out. When it comes to investigating, I'm number one chariot, and no one can deny it.

Lord Kalith is insisting that we must sail with the next tide and urgent last-minute preparations are underway. I settle back on my bunk. My mood mellows. No winter in Turai for me. No pounding my way to Minarixa's bakery through the frozen streets for a few pastries to keep me going. No hunting through snow-bound streets for debtors, robbers, murderers and assorted other degenerates. No murderous gangs carving out their dwa territory. No filth, squalor and general misery. Just a pleasant visit to the Elvish Isles where I shall no doubt clear Vas's daughter without breaking sweat and spend the rest of the time lying under a tree in the warm sunshine drinking beer, listening to Elvish choirs and swapping war stories with some of the more experienced Elves. I can't wait.

We cast off and start to manoeuvre our way out of the harbour. I've decided to keep my head down till we are well at sea for fear that Deputy Consul Cicerius or some other official might start beefing about my presence here and try sending me back, but all of a sudden a commotion breaks out on deck. I never can ignore a commotion—I'm just too nosy. It's a problem I've always had. I hurry out of my cabin and up the stairs to the deck. All along one side of the ship the Elvish crew are gathered, talking and pointing with excitement at something that's going on back on the pier.

I use my body weight to force my way through. What

I see leaves me gaping. Makri is pounding down the dock with a sword in one hand, a bag in the other and around thirty armed men in close pursuit. Makri's well in front but she's running out of room. They've chased her to the end of the pier and there's nothing in front of her but the sea. Even at this distance I can identify her pursuers. The mob comprises a large part of the local chapter of the Brotherhood. I'm astonished. I've only been gone five minutes and already Makri is waging war with the deadliest gang in the neighbourhood.

Makri reaches the end of the quay and whirls to face her attackers, drawing her second sword as she does so. The first two assailants to come near her fall beneath her blades but the others fan out and surround her, then close in with their weapons at the ready. I look on helplessly as we sail slowly away. There are cries of concern from the Elves alongside me at the sight of a lone woman up against such murderous odds, but we are powerless to help. Even if Lord Kalith turned the ship, by the time we made it back it would be far too late.

"Jump," I scream at Makri.

I can't understand why she doesn't leap into the sea. At least there she would have some chance of escape. Instead Makri stands fighting against hopeless odds. Supreme swordswoman or not, she can't fight off that number of well-armed men attacking from all sides. A pile of bodies lies prostrate at her feet but any second now one of the multiple blades facing her will find its target.

"Jump into the sea!" I scream again, but we are now more than eighty yards distant and my voice probably doesn't carry over the noise of the battle, and the waves, and the seabirds that soar over the harbour.

Finally Makri seems to realise that there is no way she's walking away from this one without getting wet.

She spins on her heel, rams her swords into the scabbards that form a cross on her back, and leaps from the quay into the water below. By this time I'm already lowering a boat from the side of the ship with the aid of several young Elves. They don't know Makri, but the sight of her battling such enormous odds has enraged their sense of fair play.

The boat hits the water with a mighty splash and I swarm down a rope into it, looking all the while for Makri's head to appear above water. Meanwhile the thugs on the dock are peering over the waters, hunting for their prey. As I start to row another body clatters into the boat. It's Vas. He wastes no energy in talking but grabs the second set of oars and starts to pull. We make our way against the tide, back towards the mouth of the harbour.

"Where is she?" I cry, alarmed.

"She must be swimming underwater to safety."

I'm dubious. Makri has been under for a very long time. We're almost at the spot where she went in and there is no sign of her. Perhaps she took a wound in the fight and is unable to swim. Perhaps she has already drowned.

"Goddammit," I growl, and stand up in the boat, scanning the waters for any sign of her. Suddenly I spot something—a dark mass like seaweed on the water. Makri's hair. Makri's head appears, twenty yards or so from our boat. Before I can yell for her to swim to us she goes under again, in a manner that suggests she won't be coming back up.

Without hesitation I strip off my cloak and plunge into the sea. I've always been a strong swimmer and it takes me very little time to reach the spot and dive under the surface. The waters are cold and grey, impossible to see through for more than a few yards. I sink deeper and deeper, hunting desperately for sight of Makri, and the thought flashes through my head that if I was any sort of Sorcerer I'd have some spell ready to help me. But I've no spell for this, nothing to help me except a grim determination that I'm not going to see Makri drown.

My lungs are bursting. I can't stay under any longer. I keep swimming. Finally I see Makri rising slowly in front of me. I kick towards her, grab her arm and head for the surface. We arrive there spluttering, coughing up water, but still alive. Makri seems in a bad way.

"Thraxas," she mutters.

I start swimming for the boat, dragging her along behind me. Vas rows towards us and soon he is helping us on board. I think I hear some cheering from the Elves' ship, and maybe some howls of anger from the dockside.

Makri retches over the side of the boat, and suddenly looks more alive.

"Nice escape," I say to her. "But it would have been better if you'd actually swum somewhere. Sinking like a stone was never going to work."

"I can't swim," says Makri.

"What?"

"I can't swim. You think I'd have hung around on the pier so long if I knew how to swim?"

"Well, maybe. You like fighting. I figured you were just enjoying yourself."

Vas brings us alongside the ship and we are helped aboard.

The Elves are full of congratulations for me at my fine rescue and there are words of admiration too for Makri for the fighting spirit she showed on the pier. Their praise dries up as the Elves suddenly notice that Makri is not the standard-issue woman they took her for.

"Orc blood!" whispers one young member of the crew, quite distinctly.

Deputy Consul Cicerius, resplendent in his best gold-rimmed toga, strides over to us.

"Investigator Thraxas!" he rasps. "What are you doing here?"

"My guest," explains Vas-ar-Methet, which surprises the Deputy Consul but doesn't prevent him from rounding on Makri.

"You cannot remain on this ship."

"Well, I can't go back there," points out Makri, quite reasonably. The dock, now receding into the distance, is still lined with armed men.

"Lord Kalith," says Cicerius, as the Elvish Captain strides along the deck towards us. "You must turn this ship around."

At this moment the wind blowing us from the harbour suddenly strengthens and the sails bulge as the ship spurts forward. Lord Kalith frowns.

"Impossible. We cannot miss this tide. To do so would make us lose a day's voyage and quite probably run into the first winter storm."

He stares at Makri. For him this is something of a dilemma. He doesn't want to turn the ship around, but there is no inhabited land between us and Avula. If he lets her stay he's going to be the first Elf Lord to arrive back home with an Orc in tow. He doesn't look thrilled at the prospect.

I'm none too pleased myself. I didn't want Makri to drown but that doesn't mean I want her along spoiling things for my visit to Avula. No Elf is going to want to talk to a man who's brought his mixed-blood friend along for a visit. The Deputy Consul is all for sending Makri back in the boat but the shore is already fading in the distance and it is just not practical.

"We'll decide what to do with you later," Kalith tells Makri. "Meanwhile, stay out of sight."

"Fantastic," says Makri, brightly. "I've always

wanted to go to the Elvish Isles. How long till we get there?"

Lord Kalith doesn't reply. As he departs to the bridge he's not looking pleased at this turn of events. He orders his crew back to their posts, and his voice is harsh.

I scowl at Makri. "Is there no end to these outrages? First you ruin my card game and now you've muscled your way on board my ship."

"Well, thanks for saving my life," says Makri. "I forgive you for the insults you heaped on my head. Could you get me something dry to wear?"

Makri tugs at the man's tunic she's wearing. In common with all of Makri's clothes, it fails to cover nearly enough of her. I hurry her off in case she commits some further outrage, such as taking it off in front of the crew. I notice that the young sailor who first commented on Makri's Orc blood has not actually departed back to his post but stands staring at Makri with some fascination. I scowl at him, then notice it isn't a him but a her, a young Elvish maid, along on the voyage for some reason. A fairly scrawny-looking specimen, not blooming with health like your standard Elvish female.

We make for my cabin. Small though it is, I will now have to share it with Makri for the voyage. I continue to complain.

"Couldn't you just let me sail in peace? What the hell were you doing fighting the Brotherhood anyway? Did you arrange the whole thing just so you could come to the festival?"

"Certainly not," replies Makri. "Although now I think about it, how come you didn't invite me?"

Makri is suspiciously cheerful about all this. For a woman who's suffering from several nasty sword cuts and nearly drowned, she's in a surprisingly good mood. I ask her what the fight was about.

"I was just trying to get your money back."

"What?"

"The money Casax took back from the pot. After all, you said yourself it wasn't fair. Once you make your bet you can't take your money back, no matter what outrage may make you wish to leave the tavern. So I went to get it back for you."

"Really? And what brought on this display of public-spiritedness?"

According to Makri it was Vas-ar-Methet. After talking for a while about the beautiful epic poem of Queen Leeuven, they came round to discussing the reason behind her wishing to kill me with an axe.

"Of course, he quite understood why I was so annoyed at you, insulting me in such a crass manner when really I was not responsible at all for anything. It's not like anyone ever mentioned to me that menstruation is strictly taboo in Turai. But after we talked for a while I did see that you were probably too upset to think clearly. Any gambler would be, and you of course do have a problem with your gambling. And you'd been drinking heavily, which always clouds your judgement. I expect you were addled with thazis as well. I've noticed it always has a bad effect on you when you smoke too much. So with the gambling, the drink and the drugs all making you crazy, I figured it wasn't really fair of me to hold a grudge, though your behaviour was bad, even by your standards. In the spirit of friendship I thought I'd get your money back for you."

I inform Makri stiffly that I was far from addled, and was certainly not crazy. "It was merely the rational response of a man who has been pushed past the limit by the ludicrous behaviour of a woman who has no idea of how to behave in polite society. What happened when you saw Casax? I take it he wasn't too keen to return the money?"

Makri shakes her head. "Afraid not. He wasn't keen to see me in the first place and I had to do a fair bit of fighting just to get to him. I grabbed his purse, but there's only a hundred or so gurans in it. And after that a battle just seemed to develop between me and his men. I didn't realise there were so many of them."

Makri grins happily, hands me the purse, and squeezes past me to peer out of our porthole.

"The Elvish Isles. Avula, birthplace of Queen Leeuven. And the festival! I can't wait. Remind me why we're going there?"

"You're not going there for anything. I'm going to get my friend Vas's daughter out of jail. She's accused of attacking a tree."

"Attacking a tree? And they threw her in prison? These Elves certainly love their vegetation."

"It was a special tree. The Hesuni Tree in fact. No doubt you have learned all about Hesuni Trees at the Guild College."

"Heart and soul of the tribe," pronounces Makri.

"Exactly. I don't have all the details yet, but Vas's daughter is in bad trouble. So kindly try not to ruin everything for me. Vas is an old friend and I want to help him. Also I can't afford to look bad in front of Cicerius and Prince Dees-Akan."

"Is he the dwa-ridden drunken Prince or the sober responsible one?"

"The sober responsible one. Well, sober and responsible as far as Turanian Princes go."

"You mean he's a lush?"

"He's not quite as bad as his older brother. And don't insult the Royal Family."

My cheerful mood has vanished. I can see this is going to be a tough journey.

"When we get to Avula I doubt you'll be allowed

to go ashore, but if by some miracle you are, for God's sake don't mention your—your—well you know what I'm talking about. You'll panic the Elves."

Chapter Four

On the second day of the voyage Vas-ar-Methet manages to escape from his official duties for long enough to fill me in on the details of the case.

"My daughter's accuser is Lasas-ar-Thetos, Chief Attendant to the Tree. He is the brother of Gulas-ar-Thetos, the Chief Tree Priest. According to Lasas, he caught her in the act of chopping into the tree with an axe, after she had previously tried to set it on fire."

"What does your daughter have to say about this?"

"She remembers nothing of the incident."

I raise my eyebrows. I don't expect all my clients to be innocent, but the least they can do is think of a good excuse. "She remembers nothing at all?"

"No. But she does not deny that she was there. Unfortunately her memory of events appears to be completely empty. She cannot remember a thing from the time she left our house till the moment she found herself in custody."

"You know that doesn't look good, Vas. Doesn't she even remember why she went to the Tree?"

Vas shakes his head. I ask him if he believes her and he is quite emphatic that he does.

"I am aware that it looks bad for her. She has no defence to present to the Council of Elders who will try her. But I do not believe that my daughter, as fine an Elf as there is on the entire island, would ever commit such a sacrilegious act. It is completely against her character, and besides, she had no reason to do it."

Despite Vas-ar-Methet's strong desire to see his daughter cleared, I can't learn nearly enough from him. He has no idea of what she might have been doing near the Tree, no idea when she ever visited it in the course of her normal life, and no idea of who else might have wished to damage it.

"Do you think her memory was sorcerously affected? Has anyone checked?"

"Yes. The case has been investigated by Lord Kalith's officials, and that includes Jir-ar-Eth, his Chief Sorcerer. I understand that he found no trace of sorcery being used in the area, although everyone knows that that would be hard to establish anyway. The Hesuni Tree creates a powerful mystical field around it. All sorcery would be affected, and it is impossible to look back in time at anything that happened there."

I nod. I'm used to sorcery not working out too well when it comes to investigating. The idea of a Sorcerer having a look at events, sorting out some clues and producing a neat answer is fine in theory—and it works occasionally in practice—but generally there are too many variables to make it reliable, or even feasible. That's why I'm still in a job. You always need a man who's prepared to pound the streets looking for answers. Or, in this case, pound the trees. The Avulans live mainly above the ground, on villages suspended in the tree tops, with walkways connecting them. Last time I visited the Elvish Isles I remember travelling briskly over these walkways, admiring the ground below, but I was a lot younger then, and a lot thinner.

As Vas leaves the scrawny little Elvish girl arrives and tells me that Lord Kalith wants to see me in his cabin. I make my way there, shielding my face against the heavy rain that pounds down on to the deck. Despite the poor weather the wind is in our favour and we're making good progress. The ship rolls gently beneath my feet and the motion brings back many memories. It's some time since I've been on a voyage, but I haven't lost my sea legs.

Lord Kalith's cabin, while comfortable, is not ostentatious. There's little by way of decoration to show that Kalith is the head of his tribe, though I cast a jealous eye at the fine furniture. All I have in my cabin is a bunk, and it makes for a very poor seat, particularly when the ship pitches into a trough.

Lord Kalith himself wears few emblems of his rank, as is common among the Elves. An Elvish Lord would regard anything more than a small circle of silver in his hair to be bad taste. His cloak, while slightly more sumptuously cut than those of the other Elves, is the same shade of green, and untrammelled by any decoration.

"I understand you have been questioning my crew."

I nod. There's no denying it, though really I have been doing little more than acquainting myself with the background of the case.

"I wish you to stop," says Lord Kalith.

"Stop? Why?"

"As master of this ship and Lord of my island, I do not have to give you a reason. I merely wish you to stop. My sailors should not be disturbed in their duties."

I shrug noncommittally. I would have no qualms whatsoever about outraging Kalith and every other Elf Lord while carrying out an investigation, but I figure there's no point in annoying him yet. If things go badly for me on Avula, I'll annoy him plenty there.

I do take the time to point out to Kalith that I am here at the bidding of Vas-ar-Methet, and was given to understand that he had his Lord's approval. Kalith concedes that this is true, but makes it clear that he never thought it was such a great idea.

"Vas-ar-Methet is of great value to me. I could not refuse his request for help in the matter of his daughter. But I am quite certain that, sad as it may be, his daughter did actually do what she is accused of. On Avula, you have my permission to ask questions, within reason. Here on my ship, I expect you to behave with decorum, and refrain from distracting my crew."

I nod. I notice that Lord Kalith has a game of niarit set out on the small table by his couch. I glance at the pieces.

"The Harper's Game," I say, recognising the formation.

Lord Kalith raises an eyebrow. "You play the game?"

"Often. But I never favour the Harper's Game. I find it's too susceptible to an attack from the Elephants and the Plague Carrier."

"I have been working on a new variation. It involves some new moves for the Hero and the Sorcerer. Perhaps we shall have a chance to play, later in the voyage?"

As I leave the cabin his farewell is friendlier than it might have been. Keen niarit players always feel some sort of bond with their fellows. Heading back to my cabin, I'm thoughtful. As a warning not to do any investigating, it was reasonably friendly. I've had far worse.

Makri is sitting on my bunk reading a scroll. She's wearing a green Elvish tunic brought to her by Isuas, the young Elf maid. While none of the other Elves on board has so much as spoken to Makri, Isuas doesn't seem to share their inhibitions. From the way she bounded into the cabin minutes after Makri arrived soaking wet, and offered to find her some dry clothes, I'd say Makri might have made a friend. Makri doesn't seem too impressed.

"At least someone on this ship likes you. I'd have thought you'd be pleased."

"She annoys me."

"Why?"

"Because she's so weedy and pathetic. Are all thirteen-year-old Elf girls like that?"

I tell her I don't think so. Isuas does seem a little on the small side, but I don't see that as any reason for Makri's dislike.

"I hate weedy little girls," says Makri, matter-of-factly. "Back in the slave pits they just used them for target practice. If I'd been runt-sized like her I'd have been dead long ago."

"Well, excuse the rest of the world for not all being demented warrior women," I say, and tell her to shove up on the bunk as I need to sit down. "Anyway, try not to alienate her. Apart from Vas, she's probably the only Elf on board with any sympathy towards either of us. You know, I've just been warned off by Lord Kalith? Not what I was expecting, I must say. I thought he'd be pleased to have an experienced investigator coming down to sort things out. It's weird the way my cases always get so difficult right from the start. Sometimes I think I'm cursed by the Gods."

Makri shrugs. She's not big on religion. "Maybe you should pray more. Are you still meant to do it three times a day, even on a ship?"

In Turai this is a legal requirement.

"A Turanian citizen should pray at the correct times, no matter where he is."

"I haven't noticed you doing it," says Makri.

"Yes, well, my knees aren't what they were. It's hard on a man, having to kneel all the time."

In truth, I haven't been out of bed in time for morning prayers for something like ten years, and for the other two daily prayer slots I generally just try to hide in my room.

"Anyway it's too late for prayer now, I'm stuck with you."

"What do you mean, stuck with me?" protests Makri.

"Exactly that. The plan was for me to go to Avula, thereby missing the rigours of the Turanian winter, quickly clear Elith-ir-Methet of Tree desecration, then spend the rest of the time lounging around in the sun drinking beer. Now you've managed to spoil everything. I'm practically confined to my cabin, and when we get to Avula I'll be lucky if the Elves will deign to speak with me—I'm a man with a travelling companion who has Orc blood. And it's no use looking at me like that, you know full well it's true. It beats me why you insisted on coming."

"I didn't insist on coming. It was an accident. I was just trying to get your money back."

I still suspect Makri staged the whole thing.

"Shouldn't you be home studying?"

Makri attends the Guild College, a place where those sons of the lower classes of Turai who wish to better themselves take classes in philosophy, theology, rhetoric, mathematics and whatever else it is they teach there. Makri is the first woman ever to study at the College. At first they refused to have her, but she gained entry by extreme force of personality and some threats of legal action by the Association of Gentlewomen. Her ultimate ambition is to attend the Imperial University. There is no chance that they will ever let her in, but she refuses to be put off.

"The College shuts for the winter. I figure this trip will do me a load of good next year. I'll be able to give my professors first-hand accounts of Elvish society."

"You'll be able to give them first-hand accounts of what it's like to stay on a ship, you mean. There's no chance they're letting you disembark, Makri."

"But I want to see the festival. Just think, there are going to be three staged versions of the tale of Queen Leeuven."

"Sounds dull to me. These Elvish plays are all full of heroes battling hopelessly against fate, and they always end in tragedy."

"What's wrong with that?"

"When I'm at the theatre I like something a little more entertaining."

Makri makes a face at me. "You mean you like it when the chorus line sings some obscene drinking song and the heroine's top falls off by accident."

"That's the sort of thing," I agree. "I never enjoyed the classics."

"They have to let me attend the festival," says Makri. "I'm the only one from Turai who'll appreciate it properly."

"You won't appreciate it if the Elves start rioting because they sense Orc blood in the audience."

"Do Elves riot?" asks Makri.

I admit I don't know. If Makri sets foot on Avula, we'll probably find out.

By the fourth day of our voyage I'm bored. The ship is making good time over a calm sea with a fast wind behind us, but I'm starting to feel more than a little frustrated. Deputy Consul Cicerius has strongly suggested that I keep myself hidden for the whole of the journey. As a free Turanian citizen I don't have to do what the Deputy Consul says, but I don't want to aggravate him more than is necessary. He could make my life very difficult back in Turai. During the past year I've done some good work for Cicerius, thereby increasing my standing with city officials, but if I end up offending him or the Prince I could have my Investigator's licence revoked and then I'd be in trouble.

I sigh. It's surprising how much of my life is spent being in trouble. I should have studied more when I was young. I could have been a proper Sorcerer.

As for Prince Dees-Akan, he has not yet condescended to visit me. Nor has an invitation to an informal get-together in his cabin come my way.

I've been explaining the case to Makri. Normally I'd do this anyway—Makri is a very smart woman—but I had planned to be mad at her for a lot longer. However, as we have now been thrown together in one small cabin, it seems easier to forget her numerous outrages and revert to being friends.

The facts, as reported by Vas, are puzzling: his daughter Elith-ir-Methet was found unconscious at the scene of the crime, the Tree was badly damaged and she still had an axe in her hand.

"Is she saying she didn't do it?" asks Makri.

"Unfortunately not. She claims not to remember anything."

"That's going to make things difficult for you."

I nod. "Even if Elith is telling the truth about remembering nothing, it doesn't mean she's innocent. I've known criminals who've blanked out all memories of their crime. Something to do with the trauma, I suppose."

"So what are you going to do? Distort the facts?

Muddy the waters till there isn't enough evidence to convict her?"

"Only as a last resort. I'll at least try to find out the truth first. It's possible she didn't do it. It sounds to me as if there wasn't any sort of proper investigation. The Elves on Avula are not used to investigating. I'm going along with the presumption that's she's been framed."

The seas have become a little rougher and the ship has started to roll. I notice that Makri is looking a little queasy.

"Feeling the effects?"

"I'm fine."

A large wave rocks the ship. Makri turns quite an odd colour and rushes out of the cabin. That will teach her to interfere with my mission.

Seasickness doesn't trouble me. My only worry is that I might run out of ale on the voyage. Back in my army days I was used to these hardships, but since I moved into the Avenging Axe I've grown used to beer being available whenever I want it. It occurs that I want beer most of the time.

"Nothing wrong with that," I say out loud, patting my belly. "In a corrupt city full of thieves, murderers and drug addicts, heavy beer consumption is the only rational response."

Makri reappears, groans and flops down on the bunk, where she lies moaning about how terrible it is to be at sea.

"You'll get used to it," I tell her. "Feel like a beer?"

Makri spits out an Orcish curse, which would sound strong even in a gladiator pit, and turns her face to the wall. I decide to leave the cabin and wander among the crew. Even taciturn Elves will be better company than a seasick Makri.

I emerge on deck to encounter a light drizzle and

a strong wind. A senior member of the crew is shouting instructions to some lithe young Elves who are swarming over the rigging, adjusting the sails to cope with the worsening weather.

I watch them with interest, noting the skill with which they carry out their tasks. I've seen Turanian sailors performing similar work on many occasions, and Turanian sailors are skilful at their craft, but the Elves seem to fly over the masts and rigging as if they are unaffected by gravity's pull.

Someone appears beside me. I'm about to comment on the crew members' expertise when I realise that it is Prince Dees-Akan. This is the first time I've met him on board. I greet him graciously. I may have been sacked from my job at the Palace after getting drunk at Rittius's wedding and generally disgracing myself, but I haven't forgotten how to address the second in line to the throne.

The Prince is around twenty years old, tall and dark, though not reckoned particularly handsome by our nation's matrons, certainly not in comparison with his older brother. The young Prince is fairly popular in our city-state however, and commonly regarded as a much more stable character than his brother, the heir to the throne. That's not saying too much really. Prince Frisen-Akan might have the good looks but he is also a drunken degenerate who'd sell the Palace furniture to buy dwa. Last year he very nearly caused the ruin of the city when he became involved in a plot to import the drug through the agency of Horm the Dead, a half-Orc Sorcerer who damn near destroyed Turai with one of the most malevolent spells ever created.

I had a hand in stopping Horm. I also prevented the elder Prince's involvement from becoming known to the public. Cicerius paid me well enough, but I figure he might have been more grateful.

I've never had any dealings with the younger Prince. As he stands next to me I sense a certain awkwardness. On a long sea journey etiquette tends to be relaxed so there is no particular reason why the Prince can't converse with even a low-life like myself, but he seems to be unsure of what to say. I help him along a little.

"Ever been to the Elvish Isles before, your highness?"

"No. Have you?"

"Yes. A long time ago, before the last great Orc War. I've always wanted to go back."

The Prince gazes at me. Is there a glimmer of dislike in his expression? Possibly.

"Deputy Consul Cicerius is worried that you may cause trouble."

I reassure him. "Nothing is closer to my heart than the well-being of our great city."

"You are conducting an investigation. Might that not lead to some unpleasantness?"

"I'll do my very best to prevent it, your highness."

"I trust that you will. It seems to me a bad idea that you are here at all. Surely our Elvish friends can deal with their own criminals?"

I've quickly gone off the young Prince, but I still try to look respectful.

"And Cicerius informs me that when you are around, bad things tend to happen."

"Not at all, your highness," I say, in my most reassuring voice. "For an Investigator, my life is surprisingly peaceful."

At this moment an Elf falls from the highest mast and lands dead at my feet. It makes a really loud noise. I swear the Prince looks at me as if it's my fault.

I'm already bending down over the body. Elves are much longer lived than Humans, but even they can't survive broken necks. Members of the crew are running towards us and more are swarming down the rigging to see if they can help. There's some confusion till Vas-ar-Methet arrives on the scene and forces his way through. He kneels over the fallen Elf.

"What has happened?" comes the commanding voice of Lord Kalith, arriving at a fast gait from the bridge.

"He fell from the rigging, sir," replies one young sailor.

"Dead," says Vas, standing up. "His neck's broken. How did it happen?"

I struggle to hear clearly as many Elves speak at once, but from what I can gather the young Elf had lost his hold on the rigging when he went to take a drink from his water bottle. The bottle, made from some sort of animal skin, is still slung from his neck on a long string.

I bend over the body, lift the bottle and sniff the contents.

"That will not be necessary, Investigator," booms Lord Kalith, sounding quite insulted at the implication that there may have been something other than water in the Elf's bottle. Without making it too obvious, the other Elves get between me and the body and lift it up to take it away.

Throughout all this the Prince has stood impassively at the side of the action, joined now by his bodyguards, and also Cicerius, who hastened to our side at the sound of the commotion.

"That was hardly tactful," the Prince says to me reproachfully as the Elves depart.

Cicerius asks what he means.

"The Investigator felt obliged to check the unfortunate Elf's water bottle, apparently suspecting that he may have fallen from the rigging while drunk. Lord Kalith was plainly insulted."

"Is this true?" explodes Cicerius.

I shrug. "Just a reflex action. After all, he fell off while trying to take a drink. You've seen how sure-footed the Elves are. I just wondered if he might have had a little klee inside him, or maybe some Elvish wine?"

Cicerius glares angrily at me. The Prince glares angrily at me.

"Well, it's my job," I protest. "What if he was poisoned?"

Cicerius, never hesitant about giving a man a lecture, proceeds to tell me in strong language that I am to stay well out of the affair.

"Let the Elves bury their own dead, and whatever you do, do not go around asking questions about the accident. You and your companion have caused us enough trouble already."

I am spared further lecturing by the reappearance of Vas-ar-Methet. He looks worried.

"Very unfortunate," he confides. "Please tell Makri to stay well out of sight."

"Why?"

"A few of the younger Elves are muttering that we're cursed because of her presence."

"That is ridiculous, Vas, and you know it. It's nothing to do with Makri that one of your crew fell off the rigging."

"Nonetheless, do as he says," says Cicerius.

A slender figure in a man's tunic with a great mass of hair billowing in the wind suddenly staggers past us at a fast rate. It's Makri, heading swiftly to the rail at the side of the ship. Once there she hangs her head over and throws up violently. The wind catches some of her vomit and blows it back over her feet. She curses vehemently, and quite obscenely, and bends down to wipe them clean. I notice that her toenails are painted gold, a fashion only worn, to my certain knowledge, by the lowest class of prostitutes in Simnia. Cicerius winces.

"Hey, Makri," I call. "The Deputy Consul wants you to stay out of sight."

Makri's reply to this is fortunately carried away in the wind. She's really going to have to stop using these Orcish insults if she wants to start making friends around here.

As soon as Cicerius and the Prince depart I start asking Vas-ar-Methet about the recently deceased Elf.

"Did anyone see anything suspicious?"

Vas is puzzled. "I don't think so. Why?"

"Well aren't you curious when one of your crew suddenly plunges to his doom for no apparent reason?"

Vas shrugs. "These things happen at sea."

"Maybe. But I seem to recall hearing that Lord Kalith has one of the finest crews in the Elvish Isles. I'd say it warranted a little digging around. Will Lord Kalith instigate an enquiry?"

Vas-ar-Methet seems genuinely puzzled by my curiosity. He doesn't seem to think that there is anything to enquire about. Maybe it's one of these different-culture things. Perhaps Elves accept deaths at sea as natural occurrences. Myself, I'm just naturally suspicious about anyone dying right in front of me.

Chapter Five

Next day they hold the funeral of the young Elf who fell from the rigging. It's a long time since I've seen a burial at sea.

"Have a nice time," mutters Makri from her bunk.

"You're coming too," I inform her.

"I'm sick."

"Everyone on an Elvish ship has to attend the funeral of a crew member. It's their custom, no exceptions allowed. So get ready."

Neither of us is much looking forward to it. I'm trying to put some sort of shine on to my salt-water-encrusted boots. It's a frustrating task and I give voice to some complaints.

"Sail down to Elfland and sort out some minor difficulty over a tree—ought to be as easy as bribing a Senator. Now Kalith is angry with me, the Prince wishes I was back in Turai and the Elves are treating me like I've got the plague. How did everything go wrong so quickly?"

"It's a flaw in your character," says Makri. "You generally offend everyone when you're on a case. Sometimes it's because you've drunk too much. Other times it's just because you're an offensive sort of person. But hey, you often get the job done."

"Thank you, Makri."

The ship's crew are joined by the Turanian delegation in a sad and solemn gathering at the stern of the ship. Makri and I skulk at the back, trying to keep out of everyone's way. Prince Dees-Akan, standing beside Lord Kalith, ignores us.

"I don't really take to that Prince," whispers Makri. "I liked his sister much better."

We encountered Princess Du-Akai a while back. She hired me under false pretences, told me a load of lies and very nearly got me killed. But she did seem like a pleasant sort of person.

Lord Kalith intones the funeral litany, much of it in the Royal Elvish language which I don't understand although I attended plenty of Elvish burials during the war. It doesn't differ a great deal from a Human funeral—formal attire, brief reminiscences of the departed, some singing—and it isn't any more cheerful. The Elves tend to look at life in a more philosophical manner than we do, but that doesn't make death easy for them.

The ship pitches gently. We're now far south and the weather is improving. The rain has ceased and the sun warms the air. At night all three moons have been visible, large and heavy in the clear sky.

The dead Elf is wrapped in a funeral cloth bearing Lord Kalith's nine-starred insignia. After the oration a singer steps forward and intones a mournful dirge. His voice is clear and strong but the lament is full of sadness and casts a further shadow over us all. When the song is finished the Elves stand in silence. I bow my head, and try not to fidget. Finally the body is lowered over the side and sinks below the waves.

Lord Kalith walks briskly back to his post. The other Elves linger, talking among themselves. I'm already heading back to my cabin, keen to get below deck before Cicerius or the Prince decides it's time to lecture me about something or threaten to take away my Investigator's licence.

"A rather unfortunate family," says Makri, as we step through my door.

"What do you mean?"

"The dead Elf. Weren't you listening to the oration?"

"Most of it was in the Royal Elvish language. I couldn't understand it."

Makri slumps on to the bunk, looking ill. She's one of the poorest sailors I've ever encountered.

"I caught most of it," she says. "Lord Kalith is a very good speaker. I'll relay his speech to my Elvish language teacher back at the College. He'll like it."

I get a beer and start hauling my boots off. "What did you mean about an unfortunate family?" I ask.

"Well, one Elf in jail and another one dead. The Elf who fell from the rigging was called Eos-ar-Methet. Vas-ar-Methet's nephew, and Elith's cousin."

I finish my beer and start putting my boots back on. I can feel some investigating coming on.

"Her cousin? How about that. An interesting piece of information that no one was rushing to tell me."

I make to leave. Before I do I ask Makri if she could keep it quiet that she understood all of the funeral oration.

"I think that the fewer people who know you can speak the Royal Elvish language, the better. You might pick up more interesting things."

I find Vas-ar-Methet in his cabin, a large area that

serves as both his living quarters and his on-board treatment area. As I arrive an Elf is leaving, smiling.

"He was looking pleased. You just heal him?"

"Yes. He was having bad dreams."

"How do you cure someone of bad dreams? No, you can tell me some other time. Right now I'm looking for some information."

Vas-ar-Methet immediately seems troubled.

"Thraxas, you know I'm grateful for your help, but . . ."

"But you've heard that with the assorted Lords, Sorcerers and important Turanians on this ship I'm about as popular as an Orc at an Elvish wedding. Don't worry about it, it's often this way. You didn't hire me to make friends. Now, how come you didn't tell me that the Elf who died was your nephew?"

Vas looks puzzled. "Is it significant?"

"Of course. Doesn't it strike you as strange that the Elf who plummeted to his death for no apparent reason was Elith's cousin?"

"No. What is the connection?"

"I can't say. But trust me, my Investigator's intuition doesn't let me down. I knew there was something strange about that accident. Why would a healthy young Elf suddenly fall from the rigging and break his neck? Doesn't make sense. How many times has he been up there? Hundreds. I saw him myself, moments before, and he wasn't looking like an Elf who was suddenly going to make the elementary mistake of not holding on."

"What are you suggesting? That he was pushed? There were other members of the crew there. They would have seen something."

"There are other ways it could have happened. I tried looking at the body at the time but I was prevented from examining it properly. My first thought was that he might have been drinking, although as far as I could see he only had water in his flask. But it could have been poisoned."

Vas is very dubious.

"I really don't think that that is likely, old friend. His companions report that he simply lost his grip when he reached for his flask."

"Do experienced sailors normally wave their hands around when they're up in the rigging? He could have got a drink any time. Speaking of which . . ."

I look pointedly at the inviting decanter on Vas's table and he pours me a glass of wine. As Elvish wine goes, it's okay, nothing more. Lord Kalith ought to take more care when he loads up with supplies.

I admit that the link may appear tenuous, but when I'm grubbing around in the city and odd things start happening I generally find they're connected somehow. I doubt things are any different with the Avulans.

"Did Eos have any sort of connection with the Hesuni Tree? Maybe help with the prayers, hymns or whatever else goes on there? And was he on friendly terms with your daughter?"

Vas considers this. "It is not impossible. But before this terrible affair of my daughter, I had very little contact with the Tree Priests. I am only slightly acquainted with Gulas-ar-Thetos, the Chief Tree Priest. Whether Eos knew him, I can't say. It seems unlikely. Young sea-going Elves do not normally spend too much time with older members of the religious order. But he was friendly with my daughter. She will be sad to learn of his death."

He promises that when we reach Avula he will be able to put me in touch with several Elves who will be able to tell me more.

"I hope they're going to be more co-operative than the crew."

"They will be. They are my friends. I may be the only Elf on Avula who believes my daughter is innocent, but I am not the only one who would be glad if she were."

An Elf arrives, apparently needing Vas's healing services. He is looking particularly unhappy. Many of the crew look unhappy. Maybe they're all having bad dreams.

The seas are now rough but we're making good progress. It is not just the skill of the Elvish sailors that speeds us onwards; Elvish shipwrights are privy to shipbuilding secrets unknown to their Human allies. Our craft cuts through the water at a rate that would be the envy of any Turanian Captain. Lord Kalith's personal Sorcerer, Jir-ar-Eth, is on the ship and could if necessary use sorcery to change the weather in our favour, but so far there has been no need. He stays below decks, swapping tales with Harmon Half-Elf and Lanius Suncatcher.

The death of the crew member has cast a pall of gloom over the ship. I'll be glad when we reach Avula. The voyage has started to bore me and I'm running short of beer. There is nothing to see apart from the endless grey seas and there is precious little to do. I've carried on with my enquiries as best as I can but because of the reticence of the Elves I've learned very little that Vas has not already told me.

Even young Isuas, for some reason quite in thrall to Makri, tells us bluntly that Vas's daughter is clearly guilty of the crime and is fortunate not to have been punished already.

"Only my father's high regard for Vas-ar-Methet has delayed it."

"Your father's high regard? What do you mean?"

Isuas looks puzzled. "Lord Kalith of course. Were you not aware that he is my father?"

"This youth is a spy!" I exclaim, and glare at her. "So that's why you've been coming here every day, is it? Reporting on my movements to Lord Kalith, no doubt. Makri, send her away immediately."

"I didn't want her here in the first place," exclaims Makri, who has notably failed to warm to the young Elf.

"Are you really the daughter of the Elf Lord?"

"Yes. His youngest daughter."

"Then what are you doing working as a cabin boy? Or should that be cabin girl?"

"Cabin Elf?" suggests Makri.

Isuas doesn't seem to think there is anything strange about it. She's been sailing with her father for the past year. "He says it will toughen me up."

"Well that would make sense," says Makri. "You certainly are a weedy kid."

Isuas looks distressed at this. I guess she already knows she got the short straw when it came to handing out health and strength. I still feel suspicious of her presence. Back in Turai, young daughters of rulers don't go around being junior sailors.

"Does no one else believe Elith to be innocent?"

"Why would they? She admits the crime."

"Not exactly. She doesn't deny it. That's different."

Isuas does not seem overly concerned with the affair. Rather, her interest is taken up with one of Makri's swords, which is lying on her bunk, a dark evil-looking weapon that Makri brought with her from the Orc Lands.

"Is that an Orcish blade?" asks Isuas, wide-eyed.

Makri grunts in reply.

"Such a thing has surely never been on this ship before. Can I touch it?"

"Only if you want to lose your hand," growls Makri, who is never keen to see her weapons pawed at.

Young Isuas again looks distressed.

"Well, could I watch you clean it?" she ventures.

Makri hisses something rude.

"Could I just touch it? Please?"

"Oh, for God's sake, pick the damn thing up," growls Makri. "Anything to shut you up. Little brat," she mutters as she lies on the bunk, groaning and complaining about the rough seas. Isuas holds Makri's sword out in front of her, and tries to look fierce.

"Will you teach me how to fight?" she says, eagerly.

Makri, unable to take any more of this, picks up one of her sandals and bounces it off Isuas's head. Isuas squawks, then flees from the cabin in tears.

"That was a bit harsh."

"Harsh? She's lucky I didn't hit her with the sword. Now stop talking to me—I'm sick."

I depart, leaving Makri to her misery. I meet Cicerius on deck. He knows I'm curious about the death of the sailor and this displeases him. The rain has obliged him to wear a cloak over his Senatorial toga but he still manages to look like an important official giving a telling-off to some hapless minion as he informs me that I am to stop making enquiries.

"I have been given strongly to understand that the Elves do not wish the matter to be further investigated."

"Tell me something I don't know. Am I the only one around here who thinks that deaths should be looked into? I take it you don't actually forbid me to try and clear Vas-ar-Methet's daughter of the crime she's accused of?"

"I believe Lord Kalith regrets giving permission for Vas-ar-Methet to extend the enquiry," says Cicerius.

Cicerius has the universal reputation of being the most incorruptible person in Turai. Despite his renowned austerity, he is not an unfair man. He tells me that he can understand my need to help my friend and wartime companion.

"Although I regret that you are on this voyage, I realise that it would have been difficult for you to refuse Vas-ar-Methet's request. Ties of friendship should not be taken lightly. But I must insist that you carry out your work without causing offence to our Elvish friends. And keep that woman Makri out of sight. Yesterday she was parading round the ship in a quite shameless manner wearing only a chainmail bikini. I do not believe the Elves were pleased."

"Well, it was certainly a novel sight for them. Though I think she was fleeing to the rail to be sick, rather than actually parading around. Did you notice the gold toenails? Odd that she's picked up that fashion, because Makri's never been in Simnia, and as far as I know the only other women who do that are Simnian—"

"Just keep her under control," says Cicerius, icily.

"You know what she's like, Cicerius. Difficult to reason with."

The Deputy Consul almost smiles. Cicerius is not about to admit that Makri is exactly a good thing, but he would be forced to allow that she had been helpful when I last worked for him. He draws his cloak tighter against the wind and the rain, and contents himself with warning me not to make things difficult.

"There are times when your doggedness has proved useful. This is not one of them. If by any chance you do discover any secrets on Avula, keep them to yourself. As a representative of the state of Turai, I forbid you to say or do anything that may upset the Elves without fully consulting me first. This five-yearly festival is an important affair and the Avulans will be highly displeased if anything bad happens while their island is full of visitors."

He pauses. "Have you been drinking?"

I don't deny it. It passes the time.

Cicerius departs with his nose in the air. I notice that he is vain enough to wear a cloak sufficiently short to display the gold edging around the bottom of his toga. Only the upper classes wear togas. I'm dressed in my standard dull tunic with a heavy cloak to keep out the elements. I wander off, wondering who I might profitably spend some time with. It makes sense at least to try to gather some background information. Elith is due to be tried immediately after the festival, which means I'll only have a week or so to investigate the affair once we land.

I decide to see if I can find Lanius Suncatcher and Harmon Half-Elf. So far I have had little contact with them on board and I wonder if they might have picked up anything interesting about the crime. Before I can go in search of the Sorcerers, an Elf I don't recognise plants himself firmly in front of me. I greet him politely. He stares at me in a hostile manner. Though most of the Elves tie their hair back whilst on board ship, his long golden hair swings freely in the wind. His eyes are a little darker than normal and he has a powerful build. We stand looking at each other in silence.

"I am Gorith-ar-Del," he says, finally.

I stare at him blankly. "Is that supposed to mean something to me?"

"Callis-ar-Del was my brother. He hired you to help him. Then he got killed."

Callis-ar-Del. I remember him. Along with his friend Jaris-ar-Miat, he was one of the Elves who hired me to look for the valuable Red Elvish Cloth last summer. They pretended they were trying to recover it for their Elf Lord Kalith-ar-Yil, our ship's Captain, but in reality they were trying to steal it. Both were eventually killed by Hanama from the Assassins Guild. They got in her way, which was foolish.

The way Gorith-ar-Del is staring at me, I have the impression he holds me responsible. I wasn't, but I don't want to go over the details of the case again. Hearing about his brother's criminal activities can only be painful to Gorith.

"I don't believe my brother was trying to steal the Cloth. I believe he was made the scapegoat after being caught up in events in a foreign city. He hired you to help him. Why didn't you protect him?"

The wind is picking up, My hair, tied back in a long ponytail, starts to swing gently like a pendulum.

"He left Turai without telling me. I did go after him, and I caught up with him before his ship left harbour. Unfortunately he was dead by then. The Assassins Guild. It was no secret."

"And was any effort made to punish the killers?"

"No one from the Assassins Guild ever gets taken to court."

"Why not?"

"That would require a longer lecture on Turanian politics and customs than you want to hear. I'm sorry your brother was killed."

Gorith leans towards me threateningly. "It seems to me that someone set my brother up with the Cloth then was able to share the profits after he was murdered." The Elf's eyes are cold. "I don't trust you, fat man."

Gorith-ar-Del stalks off, graceful despite the pitching of the ship. I look at his retreating figure. I shrug, and continue on my way to find Lanius and Harmon.

I locate them below decks in Harmon's cabin, which is a whole lot bigger than mine. The Elvish Sorcerer Jir-ar-Eth is with them and they're all seated comfortably, drinking wine. I'm irritated that no one thought to invite me, a fellow practitioner of the mystic arts, for a friendly drink. Harmon Half-Elf greets me affably enough.

"Come in, Thraxas. How are things with you?"

"Better than rowing a slave galley. Not too much better though. The Turanian delegation wishes I wasn't here, the Elves are freezing me out and my cabin is occupied by a woman who only stops complaining when she's throwing up."

Vas has given Makri soothing herbs and potions, but she seems to be unusually prone to seasickness. There is nothing to do but wait for it to pass.

I've really come here looking for some friendly company, but the sight of all the friendly company going on quite merrily without me is annoying. Even the Sorcerers are avoiding me. How come I'm the one who's suffering here? Rather than the civilised conversation I had in mind, I find myself pitching into the Elvish Sorcerer with an aggressive line in questioning.

"So, what's up with you Elves anyway?" I demand, fixing Jir-ar-Eth with an accusing look. "I'm starting to think you all have something to hide. How come no one will answer my questions? Scared I'll dig up something?"

"Not at all," replies Jir-ar-Eth. "You can hardly blame Avulans for some reticence in the face of a man they have never met, who brings with him a woman of Orc parentage. But to the best of my knowledge, all the facts about the assault on the Hesuni Tree are known."

"Oh yes?" I grunt. "Well, I'm not convinced."

I'm feeling aggressive. It feels good. I've had enough of crawling around being polite. I take a goblet of wine, uninvited, and bark a few more questions.

Unlike our magicians, who all wear a rainbow cloak as a mark of their guild, Jir-ar-Eth is clad in a standard Elf's green cloak with only a small yellow tree embroidered on the shoulder as a mark of his profession. He looks fairly old for an Elf, with his golden hair turning silver, but vigorous still.

"I understand that Elith can't remember the crime. Very convenient, don't you think?"

"You believe that someone else is responsible? Why?"

"Investigator's intuition," I reply. "And I'll trust my intuition against yours any day. Is there any chance of another glass of wine? Thank you. So, why did Vas's daughter damage the Tree?"

The Elvish Sorcerer confesses that he has no idea. Elith has not vouchsafed a motive.

"Rather suspicious, don't you think? Who might have framed her?"

"Really!" protests Jir. "This is quite uncalled for. You must not apply the standards of your Human city to those of the Elvish Isles."

"Oh yes," I state, walking around the cabin waving my hands in the air. "You Elves are always keen to brag about your high standards. Well let me tell you, I've had to help quite a few high-class Elves out of tough spots in Turai. Generally when they find themselves drunk in some low-class brothel and want it all hushed up from their Elf Lord."

Jir-ar-Eth looks at me with amazement. Possibly fearing that Jir is about to blast me with a spell for my insolence, Lanius Suncatcher tries his best to smooth things over.

"You must excuse Thraxas," he laughs. "Always has to see suspicious circumstances everywhere. Back at the Palace he was famous for it."

I am unapologetic. It's time I stirred things up a little around here. I've been on this ship for two weeks and I've learned nothing at all. You can't expect an Investigator to take that lying down. (Not this Investigator anyway. Maybe some others with lower standards.)

"I really don't see that you have any cause for suspicion, Thraxas," says Harmon Half-Elf. "And I would suggest that you moderate your manner. Cicerius and the Prince will not be pleased to learn that you are insulting our hosts."

"Cicerius and our Prince can go to hell. I'm fed up with being warned about my behaviour. Who was it saved the city from that mad Orc Sorcerer only last month at the race meeting? Me. I didn't see anyone complaining about my bad manners then."

"Everyone complained about your bad manners," retorts Harmon. "You were just too pleased with yourself to pay any attention."

The Elvish Sorcerer clams up and refuses to answer any more of my questions. Lanius suggests that perhaps I should go back to my cabin and rest.

"Fine," I tell him, and pack a bottle of wine into the bag at my side. "I will. But don't expect me to pussyfoot around when I get to Avula. If anyone tries to hide the facts from me there I'll be down on them like a bad spell."

I storm out. Back on deck the rain hits me in the face. I ignore it and stride back to my cabin. Inside Makri is sitting on the floor, not looking any better.

"Damned Elves," I exclaim. "I'm sick of them already. What can you expect? Sitting round in trees all the time, singing about the stars. Apart from the ones who are threatening me."

"You were threatened?"

"Yes. Some large Elf called Gorith thinks I was responsible for the death of his brother. You remember, one of the pair whom Hanama killed in Twelve Seas."

"Hanama. I like her."

"Yes, for a murderous Assassin she's always excellent company."

I bring out the wine and take a healthy slug. "To hell with Gorith."

The ship rolls suddenly. Makri, unable to take the sight of me guzzling wine in her present precarious state, is once more overcome with nausea. She fails to make it to the side of the ship. She fails even to make it out the cabin, and is sick on the floor. Meanwhile the sudden violent pitching makes me drop the bottle of wine and it smashes. I slip and follow it down. At this moment, while Makri and I are rolling around on the floor of our tiny cabin in a mess of beer, wine and vomit, the door bursts open and Prince Dees-Akan walks in.

He stares, incredulous, at the sight that meets his eyes. It's not the sort of behaviour he's been brought up to expect. As I'm hauling myself to my feet he seems to be having some difficulty in finding the appropriate words.

"Is it true that you just insulted the eminent Elvish Sorcerer Jir-ar-Eth?" he demands.

"Certainly not," I reply. "Possibly he got the wrong impression. Not used to being questioned, I expect."

Makri groans, rolls over and throws up over the Prince's feet.

"Eh . . . sorry, your highness . . . hasn't quite found her sea legs yet."

"You low-life scum!" yells the Prince.

"There's no need to talk to her like that!" I protest. "She's never been on a ship before."

"I was referring to you," says the Prince.

"Don't worry," says Makri, grabbing his leg in an attempt to make it back on to her feet. "I'll have him civilised by the time we get to Avula."

When Makri first arrived in Turai, fresh from the rigours of the gladiator slave pits, she showed very little sign of a sense of humour. It developed fairly rapidly, but I could have told her that with the Prince looking with horror at his ruined sandals, this was not the time to be light-hearted.

"How dare you address me, you piece of filth!" shouts the Prince.

He departs in a fury. Makri abandons her efforts to rise and lies in a pool of her own sickness. It is really, really unpleasant. I hunt for one of my remaining beers, break open the bottle and start pouring it down my throat. We remain in silence for a while.

"You think we made a good impression?" says Makri finally.

"Pretty good. I may be in for a swift recall to the Palace."

Makri laughs. I help her to her feet. She shakes her head to clear it. "I think I'm starting to feel better now. How long till we reach Avula?"

I hand her a towel to clean her face. "Another two weeks."

"I'll be pleased to walk on dry land again," says Makri.

"Me too. And it will be good to get some proper investigating done. Now we've started to make friends in important places, it should be a breeze."

Chapter Six

◆───◆

Two weeks later we're close to Avula. We should sight land tomorrow. The weather has improved. Makri's health has improved. We're bored. For want of anything better to do, Makri, with encouragement from me, has given in to Isuas's repeated requests and has given her some lessons in basic sword play. These lessons have all taken place in the cramped privacy of our cabin, partly because Isuas feels her father would not be pleased if he knew, and partly because Makri says she wouldn't like her reputation as a fighter to suffer from anyone learning that she was trying to teach sword-fighting to such a useless excuse for an Elf as Isuas. The cabin being somewhat cramped at the best of times, I haven't actually seen any of these sessions, but Makri assures me that Isuas is the most pathetic creature ever to hold a sword, and seeing the child fumbling around gives Makri the strong desire to pick her up and throw her overboard.

"Not warming to the kid, then?"

"I loathe her. She keeps bursting into tears for no reason. Why did you encourage me to teach her?"

"Because it might do us some good on Avula if we have an ally. She's Kalith's daughter—she might be able to open a few doors for us."

"Not if I break her fingers," mutters Makri.

Nothing of note has happened to me. I haven't even been threatened recently. I've seen Gorith-ar-Del several times but he has not spoken to me since his original menacing approach.

I haven't learned anything much though I picked up a little gossip while playing niarit with Osath, the ship's cook. I like Osath. He's an excellent chef. He's also one of the very few Elves who carries a little extra weight round his belly. My tremendous enthusiasm for his food overcame his Elvish reticence and we've spent a few evenings playing niarit together. Most of what I learn sheds no light on Elith's case, but it's interesting background information. Even in a place like Avula, there are political tensions. Lord Kalith has an advisory Council of twelve leading Elvish Elders, and certain of these Elders have been pushing for more influence. It's even rumoured that some wish to abandon the traditional rule of the Elvish Lord and move on to some representative system, which would be unheard of among the Elves.

Furthermore, there are some tensions around the Hesuni Tree. Gulas-ar-Thetos holds the position of Chief Tree Priest but there is another branch of the family that has claimed for several generations that the Priesthood should belong to them. Some sort of complicated dispute about the rules of succession, which never quite goes away.

Even the festival is not without its attendant controversy. The three staged versions of the tale of Queen Leeuven are each put on by one of the Ossuni Elves' islands—Avula, Ven and Corinthal—in the form of a competition, with judges giving a prize to the winning play. It is a great honour to produce the play and on each island leading Elves compete for the position. Apparently the person chosen by Lord Kalith to produce and direct Avula's play this year is not universally popular. There is a feeling on the island that the job has gone to the wrong Elf.

"Myself, I've never cared much for the plays," confides Osath. "Too highbrow for me. I like the juggling competition best. More soup?"

Other than this, I sit in my cabin and smoke thazis with Makri.

"I can't wait to get off this ship," she tells me for the twentieth time, idly prodding at the gold ring that pierces her nose, another sartorial outrage guaranteed to inflame public opinion in Turai. She's just washed her hair and the huge dark mass of it seems to take up a substantial amount of our limited cabin space.

We pass the thazis stick back and forward between us. We have the porthole open to let out the pungent aroma. This gives me the odd feeling that I'm a much younger man, a youth in fact, smoking the mild narcotic in secret. These days in Turai no one bothers to conceal thazis, though it is still technically illegal. Since the much more powerful drug dwa took its hold on the city, the authorities are relieved if thazis is the worst thing you're up to. But I don't want to offend the Elves. As far as I know, they disapprove of all narcotics.

Isuas appears, wide-eyed and timorous as usual.

"Can't you knock?" growls Makri.

I grin at the young Elf. She might be a sickly sort of kid, with straggly hair and watery eyes, but I like her well enough. She has a message for me from Lord Kalith.

"He asks if you would like to spend this last evening playing niarit."

"Niarit? I must be back in his good books."

Isuas looks doubtful. "I think he just ran out of opponents. He's beaten all the other players on the ship."

I haul myself up. "Then it sounds like a job for Thraxas. Once I'm through with him, your father will regret ever taking up the game."

Isuas looks pained. "My father is renowned as a fine player."

"Oh yes? Well, when it comes to niarit I am number one chariot. Ask Makri here."

"Will you teach me some more fighting?" asks Isuas eagerly.

Makri scowls. "What's the point? When it comes to sword play you're about as much use as a eunuch in a brothel."

Isuas gapes, shocked by this crude expression. She hangs her head. "I'll try to do better," she mumbles.

"Well, I'll leave you to it, Makri. Have fun."

"Are you going to go and leave me with this brat for company?"

"I am indeed. A true niarit player never refuses a challenge. If there's any wine going spare I'll bring you back a bottle."

I depart, keen for some action. I wonder if Lord Kalith might wish to place a small wager on the outcome? I have a package with me, just in case.

I enter Kalith's comfortable cabin for only the second time on the voyage. One might have thought that as a guest of the Elves I would have been invited there more frequently, but no. While Princes, Deputy Consuls and assorted Sorcerers have freely enjoyed the Elf Lord's hospitality, Thraxas the Investigator has sadly languished in a tiny cabin at the unfashionable end of the ship, fruitlessly awaiting an occasional invitation to socialise with the upper classes.

Stifling my resentment, I greet Kalith politely enough.

"You wished to see me?"

"I wondered if you might care for a game?"

Lord Kalith gestures with his hand towards the niarit board set out in front of him. The two opposing armies are lined up against each other, the front rank comprising, from left to right, Foot Soldiers, or Hoplites, then Archers, then Trolls. The rear rank is made up of Elephants, Heavy Mounted Knights and Light Mounted Lancers. Each player also has in their army a Siege Tower, a Healer, a Harper, a Wizard, a Hero and a Plague Carrier. A the very back of the board is the Castle, the object of the game being to defend your own Castle and storm your opponent's. Lord Kalith's board is the same as that used all over the Human Lands, except that one of the armies is green instead of white, and the Castles at each end of the board are instead represented by large fortified trees.

"I generally take green," says Lord Kalith.

"Fine. They call me Thraxas the Black. And I generally take wine."

No servant is in attendance. Faced with the possibility of actually standing up and pouring me some wine himself—which would be asking rather a lot of an Elf Lord—Kalith looks suddenly puzzled and asks me if I know where his daughter is. I tell him she's hanging around with Makri, which doesn't please him.

"All I hear from my daughter these days is Makri this or Makri that. I do not approve."

"Yeah, as a role model Makri is the woman from hell. Don't worry, she hates your daughter anyway."

Somehow that didn't come out quite as I intended. Kalith is not pacified. To save him any embarrassment I get my own wine, filling a goblet from the decanter nearby. And once again I have to say that, as Elvish wine goes, it is not of the finest. Makes me again suspect that Kalith is not liberal with his hospitality, and probably doesn't have a spare barrel of beer waiting in the storeroom for anyone who might wish to partake of it.

"Care for a small wager?"

Kalith raises his eyebrows a fraction. "I have no wish to take money from you, Investigator."

"You won't."

"I will assuredly defeat you."

"That's what your cook said before I sent his army down to Elvish hell."

Kalith smiles. "I have heard that you outplayed Osath. I, however, am a rather better player. But I repeat, I have no wish to take money from you."

I unwrap my package.

"A stick?"

"An illuminated staff. One of the finest. Given to me by the renowned Turanian Sorcerer Kemlath Orc Slayer."

I speak a word of power and the staff lights up with a brilliant golden hue. It really is a fine illuminated staff, the best I've ever had. Even to an Elf Lord, it can't be an unattractive bet.

Lord Kalith picks it up and holds it, watching as the golden light streams out of it, lighting all corners of the cabin.

"A fine staff. Though I seem to remember hearing that Kemlath Orc Slayer was obliged to leave Turai in disgrace."

"He had the misfortune to have me investigate some crimes he'd committed."

"Very well, I accept your bet. What shall I wager in return? A golden goblet?"

Elves always think that humans are slaves to gold. Fair enough. I've done plenty of questionable things for gold. But that's not what I'm looking for right now.

"Would you rather I staked some mystical item? My chief Sorcerer Jir-ar-Eth has many fine articles."

"No, I'm not needing any fine articles. I was thinking more about Makri."

Kalith frowns.

"I want her on Avula with me. She helps me investigate. If I win, I want you to let her land, no questions asked. And guarantee that the Avulans will be hospitable to her."

"There is no possibility of my people being hospitable to her."

"Well at least not openly hostile. Do you accept my bet?"

The Elf Lord shakes his head. "I cannot allow her on my island."

I stand up.

"A pity. I was looking forward to playing. It's not often you get the chance to show an Elf Lord that no matter how many excellent variations he works out for the Harper's Game, he's got about as much chance against Thraxas as a rat against a dragon. And I mean a small rat and a big dragon."

A pained look comes into the Elf Lord's face. I doubt that he has ever before been compared to a rat.

"Sit down," he says coldly. "And prepare to lose your staff."

We start to play. Lord Kalith apparently does not fully trust his new variation because he starts off with the Hoplite advance, a solid if unexciting strategy. I respond in a conventional manner by harrying them with my Light Cavalry, meanwhile forming up my own Hoplites to resist and bringing up my Trolls for some heavy support. It has all the makings of a stiff battle on the centre of the field, which will suit me fine, when

Lord Kalith surprises me by sending his Hero striding out in front of his army, straight into my Light Cavalry.

This seems foolish. The Hero carries a lot of weight on the board and can deal with most things, but not an entire division of Cavalry backed up with Hoplites and Trolls. I surround him and get ready for the kill but I'm keeping a watchful eye out for whatever else Kalith might have planned.

When I'm about to slay Kalith's Hero he suddenly advances his Archers up towards my right flank, backed by his Elephants. Coming alongside them are his Harper and his Plague Carrier. I'm momentarily puzzled. Apparently Lord Kalith now wishes to rescue his Hero, but I can't see how even this strong force can reach him in time. His Harper sings to my troops, which has the power of paralysing them, and his Plague Carrier starts to do some damage, but I form up my Trolls in a strong defensive line and send over some of my Heavy Cavalry for support, with my Healer and my Wizard in attendance. Lord Kalith's relief force fails to penetrate and I kill his Hero, which, I think, puts me at a strong advantage.

All of a sudden I notice that for some reason his Harper seems to be continuing to advance and far too many of my troops on my left flank are succumbing to his singing. In an unexpected move, Lord Kalith sends his Light Cavalry streaming through the gap. I remain impassive at the board, but inside I'm uttering a few curses. Kalith has indeed worked out a new variation on the Harper's Game, sacrificing his Hero. He apparently had no intention of rescuing him, but merely used the gambit as a distraction.

There are a tense few minutes as I struggle to reinforce my left flank. Even here I'm still a little doubtful, fearing that I may be missing something. I don't want to overcommit and find Kalith suddenly breaking through somewhere else. It takes some fine swift calculations on my part to reorganise my defences and in the process I lose the services of my Harper when he is trampled by a rampaging Elephant.

Finally, however, I hold the line, and start pushing Kalith back up the board. With his Hero gone, his Wizard nearly out of spells and his Trolls hemmed in by my Heavy Cavalry, he has no option but to retreat. As play crosses back into his side of the board I start to inflict heavy losses on his army and manage to isolate and kill his Wizard. I've got him beat. No one comes back from this position, not against me anyway.

Makri chooses this moment to burst into the cabin, followed firstly by a frightened-looking Isuas and secondly by two irate Elvish attendants. She strides over to us and plants herself right beside Lord Kalith's chair.

"What's this your daughter tells me about you issuing orders that I can't leave the ship?" she demands.

I quickly glance at Makri's hips and am relieved to see she has not actually brought a sword with her. Not that this is any real guarantee that she is unarmed. Makri is always liable to produce a dagger or a throwing star from some unexpected place. I never met anyone so keen on walking round with a knife in each boot.

"I did indeed issue such an order," says Lord Kalith, regally. If he's at all concerned about the sight of a furious Makri towering over him he's not showing it, and when his attendants hurry forward he holds up his hand to show that everything is under control.

I rise to my feet. "Don't worry about it, Makri, I've arranged things."

I wave at the niarit board, then give Kalith a look.

"I presume you do not wish to carry on with the game."

Again, I have to say that Lord Kalith takes it well. Good breeding. He can't be at all happy that's he's just lost to me at niarit, and he has made it perfectly plain that he is utterly opposed to Makri landing on Avula, but from all the emotion he shows you might imagine he was having another excellent day at the Tree Palace.

"I concede. Well played, Investigator. I see that my variation needs further work."

He turns his head toward Makri. "You may land on Avula. Do nothing that may disturb my Elves. And stay away from my daughter."

"What's going on?" asks Makri. I tell her I'll explain later and usher her out before she causes any further offence.

Back on the deck we run into Cicerius.

"Have you—?" he says.

"Yes. Thoroughly offended Lord Kalith. Major diplomatic incident. Better go and sort it out. See you on Avula."

Chapter Seven

By the afternoon of the next day we're riding inland to the heart of the island. Avula is extremely lush, densely forested with tall trees that cover the shallow hills that rise towards the centre. I'm a little taken aback by the size of the trees. I'd forgotten how large they were. Even the great oaks in the King's gardens in Turai are mere saplings in comparison. And without getting too mystical about it, the trees on an Elvish island give the impression that they're more alive than your average tree.

Landing on the island involved less ceremony than I was expecting. A delegation of important Elves, including Kalith's wife, Lady Yestar, was at the quay to greet their guests, but there was not the tedious formality that such an event would have occasioned in Turai. Brief introductions were made and we set off inland. Even Makri's appearance failed to cause a commotion. Kalith presumably had sent word of her arrival, and his subjects, while not looking thrilled at the sight of her, at least didn't make a fuss. Makri greeted Lady Yestar in her flawless Elvish, as genteelly as any lady of the court, if the Elves have a court that is, which I'm not certain about. I know Kalith has some sort of palace in the trees.

I ride beside Makri at the back of the column, far behind Lord Kalith and Prince Dees-Akan. Makri looks around her with interest but I'm too busy thinking about my work to fully appreciate the splendour of the island. I have the tiniest feeling, far away at the very edge of my Investigator's intuition, that something is wrong all around me. Something intangible that I can't put a name to. Whatever it is, it prevents me from gaping at the giant butterflies.

Avula is one of the largest of the Elvish Isles. During the last Orc War it provided many troops and ships for the defence of the west, but as we travel inland it's not exactly obvious where all these Elves live. There are no extensive settlements at ground level. Here and there wooden houses stand secluded in clearings in the forest, but in the main the Elves prefer to construct their houses high up in the trees. These are cunningly crafted so that they appear to be more like natural growths than artificial objects. Even some of the larger collections of these houses, connected by walkways high above our heads, blend in with the environment in a manner that makes it easy to believe that the land is devoid of inhabitants. Only the regular, well-maintained path we travel on betrays the fact that many Elves live in these parts.

Somewhere or other there must be some sort of industry, workshops where the Elves make their own swords, harnesses and other such things, but we see nothing of this. Just trees, treehouses and the occasional Elf looking down with interest at the procession.

We're riding on horses provided by the Elves. Vas tells me that on the far side of the island the land is more open, and their animals are pastured there. We pass several small rivers, each running with bright water that glints in the sunlight.

Lord Kalith's Tree Palace is situated at the centre of the island, the highest point on Avula. The Hesuni Tree is next to the Palace. The important guests are to be quartered nearby. I wonder how Cicerius will manage living in a tree. I notice that the sombre mood of our Elvish hosts has lightened as they find themselves once more in their familiar surroundings, but I still have the feeling that all is not well.

Cicerius is riding beside me, upright in the saddle like a man who once fought in the army. Cicerius never managed to cover himself in glory at war, but he did at least do his duty against the Orcs, unlike most of our present-day Turanian politicians, many of whom bought their way out of military service. I lean over and whisper to him.

"Is it just me or do you feel something wrong here?"

"Wrong? What do you mean?"

"I don't know exactly. I just get the feeling that something is wrong. Shouldn't these Elves in the trees be waving to us or something?"

"They are waving."

"Well maybe they're waving a bit. I still figure they should be happier to see their Lord back. Singing maybe. Don't Elves sing a lot? There's some kind of gloom over this place."

"I don't feel it," says Cicerius.

I always trust my intuition and it's kept me alive for a long time.

We pass through a clearing and view an unusual spectacle. Thirty or so Elves in white cloaks are moving around in unison under the direction of another Elf. He seems to be shouting at them in an exasperated manner.

"The chorus for one of the plays," our Elvish companions inform us.

The irate screaming gets louder.

"The directors of the plays are often given to excesses of emotion."

Passing through another clearing we distinctly hear choral singing, again from a group rehearsing for the festival, and in the distance we catch sight of some jugglers practising. The whole atmosphere becomes more festive. I wonder again if I might solve the case quickly and thereby have some time in which to enjoy myself. Along with Osath the cook, I'm quite looking forward to the juggling competition. Whatever happens, I don't have that long in which to investigate. Elith is due to be tried immediately after the festival, which begins in seven days' time and lasts for three.

Vas-ar-Methet is riding some way in front of us. Several hours into the journey he sends a message back to me that we are close to his brother's abode. The messenger is to take Makri and me there while the procession rides on. The deputation is to receive the full hospitality of Lord Kalith. We aren't.

"Would it be any use telling you not to make a nuisance of yourself?" asks Cicerius as we prepare to go our separate ways.

"You'll hardly notice we're here," I promise.

"Whatever you do," says Cicerius sternly, "don't meddle with anything that is calanith."

"Cheer up, Cicerius," says Makri, appearing beside us. "I'm an expert in Elvish taboos. In fact, I am an Elvish taboo. I'll keep Thraxas out of trouble."

Makri sits well on her horse. When she arrived in Turai she was already a good rider. Makri is good at most things. It's annoying. Since leaving the ship her spirits have improved.

"I'm as happy as an Elf in a tree," she says, laughing,

and then looks thoughtful. "Although I have noticed that the Elves up in the trees don't actually look all that happy. Good choral singing though."

Our guide leads us down a narrow path. For an Elf he seems remarkably dour. My efforts at conversation come to nothing. Apart from learning that his name is Coris-ar-Mithan and he's a cousin of my friend Vas, I learn nothing at all from him.

We don't have to endure each other's company for long. Coris brings us swiftly to another small clearing where three other Elves, two of them elderly, are waiting for us. Coris greets them briefly, bows formally to us and rides off.

"Greeting, friends of Vas-ar-Methet. Welcome to our home."

They introduce themselves to us as Vas's brother, mother, and sister.

"You must be tired after the long journey. We have prepared food and your rooms are waiting. Please follow us."

They head for a tree. Lying flush with the trunk is a ladder that goes upwards for a long way. I look at it doubtfully and turn to Makri.

"How do you like heights?"

"I'm not wild about them."

"Me neither."

We grit our teeth and start to climb. We climb a long way. I try not to look down. As a man who can have difficulty mounting the outside steps to my office, I don't find it the most convenient place for a home. I'm relieved when we reach the top and step on to a platform. The Elvish house stretches over the highest branches of the tree, and over to the next tree. We're on the very outskirts of the large central township of the Elves, and from here to the centre of the island houses are strung over most of the forest, increasing in density as they approach the centre. From here it should be possible to walk all the way to the centre of the island without once touching the ground.

Once we step inside we find a comfortable and welcoming dwelling place. The rooms, though simply constructed, are brightly lit, decorated in warm colours with tapestries and rugs. There are pitchers of water and we are invited to wash and make ourselves comfortable before our meal.

"Nice house," says Makri after they've left us.

I agree. "Pity it isn't on the ground. I'd have a hard time making it up that ladder every day."

It is now late in the afternoon. After eating I'm planning on heading out quickly to investigate.

"I'm going to see Elith. Time to question the suspect and get things moving. I figure if I can clear her name quickly I might be able to get a bit of rest before heading back to Turai. I need a rest, I've been working way too hard recently."

Vas has arranged that his brother will take me to the place where Elith is held and I'm keen to set off as soon as I can. Camith, slightly younger and less distinguished than the healer, is pleased to find I'm eager to get started.

"No one in our family believes that Elith is guilty of this terrible crime."

Leaving Makri to look around, I accompany Camith on the long journey through the walkways over the trees towards the centre of Avula, where Elith is incarcerated. He tells me that she is held in a rarely used prison building at the rear of Lord Kalith's Tree Palace.

"Have you considered a jail break?"

Camith seems shocked by the suggestion. "No. We are presuming that her name will be cleared."

"Don't presume. After all, she might be guilty. I'm planning on knocking a few heads together to find out the truth. But it never hurts to have a back-up plan."

The wooden walkways lead us past more houses. Elves stare as I pass. I'd imagine it's a long time since they've seen anyone with my impressive figure. They're a thin race, the Elves. Even in old age they rarely seem to settle into comfortable obesity. I ask Camith if there are any taverns on Avula. He tells me that there is nothing that would actually qualify as a tavern, but they do brew their own beer and gather in glades to drink it, which doesn't sound too bad. I tell him that I have now run out of beer, and instruct him that I must have some as soon as possible.

We pass over a large clearing, the largest open space I've seen since we reached the island.

"The tournament field," explains my guide. "It is often in use—Lord Kalith likes to keep his Elves well prepared. It is here that the plays will be staged. There will also be a tournament, for the younger Elves. Will you be staying for the whole festival?"

"I'm not sure. Depends how the investigating goes."

"A curious way to make a living," ventures Camith.

"Not in Turai it isn't. Where I live you can't turn round without bumping into something that needs investigating."

"Are you paid well for the service?"

"No," I reply, truthfully. "But I make up for it at the chariot races."

Camith laughs. I like him, he's affable like his brother. He's heard about my triumph over Lord Kalith at the niarit board and has the good grace to tell me that the Avulans cannot remember when their ruler was last defeated at the game, which pleases me immensely.

The evening is cool and pleasant. Walking through the tree tops isn't so bad when I get used to it and the journey takes less time than I anticipated. Camith

comes to a halt, pointing out to me a large wooden
construction visible a short way ahead.

"The Tree Palace," he informs me.

To one side there is a tree so large and impressive
that it has to be the Hesuni Tree. It seems healthy
enough, with plenty of golden foliage. Beside it are two
pools of still water, one large and one small. We walk
over a narrow suspended bridge towards the Palace, but
when we're almost there a commotion breaks out and
several Elves appear at the doorway, talking together in
an agitated manner. When they see us they run up and
start speaking to Camith accusingly. He looks confused,
and turns to me to explain, but I need no explanation.
Elith-ir-Methet has vanished from her prison.

"Escaped?"

The Elvish guards nod. They recognise Camith and
they find it very suspicious that her uncle just happens
to be strolling by at this very moment, but before they
can pursue it further a great wailing breaks out from
the direction of the Hesuni Tree. Camith and the other
Elves are taken aback and peer over the walkway in
an attempt to find out what is happening. Sensing that
his niece may be in trouble Camith starts to run in
the direction of the Palace. I follow him as best I can,
though I have difficulty keeping up. All around Elves
are shouting, torches are being lit and the general
uproar grows ever more furious. Close to the Tree
Palace Camith spots an Elf he recognises on a walkway some way below us and leans over to shout at him,
trying to find out what is happening.

"It's Gulas-ar-Thetos," shouts the Elf. "He's dead.
Murdered beside the tree. Elith-ir-Methet has killed
him."

Camith almost falls off the walkway, such is the shock
that this intelligence gives him. For a while he is incapable of speech and gasps for breath as the outcry

intensifies. The Elves' Tree Priest has been murdered and I don't need to be told that this is the most sensational event ever to happen on Avula.

"Elith!" gasps Camith. "How could she?"

"We don't know that she did," I tell him harshly. "Now, take me to the scene of the crime, and quickly. If I'm going to sort things out I'll need to know a lot of things and I'll need to know them fast."

I give him a push, none too gently. It's enough to get him back into action. We hurry round the outskirts of the Palace and make our way down a ladder to the Hesuni Tree, where already a great many Elves are congregating, and everything is noise and confusion.

I pat my sword, secure at my hip, and take out a small flask of klee I've saved for emergencies. As it burns its way down my throat, it strikes me that for the first time in over a month I'm feeling properly like myself. Thraxas the Investigator. I'll show these Elves a thing or two when it comes to investigating.

Chapter Eight

By the time we reach the ground about fifty Elves are
standing in a circle between the large pool and the
towering Hesuni Tree, and they're making enough noise
to wake Old King Kiben. Camith hangs back but I
barge my way through. Standing forlornly in the centre of the circle is a tall young female Elf I take to
be Elith-ir-Methet. Lying next to her is another Elf,
this one dead, with blood seeping from an ugly wound
in his chest.

Elith is holding a blood-stained knife.

"Elith-ir-Methet has killed the Tree Priest," say the
Elves over and over again, horror and incredulity in
their voices.

Things are looking worse for my client.

The surrounding Elves seem at a loss. No one is
making any moves to drag the culprit away, examine
the body, or do anything really. I stride forward.

"Thraxas," I announce. "Investigator, guest of Lord
Kalith."

I examine the body. The light is fading and I'm not as familiar with deceased Elves as I am with murdered Humans, but I'd say he's only been dead for a matter of minutes.

"Did you do this?" I ask Elith.

She shakes her head. Then she faints. I curse. I was hoping for a little more information. Three tall Elves wearing the nine-starred insignia of Lord Kalith's household arrive on the scene and start to take control. When the crowd apprises them of the facts one of them departs immediately, presumably to inform Kalith of events, while the other two pick up Elith. Her long golden hair trails to the grass as they start to carry her away.

"Where are you taking her?" I demand.

They decline to answer. I follow them. The crowd troops along in our wake and I lose sight of Camith. I notice that one Elf in particular seems to be doing a lot of wailing, something about his poor brother. Before we reach the great wooden ladders that lead up to Kalith's Tree Palace more of his household appear. While their manner holds none of the undisguised hostility that the Civil Guards in Turai would display in similar circumstances, they make it clear that this matter is now in the hands of their Lord and the crowd is not to advance any further.

"Thraxas of Turai," I say imperiously as they bar my way. "Assistant to Deputy Consul Cicerius."

I try to look important. It gets me through. My weight can lend me a certain grandeur. Elith is carried up the ladder and I climb up right behind her.

We ascend a long way, past platforms decorated with carvings of eagles intertwined with ivy and woven with streamers of golden leaves. The trees that support the Palace seem to reach up forever and my limbs are aching by the time we reach the top. As we clamber on to the final platform Kalith is there to greet us.

His attendants place Elith in front of him. She stirs. Lord Kalith glares down at her.

"You have killed Gulas-ar-Thetos, Priest of the Hesuni Tree!"

Elith blinks, and makes no reply. She appears dazed, maybe just from shock, but maybe from something else. Her pupils seem to me to be dilated, though with Elves it's hard to tell, the whole race generally having such big eyes anyway.

"Well, so it is alleged," I say, moving to her side. "But nothing has been proved against her."

The Elf Lord is positively displeased to see me. "Leave my Palace."

"I never desert a client. And shouldn't someone be getting her a healer? She looks as if she could do with some attention."

"What sort of attention did she give my brother?" roars an Elf behind us, and he makes an effort to rush at Elith. His companions restrain him.

I don't like this at all. My client is surrounded by a horde of hostile Elves and the ruler of the island seems in no mood to listen to pleas on her behalf. Simply because Elves have a reputation as just and tolerant, it doesn't mean that Kalith won't decide that the best thing to do with the murderess is to throw her off the highest platform and have done with it. I'm relieved when Vas-ar-Methet arrives. He doesn't do much except stand there looking anguished, but I figure that his daughter is at least less liable to summary justice with him in the picture.

Kalith orders Elith to be taken to a secure place and guarded well. He allows Vas to go with her, to minister to her sickness, then tells his guards to bring him witnesses to the event so that he can have the full story from people who saw what happened. Then he orders me to get out of his sight.

I depart without an argument. I could do with talking to some witnesses myself. I'm about to fortify myself with klee for the journey back down the ladders when I get a mental image of the Elf falling from the rigging, so I put the flask away and make the descent sober.

Back at the Hesuni Tree the crowd is still gathered. A few of them are wearing the white robes that denote their status as actors.

"More evil has befallen us," moans an Elf to her friends, and they moan back in agreement.

I can understand why they're upset. If the most important religious official in the land has to get murdered, you really don't want it to be right at the moment you have a host of foreign guests to impress. No wonder Lord Kalith is furious. That, however, is a problem for the Elves. My problem is gathering information and clearing Elith's name. Unless she turns out to be irredeemably guilty, in which case I've a jail break to plan. For desecrating the Hesuni Tree, Elith was facing banishment. For murder of the Tree Priest, she's facing execution. I will not allow Elith to be convicted of murder. For one thing, I owe her father. For another, Lord Kalith has really started to annoy me.

I introduce myself to a group of Elves and ask them if anyone actually saw Elith sticking the knife into Gulas-ar-Thetos. They don't know. It all happened before they arrived on the scene. The next group gives me a similar reply. Some Elf—no one knows quite who—arrived to find Gulas dead and Elith lying beside him with a knife in her hand.

I'm hindered in my investigations by the activities of the Elves sent by Kalith to gather witnesses, and more than once I'm just about to question someone when he or she is hustled off to the Tree Palace, but at least the attendants don't send me away, or threaten me with arrest. As darkness falls I've learned about as much as I can and I decide it's time to talk to Vas-ar-Methet. I head back towards the Tree Palace but in the gloom I bump into an Elf coming the other way. He raises his head and beneath the hood I see a face I recognise. It's Gorith-ar-Del, and he doesn't look any happier to see me now than he did during the voyage.

"Interfering again?" he demands.

I decline to answer, but as I hurry away I'm struck by the murderous look he had in his eyes. There is an Elf who hasn't been spending much time singing in the trees. There's something about him that doesn't quite add up and I make a mental note to check him out later.

Back at the ladders that lead up to the Tree Palace I have the good fortune to arrive just after Prince Dees-Akan and his entourage. The guards part to let them through and I hurry after as if I'm part of the official party. Making the climb for the second time tonight I develop the strong conviction that it is a mistake to live up in the trees. My limbs wouldn't take too much of this. Prince Dees-Akan catches sight of me.

"Were you invited to the Tree Palace?" he demands.

"Yes, your highness," I lie, and saunter past. The doormen look doubtful. An Elf with drooping shoulders and downcast gaze comes towards us and I march past crying out Vas's name.

"I'm here. Take me to the patient."

I grasp the startled Vas-ar-Methet's arm and steer us through to the first courtyard.

"Where is she?"

"Thraxas, it is all so terrible, I cannot—"

I interrupt him impatiently. "Never mind that just now. Just take me to her. If I don't get to speak to her now I might never get the chance."

Vas nods. Back in the War he wasn't an Elf to hang around dithering when action was needed. He leads me through the courtyard and up another ladder to a higher platform. From there a walkway stretches over most of the length of the Palace. Lord Kalith's attendants are dotted around, but no one tries to get in the healer's way.

"She's being held in a building at the back of the Palace. I can get us close, but I doubt they'll let you in."

"I'll think of something."

We are now high above the Palace, further from the ground than I would wish to be. I look down at the blanket of trees below us, and imagine how easily I would plummet down through them if I lost my footing. We reach the end of the walkway and descend into another courtyard, this one darker and less ornate than those at the front of the building. Vas points to a door in front of which three Elves are stationed, each of them armed. These are the first Elves I've seen on Avula to carry swords openly.

"They are guarding Elith," whispers Vas. "I didn't want to leave her, but Lord Kalith sent word that I was to be dismissed before he came to question her himself."

"Where is he now?"

"Hearing the accounts of those who witnessed the affair. I imagine that he will be here before long. The death of our Tree Priest is a catastrophic event, Thraxas. I will not wish to continue living if my daughter is found to be guilty of his murder."

"Well, don't do anything rash," I tell him. "I'm going in."

The guards challenge me. I speak the one solitary spell I'm carrying with me, the sleep spell. It works well, as it always does. The three guards sink gently to the ground. Vas-ar-Methet gasps in amazement at my action.

"You worked a spell on Lord Kalith's guards?"

"What were you expecting? A few cunning lies? I need to see Elith and I need to see her now."

"But when Kalith—"

I don't stay around to listen to the rest but hurry into the cell, where Elith is sitting on a wooden chair, gazing out of the barred window.

I greet her and introduce myself as a friend and wartime companion of her father.

"Why are you here?"

"Your father hired me to investigate the damage to the Hesuni Tree. He says you're innocent, so I believe him. Now there are a few more things I have to deal with. Fine, I'll deal with them. Tell me everything and make it quick. What happened to the Tree and what's the story of you not remembering anything? How did you escape from prison, and why were you found with the knife right beside the dead Priest?"

Elith is taken aback. Since the ministrations of her father she's looking healthier but, not surprisingly, she's extremely distracted. I look her straight in the eyes and tell her to snap out of it.

"There's no time for rambling, so get to the point. Lord Kalith is on his way here; three of his guards are outside sleeping off a spell, thanks to me, and he's not going to be very pleased about it. So in the brief time we've got I need to know everything. Don't sigh, don't cry and don't stray from the point. Just tell it like it happened."

At this, Elith-ir-Methet manages a weak smile.

"I remember Father speaking of you now," she says.

"You appear in many of his war stories. It was good of you to come. But really, you can do nothing to help me."

"I can. Tell me about the Tree. Did you damage it?"

She shakes her head slowly. "I don't think so. But I might have. I really can't remember. They said I did it."

"Who said?"

"Gulas, the Tree Priest. And his brother Lasas."

Why can't you remember?"

She looks blank and tells me she just can't. Already I'm starting to dislike her as a client.

"What were you doing near the Tree?"

"Just walking. We live nearby."

I'd like to question her plenty more about this, but time is short and there's the murder to consider.

"How did you get out of your cell tonight?"

"I wasn't in a cell. Kalith had merely confined me to a room in the Palace and I gave my word I would not try to leave."

"So why did you change your mind?"

She shrugs. I grow impatient.

"Is this hopeless-Elf-maiden routine the best you can do? You realise how much trouble you're in?"

Elith just sits there: tall, slender, golden-haired and apparently suffering from a severe attack of amnesia. I ask her what happened after she left the Palace.

"I descended to the forest and went to the Hesuni Tree."

"What for?"

"I wanted to see Gulas-ar-Thetos. It was he who was my main accuser in the matter of damaging the Tree."

She stops. Tears start to trickle down her pale face.

"What happened then?"

There's no reply. I change tack. "Your cousin Eos-ar-Methet died on the voyage from Turai to Avula. Were you friendly with him?"

Elith is startled. "No," she says. "Well, yes, I knew him. Why?"

"Because I'm wondering about his death. You know any reason he might have been acting strangely?"

Elith goes quiet, and I'm fairly certain she's hiding something. I ask her again what happened when she left the Palace earlier this evening.

"She killed Gulas, that's what happened," roars a voice as the door flies open and Lord Kalith marches in, flanked by four Elves with swords.

"How dare you interrupt an Investigator in private conference with his client?" I roar back. "Have you no idea of the due process of law on Avula?"

Kalith strides up to me and puts his face near mine, which involves some bending over on his part. His men meanwhile surround me and point their swords in my direction.

"Are you responsible for putting my guards to sleep?" he demands.

"Guards? I didn't see any guards. Just wide open space and a comfy cell at the end. Now would you mind giving me a little time alone with my client? I really must insist—"

The attendants make to grab me. Not wishing to be grabbed, I step back quickly and prepare to defend myself. Elith prevents an ugly scene by laying her hand on my arm.

"Stop," she says, quite softly. "I appreciate your trying to help me, Thraxas, but you can do nothing for me. Lord Kalith is right. I did kill Gulas-ar-Thetos."

"Disregard that statement," I say quickly. "The woman is under stress and doesn't know what's she's saying."

"She knows very well what she is saying," retorts Kalith. "She murdered our Priest. Three Elves witnessed the event. At this moment they are giving sworn statements to my scribes."

It's a bad turn of events but, as people have been known to say in Twelve Seas, Thraxas never abandons a client.

"Witnesses have been known to make mistakes," I point out.

Kalith smiles, which surprises me. He's regained his composure.

"Thraxas, I could almost like you, were you not such a buffoon. One certainly has to admire your persistence. You enter my Palace without an invitation, you sneak over to this cell and you put three of my guards to sleep with a spell. You question Elith-ir-Methet against my express wishes. Then, despite the fact that she admits the crime, and that there are independent witnesses to testify that she is guilty, you persist in standing here blustering about client–Investigator privileges. You have never thought me sympathetic to your case, but believe me, if my trusted healer Vas-ar-Methet had not spoken so highly of the character you showed during the Orc Wars, I would never have even allowed you on board my ship. And he was right, in some ways at least. He told me that you were disinclined to give up on anything you started. An admirable trait in time of war, but not so now. Elith is guilty. Nothing you can do will change that fact. And you must now leave it to me to dispense justice, as is my right and duty."

I protest, but he holds up his hand, forbidding further speech, and gestures to his guards. "Enough, Thraxas. These Elves will escort you from the Palace. No doubt we will meet again at the festival."

And that, for the moment, is that. The four armed Elves escort me out of the cell, along the courtyard, back up to the high walkways, and out of the Palace.

Once back on the ground, I turn towards the Hesuni Tree, having no intention of going home just yet. The large clearing is now empty of life. Light from the moons reflects from the still water of the twin pools and the Hesuni Tree stands majestically at the far end of the water. I decide to take a look at the Tree, and march over.

To me it looks like any other large tree. I can't pick up any traces of its spiritual power, but that's only to be expected, me being Human rather than Elf, and not very spiritual. I can't sense any sign of sorcery in the air either. I can't learn anything, in fact. Studying the grass in the area where Gulas lay dying reveals nothing except that a lot of Elves have since walked all over it.

"Are you looking for something that will save Elith?"

It can be annoying the way these Elves approach without making a sound. I whirl round and lift my staff, illuminating an Elf by the Tree.

"Lasas-ar-Thetos?"

He bows slightly. I wonder at him being here on his own. As his brother has just been murdered, I might have expected him to be comforting the family, or mourning, or something.

"I must assume my new position and minister to the tree," he says, as if in answer to my thoughts.

"Why did Elith kill your brother?"

"She is insane. We knew it from the moment she damaged the Tree."

"Is that the only reason?"

"I believe so. Now, please, leave me. I must communicate with the Tree."

"Yeah, I guess the Tree must be pretty upset, with all this going on. Do you know Gorith-ar-Del?"

Lasas scowls at me, frustrated by my persistence.

"No," he replies. "I do not."

It seems to me that Lasas is lying. I'm about to question him further when he starts chanting softly, his eyes closed, his head swaying gently from side to side.

Torchlight and voices from the other side of the clearing announce the arrival of some Elves from the Palace. I depart. It feels like a long walk back to Camith's house. I climb wearily up to my temporary dwelling and find Makri sitting in my room, studying a scroll.

"How's the case going?" she asks.

"Getting difficult," I confess. "Elith-ir-Methet has just been accused of murdering the Tree Priest."

I haul my boots off. "And I still can't find any beer. I think the Elves are hiding it from me out of spite."

Chapter Nine

———◆———

Vas-ar-Methet's brother has treated Makri and me hospitably from the moment we arrived and we're grateful for this. We can eat our meals with Camith's family or on our own if we prefer, and they make no attempts to hinder us in our coming and leaving. If they think it is strange or disreputable to have someone with Orc blood under their roof, they don't show it. Makri tells me that her faith in Elfkind is partially revived.

"After that voyage, I thought I was going to hate them all. But Vas-ar-Methet's relatives are nice. When you were out they asked if there was anything they could bring me and then Camith invited me up to the top of the tree to look at the stars."

Elves are partial to the night, rising late in the day and staying up to enjoy the pleasures of the midnight sky. Well, most of them. Perhaps farming Elves have to rise early to plant crops. I ask Makri about this, but she doesn't know.

"At the Guild College we only learn Elvish myths, stories, histories of their wars and things like that. The subject of Elves having to get up early to plant crops or milk cows never came up. Strange really, because only last term Professor Azulius was stressing how important the average citizen was in the history of the city-state. "History is not all Kings, Queens and battles," as he likes to say. Do you think there are low-class Elves who clean the sewers at the Tree Palace?"

"I expect so. They can't all be composing epic poems and gazing at the stars. You know, I've been close to losing my faith in Elfkind as well. I appreciate that I'm causing them difficulties, but right from the first day of the voyage they've been about as friendly as a two-fingered troll. Much less welcoming than my hosts on my last visit to the islands."

"That was a long time ago," Makri points out. "Maybe they became more suspicious of strangers after the last War. Do you know the whole island is suffering from bad dreams?"

"Really? Everyone?"

"Apparently," says Makri. "Camith certainly is. I don't think the Elves like to talk about it though. Discussing illness with strangers is calanith."

"Is it only the Avulans or are their guests from the other islands suffering as well?"

Makri doesn't know. She's hoping the other Elves are in good health because she's looking forward to the theatrical performances. I remain unimpressed at the prospect.

"Three versions of the tale of Queen Leeuven. Couldn't they come up with something else?"

"Of course not. The plays at the festival are always about Queen Leeuven. That's the point."

"It sounds dull to me."

"Well, they do choose different episodes from the

saga. But it's all quite formal, you know. The stories are already well known to the audience; it's the way they are told that makes all the difference. At the last festival the Venian Elves presented such a tragic account of Queen Leeuven accidentally killing her brother that the entire audience was moved to bitter tears. They won the prize. The Avulans are keen to take it this time."

I see that Makri has wasted no time in learning more about the culture of the island. I ask her if she knows anything about the juggling competition. She informs me that it's part of the light entertainment put on before the plays, to get the crowd in a festive mood.

"Is there a favourite to win? I might be able to get a bet down."

"Do you have to bet on everything?"

"Yes."

"I don't think they have bookmakers on Avula," says Makri.

"Don't you believe it. Just because the festival features high-class tragedy doesn't mean there isn't someone running a low-class gambling operation somewhere. If you can get a hot tip for the juggling competition, I've no doubt I can place some money on it."

With her mind occupied by the theatre, Makri has little enthusiasm for juggling, but she does express an interest in the tournament. She's sorry that it is only for the under-fifteens and would have preferred to see the true Elvish warriors battling it out, but considers that any fighting is better than none.

"I've never seen a tournament," she says.

She is disappointed when I inform her of the probable nature of the event.

"It's only practice really. Nothing too vicious. They use wooden swords and there are restrictions on what you can do. No stamping on your opponent's groin for instance, and no attacks to the eyes."

"No groin-stamping? No attacks to the eyes? What's the point of that?"

"They're all under fifteen, Makri. The Elves don't want to maim their kids, just give them a little practice in sword play. And don't tell me that when you were fifteen you were already killing dragons. You mentioned that already. But being a gladiator is not the same thing as entering a civilised tournament."

Makri is still dissatisfied. "Sounds like a waste of time to me."

I'm eating my dinner from a tray. Obviously realising that I am a man of healthy appetites, my hosts have sent me a great amount of food. It's not quite the gargantuan meal I'd take in back at the Avenging Axe after a hard day's investigating, but it comes close. As I drink the last of the bottle of wine they sent along with it I feel a little more in tune with the world.

"Did Camith have any idea why everyone was having bad dreams?"

"Not exactly. He thought it might have something to do with the damage to the Hesuni Tree. The Avulans are all connected to it in some way."

"Isn't it healthy again? It looked okay to me."

Makri nods. The tree healers have brought it back to full health. Something is still causing the Elves to have nightmares, though, which is interesting.

"So what now? If Elith did kill the priest, what can you do? Are you serious about breaking her out of jail?"

"Maybe. The way these Elves run things it would be as easy as bribing a Senator. Her last cell didn't even have any bars on the window. Elith just gave her word she wouldn't escape."

I pause. It is very, very unusual for an Elf to break her word. It's something they just don't do. It's calanith.

Vas would rather die than disgrace himself in such a way. It strikes me that there must have been some over-whelmingly powerful reason for Elith-ir-Methet to leave the Palace.

"But I'm not convinced she's guilty. I don't like the way she can't remember anything about damage to the tree. It means she's either lying or under pressure from someone. Or else her memory has been affected by sorcery or drugs. I'm not happy about her murder confession either. She was acting very strangely the whole time I was with her. The first time I saw her she fainted right away and you know, Elvish women don't faint a lot. They're tougher than that. I've seen them fighting Orcs. When I was asking her questions I swear her mind was somewhere else. There was a very strange look in her eyes."

"What kind of look?"

I can't exactly describe it. "Something like a person on dwa."

Makri is dubious. "You said dwa hadn't reached the Elvish Isles."

"It hasn't. Anyway, it doesn't affect them the same way it affects Humans. I've seen the occasional deca-dent Elf in Turai who's taken it, but they never get the same hit off the drug as a Human. Nothing like enough to be so out of it they'd forget about committing some major crime. I'll go and see Kalith's Sorcerer, Jir-ar-Eth, and see if he might have picked up any lingering traces of magic. Lord Kalith has probably had him examine Elith by now, though if he's found anything I doubt he'll be eager to tell me. Things would be a lot easier if these damned Elves would cooperate. Still, I knew it was going to be tough."

I consider the situation. Things look bad for Elith-ir-Methet, but things have looked tough for my cli-ents before. It's not as if anyone has provided a

motive for the killing, and I can't see why a respectable Elf would just up and kill the Tree Priest for
no reason. As for the witnesses, I'm keeping an open
mind. There are plenty of reasons why witnesses
might get things wrong. Like wanting to please an Elf
Lord for instance. I'll start nosing around the Hesuni
Tree and see who else might have had something
against Gulas-ar-Thetos. And I'll ask a few questions
about Gorith. I'm suspicious of him, if only because
he seemed so hostile towards me.

Makri stretches. "Camith gave me this scroll; it's all
about the local plants. He used to learn from it when
he was at school. Elves go to school in trees, which
is no real surprise. Tomorrow I'm going to look around
at the local plant life and then see what the Elves have
in the way of swords, knives and axes. You think they
might give me some free stuff, seeing as I'm their
guest? Thank God that spineless brat Isuas isn't here
to bother me any more."

"Eh . . . hello," says the spineless brat, entering the
room timidly. She's wearing a green floppy hat that
comes to a point at the end, rather like a pixie might
wear in a children's story. It makes her look even
younger than usual. As Isuas walks towards Makri she
catches her foot in a rug and plummets to the floor.
It's quite a pathetic sight, but Makri looks on stonily
as I help the youngster up. She rubs her head and tries
not to cry.

"I thought I'd see if you were all right," she says,
fumbling with her hat.

"I was a minute ago," says Makri sharply.

I'm still of the opinion that being friends with
Kalith's daughter would be no bad thing, so I cover
up for Makri's rudeness by asking Isuas if she's pleased
to be home.

"Feel good to be back on dry land?"

Isuas shrugs. "Okay. But everyone's busy at the Palace."

I have the impression that everyone being too busy for Isuas might not be that uncommon.

"Will you save Elith even though she killed Gulas?"

"I will. And I'm not convinced she did kill him."

"I hope not," says the young Elf. "I like Elith."

"Will you teach me more fighting?" she says to Makri, unexpectedly.

"No," replies Makri. "I'm busy."

"Please," says Isuas. "It's important."

Makri sticks her nose in her scroll.

"Why is it important?" I enquire.

"So I can fight in the junior tournament."

Makri emerges from her scroll to have a good laugh. "The junior tournament? With wooden swords?"

"Yes. For all the Elves under fifteen. My oldest brother won it six years ago. My next oldest brother won it the year after that. And my next oldest brother won it the year—"

"We get the picture," says Makri. "And now you want to enter but you can't because you're too puny and haven't a chance of making it past the first round even if your father lets you enter, which no doubt he wouldn't. You being so puny. And clumsy."

Isuas stares at the floor. Makri seems to have summed it up neatly enough.

"They never let me do anything," Isuas mumbles.

"Who can blame them?" says Makri.

"Please," wails Isuas. "I want to enter the tournament."

Makri again finds something to interest her in her scroll. I frown. I wish she didn't display her dislike of the child quite so openly.

"What do your parents say about you entering the lists?"

"My father refuses to listen."

"Well, perhaps we could have a word with your mother," I suggest. "If Lady Yestar had no objections, I'm sure Makri could continue your lessons."

Isuas's face lights up. She is of course too young to realise the cunning way in which I have just guaranteed our entrance to the Tree Palace as an aid to investigating. Unfortunately Makri isn't. She grunts at me.

"Forget it, Thraxas. I'm not getting stuck with the kid just so as you can wander about asking questions."

"Makri will be delighted to help," I say. "Would tomorrow in the afternoon be a good time to talk to Lady Yestar?"

Isuas nods, and manages to raise a smile. "I'll have the servants prepare a meal."

"Excellent, Isuas. Do you think they could rustle me up some beer?"

"Beer? I don't think we have that at the Tree Palace. But maybe we could send out for some. I know that Mother will be pleased to meet you."

I doubt that very much.

"I've practised what you showed me every day," says Isuas to Makri before she departs.

Makri places her scroll on a table and looks at me rather wryly.

"Yes, very clever, Thraxas. Now you can enter the Palace as a guest of the Royal Family and make a nuisance of yourself to your heart's content. Provided you don't just concentrate on emptying the island of beer, that is. But I'm not playing along. I refuse to teach that kid any more. She's a hopeless student. Anyway, I don't like her. It was all I could do not to knock her head off on the ship. I only went along with it because I was bored. There's plenty of other things I want to do on Avula rather than play nursemaid to the Royal Family's unwanted runt."

"I still don't see why you dislike her so much, Makri. She's not that bad."

"I can't stand the way she's always bursting into tears. When I was her age tears were punishable by immediate execution. And she keeps falling over. It's infuriating. And she's so weedy. Also, it gives me the creeps the way she keeps getting more friendly the more I insult her. It's not natural. What she needs is a good beating."

"Are you sure she doesn't remind you of yourself at her age?"

"What do you mean?" demands Makri. "I was never like that."

"So you say. But the way you take against her gives me the strong impression that at one time in your life you were an extremely frightened and weak child. And you don't like being reminded of it."

"Nonsense," says Makri, crossly. "Stop trying to be analytical, Thraxas, you're really bad at it."

I shrug. "Anyway, if you were teaching her how to fight, wouldn't that give you some reason for handing out a beating? It would certainly toughen her up."

"I've a reputation to protect," objects Makri. "You think I want to send her out to fight as my pupil and have all these Elves laugh at her? Think how bad it would make me look. I'm not going to be able to teach her enough in six days to prevent her from being a laughing stock."

"Don't forget, she's been practising every day. She might have improved. Anyway, when it comes right down to it, Lord Kalith and Lady Yestar aren't going to let her enter the tournament. So just pretend you're willing. It'll get me a day or two at the Palace. After the way I outraged Lord Kalith by putting his guards to sleep, I can't see any other way I'll get back in."

The most I can persuade Makri to do is to turn up with me there tomorrow.

"If I end up having to teach her, there's going to be trouble," Makri warns me.

"You won't," I assure her. "Kalith wouldn't let Isuas within a mile of any fighting. Okay, you're laughing about using wooden swords, but these things can still be tough. There were junior tournaments in Turai when I was young. Not big affairs, like they have for Senators' sons of course, just small affairs for the offspring of the local workers. Prepared us for life in the army. One day I went up against the son of the blacksmith and he broke my arm with a wooden axe. My father was furious. Said I'd let the family down. He made me go back out and fight with my arm in a sling."

"What happened?"

"I kicked the blacksmith's son in the groin and then stepped on his face. Which was going a bit far even by the relaxed standards of the tournament. I was disqualified. But my father was pleased with me."

"Quite right," says Makri. "I don't see why they disqualified you. You have to do whatever is necessary."

Makri tells me some stories of her early fighting experiences, most of which involve inflicting terrible damage on Orcish opponents, all much older and heavier than her. She cheers up. Talking about fighting always puts Makri in a good mood. It must be the Orcish blood. Keeps her savage, even when studying botany.

Chapter Ten

I'm planning to make an early start next day. As the Elves rise late I should be able to examine the scene of the crime without interruption. Unfortunately, after securing another bottle of wine from Camith, I find myself swapping war stories with him late into the night and by the time I wake the sun is overhead and the morning is gone.

"I did not wish to disturb you," says Camith as I struggle through for a late breakfast. "I know that Turanians are conscientious about their morning prayers."

"Yes, it often holds me back," I admit, and settle down to a loaf or two, washed down with the juice of some Avulan fruit I can't put a name to.

I ask Camith if he knows Gorith-ar-Del.

"I know of him. I don't believe we have ever spoken. He's a maker of longbows and lives on the west of the island, where the trees are suitable for his craft."

"Can you think of any reason why he might be skulking round the Hesuni Tree, looking unfriendly?"

Camith can't. He's never heard anything disreputable about Gorith although he is aware of the trouble his relatives found themselves in when they visited Turai.

"I've been wondering about this Hesuni Tree, Camith. Just supposing it wasn't Elith who damaged it, and also supposing it wasn't just some random act of vandalism, which seems unlikely, what motive might any other Elf have for doing it? I mean, who could gain from it?"

"No one."

"Are you sure? Makri tells me that not only are all the Avulans connected to it in some way, but the Tree Priests can actually communicate with it."

"In a way," agrees Camith. "Though the communication is not what you would have with another Elf. More a sense of the life around the Tree, I believe."

"What if something dubious was going on on Avula? Might the Tree be able to tell the Tree Priests about it?"

This makes Camith smile. "I do not think so. It's not that sort of communication." He looks serious. "Yet there is a relationship. Perhaps the Tree Priest might learn some things that were beyond the ken of other Elves."

"Which might be motive for someone to try and kill it. Bumping off a witness, so to speak."

Makri is sceptical. "You can't get a witness statement from a Hesuni Tree, Thraxas. You're grasping at straws here."

"Okay, I'm grasping at straws. But last summer I found myself in conversation with dolphins in Turai, so I'm keeping an open mind about a talking tree. What about this other branch of the family I heard about? The rival claimants to the position of Tree Priest?"

This makes Camith uncomfortable. "There is a rival claimant, Hith-ar-Key. The dispute over the succession goes back some centuries. I believe that their claim is weak but it is not something that would be much discussed, apart from in the Council of Elders."

"Why not?"

"Any dispute over the Priesthood is calanith to everyone except the Elders and the priestly families. It is up to them to sort it out and no other Elf would interfere or even refer to the matter."

I'm already getting the impression that far too many things on Avula are calanith, which might turn out to be awkward, given the Deputy Consul's strict admonition not to rub up against any Elvish taboos the wrong way. I let the subject drop.

Makri is eager to set off.

"I haven't seen the Tree Palace yet. Look, I painted my toenails again."

"Lady Yestar will be thrilled. Are you planning on wearing that tunic?"

"What's wrong with it?"

"The same as with everything else you wear. It doesn't cover enough of you. Haven't you noticed that the Elf women cover their legs? Couldn't you borrow some demure Elf clothes?"

"I think not," says Makri, sagely. "As the philosopher Samanatius says, 'Never try to pretend to be someone else.' "

"I don't trust Samanatius."

"Why not? You've never heard him speak."

"He teaches for free, doesn't he? If he was any good he'd charge admission."

Makri shakes her head. "Thraxas, you take ignorance to new depths. Anyway, Yestar would probably be disappointed if I turned up looking like an Elf. Isuas will have told her what a Barbarian I am."

As if to emphasise the point, Makri has her twin swords strapped to her back. I instruct her not to unsheathe the Orcish blade under any circumstances. The dark metal is instantly recognisable and waving an Orcish weapon around is liable to get us run off the island.

Camith sees us off. "You notice how he was yawning all through breakfast?" I ask Makri.

"Still bored by your war stories, no doubt."

"Camith was not bored by my war stories. Rather, he was honoured to have such a distinguished soldier under his roof. If we hadn't stood firm in Turai, there would have been no stopping the Orcs. They'd have been down here with the war ships, dragons at the ready. The Elvish Isles might well have fallen. Really, when you think about it, these Elves owe me for protecting them."

"I thought the Elves came to your rescue?"

"They helped. I expect we'd have managed anyway. But the point I was trying to make before you started interrupting was that Camith was yawning having presumably had a bad night's sleep. More nightmares, I imagine. So when we get in the vicinity of the Hesuni Tree, keep a look-out for anything that might be affecting it enough to make it start sending out bad feelings to the Elves."

"Like what?"

"I've no idea. Just look. You're well versed in Elvish lore, you might spot something I'd miss."

We set off across the walkways towards the Palace. Even at this elevation the vegetation is dense, with vines tangled over the tops of the trees. There are few places where the ground is visible and such small clearings as we cross are covered with flowering bushes. There are plenty of butterflies and small birds that make a lot of noise, and occasionally a monkey swings over to examine us before disappearing back into the forest. Makri studies them with interest but I've never been fond of monkeys.

Above our heads the sky is blue. Although this is the winter season on Avula it's still warm and pleasant, in contrast to the icy misery of Turai, far away to the north.

"Poor Gurd, he'll be as cold as a frozen pixie right now. Of course as a northern Barbarian he doesn't feel it as much as a civilised man like myself."

We pass over the tournament field. Some young Elves are practising for the big event. Camith had laughed when we mentioned that Isuas had asked Makri for fighting lessons. Isuas is not unpopular among the Avulans, but her lack of physical prowess is something of a standing joke among them.

"But Kalith has four strong sons and three hearty daughters," Camith pointed out. "No one minds that his eighth child is a weakling. I believe that Lady Yestar encourages him to take her on his voyages in an effort to harden her, but from what I saw of her yesterday it has had little effect."

Along the way we pass small settlements. When an Elvish child runs indoors in a panic at the sight of Makri, she professes that's she's starting to feel depressed again.

"Now I think about it, it might not be so great at the Tree Palace. Full of high-class Elves making comments about my toenails, I expect."

"Well, you would insist on painting them."

"I need some fortifying," she announces. "You bring any thazis out with you?"

"Thazis? This is the Elvish Isles. A paradise on earth and a drug-free environment."

"I know. So did you bring any?"

"What do you need it for? Can't you just enjoy the clean air?"

"It's wonderful. So? You bring any thazis?"

"Of course. You expect me to wander about a strange island without any thazis? Hell, who knows when I might next get a beer."

I pass Makri a thazis stick and she lights it with a satisfied sigh. I do the same. I don't know if this mild narcotic is illegal on Avula but I doubt Lord Kalith would be pleased to learn we'd been using it on his island. We finish it off on a lonely stretch of walkway. The sound of choral singing floats past us pleasantly. Entrants to the festival are rehearsing anywhere they can find space.

"Now I'm relaxed," says Makri.

Eight masked Elves carrying long vicious spears appear round the corner and advance towards us menacingly.

"Damn it," says Makri. "Why did you make me smoke that thing?"

I can't believe that we are about to be attacked right here in the middle of Avula.

"They must be practising for the tournament."

"They don't look like they're under fifteen."

The walkway is wide enough for four. The eight Elves are drawn up in two ranks, in battle formation. Eight spears point towards us, leaving no way through. They break into a run. You can't fight eight Elves with spears in a confined space like this, certainly not without a hefty shield to cover yourself.

"Got any spells?" says Makri, unsheathing her twin blades.

"Didn't think to load any in."

"Can't you just remember one?"

Unfortunately it doesn't work like that. Once you use a spell it's gone from your mind. To use it again you have to reread it from your grimoire. We've no time for further discussion. They're almost upon us. Even against such odds Makri would normally refuse to retreat. Probably she'd try and outflank them. On the narrow walkway, there's no way to do that. When the spears are only a few feet away Makri and I sheathe our swords simultaneously and leap into the trees. I offer up a prayer for a sturdy branch to hold on to, a prayer that unfortunately seems to go unanswered as I plunge down through the branches. I grab frantically at everything I can reach but nothing will support my weight and I fall a long way without making contact with anything firm enough to halt my descent. Eventually I thud heavily into a sturdy branch, only ten feet or so from the ground. I'm severely winded and badly scratched, but otherwise undamaged.

There are crashing noises above me, and some swearing. Makri found a firm handhold further up and is now swinging herself down to my level. We drop to the ground and draw our weapons, waiting for our assailants to come after us. There's no sign of them.

"Let's go," I say, and we move off, but moving off in the dense undergrowth is difficult. Makri snarls as she cuts her way through the vegetation. Fleeing from an opponent always puts her in a bad mood.

"Don't worry. I figure you'll get a chance to meet them again."

"Who were they?"

Neither of us has any idea. Eight masked Elves, all silent, with no identifying marks.

After a long period of hacking our way through the thick plant life, hunting unsuccessfully for a path, Makri rounds on me with a savage look in her eyes.

"Give me more thazis," she demands.

"Not really what we need right now, is it, Makri?"

"Just give me the damned thazis," she snarls.

"Hey, okay, don't get crazy about it. I know you hate running from opponents, it's not my fault they had us outweaponed in a narrow place."

Makri's anger suddenly leaves her and she sits down heavily.

"Now I'm depressed. In fact I'm as miserable as a Niojan whore. Damn these mood swings."

I ask her what is going on.

"It's a month since we left Turai," she replies.

"So?"

"So it's my period again. Any complaints?"

I sigh. "No. None. But try not to bleed over the Tree Palace. Kalith will be furious if that happens."

"To hell with Kalith," says Makri, lighting up her thazis stick. "Of course I don't have anything with me, seeing as I didn't get a chance to pack before I leaped into the ocean. Maybe Lady Yestar can lend me a towel or something."

By this time I'm in need of a little relaxation myself. I smoke another thazis stick and consider the situation. There has to be a path around here somewhere. There's nothing for it but to keep chopping our way through till we find one. I'm not certain if the Avulan forest contains any dangerous predators. It certainly contains a lot of insects, several of which seem to have decided that nothing tastes better than Thraxas the Investigator.

"If this blunts my blades someone is going to pay dearly," states Makri. "I hate this. My legs are getting scratched. Why didn't you tell me to wear something more suitable? You want to go in front for a while, I'm sure I'm doing all the work here. Put some effort into it, Thraxas, we're going to be here all day at this rate."

It's exhausting work and I am soon dripping with sweat. Eventually we break through into a small clearing. I slump heavily to the ground.

"To hell with this."

"Give me another thazis stick," says Makri.

I was planning to ration my thazis carefully, but the situation seems to call for it so we light up some more, smoke it, then set off again. We're heading in the general direction of the Palace. At least I hope we are. I'm trying to navigate by the sun but the sun is rarely visible through the trees. Makri's mood continues to alternate between anger and depression. I'm fairly furious myself.

"Damned spearmen. If I'd known this was going to happen I'd never have jumped."

"We should have stayed and fought them. I'll kill them when I get my hands on them. Hell, I just got stung."

After what feels like several hours of hacking, chopping, cursing and complaining, we finally find a clearing in which a ladder ascends to a walkway above.

"Thank God for that."

We climb. When we finally make the top I sit down exhausted. Makri has drawn her swords, eager for another sight of the spear carriers, but the walkway is empty. She sheaths her weapons angrily.

"I'm in a really bad mood," she says.

I pass her a thazis stick. We smoke them and walk on.

"Where are we?"

"No idea. Look, there's an Elf sitting in that tree."

We shout to the Elf, asking which way the Palace is. He points, and we head in that direction.

"I'm in no mood to talk to Lady Yestar," Makri says. "Better give me another thazis stick, mellow me a little."

I figure this is a good idea. No point in being flustered when we arrive. We light two more thazis sticks and smoke them as we walk. Wherever we are, it seems to be a sparsely populated part of the island, and we pass no further Elves.

"I hate this stupid forest," says Makri.

I pass her another thazis stick. We walk on.

"Look. Elf houses. Don't you think they look sort of funny?"

Makri giggles. "Houses in trees."

It does seem quite funny, now she mentions it.

"We better have some more thazis before we hit the Palace. Don't want to arrive there in a bad mood, what with me menstruating and everything."

"Absolutely," I agree, and light us up a stick each. I remember my flask.

"Some klee?"

"Thank you," says Makri.

The walkway brings us into the centre of the island, ending in a long ladder down to the central clearing. The Tree Palace is visible on the other side. Elves stare at us as we pass. We greet them warmly.

Once we reach the clearing Makri halts, looking thoughtful.

"You say thazis isn't used among the Elves? You think they might not like it? We'd better smoke some behind this tree, before we get to the Palace."

This sounds like a good idea.

"You are good at having good ideas," I tell Makri.

"I know. I think about things a lot," replies Makri, inhaling the thazis smoke. "Important things."

"I think about important things too."

"It's good to think about important things."

After all the thazis my mouth tastes funny. I take some klee to clear away the taste and pass the flask to Makri. She coughs as it burns her throat. We sit under the tree and gaze at the beautiful blue sky for a while. Butterflies flutter around our heads.

"I never realised how beautiful butterflies are," says Makri.

"Neither did I. Aren't they pretty?"

We watch them for a long time. A few clouds drift across the sky.

"Where were we going?" asks Makri, eventually.

I think about this.

"The Palace."

"Right. What for?"

"You know. Just to see it. Talk to the Elves."

Makri blinks. "Right."

We sit under the sun.

"Should we go?" says Makri, after a while.

"Go where?"

"The Palace."

"If you like."

Our discussion is interrupted by a furious debate. A large group of white-robed Elves appears out of the forest, all talking heatedly at once.

"We cannot omit the scene where King Vendris butchers his children," says one of the actors, angrily. "It traditionally appears after the Tree-burning scene . . ."

"Then it is time for a change," counters a grey-haired Elf, whom, from the way he seems to be taking the brunt of the anger, I take to be the director.

"And who are you to change the telling of the ancient tale of Queen Leeuven?" demands an actress, possibly Queen Leeuven herself, from the gold tiara in her hair.

"I am the man appointed by Lord Kalith to put on the play," retorts the grey-haired Elf.

"A terrible mistake!" cry several of the actors, with feeling.

"Just do as I tell you if you want that prize . . ."

The group carries on across the clearing, finally disappearing back into the forest, still arguing.

We stare at them as they go.

"You know, Makri, I kind of thought that traditional Elvish actors would be more dignified. That Elf with the tiara reminded me of a chorus girl I once knew.

I had to help her flee from Turai after she burned down the theatre."

We lapse back into silence.

"I haven't had any thazis since we landed on Avula," says Makri. "Did you bring any?"

"I think so," I reply, hunting around in my bag.

We saunter towards the Palace, thazis in hand. More Elves walk by. They stare at us, but say nothing. When we're walking between the two pools by the Hesuni Tree Makri stops to admire the view.

"I'm thirsty," she says, and kneels down to drink.

"Me too. You know, I think that thazis might have affected me a little."

Makri says she feels fine. I figure I'll be fine too after I've had some more water. I almost imagine that someone is shouting at us, but it's only a fleeting impression. Makri bends down to splash water over her face and I do the same. It's cool and refreshing. I drink some more, and feel the intoxication passing from my body. I realise that someone is indeed shouting at me. It's an Elf I recognise, looking angry.

"Don't you know it's forbidden to drink from the sacred pools that feed the Hesuni Tree?" he cries.

"Sorry," I say.

"No one mentioned it," adds Makri.

Our Elvish inquisitor looks at us with disgust. It's Lasas, brother of the murdered Tree Priest.

"Pray you are pure of body and spirit, both of you. Else be very wary of the effects of the sacred water."

Sensing that nothing I can say is going to pacify Lasas, I apologise again and make off briskly for the ladders that lead up to the Tree Palace.

"Another social blunder. How were we meant to know they were sacred pools? They should put a sign on them or something."

I'm expecting difficulty with the guards at the ladders, but they wave us up almost affably.

"Lady Yestar is expecting you."

We start to climb.

"What do you think that Elf meant by "be very wary of the effects of the sacred water"?" says Makri.

"Who knows? Just trying to scare us, I expect. I mean, it can hardly be poisonous as it's feeding the Hesuni Tree."

"Hesuni," says Makri. "That's a funny name."

She giggles. I realise that the thazis has not entirely worn off and make a supreme effort to concentrate as we reach the platform on which stand the great wooden doors to the Palace. Again we gain entry without difficulty.

"You have to hand it to Isuas," I say. "Having her put in a good word for us certainly makes things easier."

"Absolutely," agrees Makri. "She's a fine kid. I always did like her."

We pass through several well-lit rooms and corridors. The Tree Palace, while larger than the other Elvish dwellings on the island, is far smaller than the sort of palaces built for Human Kings and gives the impression of comfort rather than luxury. A pleasant aroma permeates the whole building, either from incense or natural fragrances in the wood. We're shown into a reception room, which again is far smaller than an equivalent room at the Imperial Palace in Turai, but warm and welcoming, with a tapestry on the wall depicting some deer drinking from a pool.

"Lady Yestar will be here presently," says the attendant.

"Can you get me a beer?" I ask, hopefully.

The attendant looks doubtful. "I don't think we have any beer in the palace."

At that moment Lady Yestar enters the room. A

small silver tiara is the only mark of rank she wears. Isuas is hanging on to the side of her dress. When she sees Makri the child shouts with glee and tugs at her mother's dress in her eagerness to introduce her.

"This is Makri," she cries. "She killed a dragon when she was a gladiator slave and she once fought eight Trolls at once and then she slaughtered everyone and escaped and went to Turai and now when Thraxas is out investigating she kills people as well. And she let me point her sword. She's got an Orcish sword! She got it when she slaughtered everyone. She's been teaching me how to fight. She was the champion gladiator!"

At this introduction Lady Yestar surprises me by bursting out laughing. It's the first time I've seen an Elf laugh since the start of this affair. I'd almost forgotten they were capable of it.

Chapter Eleven

Lady Yestar is not at all as I had anticipated. As she is the wife of Lord Kalith and a very aristocratic Elf in her own right, I had expected her to be cool and aloof, distant in that particular way only an Elf with a long lineage can be. Some of the great Elvish families can trace their ancestry back as far as the Great Flood, an event that, though only mythical to the Human nations, is historical to the Elves.

Yestar certainly looks the part; she's tall, pale-skinned and tending towards the ethereal. At first sight she gives the impression of being an Elf to whom the affairs of a Turanian Investigator will be well below her notice. In this I am mistaken. She turns out to be a friendly, cheerful, intelligent Elf who greets us warmly while laughing at the enthusiastic antics of her daughter. I notice that she wears eye make-up, which is rare among the Avulans.

Isuas herself seems transformed in the presence of her mother. She still trips over rugs but her shyness largely disappears and she no longer seems like the hopelessly inadequate child of a very busy and important family.

Lady Yestar rises further in my estimation when, in reply to my polite question about the availability of beer on Avula, she informs me that, while it is generally not drunk in the Palace and other similarly elegant establishments, it is brewed and enjoyed by many of the common Elves.

"I could ask my attendants where you might meet with other Elves who partake of it."

By this time I've shaken off the effects of the thazis binge but I'm not so sure that Makri has. I'm surprised to see her patting Isuas affably on the head and admiring her floppy green hat.

"Would you like it?" enquires Isuas.

Makri would, and accepts it with glee.

"Bezin hat," she says, cramming it over her head, where it looks ridiculous.

Bezin is a pidgin Orcish word that Makri uses of things she approves of. It's utterly unsuitable for use in a place like this but fortunately Lady Yestar has never encountered pidgin Orcish and it passes unnoticed.

"You must have had an interesting life," says Yestar. "Isuas is full of stories about you."

"Very interesting," agrees Makri. "Champion gladiator of the Orcs and now barmaid at the Avenging Axe. Also I'm studying at the Guild College. And I help raise money for the Association of Gentlewomen. They're trying to raise the status of women in Turai. Do the males on Avula treat the females like lower forms of life? Turanian men are dreadful; you wouldn't believe some of the things I have to put up with as a barmaid."

This is all quite inappropriate as an opening speech

to Avula's Queen, but Yestar only laughs. More than that, she conveys the impression that yes, she has met a few dreadful males in her time. I sip some wine, and let them talk. Lady Yestar obviously likes Makri and that is all to the good. I'm hoping Makri's benevolent mood lasts long enough for her to pretend to be willing to teach Isuas how to fight. Though Yestar will undoubtedly pour cold water on the idea, it will show us in a good light if Makri can at least feign some enthusiasm. It seems like the subject might never come up as Makri and Yestar talk about particularly useless males they have encountered, then move on to the tale of Queen Leeuven, till Isuas, bored with this, interrupts them.

"Tell Mother about you jumping in the ocean. You know Makri wasn't on board when we sailed? She ran on the quay, fighting all these men. And she killed most of them and then jumped in the sea and Thraxas went out for her in a boat."

"Really? How extraordinary. Did you miss the embarkation?"

"I wasn't invited on the voyage," explains Makri.

Yestar asks why she was not invited. I don't like what this might be leading to.

"Well, Orcish blood, you understand," I break in. "Didn't want to cause any embarrassment—"

"Thraxas was mad at me because I cost him a load of money gambling at cards," says Makri, interrupting me. "He's a terrible gambler."

"What did you do?"

"Opened her mouth when she shouldn't," I say, glaring threateningly at Makri.

"Makri can train me for the tournament," cries Isuas, unable to contain herself any longer. Yestar smiles. She has a beautiful smile. Perfect white teeth.

"Ah yes. The tournament. Isuas is keen to enter. All

her older brothers fared well in the junior tournament, as did one of her sisters. Unfortunately . . ."

Not wishing to say anything demeaning to her daughter, she leaves the sentence unfinished.

"You think she might do badly, not being used to sword play?" suggests Makri. "Well, if that's the only problem, leave it to me. I'll bring her up to the required standard."

I'm amazed. Makri must really be under the influence. Strange, she's normally no more liable to the effects of thazis than I am. I wonder if the water from the sacred pool might have affected her in some way.

Isuas whoops with glee and starts dancing round her mother. Lady Yestar seems dubious.

"I do not really think I can allow it. Isuas is small for her age, and inexperienced. Surely she could not put up a good showing against boys older and more experienced than her?"

"She'll do well," says Makri. "Only way to get experience, just plunge right in. I tell you, I can train that child to put up a fine show. Why, even on the ship she was making excellent progress."

Isuas beams. Lady Yestar considers it.

"Well, if you are sure . . . I would not like to risk my daughter being hurt, but I have been encouraging her to sail with my husband, to make her tougher."

She turns to Isuas. "Are you sure you wish to do this?"

Isuas bounds around, very sure that she wants to do it.

"Excellent," says Makri, adjusting her hat, which has slipped over her eyes. "We'll get started as soon as possible."

"Might Lord Kalith possibly object?" I venture.

"We won't mention it to him just yet," says Yestar. "Keep it as a surprise."

"I have a practice sword," says Isuas, still unable to control her excitement. "Come and see it."

Makri allows herself to be dragged away to see the practice sword. I know she's really going to regret this when she wakes up tomorrow.

"Do many women in Turai have pierced noses?" enquires Yestar politely.

"Only two. One's a travelling musician who dyes her hair green and the other is Makri. I expect the green hair will follow along in time."

"Such things can surely not help her in her quest to be thought a suitable candidate for the Imperial University?"

"So I keep telling her. But she's full of contradictions. All that mixed blood, I expect."

"Are you hoping to question me about the sad affair of Elith-ir-Methet?"

I'm surprised at the abruptness of this.

"Yes," I reply. "I am. Do you go along with the popular opinion that she is guilty of everything?"

The Elvish Lady sits in silence for a while.

"Perhaps. I have heard all the reports. And there are witnesses who claim to have seen her stab the Tree Priest. But I have known Elith for most of her life. I find it very difficult to believe that she would kill anyone. Have you any reason for imagining her to be innocent, apart from your desire to upset my husband?"

I assure Lady Yestar that I have no desire to upset her husband.

"Only a few days ago we shared a friendly game of niarit, and . . . eh . . ."

"You defeated him."

I apologise. Lady Yestar doesn't mind. I tell her I have a powerful desire to help Vas-ar-Methet.

"I know he'll go into exile if his daughter is found guilty and I don't want to see my old companion-in-arms reduced to hawking his healing services around some third-rate city in the west."

"Have you learned anything that may assist her?"

I admit that I have made little progress.

"I can see far, in many directions," says Yestar. "I gazed at the troubles of Elith-ir-Methet, but I was unable to penetrate the mists that surround them. Yet your presence here brings new energy to the affair, Investigator. Perhaps I should look again."

She lapses into silence. She stares into the distance. The sun streams in through the windows, and the sound of birdsong. It strikes me that of all the rooms in palaces I've ever been in, I like this one best. I like Lady Yestar too. I wonder what she is looking at. Who knows what a powerful Elvish Lady might be capable of?

Finally her attention returns. "I see that you might have been a powerful Sorcerer," she says, "had you been prepared to study when you were young."

There doesn't seem to be any answer to this so I remain silent.

"You know we have been plagued by bad dreams? I see that they are connected with Elith in some way. And the Hesuni Tree, though our healers assure us that it is again healthy."

Yestar stares into space. A smile comes to her face. "The juggling competition? Even here on Avula, you wish to gamble?"

I feel uncomfortable. If Lady Yestar possesses powers of farseeing, I'd prefer her to concentrate on the matter of Elith rather than my bad habits. Any moment now she'll be advising me to drink less.

She lapses into her semi-trance once more. From another room I can hear the sound of a child's voice, excited. Isuas is screaming about something or other.

"And Makri may regret her offer of help when her mind clears. Did you drink of one of the pools?"

I nod.

"You're not supposed to."

"I'm sorry. Is it calanith?"

"No. We just don't like it."

The Elvish Lady frowns, and concentrates some more. "Something was sold next to the Hesuni Tree."

"Pardon?"

"Something was sold."

This is interesting, but Yestar can summon up nothing more. She can't tell me who sold what, or to whom, but she has the distinct impression that a transaction was made. I ask her if in all her farsighted gazing she received any impression as to Elith's guilt or innocence.

"No. I could not see who killed our Tree Priest. But, as you know, the Hesuni Tree casts a dense cloud over all mystic effects in the area."

Yestar, now fully back in the real world, fixes me with a stare. "If you are able to clear Elith-ir-Methet I will be pleased. However, if it transpires that she is guilty, neither I nor my husband will stand for any attempt to forge evidence in her favour, or to spirit her off the island."

I don't bother to defend myself against this one.

"She will be executed if found guilty," I point out, and I can see that the prospect of this does not please Lady Yestar.

"I'd like to talk to someone who could tell me about the rival factions for the position of Tree Priest," I say.

"That would be calanith."

"But possibly very helpful."

Yestar studies me for a while longer. Whether she's influenced by my honest face, or by her abhorrence at the thought of Elith being executed, she finally tells me that Visan, the Keeper of Lore, may be willing to explain it to me, if Yestar gives him permission.

Our conversation is interrupted by Isuas, who erupts into the room with Makri in tow.

"Makri just showed me a new attack," she yells.

It's time for us to leave. Makri promises to return tomorrow to start the training. Lady Yestar will direct her to a private clearing where they will be undisturbed. An attendant leads us through the Palace.

"Still happy to be teaching the kid how to fight?"

"Guess so," says Makri.

Whatever is influencing Makri's behaviour is lasting a long time. I study her eyes, and I see that they have the same glazed sort of look I saw in Elith-ir-Methet's.

"Bezin hat," she says, still pleased.

Makri's continued intoxication leads to a brief comedy when we are led through a corridor with doors going off on each side. One of the doors opens and Jir-ar-Eth rushes out, plunging headlong into Makri, who stands there looking surprised as the Sorcerer tumbles to the floor.

"Careful," she says solicitously, helping him up.

Jir-ar-Eth is displeased and rises with the air of an Elf who feels his dignity has been encroached upon.

"Can't you look where you're going ?" he demands before hurrying off. I'm disappointed. From Lord Kalith's Chief Sorcerer, I would have expected a better rejoinder.

Our attendant leads us on. Before I follow him I bend down to quickly scoop up a slip of paper that I purposely covered with my foot when it fluttered from the Sorcerer's pocket. It's probably only the Royal Laundry List, but I always like the opportunity to study the private papers of important people. And Elves.

At the end of the final corridor, before the huge

outside doors, the attendant leans over to whisper in my ear.

"I believe that if you go to the clearing at the stream and three oaks, you will often find a convivial gathering of those who enjoy beer," he murmurs.

I thank him profusely, then ask a question.

"We saw some actors in the clearing below. They all seemed to be arguing with a grey-haired Elf. The director of the play, maybe?"

"That would be Sofius-ar-Eth, appointed by Lord Kalith to produce and direct Avula's entry at the festival."

"Sofius-ar-Eth? Any relation to Jir-ar-Eth, the Sorcerer?"

"His brother."

That is interesting.

"Didn't feel the desire to be a Sorcerer too?"

"He did, sir. Sofius-ar-Eth is one of Avula's most powerful Sorcerers. It was a surprise to many when he was appointed to take charge of our play."

The doors are opened and we stroll out, only to meet with Cicerius, Prince Dees-Akan, Lanius Suncatcher and Harmon Half-Elf, a full Turanian delegation here on business. I greet them politely and step aside to let them pass. Both Sorcerers enter the Palace but Prince Dees-Akan halts in front of me with an expression of dislike on his face.

"Have you been bothering our hosts again?"

I regret his unfriendly tone. It's going to make life in Turai difficult having a Royal Prince down on me like a bad spell.

"Guests of Lady Yestar," I explain.

"You are not to disturb Lady Yestar with your pointless questions," commands the Prince.

Makri wanders up to us, obviously still under the influence of thazis.

"The second in line to the Turanian throne," she says, benignly, "doesn't have any power to issue orders to Turanian citizens while in another country. No legal basis for it. I studied the law at the Guild College. Passed the exam only last month. Do you like my new hat? I think it's bezin."

The Prince is outraged. "How dare you instruct me on the law!" he says, loudly.

"Well, you need instructing. Cicerius will tell you. He's a lawyer."

All eyes fall on Cicerius. He looks uncomfortable as he grapples with the difficult notion of trying to grant that Makri is correct without infuriating the Prince. Prince Dees-Akan shoots him a furious glance, turns on his heel, and marches into the Palace.

"Thank you for that," says Cicerius, icily.

I apologise. "Sorry, Deputy Consul. Didn't mean to put you on the spot. But we were invited here by Lady Yestar. We could hardly refuse to come, could we?"

The Deputy Consul draws me away from the gates and lowers his voice. "Have you discovered anything?"

"Nothing startling. But I'm still suspicious of everything."

"This really is awkward for Lord Kalith you know. It's most unfortunate that all this has happened at festival time. He has many important guests to welcome and even before the murder of the Tree Priest he was in an embarrassing situation. I understand that certain members of his Council of Elders are saying in private that the disgrace of having their Hesuni Tree damaged reflects so badly on the Avulans that Lord Kalith should abdicate. Since Gulas-ar-Thetos was killed that disgrace has grown considerably worse, though Kalith is putting a brave face on it. I repeat, Thraxas, I understand your desire to help your friend and wartime companion, but one can hardly blame the Elf Lord for wishing to bring things to a swift conclusion."

"I suppose I can't, Cicerius. And I don't blame you for supporting him either. I know that Lord Kalith is an important ally of Turai. But doesn't it strike you that I may be doing him a favour? His prestige won't be helped if the wrong Elf suffers for the crimes."

"That," says Cicerius," would depend on whether anyone found out."

"Meaning a swift conviction of Elith would be best all round, whether she did it or not."

"Exactly."

I study Cicerius's face for a few moments. Over in the trees behind us colourful parrots are squawking cheerfully at each other.

"Cicerius, if we were in Turai, you wouldn't want an innocent person to be punished for a crime they didn't commit, no matter how convenient it was for the state. Even though you're a strong supporter of the Royal Family you've defended people in the law courts that the King would much rather have seen quickly hanged. Hell, you're far more honest than me."

Cicerius doesn't contradict me. He gazes over at the parrots for a minute or so.

"You would be far better leaving matters as they are," he says, finally. "Were it not for the fact that Lord Kalith knows it would only look worse for him to have a Human guest of his own favoured healer languishing in prison during the festival, you would have been locked up for putting a spell on his guards. You would be unwise to push him any further."

He pauses. The parrots keep squawking. "But you might be interested to know that Palace gossip says that Elith-ir-Methet was having an affair with Gulas-ar-Thetos. That, of course, would be a taboo affair that neither of their families would have allowed to continue. Tree Priests cannot marry outside of their clan."

"Does Palace gossip say that's why she killed him?"

Cicerius shrugs.

"I never repeat gossip," he says, then walks swiftly away through the gates of the Palace. Makri is quiet as we walk back to Camith's tree dwelling. Even the inquisitive monkeys don't attract her attention. We're almost there when she suddenly comes to a halt.

"What the hell was in that thazis stick?" she demands, shaking her head.

"Just thazis."

"I feel like I've been journeying through the magic space."

"I noticed you weren't your usual self."

Makri shakes her head again and a breeze catches her hair, displaying her pointed ears.

"Did I really agree to teach that horrible child how to fight?"

"I'm afraid so."

She sits down and dangles her legs over the edge of the walkway. "Now I'm really depressed."

"You should be. You've only got six days to get her ready."

"Give me some thazis," says Makri.

Chapter Twelve

We eat our evening meal with Camith and his family in relative quiet. Camith discusses the festival with his wife but Makri is mute and I'm too busy concentrating on the food to talk. Once again, I am well satisfied with the fare. The venison is of the highest quality and the fish is freshly caught that morning by a cousin of the family who has his own fishing boat.

In Turai Elves mean only one of two things to most people: either mighty warriors helping us against the Orcs, or makers of fine poetry and songs. We never think of them as owning fishing boats, somehow. Or having arguments when they're trying to put on a play.

Makri is unusually quiet. Later she tells me that she has been feeling strange ever since drinking the water at the Hesuni pools.

"I'm almost back to normal now. I wonder why it didn't affect you?"

"Maybe it only affects Elves? Or those with Elvish blood?"

Whatever the reason, I'm betting it has some connection with Elith's memory loss, and I'll be investigating the pools at the first opportunity. I wonder what Lady Yestar meant about something being sold in the vicinity?

"I'm heading off to the clearing at the stream and three oaks."

"What for?"

"Beer. Apparently it's a gathering point for nighttime drinking."

"Do you always have to move heaven, earth and the three moons just to find beer?"

"Yes. Do you want to come?"

Makri shakes her head. She's muttering about the injustice of being mysteriously drugged and then tricked into teaching Isuas how to fight.

I'm puzzled about this. I could see that Lady Yestar liked Makri but after all the fuss about a person with Orcish blood even landing on the island, one might have thought that the Queen would be hesitant about immediately commissioning this person to train her child in the art of war. How are the population going to react? What about the already dissatisfied Council of Elders? Surely Lord Kalith will be furious when he hears the news.

"I'm not worried about Lord Kalith," says Makri. "I'm concerned about my reputation as a fighter. How am I meant to train that child? She's about as much use as a one-legged gladiator. She couldn't defend herself against an angry butterfly."

"Well, be sure and go easy on her," I say. "Yestar won't thank you if you send her home with a black eye and a bloody nose. And remember, no attacks to the groin, eyes, throat or knees. It's against the rules."

"No attacks to the groin, eyes, throat or knees?"

cries Makri, despairingly. "This gets worse all the time. What's the point? It's hardly like fighting at all."

"I told you, they don't want their children maimed. If Isuas trots out to her first engagement and proceeds to poke a dagger into her opponent's eye she'll be disqualified, and no one is going to be very pleased about it."

"But I was depending on the dagger attack to the eyes," complains Makri. "Otherwise what chance does she have?"

"You'll just have to teach her some proper sword play. You know, the sort of thing gentlemen do."

"It's all ridiculous. These tournaments are stupid." I agree with her, more or less.

"I'd never enter one," states Makri. "If I'm going to fight, I'll do it properly or not at all. What about these fighting competitions in the far west I've heard about? Are they all pussyfooting around?"

"No, not all of them. Some of the tournaments in the far west are very vicious affairs. They fight with real weapons and no one minds who gets hurt. The warriors' competition in Samsarina used to be notorious for the number of deaths each year. Still is, I expect. It attracts the finest swordsmen from all over the world, because of the handsome nature of the prize.

Makri is interested in this. "You've been in Samsarina, haven't you? Did you see the competition?"

"I was in it."

"Really? How did you do?"

"I won it."

Makri looks at me suspiciously.

"You won the warriors' competition in Samsarina, against the world's best swordsmen?"

"I did."

"I don't believe you."

I shrug. "I don't care if you believe me or not."

"How come no one in Twelve Seas ever mentions it? Surely they'd have heard of such a notable feat?"

"It was a long time ago. Anyway, I was entered under a different name as I was on some unscheduled leave from the army at the time. What are you looking so dubious about?"

"I thought you spent your youth being thrown out of the Sorcerers' school."

"I did. And after that I learned how to fight. You think it's just an accident I've lasted so long as an Investigator in Turai?"

As I'm putting on my cloak I remember the slip of paper I filched from Lord Kalith's Sorcerer. I can't read it, so I show it to Makri.

"Royal Elvish?"

She nods. "Where did you get hold of this?"

"It fell out of Jir-ar-Eth's pocket when you knocked him to the ground. Can you translate it?"

Makri studies the paper for a moment or two and pronounces it to be a list. I guessed it would be something dull.

"What sort of list? Laundry?"

"No. This is a summary of Jir-ar-Eth's report to Lord Kalith. It's a list of all possible suspects for the killing of Gulas-ar-Thetos. He's been using sorcery to scan the area and he's identified everyone who was close enough at the time to have stuck a knife into Gulas. You're on it, and Camith."

"We were on the walkway above. Who else?"

"Elith-ir-Methet," reads Makri. "Lasas-ar-Thetos, Gulas's brother. Merith-ar-Thet, listed as a cousin of Lasas and Gulas. Pires-ar-Senth, a Palace guard. Caripatha-ir-Min, a weaver. And Gorith-ar-Del."

I take back the paper.

"Makri, did I ever say how much I valued your intellect, particularly your fine command of languages?"

"No. But you did once say that pointy-eared Orc bastards had no business learning Royal Elvish."

I chuckle indulgently.

"A joke you took in good part, as I recall. When the Association of Gentlewomen sends round its next collection plate for educating the struggling masses of Turanian women, you can count me in for a few gurans. With this paper, my investigation just became a whole lot easier."

"How come you get such a lucky break?" enquires Makri.

"I practise a lot."

I leave Makri and seek out Camith for directions to the clearing at the stream and three oaks, which he provides.

"A haunt of armourers and poets, I believe."

"Armourers and poets are fine with me, providing they have beer."

I take my illuminated staff to light my way, and set off briskly over the walkways.

"Follow the Dragon's Tail and you can't go wrong," Camith instructs me. The Dragon's Tail comprises five stars that form a line. It's visible from Turai, though I think it points in a different direction up there. I don't know why that would be.

I traverse the walkway with care, not wishing to plunge off the edge in the darkness. It's something of a relief when I come to the distinctive tree that carries a ladder down to the ground. From here I'm to keep to the path till I come to a fork, where I'm to take the left path till I reach the clearing.

Even though this is an Elvish island on which there are no evil creatures of the night and no criminal gangs—at least in theory—I still feel slightly apprehensive walking through the forest on my own in the darkness. I wouldn't admit it to anyone, but the forest bothers me in a way the city never does. It feels like it's alive, and it knows I don't belong here. I boost my illuminated staff up to maximum power and hurry along, cheering myself up with the thought that I'm finally going to get myself a beer, and that it is long overdue.

I'm concentrating on following the path so when a voice comes from right behind me I practically jump into the nearest tree.

"It's an enormous Human with an illuminated staff! How interesting!"

I spin round, not pleased to be taken unawares. Standing there, grinning at me, is a slender young female Elf of eighteen or so. Her hood is thrown back and her hair is cut unusually short for an Elf.

"How do you do?" she greets me. "Are you looking for beer, enormous Human?"

I scowl at her. "The name's Thraxas."

"I know," she says, smiling pleasantly. "Everyone on Avula knows that there is an Investigator called Thraxas going around asking questions. Are you going to the three oaks to ask questions, enormous Human?"

"No. I'm going for a beer. And will you stop calling me enormous? Is that a polite way to address a guest?"

"Sorry. I was being poetic. But I suppose 'enormous' isn't a very poetic word, when applied to a Human. Would 'impressively girthed' be better?"

"No, it would still be lousy," I reply.

"Kingly proportioned?"

"Could we just forget my weight for a moment? What do you want?"

"The same as you. Beer."

She falls in at my side and we walk on.

"I take it you are a poet rather than an armourer?"

"Definitely. I'm Sendroo-ir-Vallis. You can call me Droo."

"Pleased to meet you, Droo."

Having got over my surprise, I don't mind a little company. Droo, obviously an Elf who has no problems in talking to strangers, tells me that she comes to the three oaks most nights to meet other poets.

"And drink beer."

"I thought Elvish poets would drink wine."

"Only the older ones," Droo informs me. "And I daresay it was fine for composing epics. But poetry moves on, you know. Look, there's the clearing. There's a hill where you can look at the stars through the fine mist from the waterfall. It's very inspiring. Poets have always loved the spot."

"What about the armourers?"

"They use the fast-flowing water for their forges. I've never found that very poetic, but we get on well with them. Is it true that you travel with a woman with Orc blood and a ring through her nose?"

I see that Makri's reputation has spread as swiftly as my own. "I never go anywhere without her. Apart from tonight. She's home resting."

Droo seems disappointed, though she owns that she's pleased to meet a detective.

"I need new experiences, and there are so few opportunities for a young Elf to get off the island. I wanted to sail on the ship to Turai but my father wouldn't let me. Are you going to ask everyone questions?"

"Maybe a few. But mainly I'm looking for beer."

We arrive at the clearing and I've rarely seen a more welcoming sight. Benches are laid out under the three mighty oaks and from inside the hollow stump of a huge dead tree an Elf is handing out tankards. Two large tables are occupied by brawny Elves in leather aprons whom I take to be armourers, and a further table nearer to the stream is surrounded by younger, thinner Elves, presumably poets. They wave to Sendroo as she appears, and some of the weapon-makers also shout greetings. The atmosphere is convivial, sufficiently so that my arrival, while provoking some comment, doesn't cast any sort of shadow over the place.

I march up to the Elf in the hollow tree, take out some small pieces of Elvish currency, and request a beer. He hands it over in a black leather tankard. I drink it down in one, hand back the tankard, and request another. He fills the tankard from a barrel at the back and hands it over. I down it in one and give him back the tankard.

"More beer."

I take the third tankard, empty it straight down and hand it back. By this time the Elf is looking slightly surprised.

"Would you like to try—"

"More beer."

As I'm draining the fourth tankard there is some good-natured laughter from the armourers behind me.

"He is a mighty drinker," says one of them.

I finish off a fifth tankard, and take a six and seventh over to their table.

"Better bring me a couple more," I say to the bar-keeper, and hand him a few more coins. "Make that three. Four. Well, just keep them coming till I tell you to stop."

"Any room for a thirsty man at that table?" I ask.

I figure that while the poets might be interesting in their own way, the armourers will make for better company while I'm in such desperate need of beer. They look like the sort of Elves who enjoy a few tankards themselves after a hard day at the forge. They're brawny, as Elves go. Not as brawny as me, but at least they don't make me feel quite as oversized as most of the Elves do.

The weapon-makers move up, letting me in at the bench. I drink down one of my tankards, make a start on another, and look round to check that the barkeeper is on his way with more.

"A hard day?" enquires the nearest Elf jovially.

"A hard month. I ran out of ale on Kalith's ship and I've been searching ever since."

When the barkeeper arrives I order a round of drinks for the entire table, which goes down well.

"He's trying to bribe us with drinks," cry the Elves, laughing. "Are you here to ask the armourers questions, Investigator?"

"No, just to drink beer. And isn't it time someone was calling that barkeeper over? Anyone know any good drinking songs?"

You can't ask an Elvish weapon-maker if he knows any good drinking songs without getting a hearty response. I know that. I remember these Elves, or Elves very much like them, from the war. I feel on much firmer territory than I have been with Lord Kalith-ar-Yil and his retinue. A drinking song starts up, and after it's gone round a few times one of the Elves further down the table actually shouts that now he remembers me.

"I was up in Turai during the War! You used to fight with that Barbarian—what was his name?"

"Gurd."

"Gurd! Bless the old Barbarian!"

The Elf slams his tankard cheerfully on the table.

"Thraxas! When I heard we had a Human Investigator heading our way, I never realised it was you."

He turns to his companions.

"I know this man. Fought well and never let us run out of drink!"

It's true. I raided the cellars after the Orcish dragons burned down the taverns.

"Is that you, Voluth? You didn't have a beard back then."

"And you didn't have such a belly!"

Voluth roars with laughter. I remember him well—a shield-maker by trade, and a doughty warrior. He calls for more beer, and starts telling war stories, stories in which I'm pleased to see I feature well. I smile at everyone genially. This is more the sort of thing I had in mind when an expedition to the Elvish Isles was mooted. Beer, drinking songs and convivial company.

Which is not to say I'm not alert for anything that may be helpful. Talk naturally swings round to the matter of Elith-ir-Methet's killing of Gulas. If they were having an affair, word of it hasn't reached the armourers, though several of them do say that Gulas was very young to be Tree Priest. His brother is younger, and, I gather, less popular.

The poets are meanwhile sprawled over the ground at the foot of the small hill, looking at the moons and reciting lines to each other. Droo is talking animatedly with another Elvish youth. In fact they seem to be arguing. I can't hear their conversation, but it seems to be growing more heated. Suddenly the sound of singing fills the glade.

"Choirs are practising late," say the armourers, and listen with the air of Elves who have a fine judgement of such things.

"Sounds like the choir from Ven. Not bad, though I fancy Corinthal may have the edge this year."

"Is competition fierce in all the events?" I enquire, reasoning that if it is I may well find out if there's any gambling in these parts.

"Very fierce," says Voluth. "With the festival only taking place every five years, these choirs spend years practising and no one wants to put up a bad performance on the day. It's even worse with the dramatic companies. It's an immense honour winning the first prize. Ten years ago the Avulans won with a spectacular rendition of the famous episode where Queen Leeuven goes to war against her stepbrother. Lord Kalith made the director an Honoured Knight of Avula, an award previously only given to Elves who distinguished themselves on the battlefield. He's never had to buy himself a goblet of wine or haunch of venison to this day."

"We didn't do so well last time though," another Elf puts in. "Staid performance. No emotion. The whole island was disappointed."

"What happened to the director?"

"He sailed off in a bad mood, saying the judges wouldn't know a good play if Queen Leeuven herself handed it down from heaven. We haven't seen him since."

This leads to a lot of talk about the relative merits of the three entrants in this year's competition. As far as I can gather there is no clear favourite, but public opinion slightly favours the Corinthalians.

"But Ven will put up a good show too. Some singers from Avula went over there earlier this year and they came back with some very impressive reports of a rehearsal they'd seen."

"What about Avula this year?" I ask.

All around the table there are pursed lips, and a general air of disgruntlement.

"Not giving yourselves much chance?"

"Not much. We've got some fine performers, but who ever heard of a Sorcerer for a director? I don't know what Lord Kalith was thinking of, appointing Sofius-ar-Eth to the post."

The Elvish armourers are unanimous on this point.

"Not a bad Sorcerer, we admit, but a director? He's had no experience. No chance of winning the prize with him at the helm. There's been dissatisfaction in

Avula ever since it was announced. There's talk of some fierce arguments in the Council of Elders over the affair. No one wants to see our play turning into a shambles, and from what we hear that's what's going to happen."

It's odd. No one can explain why Lord Kalith made such an unexpected appointment.

"It's said that Lady Yestar was far from pleased. But they're always arguing, everyone knows that."

I turn the conversation round to the question of juggling, and this produces some furious debate. The merits of various jugglers from Avula, Ven and Corinthal are discussed at length, with no clear favourite emerging. The best Avulan juggler is apparently a young woman called Shuthan-ir-Hemas, but opinion is divided as to whether she can defeat some of the more experienced practitioners from the other islands.

I lower my voice, and mutter a few words in Voluth's ear. He grins. "Well, you might be able to place a bet though Lord Kalith doesn't approve of anyone gambling on events at the festival."

"Is it calanith?"

"No, he just doesn't like it. But it's been known to happen. I can't really recommend anyone for the juggling, but if you want a safe bet on the junior tournament, go for Firees-ar-Key. Son of Yulis-ar-Key, finest warrior on the island, and a chip off the old block. Firees won the tournament for under-twelves when he was only nine, and he's practically fully grown now, though he's only fourteen years of age."

I file that away as a useful piece of information. I'm about to cast around for some more betting tips when Droo interrupts by squeezing in beside me at the table. She's looking rather unhappy but her expression brightens as the armourers greet her genially.

"It's young Droo! Up to no good, no doubt."

"Do your parents know you're out writing poems and drinking ale, youngster?"

Droo returns their greetings, equally genially. They all seem to know her and like her. I try to think of anywhere in Turai where weapon-makers and poets mingle happily together. I can't. The race track, maybe, except poets never have any money to place a bet.

"You've met Thraxas already? Are you writing a poem about him?"

"Certainly," grins Droo.

"Better make it an epic," calls Voluth. "There's a lot of him to write about."

They all laugh. I call for more beer.

"I came over so I could be questioned too," says Droo. "I didn't want to miss out."

"He hasn't been questioning us," the armourers tell her.

"Why not?"

Everyone looks at me. I tell them frankly that as this is the first time I've been able to relax with a beer for weeks, I can't be bothered doing any investigating. This seems to disappoint them. In fact, as the ale keeps flowing, almost everyone seems to be keen to express an opinion about the case, and I find myself drawn into some investigating anyway, pretty much against my will. A chainmail-maker at the end of the table knows Vas-ar-Methet well and refuses to believe that his daughter is responsible for any crime. A blacksmith's apprentice beside him is of the opinion that some odd things have been happening around the Hesuni Tree for some time, and everyone knows that this is why the Elves have been having bad dreams. Maybe, he suggests, it was bad dreams that drove Elith to commit the crimes?

There is some sympathy for Elith, mainly because of the high opinion in which her father is held, but the general view is that she must be guilty as charged. Indeed, a blacksmith, who is, incidentally, the largest Elf I have ever seen, tells us that he knows Elith is guilty of the murder because his sister was close to the Hesuni Tree at the time and she was certain she'd seen the fatal blow being struck.

"You should talk to her, Thraxas. She'll tell you what she saw."

I learn something of note about Gorith-ar-Del. As a maker of longbows he's known to the armourers but he isn't making fine longbows any more. He's given up the business. No one knows why, or what he does with himself these days when he's not sailing with Lord Kalith-ar-Yil.

Some white-robed actors appear in the clearing, leading to more general good-natured greetings. I recognise them as members of the Avulan cast I saw earlier close to the Tree Palace. They've been rehearsing in the vicinity.

"How is the tale of Queen Leeuven coming on?" call the weapon-makers.

"Badly. We need ale," reply the actors, making comic faces and hurrying to the hollow tree for refreshment. They mingle with the poets and, from the fragments of their conversation I can catch, they're feeling no happier with their director.

I turn to Droo, and notice that she has a rather sad expression on her face.

"Bad time with the boyfriend?" I say sympathetically. She nods.

"He left after we argued."

"What were you arguing about?"

"Are you investigating me?" says Droo, brightening at the prospect.

"No. Well, not unless you or your boyfriend defaced the Hesuni Tree and murdered the priest."

"He didn't," says Droo, and looks gloomy again. "But his behaviour is so erratic these days, it wouldn't surprise me if he did something equally stupid. And he was really mean about my new poem."

I sympathise, which just goes to show how mellow this evening's gathering has made me. Under normal circumstances, I don't have much time to spare for the problems of teenage poets.

Elves start drifting away as the night wears on. Droo departs with her friends and I decide that it's time to go. I have drunk a great amount of beer, and it's a fair walk back to Camith's house. I ask at the bar if they have any beer in flasks or bottles I can take away with me.

"We can let you have a wineskin full, if you like."

"That'll do fine."

I pay for my drink, say goodbye to my fellow drinkers, and start off on the journey home. I don't want to admit that I can't see as well as the Elves at night so I wait till I'm some way along the path before lighting up my illuminated staff. On the way home I'm merry. The forest no longer feels threatening.

"Well, of course, that was the problem," I say out loud. "How's a man meant to relate to an Elvish forest without a few beers inside him? Now I'm in the right state of mind, it's quite a cheery place."

I greet a few of the trees as I pass. I'm quite close to home. I remember that I have to climb up a long ladder to get there. Damn. I'm not looking forward to that. The path becomes narrow. I'm humming a bright ditty as I turn the next corner. There, in front of me, are four masked Elves with spears. They let out a battle cry, and sprint towards me, weapons lowered for action.

I'm startled. I'd forgotten all about the hostile spear-carrying Elves. Once more I'm at a severe disadvantage on the narrow path. I mutter the word and my illuminated staff goes out and I hurl myself sideways into the trees. Here in the forest, they won't be able to attack me in formation. I scramble some way into the depths, then halt and listen. There is no sound.

I'm not in the mood for skulking. I'm not in the mood for struggling through the trees either. I had enough of that on the first occasion they forced me off the walkway. I get angry. A man should be able to walk around Avula without being chased by spearmen everywhere he goes. I decide to risk creeping back towards the path. I go as quietly as I can, which is very quietly. When I'm close to the path, I stop, hardly even breathing for fear of making a sound. The moonlight illuminates the path in front of me. There, easily visible, are the four Elves, standing silently, waiting.

I'm unsure what to do. Attacking them would be rash. I'm scared of no one in a fight but back on the path they would have the opportunity to form their phalanx against me. Besides, even if I hurled myself on them and managed to cut them down, Lord Kalith isn't going to be too pleased with me. I wasn't invited here to kill Elves.

All of a sudden the Elves vanish. Just like that. They disappear into thin air. I'm stunned. I've seen plenty of sorcery in my time, but it was the last thing I was expecting. I'm seriously perturbed. If four invisible Elves start hunting for me in this forest I'm doomed. I strain my senses, trying to catch any scent of them. I can't pick up anything but get the faint impression of voices receding into the distance.

After a while I venture back on to the path. Nothing there. I light up my staff and bend down to examine the grass. It looks to me as if the Elves just went on their way after becoming invisible. I don't understand any of this, but I'm not going to hang around and wait for them to come back. I set off homewards rapidly, not stopping till I reach the welcoming sight of the ladder that leads up to Camith's treehouse, which I ascend a good deal more briskly than I had anticipated.

Chapter Thirteen

—◆—

Next day I'm feeling sprightly, despite the hefty intake of beer.

"Must be the healthy air," suggests Makri. "I'm feeling good myself. What are you doing today?"

"Questioning a blacksmith's sister who saw the fatal stabbing. And talking to Visan the Keeper of Lore, whoever he may be. Yestar suggested he might be able to tell me more about the rivals for the Tree Priesthood."

"Wouldn't that be calanith?"

"What isn't on this damn island? You'd think it might be calanith to execute a woman without a proper investigation, but apparently not."

"Does Elith really face execution?" asks Makri.

"So they say. It would be the first on Avula in over a hundred years, and it's going to happen right after the festival unless I come up with something quick."

"Well, have fun. I'm teaching that idiot child how to fight." Makri is wearing her swords and has thrown a few other weapons in a bag. "I only had two knives when I jumped in the ocean, but I've borrowed a couple more from Camith. And a practice sword."

Makri looks at the wooden blade with frank distaste. I tell her not to worry, she can still kill Isuas with it if she hits her hard enough.

Makri is meeting her pupil some way over to the west of the island, at a clearing used only by the Royal Family, where they will not be disturbed. Although we've seen young Elves practising their fighting all over the island, Makri is to teach Isuas in private. This suits Makri.

"If no one sees anything, my reputation might survive the debacle."

She is still unhappy at the way things have turned out but supposes she should just make the best of it.

"Okay, teaching the brat will be a disaster, but I'll get some exercise and weapons practice myself. And maybe a chance to use the Royal Elvish language."

After some study of my grimoire, I load the sleep spell into my mind, and another one that may prove useful. We leave together, heading west. Rather than tramp over the walkways we borrow two horses from Camith and make our way round by means of one of the main paths in the forest. As we travel we pass performers of various sorts at regular intervals, all rehearsing for the festival, now only five days away. I pause to look at a young Elf who is putting on a fine juggling performance under a tall silver tree. She's keeping four small wooden balls in the air at once and her partner, or possibly her trainer, tosses another one at her, and then another, so that she now has six balls flying in an arc from one hand to the other.

"She looks like a woman who might be worth a wager," I mutter, and trot over to ask her name. She's called Usath, she's from Ven, and her green tunic is decorated with silver crescent moons. Although she is at first surprised at our approach, and visibly sniffs the air as she catches scent of Makri's Orc blood, she is not distracted for long and soon gets back to practising. Obviously a dedicated performer. Her assistant, another young female Elf, throws a seventh ball to her, but it goes wrong and the balls cascade on to the grass.

The young juggler lets out a coarse oath, and stoops to pick them up. Already she's forgotten our presence.

"Well, she made a hash of the seventh ball, but even so, she was pretty impressive with six," I say.

"Might be worth a bet," agrees Makri. "I'll see if Isuas has any information about the other jugglers."

Realising what she has just said, Makri frowns.

"How come I'm keen to bet on a juggling competition? I used to disapprove of gambling." She twists in her saddle. "It's your fault, you corrupted me."

"Nothing corrupt about it, Makri. Gambling is good for you."

"How?"

"I don't know. But I'm sure it is. You know, thanks to me, you are a much finer person than the raw young gladiator who arrived in Turai only a year and a half ago. Beer, klee, thazis and gambling. I taught you them all. Now I think about it, you weren't very good at lying till I showed you how."

Soon after this we go our separate ways, Makri to Lady Yestar's private clearing and myself on to the collection of treehouses where the blacksmith's sister dwells. She is a weaver by trade and should now be working at her loom. A few enquiries lead me to her place of work, a small wooden hut at ground level that contains four looms and two elves. One of these is Caripatha, the Elf I'm looking for. She's sitting at her loom, though rather than working she's staring into space. I introduce myself, mention my conversation with the blacksmith, and ask her if she'd mind answering a few questions.

She nods, vaguely. I'm surprised at her lack of reaction. From her indifference you might think that a Human detective appearing at her workplace to investigate a murder was an everyday occurrence.

"You were in the clearing when the murder took place?"

She nods.

"Would you mind telling me what you saw?"

"Elith-ir-Methet sticking a knife into Gulas-ar-Thetos."

"Are you sure it was her?"

"I'm sure."

"It was dark when it happened. Could you have been mistaken about her identity?"

Caripatha is quite certain that she was not mistaken. I ask her what she was doing in the clearing. She tells me that she just likes to be close to the Hesuni Tree every now and then, the same as all Avulans.

"Do you know of any reason why Elith-ir-Methet might have done it? Can you tell me anything about her relationship with Gulas?"

"I have to go now," says Caripatha suddenly.

She rises from her stool and walks out. I'm astonished.

Her friend, or workmate, has so far sat in silence.

"Where did she go?" I ask her.

The other Elf shakes her head. "I don't know. Her behaviour has been erratic recently. She hasn't woven anything in a month."

"Does she often just disappear like that?"

Apparently she does. I'm puzzled. One minute she was answering my questions, the next she suddenly departed. There was no sign that my questions had perturbed her. It just seemed like she'd remembered something more important she had to do.

Outside my horse is waiting for me. I mount up and ride off, deep in thought. These Elves. Is it just me, or are they all acting strangely?

I ride back towards the centre of the island. Two groups of mounted Elves pass me, each with cloaks and tunics a slightly different shade of green than those of the Avulans. The island is filling up as guests and spectators arrive from the nearby islands for the festival. As I pass the turning that leads to the Queen's private clearing, I'm overcome with curiosity about Makri and Isuas. I lead my horse up the path. As far as I know, Makri has never taught anyone before. I wonder if she has an aptitude for it. I hope so. As long as Isuas is happy, I'm guaranteed entry to the Palace.

There are no guards or fences to prevent other Elves from entering the clearing. They just don't. Avulans are, on the whole, far better behaved than the people of Turai. The murder of Gulas-ar-Thetos is the first killing to happen on the island for twelve years. In Turai someone is murdered every four hours.

When I sight the clearing I dismount, tether my horse, and advance softly, wishing to arrive unannounced. I poke my head quietly round the last tree at the edge of the path.

Makri and Isuas are facing each other. Each has a wooden sword in one hand and a wooden dagger in the other. Isuas is wearing a green tunic and leggings, which look new. Probably her mother provided her with new clothes for the venture, which would be regarded as lucky by the Elves. Makri has discarded her Elvish tunic and sandals and is looking exotic, though not very savage, in bare feet, chainmail bikini and floppy green hat. Her hair is as voluminous as usual but she's plaited the strands at the front into braids to prevent it from flying into her face while in combat.

Makri is giving instructions. I remain silent, and

strain to hear her words. Her voice sounds aggrieved, as if things have not been going well.

"Attack me. Sword then dagger, and try to get it right this time."

Isuas lunges gamely at her. It's not a bad effort for a beginner, but Makri parries her blow with some contempt and Isuas's sword flies from her hand. The young Elf has made an effort to follow through with the dagger as instructed, but Makri simply twists her body to avoid it then hits Isuas on the head with the pommel of her own dagger. Isuas falls down heavily.

"That was terrible," says Makri, raising her voice. "Now, get up, and do it right."

"You hurt me," wails Isuas.

Makri reaches down, yanks the kid to her feet and tells her to stop complaining and pick up her sword.

"Attack me again and try not to throw your sword away this time."

Even at this distance I can see the glint of tears in Isuas's eyes, but she does as she's told and again executes a reasonable thrust in Makri's direction. Makri is a master of the twin-bladed technique, which is not so common in the west or the south as it was in her gladiator days in the east. She parries both of Isuas's blades simultaneously, steps forward, smashes her right hand into Isuas's face, kicks her legs from under her and whacks her with the flat of her sword as she's on the way down. The young Elf crumples as if hit by a bolt from a crossbow and starts to scream, a scream that is cut off as Makri places her foot on Isuas's throat and glares down at her in a very hostile manner.

"What the hell was that?" she demands. "I didn't tell you to wave your sword at your mother, you useless little brat. I said attack me with it. You're pathetic. I used to have a little puppy dog that could hold a weapon better than you."

Makri has abandoned all efforts to practise her Royal Elvish language, instead choosing to curse and abuse Isuas in an ungodly mixture of Common Elvish and Orcish, and even the Orcish epithets she chooses belong not to the Common Orc tongue but to the much cruder pidgin Orcish that was the lingua franca of the gladiator pits. All in all it makes for a terrifying verbal assault. I am meanwhile standing open-mouthed at this exhibition. I did foresee that Makri would be no easy task master, but I wasn't expecting her to half kill her pupil on the first day.

Possibly sensing that the youngster is about to expire, Makri removes her foot from Isuas's throat. Isuas sobs. This seems to infuriate Makri even more.

"Stop crying, you ignorant little whore. You wanted to learn how to fight. Well, get up and fight, you cusux."

Cusux is pidgin Orcish. It's about the rudest thing you can possibly say to anyone. If Isuas ever repeats it to Lord Kalith he'll send up his fleet to sack Turai. Isuas, having made two game attempts at attacking, now seems a little unwilling to try a third. She rises, but slowly, so Makri kicks her savagely in the ribs, making her howl, as she falls over again.

"Don't hang around on the ground, stupid. You think your opponent is going to wait all day for you to get ready? Pick up your weapons and attack me and this time you better do it properly or I swear I'll put this sword in through your mouth and out through the back of your throat."

Feeling that this is going rather too far, I hasten forward.

"Makri," I call, endeavouring to make my voice jovial rather than appalled. "Just called in to see how things are going."

Makri whirls round. She's not pleased to see me.

"Can't talk, Thraxas, I'm busy."

"So I see."

Isuas is lying on the ground, holding her ribs and sobbing.

"Possibly time for a little break?" I suggest. "Maybe smoke some thazis?"

"No time for that," says Makri dismissively. "I have to teach this imbecile to fight. Goodbye."

Makri turns back to her pupil and screams at her to get up. Isuas breaks down completely, and starts bawling. I lay my hand on Makri's shoulder.

"Don't you think you're being a little—"

Makri spins to face me again, a truly savage expression on her face.

"Get out of here, Thraxas," she yells angrily. "Go investigate. And don't bother me again."

I'm taken aback. I've seen Makri in a foul mood plenty of times before but I wasn't expecting such passions to be raised in the matter of the junior tournament. I decide to withdraw. After all, it is really Makri's business and not mine. I just hope Lady Yestar doesn't ban me from the Palace when she learns of Makri's barbaric behaviour.

I walk back to the path, turning my head for a last look before leaving. Makri has hauled Isuas to her feet and forced her to attack again. As I watch, Makri smacks her practice sword on to Isuas's fingers, making her shriek with pain and once more drop her blade.

"Keep hold of your sword, you miserable cusux!" yells Makri, accentuating each word with a vicious blow. I shudder.

Riding back along the path, I try to remember what my early weapons training was like. Quite rough I think, but nothing in comparison with the lessons Isuas is receiving from Makri the madwoman. I pray that Isuas makes it through the day in one piece. If she does, I'm certain she won't be back for a second.

I ride round the island till I reach one of the paths that lead towards the middle of Avula. It runs along the banks of the river that rises in the central hills. From here I can ride most of the way to the Palace, though I'll have to walk the last part as it is forbidden to take horses into the central clearing. I haven't seen this part of the island before. It's less heavily wooded, with some areas of grassland and a few cultivated fields. Although the majority of the houses I pass are still high up in the trees, there are a few more buildings at ground level. These are of simple construction, but all bear the signs of fine craftsmanship. Everything on Avula does. They don't seem to build anything shoddily.

"The Ossuni Elves perform all work with love and perfection," I remember Vas-ar-Methet saying a long time ago.

I wonder about his daughter having an affair with Gulas-ar-Thetos. If she was, does it make her more or less likely to have damaged the Tree? Get back at your lover by damaging his precious Hesuni Tree? Maybe. I've known stranger ways of taking revenge. But then, why kill him later? It seems like far too extreme a thing for Elith to have done.

Much as I hate to admit it, I can't run away from the fact that I have now spoken to a witness who actually saw the murder. Though the weaver Caripatha showed some signs of erratic behaviour, she didn't sound to me like an Elf who was lying or unsure of what she saw. Things are looking worse for Elith. I might yet be forced to fall back on finding some extenuating circumstances to save her from execution.

Cursing all witnesses who make life difficult for my clients, I ride on. Why are so many of the Elves acting strangely? It's not just Elith. Gorith-ar-Del, for instance. I can understand his dislike for me, but why did he suddenly quit his work as a longbow-maker? Most un-Elf-like. I think back to the sailor who plunged to his death from the rigging. Very strange. As was the behaviour of Caripatha, who hasn't woven anything for a month, and suddenly decided she had to be somewhere else, rushing off without a word of explanation to her companion. What's the matter with them all?

An Elf on horseback approaches me on the path. Rather than riding past he draws his horse up in front of mine and halts, staring at me intently. He's an old Elf, the oldest I've seen on the island. He sits upright in his saddle but his hair is white and his brow is a mass of fine wrinkles.

"I am Visan, the Keeper of Lore," he says. "I believe you wish to talk to me?"

"I do."

"Then talk."

"I'd like to know about the disputed succession of the Tree Priesthood."

"Talking about that to a stranger would be calanith. Also, it is a very old and obscure story regarding junior branches of cousins' families that you would neither understand nor enjoy."

"I haven't enjoyed much since I arrived here. I don't need to know the whole history, just what might be happening now. For instance, did anyone have it in for Gulas?"

"Yes," says Visan, surprising me with his directness. "Hith-ar-Key, who claims that the Priesthood should be his. His complaints to the Council of Elders are neverending."

"How strong is his claim?"

"That is calanith."

Visan declines to answer my next few questions on

the same grounds. I can see I'm not going to learn any
secret details here.

"Well, might Hith have damaged the Hesuni Tree
to discredit Gulas?"

Visan sits astride his horse, elderly and sedate, and
considers my question.

"Yes," he says finally. "He might."

"Was it looked into at the time?"

Visan shakes his head. "Certainly not. Such an outrageous idea would not have occurred to anyone on
the island."

"But now I've suggested it . . . ?"

"It's possible."

Visan nods to me, then rides off. Whether I've
upset him by trampling on something calanith or just
tired him out with my questions, I can't say. At least
I've dragged another suspect on to the scene.

I ride on till I reach a place where nine or ten
horses roam free in a large paddock. Here I have to
leave my mount and continue on foot. I don't travel
far before I run into a large crowd of Elves who are
staring expectantly at a tree. Thinking that this is
probably some private tree matter that only Elves will
fully appreciate, I make to walk on by till suddenly a
voice calls out, "Avula's greatest juggler—in prepara-
tion for the festival—Shuthan-ir-Hemas!"

The watching Elves applaud as Shuthan-ir-Hemas
steps nimbly out along a branch and bows to them all.
She's a slender young Elf with bare feet and extremely
long hair, and from the excited words of the crowd I
can tell that they're expecting great things of her. Still
keen for some information on which way to bet, I hang
around to study her act.

Shuthan starts confidently, juggling three balls and
performing some standard tricks while making faces at
the crowd. I've seen this sort of thing often enough

in Turai, but she quickly ups the tempo, adding fourth
and fifth balls, still juggling easily while hopping back
and forward along the branch. The crowd cheers and
shouts encouragement. Obviously Shuthan-ir-Hemas is
a popular favourite.

Unfortunately things go badly wrong when she tries
to add a sixth ball to the routine. She fails to catch
it, the sequence goes wrong, and the balls tumble from
her hands. In an effort to retrieve the situation Shuthan
trips clumsily over her feet and plunges to the ground,
landing heavily on the heads of the onlookers. There
are groans of disappointment from the audience.

"She's not at her best," they say with disappointment.

"Just hasn't got the same skill she used to have."

Others mutter that this is going to be a bad festival
for Avula. Their play is being directed by an incompetent
Sorcerer, their choir is nowhere near the standard of that
of the Venians, and now even their top juggler is about
to let them down.

"If Firees-ar-Key doesn't win the junior tournament
we'll be the laughing stock of the Ossuni Islands,"
mutters one disconsolate Elf to his companion.

I walk on. I feel sorry for the Avulans, but that's one
juggler I won't be placing a bet on.

It's late in the afternoon. The weather is mild and
a light breeze blows small ripples over the pools of
water at the Hesuni Tree. The clearing is busier than
usual, with Elves from other islands paying their
respects to the Tree. They ignore me as I stroll over
the grass. I'm not the only Human in view. Over by
the smaller of the pools some Elves are pointing out
features of the local scenery to a delegation of visitors from Mattesh.

I've been suspicious of the large pool ever since
Makri found herself so powerfully affected by drinking the water. I'm here to work a spell. I know the

Elves won't like it. I considered coming here in the early hours of the morning when it might be quieter, but I suspect that Kalith will have set his attendants to watch over it and I'd be easily spotted. Here in the crowd I'm hoping I might just work some sorcery unnoticed.

I sit down next to the pool. I casually dip my finger into the water then sprinkle a few drops on to a small scrap of parchment. I look round. No one is paying any attention to me. Just another large detective taking a rest from his exertions.

I drift slowly into a state of concentration. I utter the arcane words of the Spell of Not Belonging. I've used this spell in the past and found it simple and effective, though it's possible that the mystic field projected by the Hesuni Tree will render it useless. I watch the pool, and wait. After a minute or so I notice something bobbing to the surface, quite close to me. I get up, stretch and saunter round the edge, a man without a care in the world. Floating on the surface is a small package. I reach down to adjust my boot, quickly scoop up the package, then walk on.

I'm well pleased with myself. I might not be much of a Sorcerer, but it takes a cool head to successfully work a spell like that in public without a soul noticing anything.

"Easy as bribing a Senator," I mutter, strolling over the grass.

I duck behind a tree and take out the package. I unwrap the waterproof oilskin. Inside is some white powder. I dip my finger in, taking a tiny pinch to my lips to taste it.

It's dwa. The most powerfully addictive drug on the market. The scourge of the Human Lands, and now available at the most exclusive locations in Elfland. I'm just congratulating myself on finally making some progress when a hand falls heavily on my shoulder.

"I arrest you in the name of Lord Kalith-ar-Yil."

I'm surrounded by nine Elves in Kalith's regalia, swords at the ready.

"Try to say a spell and we'll run you through before you utter a word."

Their leader snatches the packet from me.

"Do you have an explanation for this?" he demands.

I do, but I'm not going to waste it on him. They're going to take me to Kalith-ar-Yil anyway, so I might as well save my breath till I get there. I'm led through the clearing and up the long ladders to the Tree Palace, where they put me in a small cell with one chair and a nice view of the tree tops through the barred window.

"There are guards outside the window with bows. If you try to escape they have instructions to shoot. We do not take kindly to peddlers of drugs on Avula."

I'm left alone. I sit on the chair. Somehow none of this has come as a surprise. I've been thrown in jail so many times in Turai and elsewhere in the west that it was probably only a matter of time before I ended up in an Elvish prison.

Chapter Fourteen

The prison cell is clean and airy. There's a pitcher of water on the table and shortly after I arrive a guard brings me a loaf of bread. The sun streams in through the window and from somewhere in the forest below I can hear a choir practising. In terms of comfort it doesn't compare too badly with my rooms in the Avenging Axe.

The first person to visit me is Ambassador Turius. I have not yet encountered our Ambassador to Avula, so I greet him warmly and thank him for arriving so swiftly.

"It's reassuring to know that our Ambassadors are resolute in their task of protecting Turanian citizens unjustly incarcerated in foreign lands. Once you get me out of here, I shall speak very highly of you to Deputy Consul Cicerius."

"I haven't come to get you out," says the Ambassador.

"You haven't?"

"No. As far as I'm concerned you can stay here for the rest of your life. Everyone advised you to keep out of Elvish affairs. You refused to listen to this advice. Now you're in a cell, which is exactly what was to be expected."

"Aren't you bothered about whether I actually committed a crime?"

The ambassador shrugs. "If you did, Lord Kalith-ar-Yil will punish you. If you didn't, he'll let you go in due course. He's a fair-minded Elf."

"Then why the hell did you bother coming to see me?"

"A Turanian Ambassador always does his duty. I see you have food and water. Excellent. Your needs are being well catered for. Now goodbye."

Turius departs. I swear he enjoyed that conversation. I sit down and listen to the choir, and wonder who Turius bribed to get his cushy job as Ambassador to Avula.

My next visitor is an Elf of advanced years who informs me that his name is Rekis-ar-Lin and he is a member of the Council of Elders. He's accompanied by a scribe who takes down our conversation.

"I have been given responsibility for investigating this matter. Why were you found with a package of dwa?"

"I took it out of the pool."

"How did it get there?"

I tell him I've no idea.

"And how did you come to find it?"

"I looked."

"Why?"

"Investigator's intuition."

Councillor Rekis is dubious, but I don't want to tell him that I used a spell to locate the dwa because I know that will only lead to more trouble. However the Councillor has difficulty believing that, with all the

Elves in the area, it just happened to be me who found a packet of dwa in the pool.

"It seems to us more likely that you brought the dwa with you from Turai."

"Why would I do that? Everyone knows Elves don't go for dwa. Doesn't work on them."

"You would no doubt be aware that there would be many Humans on the island at the time of the festival. Perhaps you wished to sell it to them. Perhaps you yourself are so addicted that you were unable to travel without it. Either way, you are not telling me everything you know. You will provide me with a precise description of your actions since landing on Avula."

I clam up. Any time I'm in a cell, I just get wary about giving precise descriptions of my actions. We're interrupted by the arrival of Jir-ar-Eth, Kalith's Chief Sorcerer. He stares at me for a few seconds.

"He used a spell," he says. "But I can't tell which one."

Councillor Rekis stares at me coldly.

"You used a spell in the vicinity of the Hesuni Tree? On Avula, that is calanith. It is also a crime. What was it?"

"A love spell. I'm looking for romance."

Jir-ar-Eth speaks a few words and there is a slight cooling of the air in the cell.

"I've dampened the area," he says to Rekis. "The prisoner will not be able to use sorcery to escape. He has very little power anyway."

The Sorcerer stares at the necklace I'm wearing.

"A spell protection charm? With Red Elvish Cloth? Where did you get that?"

"Just picked it up along the way."

They leave me alone. I eat bread. I'm feeling hard done by. For the rest of the day my only other visitor is the guard who brings me some food. I demand to see Lord Kalith. The guard, rather politely, informs me that Lord Kalith is busy.

Night falls. I've been in so many cells it doesn't particularly bother me, but I'm annoyed at the waste of my time. Shouldn't someone have been here to help? Deputy Consul Cicerius for instance. Or Makri. She ought to at least have visited me. Maybe she's still tormenting the unfortunate Elf child. I go to sleep madder than a mad dragon and I wake slightly madder.

It's approaching lunchtime and it's getting to the stage where I'm seriously considering slugging the next person who comes into my cell and risking a jail break when Lord Kalith finally gets round to paying me a visit.

"Dwa is a filthy drug," he says, getting right down to business. "It is a curse on the Human Lands. It has never been seen on Avula before."

"Only because you didn't bother to look. And don't lecture me about using a spell in the vicinity of the Hesuni Tree. If I hadn't done that you'd never have known about the dwa."

"You still claim that you did not bring the substance with you?"

"Of course I didn't. Do you seriously believe I did?"

"Why would I not?" says the Elf Lord. "You have hardly shown yourself to be a man of sober habits. You brought a barrel of beer on to my ship and when you finished that you resorted to theft to meet your craving. You may have thought you were unobserved when you removed three large wineskins from Osath's kitchen, but I assure you that you were not. Since arriving on Avula you have mounted an almost continual search for beer, culminating in what I am reliably informed were scenes of unheard-of excess at the haunt of the armourers. And this only the day after you and your female companion ingested so much thazis as to be unable to remember your own identities. The story of you talking to the butterflies has been widely reported all over Avula."

"I was not talking to the butterflies," I reply, with some dignity. "And is there any point to all this?"

"The point is that you are a corrupting influence. Thazis is not illegal on Avula, but we discourage its use. Now one of my most respected councillors informs me that not only did he find three thazis sticks in his daughter's room, but she has informed him that she wishes to travel to Turai to write poetry. His wife is now terrified that their daughter will return home with a pierced nose and an Orcish love-child."

We seem to be straying from the point here. I tell Lord Kalith-ar-Yil that he can criticise me as much as he likes, but he can't deny that I've dug up evidence of some strange goings-on on his island.

"And what exactly are these goings-on?"

"I need to investigate more."

"Nothing you find will change the fact that Elith-ir-Methet was seen stabbing Gulas-ar-Thetos. You yourself have talked to a witness."

"I still need to investigate more."

Lord Kalith is not minded to let me out. There are three days left till the start of the festival and I'm running out of time.

"You cannot execute Vas-ar-Methet's daughter without the fullest investigation," I insist.

"Her punishment has not been decided."

"But her guilt has. You must allow me to continue with my investigation."

Kalith is offended by my tone and tells me sharply that his patience with me is wearing thin.

"Fine," I say. "Though I must admit to being very surprised at an Elf Lord being such a poor sport. In

Turai, the aristocracy does not stoop to such low tactics when faced with defeat."

Kalith's head jerks in surprise.

"What do you mean by that?"

"Well, it's pretty clear that this is all down to me
beating you heavily at the niarit board. Ever since then
it's been nothing but trouble all the way for me. You've
hindered my investigation at every turn simply because
you can't stand losing to a Human."

I move towards the window, raising my voice so the
guards outside can hear.

"I guess it was just too embarrassing for the niarit
champion of the Ossuni Elves to have his conqueror
walking around the island, telling everyone about the
bad variation of the Harper's Game he'd played. The
armourers warned me you'd probably throw me in jail
rather than risk facing me over the board again . . ."

From outside my cell comes something that sounds
very like muffled laughter. Lord Kalith, an Elf who
proved his bravery and honour time and again against
the Orcs, can't take any more of this. And so it is that
minutes later I find myself sitting at the table facing
an angry Kalith-ar-Yil over a niarit board, hastily
brought by a guard in response to his Lord's furious
instructions.

"Don't bother locking the cell," I call after the jailer.
"I'll be walking out of here soon enough. So, Lord
Kalith, are we—"

"Enough talking," says Kalith. "Play."

I start moving my Hoplites forward. Kalith counters
warily. But I notice he's getting his Elephants ready,
and his Heavy Cavalry.

The sun shines cheerfully into the cell. Parrots
squawk merrily in the trees. Outside it's another bright
day in Avula. Inside, things are not so good, at least
for Lord Kalith. Not too long after the start of the

game his forces lie in ruins, mere dust under the wheels of the unstoppable Thraxas war chariot. Kalith, after his tentative opening, was unable to resist a wild assault on my forces using his heaviest troops, an assault that I withstood for just long enough to bring his army exactly where I wanted it before falling back with my centre, outflanking him on both sides and carrying out what could only be described as a massacre. His Hero, Plague Carrier, Harper, Wizard and Healer lie dead beneath a sad tangle of dead Elephants and decimated Trolls.

Kalith looks grimly at the miserable remains and concedes defeat. I am now free to go, as per our pre-game agreement.

"Any chance of some food?" I ask, as I sling my cloak over my shoulders.

"You may visit the kitchens," replies Lord Kalith, summoning up the last reserves of his good breeding. "The guards will show you the way."

"Thank you. I take it that I will be allowed to speak with my client again?"

Lord Kalith allows that I can, which is a relief. I wasn't looking forward to trying to break back into prison.

In the short walk between the cell and the main Palace building, I pass two stern-looking Elves marching another prisoner into the lockup. I recognise the captive, though I don't know his name. It's the young Elf whom the poet Droo was arguing with in the clearing at the three oaks and river. His eyes are blank and he isn't walking very steadily. The guards help him along, shepherding him into a cell.

I'm shown to the kitchens. There I find Osath the cook, whom I haven't seen since I disembarked. He's delighted to see me. He knows how much I appreciate his cooking.

"Thraxas! They let you out? The word in the kitchens was that Lord Kalith was going to throw away the key. What happened? Did your Ambassador stand bail?"

"The Turanian Ambassador is about as much use as a one-legged gladiator. No, I was forced back on my own resources. I beat Kalith at niarit again."

Osath laughs heartily at this, as do his assistants. Again the Elves are amused at Kalith losing. Which just goes to show that even a well-loved and respected Elf Lord shouldn't go around bragging about his prowess at the niarit board. It annoys everyone.

Osath begins to pile up food in front of me and I start shovelling it in.

"I have to ask you a few questions, Osath."

The chef looks doubtful. "We can't tell you anything about Elith, Thraxas. It would be awkward for us to discuss it . . ."

"I wasn't talking about Elith. Are you and your fellow low-lives in the kitchens planning to bet on the juggling competition?"

This brings Osath and his helpers clustering round keenly.

"We are. I was going to bet on young Shuthan-ir-Hemas," replies Osath. "I've seen her put up some sensational performances. But I hear she's gone off the boil."

"She has. Yesterday I saw her trip over her own feet. Didn't look like a woman who was about to win. I did see a young woman called Usath, from Ven, juggling seven balls and looking good for a few more. You know anything about her past form?"

"Junior champion at the competition two years ago in Corinthal," says a young cook. "She's still inexperienced, but she might do well. I think she might be worth a gamble, but there's another juggler from Corinthal called Arith-ar-Tho who's built up a fine reputation recently. Be best to check him out if you get the chance."

I thank them for their help.

"What's this we hear about Makri teaching Isuas how to fight?"

"I thought that was meant to be a secret."

"There are no secrets in a Palace kitchen," says Osath. "Lady Yestar might not have told Lord Kalith about it, but we're the ones that have to make up food for them every day. Is there any chance of Makri teaching the kid well enough to enter the tournament? Would it be worth a bet? Isuas is so weak we'd get a good price on her winning even one fight against the most hopeless opponent. In fact, you'd get a good price on the kid even staying on her feet for thirty seconds."

I consider this, while mopping up some fragments of venison pie with a hunk of bread.

"I think Isuas will give up before the tournament. Makri's treating her pretty rough. But if things change, I'll let you know. Make sure you don't let on to anyone that Makri's teaching her though, or the price will drop."

Having cemented my good relations with the lower Elvish order by some solid gambling talk, I emerge from the Palace well fed and in good shape for investigating, which is just as well as I've lost time I couldn't afford and have a great deal to do.

I find Lasas-ar-Thetos in a small hut in a tree near to the Hesuni. Around his head he has a yellow band denoting his new rank as Chief Tree Priest. He's heard about recent events and displays a deep sadness.

"To think that such a substance could be polluting the sacred water of the Hesuni Tree. It brings shame to the whole island. I cringe at the thought of what my dear brother would have made of it."

At least Avula's new Tree Priest doesn't blame me.

"When Lord Kalith informed me of the matter I told him that you were not a man who would bring dwa to our island. Indeed, we should be grateful to you for uncovering it. Do you know where it came from?"

I admit that I don't, but I'm still working on it. It's something of a relief to find an aristocratic Elf who doesn't seem to hold me responsible for everything that's been going on around here. Now that Lasas has got over the immediate shock of his brother's death, he's proving to be a calm and responsible Elf. I ask him again if there's anything he might have forgotten to tell me.

"No strange goings-on? No hint of who might have been in the vicinity with dwa?"

"Nothing, I am afraid. I have been keeping my ear to the ground, but really since my brother was killed I have been too busy with preparations for the funeral and with taking up the reins of the Priesthood."

At least we seem to have got to the root of the bad dreams the Avulans have been suffering from. Lasas is firmly of the opinion that a powerful alien drug, contained in the water that feeds the Hesuni Tree, would be more than enough to give the Elves nightmares.

"All Avulans communicate with the Tree. As it was ingesting poison, so it produced nightmares. We must be grateful to you for finding it. I am now attempting to cleanse the area by means of ritual."

Tramping back across the clearing, I'm frustrated. Everyone knows that something strange has been going on but no one quite knows what. And no one can suggest a motive for Elith killing Gulas. Even Elith, who admits to doing it, can't think of a motive. Before I leave I ask Lasas if he has encountered Gorith-ar-Del yet.

"Should I have?"

"Probably not. It's just I keep noticing him hanging

round the area. Would you let me know if he contacts you in any way?"

Lasas says that he will, and I depart. I find Harmon Half-Elf and Lanius Suncatcher in the enclave of houses next to the Turanian Ambassador's residence. I know that Harmon Half-Elf has seen the prisoner and I want his opinion on whether she has been attacked or bemused by sorcery.

"I did not get that impression," he tells me. "Although with the Hesuni Tree in the vicinity, it is impossible to be certain. However, I think that if she had had her memory wiped or been victim of some spell that overpowered her will, forcing her to kill the priest, there would be some trace of it remaining. I know that Jirar-Eth has searched very thoroughly for any sign of this and has been unable to locate anything."

"And congratulations on getting out of jail," adds Lanius Suncatcher.

The two Sorcerers are not entirely unsympathetic to my cause.

"If only because you are refusing to give up. Despite the fact that everyone knows Elith is guilty, I think the Avulans are starting to respect you for the way you keep on trying to help Vas-ar-Methet. They value friendship. But really, Thraxas, what can you hope to achieve now? Elith-ir-Methet is guilty. People saw her kill Gulas. She admits it."

They offer me some wine. I drain the goblet and rise to my feet.

"If I find some reasonable motive, she might not be executed."

Stuck for inspiration, I seek out Makri. My horse is in the paddock where I left it, so I saddle up and ride round the island. Every clearing is now filled with choirs, actors, jugglers, all practising for the festival. As the path narrows between the encroaching trees I

keep a keen eye out for masked Elves with spears who
might be about to attack me, but none appear. So far
I have not managed to gather the slightest clue as to
who they are or who they might be working for. As
far as I know, the Elves have nothing that is equivalent to the Assassins in Turai, but someone is certainly
out to get me. Someone with powerful sorcerous backing. Once more I'm grateful for my excellent spell
protection charm. It will protect me from most magical
attacks, though not from invisible Elves suddenly
appearing and gutting me with their spears.

I dismount near the private clearing and again
advance cautiously. I'm wondering if Isuas has given
up. Before long I hear Makri's voice raised in anger.

"Fight, you cusux! If you trip over your feet one
more time I swear I'll kill you. You want to see my
Orcish blade? I'll let you see it, you useless brat, I'll
pin you to that tree with it."

This is followed by the sound of a wooden sword
cracking over a young Elf's head, and some wailing.

I peer into the clearing. Isuas has shown some spirit
in returning for more lessons, but Makri doesn't seem
to appreciate it. The young Elf is struggling to her feet
under a rain of blows, while Makri continues to scream
abuse at her.

"Didn't I show you how to parry? Well, parry this!"

Makri hits Isuas with a stroke that must come close
to breaking her shoulder. Isuas yells in pain. This
annoys Makri even more.

"I didn't say cry like a girl, I said parry. Now do it."

Makri slashes at the young Elf. Isuas makes a
reasonable attempt at deflecting the blow, but Makri
simply uses her other blade to whack Isuas on the side
of the head, sending her once more thumping to the
ground.

I'm fairly aghast at this. The sight of Makri using

her full fighting skills against the weak little Elf would distress the hardest of hearts. Isuas lies on the ground sobbing, where she is in receipt of a further torrent of abuse.

"You useless exin miserable zutha pathetic cusux," screams Makri, using a string of vile Orcish epithets, some of them unintelligible to me and some quite possibly never heard in the western world before.

Makri drops her swords and yanks Isuas to her feet.

"Are all Elves as pitiful as you? God help you if the Orcs ever sail down to Avula. Pah! You're so pathetic I don't even need a weapon."

Isuas suddenly looks angry. The insults are getting to her. She leaps to attack Makri, showing a surprising turn of speed. Makri stands her ground, merely twisting her body to avoid the blades before stepping lightly to one side. Isuas tries to turn and face her, but Makri, displaying new heights of savagery, actually kicks her in the head. Isuas crumples, which doesn't prevent Makri from getting in another two kicks before she hits the ground. This time the young Elf lies still. I hurry forward, alarmed.

"Goddammit, Makri, you've killed her."

Makri looks round, unconcerned.

"No I haven't. She's just dazed. What are you doing here?"

"I came to talk to you. If you can spare a moment in between tormenting that unfortunate youth."

"Unfortunate?" says Makri, puzzled. "She's being taught to fight by the undefeated champion gladiator of all the Orc Lands. I'd call that a privilege."

Isuas groans. Makri, who possesses surprising strength despite her slender frame, hoists her into the air and tosses her in the direction of a water bottle under a tree.

"Take a drink," she says. "And stop crying."

"Is it really necessary to be this brutal?"

Makri shrugs. "I'm trying to teach her a lot in a hurry. Anyway, we're using wooden swords. How brutal can you be with a wooden sword?"

"Pretty brutal, from what I saw. When Lady Yestar gave her permission for this I doubt very much if she quite foresaw that you would be kicking her daughter in the head. Shouldn't you be doing something about the bleeding?"

"The island is full of healers. They'll sort her out later. What are you here for?"

"To talk. I'm still baffled by this case and I'm running out of time. I figured I might get some inspiration if we talked it out."

"I can't spare the time right now. I'll be back at Camith's after dark—can it wait till then?"

I suppose it can.

"Try not to kill Isuas."

"Death in training isn't so bad," states Makri, firmly. "Better than disgracing yourself in the arena. Which," she adds, turning menacingly back to the young Elf, "no pupil of mine is going to do. So get up and fight."

I leave them to it.

I call back to Makri from the edge of the clearing. "What does zutha mean?"

Makri gives me a translation. I wince. It's even worse than cusux.

Chapter Fifteen

———— ❦ ————

I return to Camith's peaceful home, where I wash, eat and stare out of the window. I'm in need of some inspiration. None is forthcoming. Somewhere outside, an Elvish choir is singing, a long slow tribute to one of Lord Kalith's ancestors. It's meant to be soothing, but I'm too pressurised to appreciate it.

It's late into the night when Makri returns. She brings a tray of food into my room and tells me with a disgruntled air that she again encountered masked Elves with spears.

"On that quiet bit of walkway where you never see anyone. I turned the corner and there they were, marching towards me, spears at the ready."

Makri, unwilling to flee again, had drawn her swords and made ready to repel her attackers.

"But then they disappeared. Just vanished into the air."

I nod. A similar experience to mine.

"So what's going on with them?" demands Makri.

"Do they want to attack us or not? I wish they'd just get on with it. I can't be doing with all this appearing and disappearing. It's no way to fight."

"Speaking of fighting, how is Isuas?"

"Bruised and bloody," replies Makri. "I told her to visit Vas-ar-Methet for some healing before she saw her father. Lady Yestar is still keeping it all a secret."

I again express my doubts about the ferocity of Makri's training and Makri is again unrepentant. With so little time to prepare she is of the opinion that there is no alternative.

"And that's not the only reason. I'm strengthening her spirit. If she ever gets in a fight for real, she'll be glad I showed her the Gaxeen."

"Gaxeen? What's that?"

Makri puts down her tray, her meal unfinished. She is rarely an enthusiastic eater.

"Orcish. The Way of the Gaxeen. It translates as something like the 'Spirit of the Insane Warrior.' It's what you do when you find yourself faced with insurmountable odds. Or up against an opponent whom you can't beat with skill or craft. You go Gaxeen, as we used to say. A fury in which you do not fear for your life."

I'm interested. Much of Makri's experience of Orcish ways is unknown to us in the west. A few months ago she helped me solve a case with her knowledge of Orcish religion and prior to that I didn't even know they had a religion.

"How long does it take to learn the Way of the Gaxeen?"

"Depends on the person, or the Orc. When I first started fighting I picked up skill with weapons easily enough, but one day my trainer said I hadn't enough spirit so he'd decided to execute me. He took away my swords and told the four gladiators standing nearby that whoever killed me would get a reward. And after I'd scaled the wall of the pit, slain a guard with my bare hands to get his sword, then massacred the four gladiators in a blind fury, my trainer clapped me on the back and said, 'Well done, you have learned the Way of the Gaxeen.' I rather liked that old trainer. I had to kill him later, of course, when I made my escape."

"Well, Makri, this is a fabulous gift for Isuas. When she starts slaughtering her playmates I imagine Lord Kalith will be beside himself with joy. How is she doing? If she can win one fight I might be up for some good winnings, which of course I'll share with you."

Makri shakes her head.

"Don't bet on her. She's still hopeless. If her first opponent has two legs and two arms she won't last thirty seconds."

"What if he's only got one arm and one leg?"

"She still won't win."

Not wishing to let good food go to waste, I pick up Makri's tray and finish off what's left.

"I'm stuck in my investigation. I've managed to uncover some strange things but none of it is helping to clear Elith. You've heard about the dwa in the pool? That's what was polluting the water and giving the Elves bad dreams. And I'm sure that's what made you so stoned when we visited the Tree Palace. Someone has discovered that dwa mixed with the sacred water makes for a powerful drug that affects Elves. No doubt that's why all these young Elves have been acting so strangely, going around with glazed eyes, not working, breaking their word and so on. And though Kalith will never acknowledge it, I'm certain that the Elf who fell from the rigging did so while under the influence. Took his supply with him on the voyage."

Makri nods. "Makes sense. I can see why they'd all go for it. I felt great after I drank the water. Do you have any more?"

I frown. "That's not quite the reaction I was looking for, Makri. You're supposed to be outraged that the foul substance dwa is now polluting the world of the Elves."

"Oh well, that too. Yes, it's a shock. The Avulans will have to take swift action to prevent it spreading. Maybe we should hunt around, see if anyone else has some of the mixture and confiscate it?"

I glare at Makri. Back in Turai I have more than once suspected that she has been experimenting with dwa and I strongly disapprove.

"Never mind confiscating drugs. We already have a reputation as people of immoderate habits. Lord Kalith was fairly cutting on the subject, and that was before I beat him at niarit again. Now he's as miserable as a Niojan whore and will be down on us like a bad spell if he catches us doing anything disreputable.

"If Elith-ir-Methet would just tell me exactly what was going on between her and Gulas, I might be able to get to the bottom of the affair. I should look into who is bringing the dwa into Avula, but with so few contacts it could take me a long time to find out, and I'm short of time. I'll suggest to Jir-ar-Eth that he does some sorcerous scanning of the harbours. He might be able to pick up something. And I'd like to have someone examine Gorith-ar-Del's movements over the past few months. There's an Elf who's a strong suspect. He gave up his job and now he keeps hanging round the Hesuni Tree acting suspiciously."

"Do you think whoever is dealing dwa is responsible for attacking us?" says Makri.

"Yes. Back in Turai it's the first thing I'd have suspected, but I just never expected it here."

Makri wonders if Elith-ir-Methet is clamming up just to avoid the disgrace of having a calanith relationship with a Tree Priest.

"Surely her being executed is more of a disgrace for the rest of the family?"

"Who knows? Taboos are funny things when you're outside them. I can't work out what they'd find most important. Every other Elf who's involved is running for cover. There's no chance of any co-operation there."

Inspiration suddenly strikes.

"I know someone I might be able to put a little pressure on—Droo's boyfriend. Name of Lithias, I think. A poetic young Elf, last seen being tossed into a cell at the Tree Palace. From the way he was swaying around I'd say he was one rebellious youth who'd been dabbling with foreign substances. Perhaps Droo would persuade him to come clean about everything and that might give me some sort of lever over Elith."

"Will Droo help you?"

"She might. She seemed to like me. Anyway, I'll tell her it's the best thing she can do for her boyfriend. That usually works, even when it isn't true."

And so it proves the next day when we locate Droo at a treehouse not far from Camith's. She's not actually in the house; she's perched at the end of a slender branch high above the ground. Lithias's incarceration has plunged her into gloom and she has not moved from the spot for twenty-four hours. Her parents are so worried that they are actually glad to see Makri and me climbing up their dwelling place, although, as with most of the Avulans, they cannot prevent themselves from examining us with interest and some suspicion. Particularly Makri. Everyone still gapes at her, though less impolitely than when we first arrived. The mother is in tears, the father is raging, and they're cursing the fate that made their daughter fall in love with such a hopeless specimen as Lithias.

"Why couldn't she have fallen for a warrior?" wails her mother. "Or the silversmith's son?"

"You aren't planning to jump, are you?" I call, from the safety of the treehouse.

"Maybe," replies Droo.

"It's not that bad. Lithias hasn't done anything serious, Lord Kalith will let him go in a day or two. We're going there now. Come with us and we can sort things out."

Droo looks up.

"You're really going to see him?"

"Yes. We have free access into the Palace, courtesy of Lady Yestar."

Droo rises and hops nimbly along the branch. She ignores the admonitions from her parents and rushes inside the house, saying that she has to brush her hair before seeing Lithias.

"Lithias is a fool," says her father. He turns to Makri. "And your nose ring is disgusting."

"Well, we'd better get going," I say.

The Elf gives me a stern look. "You are the Investigator? You look like you would have difficulty finding a large tree in a small field."

This is one rude Elf. I start to understand why young Droo might not be that happy at home.

"I'd have let her stay on the branch," he mutters as a parting shot, then departs into the house.

Droo reappears. Her short yellow hair is sticking up from her head. It's an odd style for an Elf.

"You know why Lithias was arrested? He tried to start a fight with the blacksmith over a poem. How ridiculous. He's been like that for weeks. Just one irrational action after another."

Droo studies Makri as we take the walkway towards the Tree Palace.

"Are your toenails really golden?"

"Of course not. I've painted them."

Droo, unfamiliar with the concept of painted

toenails, is impressed. "Did it hurt getting your nose pierced?"

"Not really. But it was sore when the Orcs ripped it out during a fight."

"I wanted to get my ears pierced, but my father wouldn't let me. It's calanith for Elves to pierce their bodies."

I hasten to change the subject. Makri has an unfortunate habit of wondering out loud about getting rings put through her nipples and I never like to hear this sort of thing.

"How long has Lithias been acting strangely?"

"Months. Of course, he never did act entirely normally. That's why I like him. But recently he's just been out of control."

"You know he's been taking dwa?"

Droo's face falls. "I told him it was stupid."

I ask the young poet if she knows whom he buys it from, but she says that she doesn't. Nor does she know who has been bringing it to the island.

"I stayed well away from the whole thing."

I'm not sure if she's telling the truth, but I let it pass. Halfway to the Palace we come across an Elf I recognise. It's Shuthan-ir-Hemas, Avula's favourite juggler. She's lying on the wooden pathway, sleeping. Her juggling kit is strewn around her in disarray.

"Oh dear," says Droo, who obviously recognises the symptoms. So do I. You can't walk around Twelve Seas without stumbling over addicts lying unconscious on every street corner, but I never thought I'd see it spreading like this among the young Elves.

We have some difficulty getting in to see Lithias and are denied access till Makri sends a message to Lady Yestar requesting permission as a favour to me. She smiles smugly.

"You'd be lost without me, Thraxas."

"I can't think how I ever managed. Okay, let's question the errant poet."

Lithias's cell is as clean and airy as was mine, but Lithias, unused to incarceration, is slumped in despair by the wall. When he sees Droo he leaps to his feet with a cry of joy and they embrace. I let it go on for a few seconds before getting down to business. I ask Droo to leave us alone. She departs unwillingly, promising Lithias that she'll wait for him.

"Lithias, I have some questions for you. Answer them, let me sort things out, and nothing much will happen to you. If you refuse to answer, Lord Kalith will be down on you like a bad spell. It's going to dawn on him soon how large a problem he has with dwa and I get the feeling he might just exile everyone who's touched it."

Lithias hangs his head.

"I can't tell you anything," he says.

"You have to. Otherwise you'll be banished from Avula and Droo's mother will marry her off to the silversmith's son."

This gets to him. "The silversmith's son? Has he been hanging around Droo again?"

"Like bees round honey. And if you ever want to get out of this cell, you better talk to me. I want to know everything about the dwa in the sacred pool and I want to know everything you can tell me about Elithir-Methet, Gulas-ar-Thetos and his brother. Start at the beginning and don't stop unless I tell you to."

Lithias begins to talk; what he has to say is very interesting indeed, and long overdue. It turns out that young Lithias has been filling himself up with happy juice for the past three months, since a friend of his, another young poet, told him that if he wanted to have an experience that was worth writing a poem about he could show him how.

Lithias never wrote any poems. The drug made him too crazy to concentrate on poetry. "It felt good at first. After a while I didn't like it so much, but I couldn't stop."

He claims that only ten or so Elves were regular imbibers of the mixture of dwa and Hesuni water, but even so I'm surprised that such a thing could go on unnoticed right in the middle of the island. Lithias claims that they didn't actually have to go to the Hesuni Tree as the supplier would bring the mixture out to a clearing in the forest where he'd sell it to the Elves. Fairly cheaply, it seems, which would be standard behaviour at first. They'd soon find the price was on the way up.

"Who brought it to the island?"

Lithias doesn't know. He's frustratingly vague about the details and claims not even to know the identity of the Elf he bought it off.

"Would you recognise him again?"

Lithias shakes his head. "He wore a cowl and stood in the shadows. I never saw his face. Everything was very secret."

"It might have started off as a secret, but these things never stay that way. Earlier today I stepped over the unconscious figure of Avula's best-loved juggler and she wasn't making any attempt to hide what she'd been doing. How did Elith get involved? Was it through Gulas?"

Lithias doesn't know. He thinks that Elith was already taking dwa when he started.

"She was always hanging around the Hesuni Tree because she had a passion for Gulas. They were lovers before his father's death made him the Priest. He didn't want to be Priest, but he didn't have a choice. So they weren't meant to see each other any more, but I don't think they ever stopped. I used to hear some gossip about it. Lasas was never happy about it."

"Lasas? His brother? Why not?"

"Because he was in love with Elith as well. It drove him crazy that she was in love with his brother. Didn't you know that?"

Chapter Sixteen

Makri is waiting for me outside the cell.

"Learn anything?"

"Yes," I reply. "But nothing I like."

Lady Yestar appears as we approach the rear entrance to the Palace. She dismisses her attendants and greets us in her amicable well-bred manner and asks me if I still have hopes of clearing Elith, to which I reply that I do. She looks at me in her farseeing manner.

"You do not," she says.

"Well, I'm still going to try."

Yestar turns to Makri. "How is my daughter progressing?"

"Quite well."

"I notice that she has been very tired when she returns home at night."

"We've been practising hard."

"I also notice that her clothes are torn, her eyes are red and she has been in need of the services of a healer."

Makri shifts a little uncomfortably. "We've been practising hard," she repeats.

Lady Yestar nods. "Please remember that Isuas is delicate. I do not really expect that she could ever win a fight. We will be grateful if you simply manage to strengthen her up a little."

"Absolutely," says Makri. "That's precisely what I'm aiming for."

Isuas trots out of the Palace. While not exactly the eager young Elf of a few days ago, she shows no sign of giving up and greets Makri brightly enough, and they depart.

"You might be pleased to learn," Yestar tells me before I go, "that both Deputy Consul Cicerius and Prince Dees-Akan expressed some satisfaction that you and Makri were in my favour. Of course, I have not explained exactly what Makri is doing for me."

"I am pleased. It might get them off my back."

Lady Yestar smiles as she digests this unfamiliar phrase. "From their previous conversation, I'd say there had been every danger of them 'getting on your back' in a, eh . . ."

"In a big way?"

"Exactly. I understand that there are many people you must stay on the right side of in Turai. Life would be difficult with both the Prince and the Deputy Consul against you, I imagine?"

"Very difficult, Lady Yestar. The Prince doesn't take to me at all. Fair enough, I don't take to him. I don't want to get on the wrong side of Cicerius though. He's been helpful to me in the past, if only because I've been helpful to him. I couldn't say I like him all that much, but for an important politician he's honest, and there's no denying he's as sharp as—"

I pause.

"Sharp as an Elf's ear?" says Yestar, filling in the

blanks. She laughs. "I have always enjoyed that Human expression."

I reluctantly decline an offer of food and head back to the cells to interview Elith. One thing I dislike about life as an Investigator: there are times when you have to skimp on the foodstuffs.

My session with Elith-ir-Methet is short and depressing. She has accepted her fate. I tell her that this won't get her out of jail.

"I have no wish to be released."

"Your father wants it, and I'm working for him. So let's get down to business. I know what's been going on. I talked to Lithias, an Elf you are no doubt familiar with from your days of intoxication. Don't protest, I know all about it. Is that why you've clammed up about everything? Because you didn't want your proud father to know you were one of the first Avulans to enjoy the effects of dwa? Congratulations on finding a way to get it to affect Elfkind by the way. Very ingenious. Whose idea was it to mix it with the Hesuni water?"

Elith has risen from her chair and now stands gazing out of the window.

"I can see you've a lot to feel bad about. That's a strong habit you've developed in a short space of time. I wondered why you broke your word to Lord Kalith about not leaving the Tree Palace. You just couldn't wait to get your next hit."

Elith turns to face me, some anger in her eyes. "That's not true. I needed to see Gulas. I needed to know if it was true that he had accused me of damaging the Hesuni Tree."

"And once you found out that he had, you killed him?"

"Yes."

"Why don't you tell me the full story? You can't prevent disgrace from touching your family, or that of Gulas."

"Gulas had no part in the affair."

"Affair being the correct word. Why didn't you tell me before that you were having a relationship with him?"

"Because it is calanith for the Tree Priest to marry anyone outside of his family. There would have been disgrace."

"You think this doesn't count as a disgrace?"

"I would not expect you to understand," says Elith witheringly.

"I won't give up on this, Elith. You see how far I've already got. I'm going to find out the whole truth and tell it to your father. I owe him that."

Elith shrugs, the slightest movement of her shoulders signifying that she is beyond caring.

"I am tired of this, Investigator. You can do nothing to help me and I would far rather be left to my thoughts. If I tell you my story, will you leave me alone?"

"Yes."

"Very well. I got involved in taking dwa through my cousin Eos. I was unhappy at the time, because Gulas had just been made Tree Priest and our relationship had to end. Gulas would have strongly disapproved had he known. At first it made me feel better, but later it sent me into madness. One day when I went for my supply I collapsed beside the Tree and when I woke it had been damaged. I could remember nothing about it, but by this time many Elves knew that I had been acting strangely. I was put in prison while the matter was investigated. And there I learned that the main witness against me was Gulas, Gulas who had been my lover of more than a year. I couldn't believe he would do that to me. I thought he would have supported me.

"He never even came to visit. His brother did, and was kind to me. But I needed to see Gulas again. And

I also admit I needed more dwa. As you can see, I am not worth defending. If they execute me it will be well deserved. I left the Palace. I took more of the drug, and then went to find my Gulas. He wasn't pleased to see me. He called me foul names and said that my behaviour was threatening his position as Tree Priest and that if he'd known what manner of things I was involved in he would never have become entangled with me. He said that no person who had defiled the water of the Hesuni Tree with a foreign drug was worthy of living. And then he told me that he had never loved me and was pleased that I was in prison. I was still insane from the dwa, so I picked up a knife that was lying on the ground and I stabbed him. That is the whole story. Everything that is alleged against me is true. The best thing for everyone will be my death."

A tear forms in her eye but she brushes it away and refuses to cry.

I've plenty of questions left, but Elith absolutely refuses to continue. "I have nothing more to say, and no matter how many times you return I shall have nothing more to say. Please leave."

I leave. I descend to the ground beneath the palace. A choir is singing nearby. Two jugglers walk past, practising as they go. Parrots squawk merrily overhead. Three actors in white cloaks appear from the trees, declaiming with vigour. Some Elvish children race by, laughing and screaming with glee at the sight of all the preparations for the festival, due to start in just two days' time. On Avula everything is beautiful.

I'm in the worst mood I can ever remember. I stare at the Hesuni Tree and when I think of the story I'm going to have to tell my friend Vas-ar-Methet I develop the urge to attack it myself for getting his daughter into such trouble. Trouble, it seems, from which I will not be able to extricate her.

I walk along the path till I reach the paddock where I left my horse. I offer the groom a small coin, but he declines it with distaste. Too late, I remember that Makri told me it was calanith on Avula to offer money for care of a horse. It makes my mood even worse.

I ride on for a while till I reach the end of the outward path and turn left to circle the island. Just before the junction a horseman appears in front of me with a sword in his hand. I watch dumbly as he approaches. After the experiences with the masked Elves, I'm half expecting him to vanish into thin air. He doesn't. He keeps on coming. Though he's hooded I have the impression that my assailant is Human rather than Elvish. I draw my sword. Fighting on horseback is not my speciality, but I had enough experience in the army not to do anything foolish. As my attacker reaches me he tries to sweep me to the ground with a great clumsy blow that I parry easily. As he slides past I turn and cut him in the back of the neck. He slumps from his saddle, dead.

I stare at the corpse, puzzled. The whole affair lasted only a few seconds. I pull back his hood, study the man's bronzed face, look through his pockets for some identification, but I can find nothing. Just a mysterious horseman who tried to kill me, and wasn't very good at it. He looks like any common thug from any city in the west.

I ride off, leaving the corpse where it lies. Someone else can sort out the formalities. I'm not far from where Makri is training Isuas. I dismount before the clearing and advance softly. Makri is in the centre of the clearing facing Isuas and if she hasn't actually got round to killing her yet it sounds like it might not be far away. Her face is grim and her voice is venomous.

"You stinking little Elf cusux," she sneers. "This is where it ends. You wanted to try out my Orc blade?

Here—" Makri takes it from the scabbard at her back and tosses it to Isuas, who catches it by the hilt and stands awkwardly with the evil-looking black metal blade pointed at the ground.

"Now I'm going to kill you," says Makri, drawing her second sword.

"What?" stammers Isuas, and starts to tremble.

"You heard, brat. I'm going to kill you. You think I'm here because I'm a friend of the Elves?"

Makri spits in Isuas's face. Isuas shudders like she's been touched by a plague carrier.

"Think again, cusux," sneers Makri. "My allegiance is to the Orcish Lands. I was sent to wreak havoc on their enemies and everything I've done since that day has been for the sole purpose of spreading destruction on the Elvish Isles. You will be the first to die. After I've set your head up on a spike I'm going to gut your mother like the Elvish pig she is and then I'm going to burn the Palace."

Makri, now wearing a hideous expression of rage and loathing, leaps forward. Isuas jumps backwards to avoid the murderous blow.

I watch with interest. I have no fear of Makri killing Isuas—if she'd meant to do that, she would have connected with the stroke—but I'm impressed with her performance. Young Isuas, innocent of the ways of the wicked world outside her island, firmly believes that her head is about to be cut off and takes action to prevent it. She appears to forget how to be clumsy or weak or awkward, and actually parries Makri's blow and counters it with an assault of her own.

Makri, without appearing to fake it, starts trading thrusts with her young opponent, all the while continuing to taunt her with the foulest of insults, which further enrage Isuas so that she finally screams out the ancestral battle cry of her family and hurls herself upon

Makri with a rain of blows that, though not delivered
all that skilfully, are not lacking in spirit.

Makri traps Isuas's blade with the hilt of her own
and flips it away. She delivers a cruel kick into the
young Elf's midriff. Isuas crumples on to the grass.

"Die, cusux," roars Makri, raising her blade. Isuas,
shaking off the effects of the kick, rolls out of the way,
leaps to her feet, picks up a fallen branch and actually flings herself at Makri in an attempt to batter her
senseless. Makri catches hold of the Elf's wrist, puts
the point of her sword at Isuas's neck and stares at her
coldly. Isuas, unable to move, stares defiantly back at
her.

"Orc pig cusux," she says, and spits in Makri's face.

Makri nods meditatively, and grabs Isuas by the
throat. Again displaying her surprising strength, she
hoists her into the air with one hand and pulls her
forward so that their noses almost touch.

"That's a little better," says Makri, calmly. She lets
go of Isuas and turns away.

Isuas, still not understanding what's going on, swiftly
gathers up the Orc sword and leaps at Makri's retreating figure, at which Makri, displaying the sort of skill
and precision that sometimes startles even me, whirls
round and deflects the blow with the metal band she
wears round her wrist. She knocks the sword from
Isuas's grasp and again lifts her off the ground.

"Good," she says to the discomfited Elf. "Never hesitate to stab your opponent in the back. You're learning. You've got five minutes to rest."

She tosses Isuas into a nearby bush then picks up
her Orcish blade. I advance into the clearing.

"Nice going, Makri. If we are fortunate she might
get over her hysterics some time next year."

Makri shrugs. "She's all right. Good progress in fact,
by her standards anyway. What are you doing here?"

"I was just attacked by a mysterious mounted swordsman. Human rather than Elf. I had to kill him. Anything happened here?"

Makri shakes her head.

"It sounds like you're getting close to something, Thraxas."

"Seems like it. For all the good it will do."

I tell Makri that after talking to Elith there just doesn't seem any way out for her.

"She did it. End of case."

"What now?"

"I guess I'll keep ferreting around. Maybe if I can take details of what's been going on to Lord Kalith he might show some mercy. After all, Elith was under the influence of dwa when she killed Gulas, and under a lot of stress."

I'm not sounding very convincing here. I need a beer. Or maybe some good news. "You know we can get fifty to one on her making it past the first round of the tournament?"

"Who from? She isn't officially entered yet, it's meant to be a secret."

I inform Makri that I have been making discreet enquiries of the Elvish betting fraternity. "Don't worry, I couched my enquiry in the most cautious terms. So, is it worth a bet?"

Makri shakes her head. "No. Not yet anyway."

I'm disappointed.

"Has it occurred to you," says Makri, "that I'm actually taking this training seriously? I have a reputation to protect, not to mention a gladiators' code to live up to. And all you're interested in is gambling."

"Who wouldn't be at fifty to one? I've got to make a profit somewhere; the juggling contest is too close to call."

Makri promises to let me know if Isuas makes it to

the point where she's worth backing. I remind her that Gulas's funeral is to be held this evening near the Hesuni Tree.

"I've never heard you mention the gladiators' code before."

"There wasn't one," admits Makri. "I made it up. I was just trying to remind you that fighting involves more important things than betting."

"Okay, I'll believe you. You're the philosophy student. If you get her up to scratch, how much do you want to bet?"

"Everything I have," says Makri. "You can't turn your nose up at odds of fifty to one. That would just be foolish."

The slightest of sounds makes us turn towards the trees. A green-cloaked masked and hooded Elf steps out with a sword in his hands. I sigh. I'm getting fed up with this.

"Is he going to disappear?" says Makri.

"Who knows? If he can't fight any better than the last one he might as well."

I saunter forward, sword in hand, and am instantly beaten back by one of the most skilful and lethal assaults I've ever encountered. I'm forced to give ground immediately and am frankly relieved when Makri hurls herself into the fray and distracts our assailant's attention by attacking him from the flank. He parries her blade and even though I'm not slow to join in, again I can't find an opening. We trade blows for a while and though the superior forces of myself and Makri drive him backwards we can't succeed in landing a telling stroke. I've rarely seen the like of this warrior. Our assailant keeps us both at bay till, realising that he has encountered rather more than he bargained for, he spins round and sprints for the trees. We watch him go.

"Who was that?" demands Makri.

"I've no idea."

"He was certainly one hell of a swordsman. This is some Elvish paradise. Do they treat all their guests like this?"

She turns to Isuas, who is still wide-eyed after witnessing the fight.

"You see what happens when you get caught unawares?"

Makri is actually so impressed with the Elf's skill that she forgets to be annoyed about not vanquishing her adversary and looks forward to meeting him again. I'll be happy if I don't. I depart, heading home for food, refreshment, some serious thinking and a long nap before the funeral of Gulas-ar-Thetos, late Chief Tree Priest of Avula.

Chapter Seventeen

It suddenly strikes me as odd that there was a knife lying conveniently on the ground for Elith to stab Gulas with. Why? Knives are valuable items. Elves don't leave them lying around for no reason. I puzzle about it for a while without making anything of it, and file it away for later.

I eat at Camith's house, but more thoughts crowd in to disturb me. Why did Gulas suddenly go so cold on Elith? Was he really outraged at her behaviour? Maybe. He might have felt obliged to be thoroughly respectable once made Tree Priest. But that's not really the impression I have of him. More the passionate young lover, and only a reluctant priest.

And how come everyone around the Hesuni Tree suddenly got caught up in a dope scandal anyway? Who started it? Who benefits? Was there enough profit in it to make it worth the risk? I get round to thinking about the branch of the family who covet the position of Tree Priest. Might they have been trying to discredit

Gulas-ar-Thetos? It can't look too good for the Tree Priest if all of a sudden Elves are dropping like flies because they've been soaking their drugs with the water that feeds the sacred Tree.

None of this is going to help Elith, but it serves as a distraction. I want to be distracted because after the funeral I'm going to have to make a report to Vas-ar-Methet and I don't want to think about that.

I visit the Turanian Sorcerers Harmon Half-Elf and Lanius Suncatcher. It takes me a while to persuade them to do what I want.

"Working any sort of spell at a funeral is calanith," objects Harmon.

"Everything on this damn island is calanith."

Harmon Half-Elf points out with some justification that if the Elves have many taboos, they have far fewer written laws than we do, and are a more peaceful society.

"Calanith works well for them. It keeps the wheels ticking over without the need for too much heavy-handed authority."

"Spare me the lecture. I need someone to check out Gulas's body and it's way beyond my sorcerous powers."

They both look puzzled.

"Check the Tree Priest for dwa? Wasn't Gulas the clean-living one?"

"So they say. I just want to check."

"Surely Lord Kalith's Sorcerers will already have done so?"

"Who knows? If there is a Sorcerer's report on the body, no one's making it available to me, even though I'm working for the chief suspect."

Lanius Suncatcher raises his eyebrows. "Don't you mean 'person who admits the crime'?"

"Okay, she admits it. But there are extenuating circumstances. I won't see her executed."

I remind Harmon Half-Elf that I saved his life during the city-wide riots last summer.

"Not only that, I've saved the skins of more than one Turanian Sorcerer. If it wasn't for me, Astrath Triple Moon would be languishing in a cell in the Abode of Justice. And who hushed things up when Gorsius Starfinder got drunk in that brothel in Kushni? Who was it that cleared Tirini Snake Smiter when she was accused of stealing the Queen's tiara? The Sorcerers Guild owes me plenty. If I was ever to report what I know about the dubious dealings of Turai's Sorcerers to the proper authorities, half of the Guild would be in jail before sundown and the other half would be high-tailing it out of town. And I can feel an attack of public-spiritedness coming on."

My powers of persuasion win the day, though Lanius comments that if I ever do suffer from such an attack of public-spiritedness, I'd do well to make sure I never leave my house without my spell-protection charm.

"Because I seem to remember that not long after Senator Orosius accused Tirini Snake Smiter of theft, he found himself on the wrong end of a bad attack of the plague."

Harmon and Lanius agree to do what they can as long as they're sure they can manage it without being detected. I thank them, help myself to a bottle of wine, and we set off for the funeral.

I'm certain that Lord Kalith would much rather not have been obliged to hold a state funeral for his murdered Tree Priest while his island was so busy with visitors. Needs must, however, and there are an impressive number of important guests at the affair, not only Elves from Ven and Corinthal but others from further afield, along with representatives from all the Human Lands who were invited as guests to the festival. A very impressive gathering. As the Ossuni custom is that burial must take place within five days of death, and the Human Lands are all several weeks' sail from here, it is a rare occurrence for Humans to witness such an event.

My two sorcerous companions go off to join the official Turanian party at the front, leaving me to hunt for Makri round the fringes. I find her at the edge of the crowd, talking to three young Elves. Makri appears interested, but hesitant. Her posture reminds me of the few previous occasions in Turai when she has encountered Elves, particularly handsome young Elves. Makri claims never to have had a lover and has been wondering recently if something should be done about this. Unfortunately she regards almost all men in Twelve Seas as scum and thinks that Elves might be a far better option. I've noticed signs of attraction on their part as well, although the Orcish blood in Makri's veins does present something of a problem for them.

Makri would probably have faced this dilemma already were it not for the fact that when we arrived we were pretty much in disgrace with Lord Kalith and no Elf was keen to talk to us. Since then she's been busy with Isuas. Now, however, with Makri being in favour with Lady Yestar, it seems like the young Elves are plucking up their courage. Some of them are now of the opinion that they really should be paying more attention to the exotic creature currently walking around Avula displaying a confident charm plus a figure rarely seen on an Elvish maiden.

The three young Elves who face her certainly seem to be doing a good job of forgetting calanith, not to mention any admonitions their parents might have given them about being careful with the sort of girl you talk to at funerals. Makri—dark-skinned, dark-haired, dark-eyed and underdressed—seems to be casting a powerful attraction over them.

I'd be pleased to see Makri having a little fun. The woman does far too much studying. It's unhealthy. So I'm intending to walk off and leave them to it, but when Makri catches sight of me she mutters an abrupt goodbye to the Elves and hurries over. I tell her she needn't have bothered.

"Should've stayed with your admirers."

Makri looks doubtful. "You think they were admiring me?"

"Of course. Hardly surprising, in that tunic. Didn't it cross your mind to dress formally for the funeral?"

"I painted my toenails black."

"So which young Elf takes your fancy?"

Makri blushes, and suddenly becomes tongue-tied. Having spent her youth hacking up opponents in the arena, she missed out on any romance and the whole subject still makes her uncomfortable. She tells me that three of the Elves each seemed to be hinting that if she would like to see some of the more beautiful, not to say secluded, parts of Avula, they would be pleased to take her.

"What do you do if three Elves all want to take you somewhere?" she asks, quite seriously. "Do I have to pick a favourite right away?"

"I wouldn't have thought so. We're going to be on Avula for a while yet. You can play the field."

Makri considers this. "Is that good advice? Do you know about these things?"

I shake my head. "Not really. I never had a relationship where the woman didn't leave in disgust. Several of them actually tried to kill me. My wife swore she'd hire an Assassin. Fortunately she was exaggerating, though she did did smash eighteen bottles of my finest ale before she departed."

Makri sees that I am a poor person to ask for this sort of counsel, and wonders about talking to Lady Yestar.

"Except I think Yestar might not be too pleased with me. I forgot that Isuas would have to attend the funeral and I bloodied her nose and blacked her eyes and I don't think there was enough time for the healer to fix things properly."

We crane our necks to see over the crowd, but the Elves are tall and we can see little except for a sea of green cloaks and tunics and a lot of long blond hair. Light cloud has blown in from the sea and the day is dull and slightly chilly. The crowd is quiet, as befits the sad occasion.

"Do you think I'd look good with blonde hair?" asks Makri.

"I've no idea."

"It looks good on the Elves."

"Maybe. But only whores have blonde hair in Turai."

"That's not true," objects Makri. "Senator Lodius's daughter has bright golden hair, I saw her at the chariot races."

"True. Blonde hair is sometimes affected by our aristocratic females. But no one is going to mistake you for an aristocrat with your red skin and pointy ears."

"You think I should buy a dress when we get home?"

"Makri, what is this? I don't know anything about hair and dresses. I have enough trouble remembering to button up my tunic in the morning. Weren't you going to take notes about the funeral for your Guild College?"

"I am. Mental notes. I just wondered if maybe I should get a dress. You notice how Lady Yestar has that blue eye make-up and she kind of fades it into grey at the edges? How does she do that?"

"How the hell would I know? Is this all connected to those young Elves? They seemed to like you fine the way you are."

"Do you think so? I thought they might be laughing

at me. I noticed when I was talking about rhetoric their eyes were sort of glazing over. I think I might have been boring them. And when I said I was champion gladiator I wondered if they might think I was boasting. It probably put them right off."

I glower at Makri.

"Excuse me, I'm going to go and investigate something."

"What?"

"Anything."

"But I need some advice."

"Pick a favourite and club him over the head."

I walk off, keen to make an escape. Any observer might reasonably have assumed that Makri was a confident woman. Why a bit of Elvish attention should reduce her to a babbling idiot is beyond me, but I can't take any more of it. I drift around the edges of the crowd, not paying much attention to the funeral oration or the Elvish singing. I notice Gorith-ar-Del. Like me, he seems to be skulking round the fringes of the crowd.

Someone snags me as I pass. It's Harmon Half-Elf. He bends over to whisper in my ear, trying and failing to look inconspicuous. "I did the testing spell," he whispers. "A difficult procedure, without letting anyone notice."

"And?"

"The Tree Priest's body was full of dwa," he says.

Lanius Suncatcher is right behind Harmon. The pair of them look pleased with themselves. For all their protestations, I'd say they enjoyed the opportunity to act surreptitiously. Sorcerers generally like a bit of intrigue.

It's always gratifying when a hunch pays off. Elith said that Gulas abused her cruelly for using dwa. Yet there he was, enjoying it himself.

"How much dwa had he taken?"

"Difficult to judge. Enough to put him to sleep, I'd say."

Strange. He wasn't sleeping when Elith stuck a knife in him. And somehow I doubt he'd be able to ingest much dwa after that. It would be good to know if my number one suspect, Gorith-ar-Del, has been in recent contact with dwa. Now that Harmon has used his spell he won't be able to do it again till he relearns it, so I ask Lanius if he also loaded in a suitable spell. He tells me he did. I discreetly point out Gorith.

"Could you use it to find out if that Elf has been in contact?"

"My spell is for using on a corpse. You never said you wanted a live person tested."

"Can't you improvise?"

As an Investigating Sorcerer at the Abode of Justice, Lanius often encounters dwa, and must have had to adapt his spells before. He agrees to give it a try, and sidles off. Gorith-ar-Del pays him no heed as he walks up behind him. The spell might lower the temperature around them slightly, but on a cold day like today Gorith might not notice. Lanius concentrates for a second or two, then heads back towards us.

"Been in contact," he says. "Definitely."

It's a damning piece of evidence against Gorith. I'm delighted to finally have confirmation that he's been involved in this business.

After the funeral I wait around, wondering what to do. I should go and report to Vas-ar-Methet, but I can't face telling him that his daughter really is a murderer. I'm standing aimlessly in the clearing when Makri appears.

"I'm in trouble," she says. "Lord Kalith was as angry as a Troll with a toothache about his daughter appearing at the funeral looking like she'd just fallen out of a tree. Which, fortunately, is what she had the presence of mind to tell him had happened. She's been banished to her room and forbidden to leave the Palace."

"At least you won't have to spend the rest of the day teaching Isuas to fight."

Makri shakes her head. "She's still coming. She sent me a message saying she'll meet me at the clearing in thirty minutes."

"Is she going to exit via a window and shin down a tree?"

"Something like that."

I congratulate Makri on improving the child's spirit in such a short time.

"Possibly the first ever Elf child imbued with the—what was the word for insane Orc warrior?"

"Gaxeen. Yes, she's learning all right. Too much Gaxeen in fact. Now I have to show her the Way of the Sarazu."

"Sarazu?"

"The Way of the Contemplative Warrior. It's a kind of meditative trance for fighting. Very peaceful. You must be at one with the earth, the sky, the water and your opponent."

"And then you kill him?"

"Sort of," says Makri. "Although in the Way of the Sarazu, time doesn't exactly flow in a straight line."

I shake my head. It doesn't take much of this sort of thing to confuse me.

"I liked the Way of the Gaxeen better. Good luck with the kid."

Makri isn't listening. She's staring intently at the Hesuni Tree. This goes on for quite a long time. Finally she shakes her head and looks puzzled.

"You know, I could swear the tree was communicating with me."

"What did it say? Anything interesting?"

"I'm not sure. I'm only partially Elf. But I thought it was saying you should stay around here for a while."

"It was a message for me?"

I'm not too surprised. On an Elvish island it was bound to happen sooner or later. Makri departs. I take her advice and stick around, slinking into the shadows, where I can watch unseen. At least it will delay having to see Vas. I have a feeling that something is about to happen, though whether that's my investigation or Makri's suggestion I'm not sure.

Darkness falls. I've finished my wine. I've been puzzling over the significance of Gulas taking dwa. Elith swore he didn't. Something moves in the trees behind me. I sit up and listen, then crawl forward, careful not to make a sound. By the time I've advanced twenty yards or so I can make out two voices though I can't see anyone.

I sense some dwa dealing going on here. Lord Kalith is even more hopeless about policing his island than I'd realised. He doesn't seem to be making any effort at all to stop it. I rise to my feet and command my illuminated staff to burst into light, which it does, quite spectacularly. Two hooded Elves and one bare-headed man look round in surprise and at the sight of me with my sword in my hand they flee. I'm about to pursue them when another Elf steps out of the shadows. I whirl round and put my sword point at his throat.

"Well, well, Gorith-ar-Del. Sorry to interrupt you about your business. Not that you've been very discreet about it. In Turai you'd have been in jail a long time ago."

Gorith is speechless with anger.

"I imagine Lord Kalith will be pleased to find out what you've been up to."

Rather to my surprise, Lord Kalith chooses this moment to step out of the bushes.

"Lord Kalith desperately wishes that you had never come near Avula," he says, frigidly. "Congratulations on scaring off the dwa dealers. And would you mind telling me why you have been continually interfering with my agent Gorith-ar-Del in the conduct of his investigations?"

Chapter Eighteen

I'm picking moodily at my food. Camith, used to my hearty appetites, enquires solicitously if there is anything wrong with the fare. I tell him no, the food is excellent.

"But it was a poor day, investigation-wise. Elith-ir-Methet is guilty of murder and I have shown myself to be an irredeemable idiot."

My number one suspect in the case turned out to be Lord Kalith's special agent with responsibility for sorting out the dwa problem on Avula.

"A job rendered considerably more difficult by your interference," as Lord Kalith pointed out to me. He further informed me that, far from ignoring events, he was well aware of the problems his island faced, and had been trying to deal with them discreetly.

"Gorith-ar-Del has more than once been on the verge of eradicating the dwa problem, aided by my extremely able Sorcerer Jir-ar-Eth. In this they have been severely hampered by you blundering about, alarming everyone. Had it not been for you we would now have whoever is behind the importing of dwa safely behind bars."

I doubt this very much. I defend myself, but without too much spirit. Kalith might be using me as a scapegoat, but I can't deny I've made something of a blunder in pursuing Gorith-ar-Del and quite probably alerting the suspicions of the dwa dealers.

Makri arrives home late. She's sympathetic.

"He didn't even seem to believe we'd been attacked. When I described the masked Elves with spears he strongly implied that they were a thazis-induced hallucination. Seemed quite upset about it in fact. I don't think Kalith really knows who's behind it all, but whoever it is, I'm withdrawing from the affair. I can't do any more."

After the painful interview with Kalith I had to tell Vas-ar-Methet that his daughter was guilty as charged. A tree desecrator and a murderer.

"I'll put the mitigating circumstances to Kalith before the trial. It might do some good."

Vas thanked me for my efforts, but his eyes had a haunted look I never saw in them before.

"Are you really withdrawing?" asks Makri. "You never do that. Even when your client is guilty. And you've found out some odd things."

I raise my hands hopelessly to heaven.

"What have I found out? Almost nothing. The Tree Priest was full of dwa when he died. Enough to put a man to sleep. Seems strange, but maybe Tree Priests can take a lot of dwa. Elith swore he didn't use it, but she'd lie to protect his reputation. And Elith found a knife where no knife should have been, but what of that, really? Maybe someone dropped it. The rest—the Tree desecration, the Elves acting strangely—can all be accounted for by dwa and hopeless romance. I'm nowhere on this. I've let Vas down."

I make a late visit to the drinking den of the armourers. I drink a lot of beer, but it fails to raise my spirits. The armourers are cheerful at the prospect of several days away from their forges but still pessimistic about Avula's chances in the dramatic competition.

"I saw the Corinthalians rehearsing the scene where Queen Leeuven leads an assault on the Enchanter's tree fortress and it was nothing short of sensational," reports a shield-maker. "It had everything. Music. Drama. Excitement. Beautiful costumes. And as for their Queen Leeuven . . ." The Elf makes a comically lustful face which makes everyone laugh. "I can't see the Avulan company coming up with anything to match that."

No one has actually seen the Avulans rehearsing. It is all being carried out in great secrecy.

"No doubt to hide the extreme incompetence of Sofius-ar-Eth's production. What ever induced Lord Kalith to appoint that old Sorcerer as director is beyond me."

The Sorcerer seems to have even less support than before.

"He should've stuck to his trade. Okay, I admit he protected us from that tidal wave six years ago. He's good with the weather. And he made a cloak of protection for Lord Kalith so fine that no blade has ever penetrated it. No one's denying he's an excellent Sorcerer. But direct a play? Pah!"

There is still no clear favourite for the juggling competition, although Shuthan-ir-Hemas is commonly thought to be out of contention. Firees-ar-Key is still hot favourite to win the under-fifteens tournament. No one has heard about Makri training Isuas. This at least is a relief. I'm still hopeful that I might pick up a few winnings.

Perhaps tactfully, the subject of Elith-ir-Methet is avoided. Her guilt is now firmly established, but no one wants to talk about it. Not to me, and not with so many visitors on the island.

Droo, the young poet, makes a late appearance. She's more cheerful than the last time I saw her, and she tells me that Lord Kalith has released Lithias from prison with a warning that if he ever touches dwa again he'll be banished from the island. Droo is grateful to me for getting her in to see Lithias in his cell.

"If I can ever do you a favour, let me know."

"I will."

She goes off to talk and argue with her fellow poets on the hill. I leave soon afterwards, taking with me a quantity of beer. Enough to get me through tomorrow, I hope, because I've no investigating to do and I've lost my appetite for Elvish holidaying. I wish I was back in Turai, cold as a frozen pixie or not. If Elith is executed straight after the festival, I'll still be on Avula. The prospect of seeing my client hanged puts me into a mood of bleak depression and no amount of beer will chase it away.

Next day I find myself wandering aimlessly. Everywhere there are crowds of happy Elves. Bad things may have happened on Avula, but their nightmares have gone and there is a festival to be enjoyed. Whole families gather in the clearings to watch the jugglers practising or listen to the choirs. The temperature rises a few degrees and the sun shines on the island.

"I hate this place," I say to Cicerius.

"I have found it to be congenial," replies the Deputy Consul.

We're standing in the shadow of the Tree Palace.

"You don't have a client facing execution."

Cicerius looks pained. Before his duties as Deputy Consul started to take up all his time, he was famed as a lawyer. He's the finest orator in Turai but he has very rarely used his powers of speech to get a person condemned. Despite being a bastion of the traditional elements in the city, his role in the courts has almost always been that of defender. He no more likes to see a man, woman or Elf go to the scaffold than I do.

For the first time ever, Cicerius seems to be lost for words. We stare at the Hesuni Tree.

"You did your best," he says, eventually.

The festival officially starts tomorrow. The juggling will take place around noon and will be followed by the tournament. Next day it's the turn of the choirs and then there are three days of plays. Which means that this is Isuas's last day of training. Having nothing better to do, I call in at the clearing to watch. Makri and Isuas are sitting cross-legged on the grass, facing each other, eyes shut. Each has a sword on her lap. They sit motionless for a long time. The Way of the Sarazu, I presume. At least it doesn't seem to involve Isuas being beaten half to death.

Suddenly Isuas makes a move, grabbing for her sword. Before her fingers can even close on the hilt Makri lifts her weapon and brings it down with great violence on her pupil's head. Blood spurts from Isuas's forehead and she slumps forward on to the grass. Makri, still cross-legged, reaches forward, grabs Isuas's hair and hauls her upright. She slaps the young Elf's face three or four times till eventually Isuas regains consciousness.

"Poor technique," says Makri. "Get back in position."

"I'm bleeding," moans Isuas, wiping her forehead.

"Stop talking," says Makri. "And start meditating."

Isuas, still groggy, forces herself back into position. They both close their eyes. I make a mental note never to take meditation lessons from Makri, and leave them to it. I walk back to Camith's, where I spend the rest of the day sitting staring out of the window till the sun goes down over the trees and the moons appear in the sky. I don't feel any better. As miserable as a Niojan whore would be the appropriate expression, I imagine.

Chapter Nineteen

On the first day of the festival Elves from all over Avula stream towards the tournament field. Singers and lute players serenade the crowds. Isuas is due to fight in the afternoon and Makri confesses to feeling tense.

"If she lets me down I'll kill her."

She still won't say whether or not we should bet on her pupil.

"Wait till I see what the other fighters are like."

After packing a spare wooden sword in a bag for Isuas, she complains about not being able to bring a real blade, but it's calanith to take weapons to the festival.

"Who knows what might happen at the tournament? If some of these fifteen-year-olds get out of hand we'll regret not having swords with us."

Makri is still wearing the floppy pointed hat she got from Isuas. Only Elvish children wear them, but Makri likes it. She's painted her toenails gold and is wearing a short green tunic borrowed from Camith. Through her nose she has a new gold ring with a small jewel in it, borrowed from Camith's wife. All in all, it's a notable get-up and even though the Elves are getting used to her it doesn't prevent them from staring as we pass.

Some stands have been set up for the convenience of important guests such as Prince Dees-Akan, but the great mass of the audience just perches on the grass round the clearing, which, dipping slightly towards the centre, acts as a natural amphitheatre. Makri is politely accosted by one of the Elves who showed such an interest in her at the funeral. I slip away and look for Voluth the shield-maker, who has promised to introduce me to the local bookmaker. Whilst searching I meet the young poet Droo, who beams at me in a friendly manner and tells me I'm just the man she's been looking for.

"I want to do you a favour, large Human," she says.

I frown. I thought she'd got over the "large Human" bit.

"Okay, I could do with a favour. What is it?"

"Last night at the clearing I heard you talking about making a bet."

I start to get more interested. I had feared that the favour might turn out to be a poem in my honour. Droo informs me that while it is a surprise to her that betting goes on at the festival, she thinks she might be able to give me a hint.

"What do you mean, a hint?"

"On a winner."

"You mean a tip?"

"That's right. A tip." Droo beams. "Do you gamble much in Turai?"

"All the time."

"And you get drunk?"

"Every minute I'm not gambling."

Droo looks wistful.

"I wish I could visit a Human city. It sounds like fun. You know my father won't even let me smoke thazis? It's not fair."

"You were saying something about a tip?"

"That's right. You should bet on Shuthan-ir-Hemas to win the juggling."

I make a face. That's not much of a tip.

"What about her dwa addiction?"

"That's the point," says Droo, brightly. "She hasn't had any dwa for three days. I know, because she's been staying at Lithias's house since her parents kicked her out of the family tree. She says she's determined to make a new start and has renounced dwa and she's been practising her juggling like mad, and really, last night I saw her give a sensational performance when no one else was around. And I heard the armourers say how no one will be betting on her because everyone thinks she'll be useless. So won't that mean you get good odds?" Droo looks doubtful. "Unless I've got that wrong. I don't really understand gambling."

"No, you've got it exactly right. The odds on her will be high. You're sure she's going to put on a good performance?"

Droo is sure. I'm still not certain, because it takes a lot longer than three days to kick a dwa habit. Still, if she's determined to do well, it might be worth a wager. I thank Droo, and hurry off to find Voluth. I've got a bag of gurans plus some Elvish currency. Makri has entrusted me to place bets for her.

Voluth introduces me to a bookmaker who's situated himself in the hollow of a large tree just far enough from the clearing to avoid giving offence to Lord Kalith and the Council of Elders. The bookmaker—an elderly Elf, and a very wise-looking one at that—is offering twenty to one on Shuthan, with few takers. It's a bit of a risk, but at these odds I take it.

With so many of Avula's lower-class Elves in attendance, there is more than one stall selling beer, so I pick up several flagons and hunt for Makri. I find her on a slight hillock, a good position to view the event. Her Elvish admirer is not that pleased to find me barging in, but he's not making much progress with Makri anyway. She's too preoccupied with Isuas's fate.

I inform Makri that I've bet on Shuthan-ir-Hemas.

"Bit of a risk, isn't it?"

"Good tip from Droo the poet."

Makri is less confident, but too busy thinking about the tournament to give me a hard time. Personally, I'm starting to feel more alive. Things in the case of Elith-ir-Methet may be disastrous, but any time I get round to gambling I find my problems just fading away.

Singers and tumblers are strolling through the crowd as the jugglers take the field. As this competition serves merely to introduce the festival, and is not considered to be on the same artistic plane as the later dramatic events, it gets underway with very little ceremony. Jugglers, mainly young, march into the centre of the arena and do their act while the audience cheers on their favourites. I'm impressed with the performances. I've seen a lot of this sort of thing in Turai, but the Elves seem to have taken the art further. Usath, the juggler whom we saw practising earlier, has the crowd roaring as she keeps seven balls looping through the air, an incredible performance in my opinion, though Makri professes herself to be uninterested.

"Wake me up when something cultural happens," she says.

Despite her protestations Makri is all attention when Shuthan-ir-Hemas takes the field. We have a hefty bet on this young Elf, although the opinion of the crowd is still that Shuthan will certainly trip over her own feet and embarrass the whole island.

Shuthan does exactly the opposite. She comes on in her bright yellow costume with a determined air, hopping and tumbling for all she's worth and, despite a shaky start and a little trouble with her early rhythm, she goes on to give a performance that thrills the audience. Great cheers go up when she equals Usath's tally of seven balls in the air at once and when she adds an eighth and keeps it going for a full minute the crowd are up on their feet shouting their approval.

No one is shouting louder than me. I rush to pick up my winnings. An excellent start to the festival. And it is at this moment, while I am re-energised by a substantial win, that it suddenly becomes clear to me what has been going on with regard to Elith-ir-Methet and the shocking murder of the Tree Priest. Two Elves, complaining about some early gambling losses, are saying to each other that Shuthan's unexpectedly good juggling has cost them the cloaks off their backs. I get to thinking about cloaks and it strikes me that firstly I may well be able to save Elith's life, and secondly I am still number one chariot when it comes to investigating.

I hurry back to Makri with our winnings. She's about to meet up with Isuas and accompany her to the field of combat. I wish her good luck.

"I'd still like to know if Isuas is worth a bet."

Makri motions for me to go along with her. When we near the centre of the field where the combatants are gathering, Makri halts and points out one of the fighters to a nearby Elf.

"That one. How does he rate?"

"One of the best," the Elf informs her. "The under-fifteens champion of Corinthal."

Makri takes the wooden sword from her bag, strides

up to the Corinthalian youth and without warning makes a cut at him. The Corinthalian, taken by surprise, still manages to parry the blow. Makri backs away, leaving the young Elf looking puzzled.

"Bet your cloak on Isuas," says Makri.

"What?"

"If he's one of the favourites, then bet everything we have on Isuas."

I can't see how Makri can possibly have made such a judgement after only one stroke, but I trust her when it comes to fighting. I retrace my steps to the bookmaker's, stopping on the way to tell Osath the cook that, in the opinion of her esteemed trainer, Isuas stands not only an excellent chance of winning her first bout but will do well in the rest of the tournament. The cook and his companions are sceptical.

"Well, that's what Makri says, and when it comes to single combat she's an excellent judge."

By this time the entrants for the tournament have been announced. I'm too far away from the field to see Lord Kalith's face when he learns for the first time that his youngest daughter has made a late entry into the lists, but I can imagine his surprise. I can foresee some heated domestic arguments in the near future between him and Lady Yestar, but what is done is done, and family honour will not allow him to withdraw his daughter once the announcement has been made.

I arrive back at the clearing with a slip of paper in my pocket acknowledging that I have a large wager on Isuas at the excellent odds of five hundred to one to win the tournament outright, with another bet on her winning her first fight. Normally, for an event like this I'd have a large-scale plan of campaign worked out and I'd be betting on several of the contestants to cover myself, but I haven't really had time to organise such a strategy, nor the opportunity to study every entrant's form. I'll just have to cope with any emergencies as we go along.

There are sixty-four entrants, eight of them female. It's a straight knockout competition, so to win the tournament a fighter will have to defeat six opponents. The first bout is already under way. I watch with interest as the two young contestants engage rather tentatively with their wooden swords. The fighters are meant to hold back slightly and not deliver blows that might severely damage their opponent. An experienced Elf judges each fight. The first fighter to inflict what would be lethal damage, were a real weapon being used, is declared the winner. The spectacle takes place right in front of Lord Kalith and Lady Yestar, and I can tell from Kalith's face that he was not pleased to learn of his daughter's entry. Around me the crowd are still talking of little else, and the common opinion is that their ruler has lost his senses in inflicting such an ordeal on his notoriously weak daughter.

The first bout comes to an end when the fighter from Ven delivers a neat cut to the throat of the Avulan and the judge waves a small red flag indicating that the affair is over. The winner departs to generous applause. For all their fondness for poetry and trees, Elves are keen swordsmen, and appreciate any display of martial skills.

Makri and Isuas are sitting on the grass at the front. I use my body weight to force my way through till I'm close enough to lend assistance if necessary. Makri, lone bearer of Orcish blood in a huge crowd of Elves, might possibly find herself in some trouble if anything goes badly wrong. Isuas looks nervous but doesn't have long to wait. Her opponent is a fellow Avulan, a tall lad of fourteen who advances with a grin on his face that implies that he knows he has easy passage into the next round. He has a wooden sword in one hand and a wooden dagger in the other. From the way he holds them I can tell that he's thinking that while he had better not seriously damage the daughter of Lord Kalith, he isn't going to have to try too hard to defeat her. The crowd crane their necks in anticipation, but as it turns out there is little to see. Isuas's opponent makes a lazy attack and Isuas quickly and confidently parries the blow and runs her sword up his arm to his neck. The lad looks surprised, the judge holds up his red flag, and the fight is over. Isuas trots back to Makri an easy winner with the crowd wondering if Isuas just got lucky or whether her opponent let her win.

"Daughter of Lord Kalith or not," says the Elf next to me, "she won't get it so easy in the next round."

I collect up my winnings, place another bet on Isuas for the next round, then cut through the crowd in the direction of Lady Yestar. I have some trouble reaching her and am obliged to elbow a few attendants out of the way. Yestar smiles as I arrive.

"An excellent victory. Who would have thought Makri could do so much in such a short time?"

Beside us Kalith is being congratulated by the Turanian Ambassador. He acknowledges the compliment but he sounds like an Elf Lord who's suffered a severe shock. I lower my voice to a whisper.

"Lady Yestar, I need a favour. It concerns Elith-ir-Methet. And whoever is in charge of Lord Kalith's wardrobe . . ."

Lady Yestar leans forward, and listens to what I have to say.

The sixty-four entrants are whittled down to thirty-two. I see quite a lot of good fighters, and several excellent ones. Each island has sent their junior champions and the combat is of a very high standard. Best by far is Firees-ar-Key, the son of Yulis-ar-Key, finest warrior on Avula. Firees is large for his age and wouldn't look out of place on the battlefield. His first opponent is swept away in seconds and the crowd bays in appreciation. Firees is the firm favourite and is being offered at odds of just two to one, by no means a generous price in a competition of this nature.

The second round gets under way. Firees skilfully dispatches one of the favourites from Ven and another bright hope from Avula is defeated in a long struggle by a girl from Corinthal. The sun shines down on the arena and the watching Elves burst into applause each time they see a skilful manoeuvre. Makri sits quietly with Isuas, offering a few words of encouragement. Soon it's her turn again and there is some collective intaking of breath from the crowd when it is seen that her next opponent is Vardis, a youth of striking size from Ven who carries a wooden sword that appears to have been made from the branch of a particularly large tree. He towers over Isuas and looks like an Elf who does not intend to show any mercy to his opponent, daughter of a Lord or not.

He leaps at Isuas and beats her back with a series of heavy blows. Isuas gives ground, retreating step after step till it seems like she must soon run out of room. However, as Vardis thrusts forward with a stroke that would gut an ox, Isuas calmly takes the sword on the edge of her dagger and uses Vardis's momentum to turn him round, an advanced technique of which Makri is a master. Vardis finds himself looking in the wrong direction and Isuas wastes no time in stamping viciously on the back of his leg, which brings him down on one knee. She smashes her forearm into the back of his neck, sending him slumping to the ground, and then runs her sword over his back in a motion that, if performed with a real weapon, would let daylight into his vital organs.

There is pandemonium in the crowd. The Avulans cheer with delight and the Venians complain about the brutal manner in which Isuas has won the fight. Nothing she did was against the rules, however, and the judge declares her the winner. Lord Kalith's mouth is hanging open in shock. Beside him Lady Yestar has a broad smile, and applauds along with the other dignitaries.

As the second round continues I consider what else needs to be done, and go in search of Gorith-ar-Del. I find him close to the bookmaker's.

"Making a bet?" I enquire politely.

"No."

"You should. I've picked up a bundle. I'm starting to enjoy life on Avula. And I'm soon going to enjoy it more. After the tournament, I'm going to unmask the killer of Gulas-ar-Thetos."

"The killer is already known," says Gorith.

"Wrong. The killer is not known. But if you want to be one of the first to know, stick close to me."

Gorith tells me sharply that if I have any information regarding crime on Avula I should inform Lord Kalith immediately.

"It can wait till after the tournament. Makri's student is putting up a fine performance, don't you think?"

I return to the wise old Elf in charge of the book to relieve him of a little more cash. Osath is there, and he's mighty pleased with me. Despite Isuas's good showing so far, few other Elves are backing her and we still manage to get twenty to one on the third round. No one else can really believe that Isuas can possibly make any further progress.

Isuas, however, is making an excellent attempt. With Makri keeping her calm between bouts, she dispatches her next two opponents in a skilful if somewhat brutal manner. The trainer of a Corinthalian fighter actually complains in public to Lord Kalith after Isuas leaves him rolling round in agony with a series of wicked blows to the shins and ankles, followed by a sword pommel full in the face. The fighter from Corinthal has to be carried from the field and there are some fairly aghast expressions on the faces of the onlookers, the Corinthalian supporters howling their disapproval. Makri is unperturbed. Anything not actually illegal is fine in her eyes. The Avulans don't seem to mind either. They may be astonished at the sight of gentle young Isuas dealing out destruction on all sides, but they're with her all the way.

Isuas progresses without too much difficulty through her next fight and is now in the final. I am reliably informed by those close to me that there has never been such excitement here before. It's unprecedented for a rank outsider like Isuas to make such a showing. As the final bout between Isuas and Firees-ar-Key approaches, the crowd is in a state of extreme animation. The only person still sitting is Lord Kalith, who remains motionless, unable to believe that the Orc woman has trained his daughter to fight like this in just over a week.

Firees himself has shown excellent form. In the semi-final he faced a youth from Ven who was favourite with many of the crowd and a fighter of unusual skill. The adroitness that Firees showed in overcoming him leaves the majority of Elves still certain that he must be the winner. The bookmaker has Firees as favourite at eight to eleven but is now only offering five to four on Isuas. I've already picked up plenty on Kalith's daughter and I back her again in the final, but I also bet against her to cover myself, which is the prudent thing to do in the circumstances.

Right now I'm about as happy as an Elf in a tree. In fact I'm happier than most of the Elves in the trees.

Successful gambling and a solution to the mystery, all in one day. I shouldn't have succumbed to depression, really, but I don't blame myself. If you put a man in a strange land, deprive him of beer and give his client a really hard time, you can't expect him to remain cheerful in all circumstances.

The fighters walk out. The crowd bellows in anticipation. Lady Yestar has long ago abandoned all aristocratic reserve and is up on her feet cheering. The Council of Elders show every sign of equally enjoying the event. I'd say that Kalith's daughter's performance can only raise his status with his subjects. Even our Turanian Prince, not well disposed towards Makri, cheers as Isuas, thin, puny but determined, raises her sword against the formidable Firees-ar-Key.

Both fighters make a cautious start. Having got this far, neither wishes to make a foolish mistake early on. Makri, who up till now has remained impassively on the sidelines, finally gives in to the tension and rises to her feet to yell encouragement to her pupil. Beside her is a man who, from the family resemblance, I take to be Yulis-ar-Key himself, the mighty warrior.

The fight quickly heats up, with Firees having slightly the best of it. He gradually forces Isuas back, always searching for an opening. Isuas defends stoutly, but at no time does she have the opportunity to attack. After several minutes of fighting I can see that if it goes on like this, Isuas will tire long before her stronger opponent.

Misfortune strikes. Isuas drops her dagger when she mistimes a parry and suddenly finds herself at a disadvantage. Firees senses victory and moves in with renewed vigour. He forces Isuas back to the edge of the crowd, but just as it seems that he must soon overwhelm her, something seems to go off inside the younger Elf and she abruptly mounts one of the most furious attacks ever seen on the tournament field. She flies at Firees with a fury that whips the crowd into a frenzy, a frenzy that becomes even greater when she lands a stroke on Firees's sword hilt, which causes him to drop his guard for a fraction of a second. In one fluid movement Isuas kicks him in the ribs, sending him flying backwards, and she takes the opportunity to quickly retrieve her dagger from the grass. The fighters again hurl themselves at each other. It seems to me that the fight has in fact got rather out of hand, though neither the judge nor the audience seems to mind.

The fighters tire, but neither of them loses spirit. No longer moving so freely, they stand facing each other, thrusting and parrying. Isuas looks close to exhaustion. Under a furious barrage of blows her legs start to give way. Firees rains blow after blow down on her till Isuas is on her knees. Finally Firees brings his sword down in a tremendous cut that shatters Isuas's sword. He tries to follow up, but Isuas twists her body to avoid the strike, leaps to her feet and sprints towards the stands. Firees, momentarily puzzled at her flight, sets off in pursuit.

The crowd, thinking that Isuas is fleeing the field, cheer and clap in anticipation of Firees's victory, but Isuas is not leaving. Rather she reaches the stands, grabs an elderly member of the Council of Elders by his tunic and hauls him off his chair. She then picks up the chair, whirls round and lands a crushing blow on the head of the advancing Firees-ar-Key. The chair splinters into tiny pieces. Firees is stunned. His arms drop to his sides.

"Die, cusux!" roars Isuas, then kicks him in the groin, stamps on his knee, and manages to chop him in the throat and claw his eyes as he falls unconscious to the ground.

For a second or two the only noise to be head is Makri whooping in triumph from the sidelines. Then chaos erupts in the crowd. Isuas has set new standards in foul play. She's destroyed her opponent by the use of practically every illegal tactic in the book, and she's roundly condemned for her tactics. On the other hand, no one can deny that she showed a lot of spirit.

Firees's father is outraged. He rushes on to the field and in his haste to reach his son he bats Isuas out of the way. Makri cries in protest and races after him. I'm already on my way, fearing the worst, but the next thing anyone knows Makri and Yulis are facing up to each other, wooden swords in hands, and trading blows. Fortunately the Elves in attendance bring it to a swift halt, rushing on to the field to drag them apart.

I keep close to Makri, who throws off the Elves who try to hold her, and pushes her way through to Isuas. When she reaches the young Elf she picks her up and hugs her.

"Well done," she says.

Isuas looks happier than I've ever seen her. Neither she nor Makri seems at all concerned that she will be disqualified, and Firees proclaimed the winner.

"Who cares?" says Makri. "He's unconscious and Isuas is still on her feet."

Makri turns to me.

"You remember the Elf who attacked us in the clearing? It was him, the father, Yulis-ar-Key."

"Are you sure?"

"Of course. As soon as we traded blows again I recognised his style."

Lady Yestar appears, smiling broadly. She sweeps Isuas up in her arms and congratulates her.

"I'll see you both at the reception at the Palace," she says to us, before taking Isuas off to have her cuts and bruises treated by a healer.

The whole day has been so exciting that it only now strikes me that Isuas's disqualification has cost me a great deal of money.

"A shame," agrees Makri. "But it had to be done. Did we win anything?"

"Sure. I bet on her for the previous five fights. We won plenty. I'm back on top form. When we get to the Tree Palace, I'm going to unmask a murderer."

Chapter Twenty

Lord Kalith hosts a post-tournament reception at the Tree Palace. As the attendants open the doors for us, Makri receives plenty of congratulations for her success with Isuas. I'm not really surprised. Isuas might have been disqualified, but the Elves can tell a good fighter when they see one. When the next Orc War happens along, no one will care about fighting fairly.

The Palace is full of dignitaries. I see Lord Lisith-ar-Moh, who previously encountered Makri in Turai, congratulating Kalith.

"It was clever of you to hire her to train your daughter."

"Indeed," replies Kalith weakly.

Lady Yestar seeks us out.

"How is he taking it?" I ask, indicating her husband.

"Still getting used to it. The incident with the chair was a terrible shock. And no Elvish father likes to hear his daughter using Orcish oaths. But he is pleased, really. He used to worry terribly about Isuas's weakness."

"He won't have to do that any more."

Lady Yestar knows I'm not here to make polite conversation. I ask her if she can arrange for me to speak privately with Lord Kalith. A few minutes later Makri and I find ourselves ushered through a door on to a secluded balcony that overlooks the pools by the Hesuni Tree.

"What is it that is so important?"

"Elith-ir-Methet is innocent."

Kalith's eyes gleam with annoyance. "I have told you already—"

I interrupt him, rudely. "You can hear it first or you can hear it after I tell everyone else. Either way is fine with me."

"Very well, Investigator."

"Elith became addicted to dwa. It made her crazy, as you know. But she didn't damage the Tree and she didn't kill Gulas. Both crimes were committed by Lasas, Gulas's brother. He damaged the tree to discredit Gulas because he was insanely jealous of his brother's relationship with Elith. He loved her too, unfortunately. When you threw Elith in prison, Lasas spread it around that it was Gulas who accused her, which wasn't true. Lasas had done the accusing after he found Elith conveniently unconscious at the scene of the crime. I don't know if that was just lucky for Lasas, or if he saw to it that she had plenty of dwa at just the right moment. Either way, he harmed the Tree and made sure she took the blame. But that wasn't the worst. He encouraged Elith to leave her confinement and confront Gulas, but Gulas was dead by the time she got there. Lasas drugged him and stabbed him. If you want proof, I've two Sorcerers who will testify that the priest was so full of dwa before he died he couldn't have stood up, let alone talked."

"This is insane," protests Kalith.

"Not at all. I'm giving you a precise account of what happened, which I would have been able to do much earlier had you not obstructed me at every turn. When Elith arrived at the Hesuni Tree, Gulas was already dead in the bushes. Lasas then did something very cunning. He put on a hooded cloak and pretended to be Gulas, which wasn't too difficult, given that Elith was again full of dwa, and only barely in touch with reality. He tormented her till she couldn't take it any more. She picked up the knife that Lasas had left for her and lashed out at him. I don't know if her stroke would have been lethal or not, but it didn't matter. Lasas had taken the precaution of stealing one of your excellent cloaks of protection from the Tree Palace. A cloak that will turn any blade. And, as proof of that, I've already checked with your wardrobe attendant. He confirms that one of the protection cloaks that Sofius-ar-Eth made for you is missing. Lasas then crawled off into the bushes, hid the cloak, and pretended to arrive at the scene of the crime along with everyone else. Including Elves who had seen Elith stab Gulas, or so they thought.

"Which makes Elith innocent of all crimes. I admit she might be held to have attempted to murder someone, but that someone was dead long before she got there. Lasas, however, is about as guilty as an Elf can get. He damaged the Tree to discredit his brother and then he killed his brother through rage and jealousy and tried to pin the crime on the woman who had spurned him. I suggest you lock him up as soon as possible."

Lord Kalith is doubtful.

"I believe it to be true," says Gorith-ar-Del, stepping forward. "At the very least, we should subject Lasas-ar-Thetos to some stringent interrogation and have our Sorcerers investigate him in the greatest detail."

"Are you telling me that my new Tree Priest is the one behind all my recent troubles? Did he initiate the importing of dwa on to Avula?"

"Interestingly enough, he didn't," I reply. "While he was busy trying to discredit his brother, the rival branch of the Tree Priest's family was trying to discredit them both. They brought it in to start a scandal around the Hesuni Tree. I imagine they hoped that once it was known that Gulas couldn't prevent the sacred Tree from being besmirched and abused, their claim to the Priesthood would be taken more seriously."

"Do you have any proof of this allegation?"

"Not exactly. But ever since I started digging into the affair I've been under attack from various persons. Some of them were Human, probably sailors who've called here on the pretext of trade, but one of them was a very fine Elvish swordsman. Best swordsman on Avula in fact. Yulis-ar-Key. He was masked, but Makri recognises his style."

Makri, quiet up till this moment, confirms this. Kalith considers my words.

"Yulis is head of the branch of the family who contest the Tree Priesthood," I point out. "I think you'll find it all adds up."

"Have them brought to me—" commands Kalith, but that's as far as he gets. No one has noticed the appearance of Yulis-ar-Key on the balcony. We soon notice that, while we are all without weapons, Yulis has somehow managed to procure two fine swords, which he brandishes menacingly.

"I will not be subjected to sorcerous examination like a common criminal," he snarls.

"Why not?" I retort. "It would be entirely fitting."

Yulis rushes at us. Things look bad till Makri steps into his path. Yulis brings each sword down at her. Almost quicker than the eye can see, Makri raises her arms, deflecting each blade with her metal wristbands. She then steps in and butts Yulis with her head. Yulis howls and drops his swords. As he goes down he grabs Makri by the leg and they crash through the thin fence at the edge of the balcony. They plunge over the edge into the pool, far below.

We stare over the edge. Elves are already running from all directions towards the water.

"She can't swim," I yell. There are some tense moments before Makri is hauled out by her rescuers. Moments later, Yulis struggles out of the pool and is immediately apprehended.

Lord Kalith looks down at the scene below. He frowns, and utters an Elvish oath.

"Did she have to fall right into the sacred pool?" he says. "I just had it ritually cleansed."

Two days later I'm lounging on the grass in the large clearing, feeling satisfied. The plays have commenced. As I expected, I'm finding them a little highbrow for my tastes but I've a plentiful supply of beer and a fine reputation as an Investigator. Number one chariot, and no one can deny it. Elith is out of jail. It couldn't be said that her name is exactly cleared. After all, she did go wild under the influence of dwa, and she did make an attempt on the life of an Elf she believed to be Gulas. But there are plenty of mitigating circumstances. Besides, whatever she might have meant to do, she didn't actually kill anyone, and is innocent in the eyes of the law. Vas-ar-Methet has taken her home and has high hopes of rehabilitating her with his healing powers and the love of his family.

Yulis and Lasas are in prison. Both branches of the priestly family are now in disgrace. Lord Kalith will have some serious thinking to do before he makes a new appointment, but it can wait till after the festival, when the island is empty of visitors. Cicerius has expressed his satisfaction at the services I've performed on the island, and Kalith is too fair-minded not to be grateful.

Makri is now something of an Avulan hero, and not only for her amazing results with Isuas. The story of how she defeated the finest swordsman on the island without the aid of a weapon has been the talk of the festival. Isuas wishes to learn how to head-butt her opponents, and Droo has already composed several poems about the affair. She has also composed one about my investigating triumph, which she brought to my house.

"Droo likes you," says Makri. "Strange, I never saw you as a father figure to disaffected young Elves."

"Very funny. Is anything ever going to happen in this play?"

I'm bored with the drama. The Avulan version of the tale of Queen Leeuven is not stirring. Makri tells me that I'm missing the finer artistic points, but I long for something exciting to happen. I'm starting to agree with the Elves who regarded Sofius-ar-Eth as a poor choice of director.

"I'm puzzled about something," says Makri, sipping beer. "Who were those masked Elves who kept chasing us round?"

"I don't know. I'm puzzled myself. Part of the gang, I suppose, though they don't seem to fit in."

In front of us, Queen Leeuven is rallying her army. Suddenly, from nowhere, a huge crowd of spear-wielding villains appear on stage, march around for a few seconds, then disappear again. The crowd gasps. The masked Elves appear again and there is some frantic dramatic fighting as Queen Leeuven's supporters battle with the spearmen, who magically vanish, only to reappear at the other side of the stage.

The crowd go wild, clapping and cheering at this new dramatic innovation.

"Right," says Makri.

"Indeed. They were part of the play."

"That must be why Kalith appointed a Sorcerer as his director."

"He was trying to beef up the production."

We stare at proceedings. I'm feeling a little foolish. All the time I thought they were after us they were just rehearsing for the festival.

"It's low culture," objects Makri. "Cheap stage effects detract from the drama."

"I like it. But when I get back to Turai, I'm leaving this bit out of the story."

Got questions? We've got answers at
BAEN'S BAR!

Here's what some of our members have to say:

"Ever wanted to get involved in a newsgroup but were frightened off by rude know-it-alls? Stop by Baen's Bar. Our know-it-alls are the friendly, helpful type—and some write the hottest SF around."
—**Melody L** *melodyl@ccnmail.com*

"Baen's Bar . . . where you just might find people who understand what you are talking about!"
—**Tom Perry** *perry@airswitch.net*

"Lots of gentle teasing and numerous puns, mixed with various recipes for food and fun."
—**Ginger Tansey** *makautz@prodigy.net*

"Join the fun at Baen's Bar, where you can discuss the latest in books, Treecat Sign Language, ramifications of cloning, how military uniforms have changed, help an author do research, fuss about differences between American and European measurements—and top it off with being able to talk to the people who write and publish what you love."
—**Sun Shadow** *sun2shadow@hotmail.com*

"Thanks for a lovely first year at the Bar, where the only thing that's been intoxicating is conversation."
—**Al Jorgensen** *awjorgen@wolf.co.net*

DEC 0 9 2016